~y

Garden

Winds of Change

Pam McDonald

Moonshine Press • Franklin, North Carolina

Published by:
Moonshine Press
162 Riverwood Drive
Franklin, NC 28734
www.moonshinepressnc.com

International Standard Book Number : 978-1548663483

The Bible scriptures reference in this book are quoted from the NASB and KJV versions.

Acknowledgments

I am beyond grateful for the story of Windy Garden that the Lord placed on my heart and pray that, in my simple writing and lack of experience, there is a story that honors His love.

Thank you to my wonderful husband, Dave, who had faith in me to achieve a lifelong dream and cheered me on to the finish. I could not have made it through without your love and support.

To my mom and my sister, Trish, who had no idea what I was writing but supported me along the way. To all my family and friends who prayed for me. To Brenda Faulkner who encouraged me not to give up. To Sharol Ellis who has never stopped believing in me.

To the Writing Club who listened to my readings and supported my efforts even when I felt silly and inadequate. To Deanna Lawrence, who helped me find the writer within. To the porch days when Eva McCall and I poured over my story.

Thank you to Stephanie Davis who drew the leaves and is a very talented and sweet young lady.

A heart full of gratitude to Ellen McVay, "my word whisperer" and editor, who has embraced my characters into her own life and handled my story with love. To Tyler Cook, my publisher, who picked up the baton and carried my first book to completion.

"If you continue in My word, then you are truly disciples of mine; and you shall know the truth and the truth will set you free."

1

Nettie Pegram left her home in a huff, walking quite spry for a woman of 74. She was not at all pleased with yesterday's sermon at the First Baptist Church of Windy Garden, the church she had attended since she was in her mother's womb. This was *her* church after all and what was preached on Sunday mornings had better be what she believed as gospel all her life or someone would hear about it. Nettie was not one to hold her tongue. Never had been and felt she was too old to change. Besides, it took too much effort.

"There she goes!" remarked Sam, the next door neighbor, sitting in his chair on the front porch reading the daily newspaper. The neighbors knew better than to interrupt Nettie's determined gait when she was in this frame of mind.

Sam's sweet wife Carol set her crocheting project in her lap and leaned forward in her rocking chair to see who Sam was gawking at. She spotted Nettie, and shaking her head said, "Oh dear, I pity the poor target she has her arrows set on today."

Nettie lived a short three blocks from the church and downtown area, which was very convenient since she did not like to drive. Everything she involved herself in was usually within walking distance. She steeled herself for the confrontation that was forthcoming. This was not the first time she had to correct a preacher. And she had no qualms about doing so.

Nettie was determined to give a piece of her mind to this unsuspecting man of God.

"Hi, Ray!" Randy Gardner shouted in greeting to a church member getting in his car in front of the barber shop across the street from the Baptist church. Randy was more than a pastor to Ray. He was a friend. Randy had seen him through many heartaches and losses. Ray smiled and waved back at the preacher.

Just before Randy was about to cross the street, he spotted Nettie Pegram making a beeline for him. He was certain he could see her nostrils flaring in and out with each step.

As Nettie entered the church parking lot, she locked eyes with the pastor. She could tell by the look on his face that he was surprised to see her. This pleased her as she felt the element of surprise was to her advantage.

Pastor Randy greeted her with a smile and an outstretched hand in welcome. He could tell by the look on her face and the refusal to take his hand that she was really miffed about something this time. He had not missed the cold, icy stare he received from her yesterday morning during church service. "Good morning, Mrs. Pegram. How are you this fine day?"

"Don't 'fine day' me. I have a few words for you. In private, please."

A few words? Randy thought to himself. *Nettie wants to have a few words? Why, that's like asking a chocoholic to eat only one M&M. It's impossible!* He chuckled under his breath as he dutifully followed his soon-to-be attacker into the church. The pastor opened his office door for Nettie and motioned her in. He felt her 'tude enter the room minutes before her body did. His secretary, Joy, just shrugged her shoulders as Nettie passed by. Randy followed and left the door ajar, as was his custom when counseling or speaking with any woman. He motioned for her to take a seat and circled his desk to his chair.

Nettie tossed her hefty purse down in the wingback chair opposite his desk and placed her hands on her skinny hips, facing her pastor. Her penetrating steel-grey eyes peered over the large, round rim of her Gloria Vanderbilt eyeglasses.

Nettie took in a deep breath in an effort to regain her composure. She had fretted all night and all morning over yesterday's sermon. It was time she set her pastor straight on his theology. Someone had to. Her mother had taught her to speak her mind, no matter how holy the person might be. After all, it was her duty, passed on by mother.

Pastor Randy was concerned for Nettie. She was always upset about one thing or another. Many times in the past he had made an attempt to calm her down but to no avail. He worried her high strung nature would frighten off newcomers to the church, not to mention damage her own health.

"Well, why don't you sit down and we can discuss what has you so clearly upset." He motioned for the other wingback chair that did not hold the crumpled purse and looked her in the face with such compassion that the frailest flower in the garden would have bloomed at his love. But not Nettie. It only fueled the fire within her.

"I do not care to sit. I will stand right here! Let me get straight to the point. Yesterday's sermon was most certainly not a Baptist sermon and I know Baptist sermons. I've listened to them all my life. It was so far outside the lines of our beliefs. You took great liberties with that message and I am appalled that you would preach a message with such far-fetched ideas."

She picked up her bulky purse from the adjacent chair, snapped it open and rummaged through its endless contents until she found the used envelope with writing on the back. Straightening the envelope she said, "Here it is, and I quote, 'We must first be able to trust God's unfailing love for us, before we will ever be able to love ourselves properly, or others.' What is this 'loving ourselves' message? That is so arrogant and self-righteous! Everyone knows being self-absorbed is a sin.

"I just don't understand you any more. Ever since you got back from your sabbatical in the mountains and had your so-called 'encounter with God,' you seem to have lost touch with all that's been holy and right for centuries!"

Tapping her foot, she felt she had made her point and reached over to slip her notes back into her purse. "It is so exhausting keeping you people straight. Whew! That tired me out. I'll sit now," and she dropped her boney behind in the chair. She let out a breath that blew her bangs up off her face and stared at him expectantly, waiting for a response.

Attempting a little humor to break the tension in the air, the pastor smiled sweetly and said, "Well, I am glad to hear that some in the congregation listen to what I say, and take notes!" Randy hoped his humor might lighten the mood in the room. It did not. Nettie kept her smug expression, seemingly convinced she had the upper hand and that he would admit his error.

"Ahem. Well, Mrs. Pegram, let me try to explain," the kind pastor said patiently. Searching Nettie's face for understanding, he continued. The Pharisees asked of Jesus, "Teacher, which is the great commandment in the law?" To which Jesus answered, "You shall love the Lord your God with all your heart, and with all your soul, and with all your mind. This is the first and foremost commandment. The second is like it, "You shall love your neighbor as yourself. On these two commandments depend the whole law and the prophets.

"I had to ask myself, how do I love my neighbor? *As I love myself*, the word says. In our society today we have been taught it is wrong to love yourself; that loving yourself is arrogant and self-centered. But I don't believe that's what God had in mind for us. What He has in mind is that we accept his love. It is not edged in demands or commands. It is freely given. He loved us *while we were yet sinners*. Before we even accepted Him into our lives." The pastor paused momentarily searching her face for some recognition of understanding. Nettie's set jaw and raised eyebrow clearly demonstrated she was not willing to understand. Pastor Randy plunged ahead. "Please, hear me out. I was raised in a Baptist church. I was taught the do's and the don'ts, the ten commandments. I memorized them all. I knew if I did good, I got good. And if I did bad, bad is what I got. I preached that for years from the pulpit. I thought that if I reminded everyone of their sins and told them how they could do better, they would live better lives. I was wrong, Nettie. So wrong. I believed that when I failed, God was angry with me and did not want fellowship with me until I made things right. I thought He was never satisfied with me because I messed up so much. I was convinced that I was not good enough for God to love. You see, Nettie, what I believed was based on me. It was based on my performance, whether I did good or whether I did bad. That's how I thought God saw me. And I noticed that same wrong belief system in the people of my congregation. We were all condemning ourselves over our sins. Romans 8:1 says "There is therefore now no condemnation to those who are in Christ Jesus."

"Yet I could condemn myself worse than anyone else could condemn me. I was at a breaking point. That's when I decided I had to get away from the church for a while and get alone with God. So I packed up my Bible and headed for the mountains. For several days I poured my heart out asking Him to show me why I am such a failure. The third day I fell on my face and emptied myself before the Lord and I pleaded with him to tell me what was so wrong in my life. I lay there for hours waiting to hear something, *anything*. Then, in that moment, my heart started beating wildly --- and that day on the mountain, God revealed his heart to me.

"I sat back on my heels and looked to heaven, as I heard Him speak so clearly to my heart. He said, "Randy, do you know how much I love you?' I said, "Yes, Lord, I know you love me. You gave your Son for me." Again God said, "Randy, do you know how much I love you?"

"I couldn't believe He asked me that again! 'Yes, Lord, I know you love me.' I felt like Peter in the Bible at that moment. And Peter I was. But God was not finished with me yet. He said, "Then feed my sheep." 'But I am feeding Your sheep, Lord. Every week I feed them.' I was confused, but kept listening. Then he asked me what I thought was a silly question, but it turned out to be the most crucial question of my life. "*What* are you feeding them?"

"I was sure I had been teaching God's Word correctly. I studied hard every week. I had taught so much on what I had heard other pastors preach, and what other writers had written. And I had researched Scripture based on what I had learned from others. But I was missing something.

"At that moment--- God opened my eyes. I wasn't feeding the sheep His love. I was feeding them how to *behave*. And because I did not really know His love for me, I couldn't love all of you properly and nurture you with His love. I was believing wrong, so I was living wrong and, yes, preaching wrong. *That's* what God revealed to me in the mountains. I can only give out of what I have. Oh, Nettie, there is so much more!"

Randy saw Nettie's face turn crimson red. She stood up, grabbed her purse, threw it over her shoulder and spouted, "My Henry, God rest his soul, was a man of God, a deacon and a wonderful Sunday school teacher. He taught the Bible for over 40 years and I never heard him teach such a thing. He was a good man, who loved God and studied hard each week to present his lessons on Sunday. If all those sinners in the pews don't know how bad they are, they'll keep on sinning. That's what they need to hear. I do not understand what you are saying at all, preacher. And I am quite sure I'm not alone in this church on that!"

"Mrs. Pegram, before you go, let me ask you just one question, if I may." He stood and walked around his desk looking deep into her eyes, "Do you know, *really* know, how much God loves *you*?"

Before the pastor could catch his breath, with a flourish and a self-righteous grunt, Nettie stormed out of his office, past the bewildered secretary and slammed the door.

As Nettie made her way down the steps and into the parking lot, tears welled up in her eyes. She quickly wiped them away, looking about to see if anyone had noticed. Tears were a sign of weakness and she would never allow herself to be that exposed. She willed the tears to stop.

Nettie drew a deep breath and pondered Randy's response as she marched across the church parking lot. She could not embrace such a love. *I know God loves. I've heard it all my life. 'God is love.' But how can he possibly love all those sinners out there? Everyone knows we will only have that kind of love when we get to heaven. Until then, we just have to do the best we can with what we've got. How can he possibly expect me to believe such nonsense?*

Her pace quickened as she headed to the downtown area. The faster she walked, the more irritated she became.

Nettie let out a heavy sigh, *Besides, if God loved me so much, why did He take my Henry from me?*

2

Bonnie McDaniel took in the sights and sounds on Main Street, where she stood ready to meet her new town. She had lived in Windy Garden almost a month now, and decided it was time to explore. Bonnie ambled through the picturesque little downtown area with its varied shops and inviting little cafes. Even though it was 1984, this quaint little town felt more like a bygone era. It had storefronts on each side of the road with a railroad track that ran right through the middle of town. Presently, she felt the ground rumble slightly beneath her, announcing the arrival of a train about to enter downtown Windy Garden.

Windy Garden was strangely similar, yet bigger, than the little farm town of Blodgett, Missouri where she grew up. The buildings she passed as she walked along the downtown sidewalks stirred a melancholy ache in her heart. She missed home. Bonnie and her husband Will had been married only three years when Will found a job thirty minutes from Windy Garden. Leaving family and childhood friends was extremely heart-wrenching for Bonnie, but she was determined to make Windy Garden her new home.

She stopped in front of a store where a sign for hand-dipped milkshakes caught her attention, and suddenly felt hungry. Bonnie was fascinated with the name of the soda shop, The Apothecary. *Interesting*, she thought. *Sounds old and charming.*

The time had gone by so quickly this morning that Bonnie was ready for a bite to eat. "I think I'll check out this place for lunch. Sure hope the food is good," she said aloud to herself.

The rumble of the earth grew more pronounced as Bonnie anticipated the train's arrival. She turned and could see the large black engine rounding a curve, entering town from the west. Slowly approaching, Bonnie watched in fascination as an engineer hopped down with a red flag. The screeching metal brakes brought the long train to a halt. It was a small town sight to savor.

From her perspective of the depot, her eyes were drawn down the street to an impeccably dressed woman walking across the Baptist church parking lot in her direction. She couldn't help but notice the attitude that preceded the woman's pace. There was a sense of urgency and irritation emanating from her face. "Sure hope she isn't headed this way," Bonnie gulped. But, indeed, she was. She couldn't help but wonder what could have upset this determined woman whose stride indicated she was fuming about something. The woman crossed the street to the same side as Bonnie.

The train engineer's voice called for passengers to disembark. Bonnie could not see the people stepping off the train but her wild imagination pictured a movie star or a famous singer taking a break from the long train ride and walking the same sidewalks she was standing on now. Smiling, she shook off the silly notion and turned to enter the Apothecary, when her focus was redirected back to the woman quickly approaching. Before her hand reached the doorknob, the angry woman jerked the door open and marched right in. The door slammed hard in front of Bonnie's face. Peering through the closed glass door window, she could see the elderly woman march straight to a booth where two other ladies sat, motioning her to join them.

Bonnie was stunned by the rudeness of the woman who had

totally ignored her and stormed into the Apothecary. She stood dumbfounded and frightened at the rude woman's behavior. Her quiet stroll down Main Street had come to an abrupt halt, as she wondered if all the people in Windy Garden were as ill-mannered as this one. Those few moments had changed her serene and leisurely walk around town to a gnawing fear in the pit of her stomach. Maybe they had made a mistake moving to this town.

Bonnie drew a deep breath, steadying herself to enter the Apothecary. She was not sure what she'd find on the other side. As she opened the door, she noticed several customers sitting at various tables and booths, their conversations hushed and eyes fastened on her, as they examined this newcomer who had just entered into their domain. She felt downright stuck to the floor, unable to move a step. She wasn't even sure she was breathing.

"Hydie there, can I hep ya?" asked the country-sounding waitress.

Bonnie swallowed hard but no words could make it past the lump in her throat.

Noticing the stares and looks from her regulars, the waitress turned in their direction and said, "Whatcha staring at? Ya look like a bunch of deer caught in a set of headlights."

At that remark, everyone turned back to their lunches and chit-chat, quickly picking up where they had left off in their conversations, more hushed than before, seemingly embarrassed to have been caught staring a hole through this newcomer.

"Uh, uh, I would like an old-fashioned hand-dipped shake like it says on the window out there, please," Bonnie said as she pointed to the front window display.

"Well, come on over here, sweet thang, and have a sit." The waitress motioned her over to the soda counter where five stools sat empty.

Bonnie broke into a sweat but dutifully followed the petite lady with a pencil behind her ear. Sitting down carefully on the counter stool as if it might break into a thousand pieces, she tried gathering her thoughts as how to respond to this kind waitress.

"What flavor, honey? We got chocolate, vaniller, strawberry and surprise." The chipper waitress held up a stainless steel container in one hand and an ice cream scooper in the other, smiling at Bonnie.

"What's ....surprise?"

"That's what's so funny. We mix a little of this and a little of that and stand back and watch the face of the one drankin' it to see the look of surprise come all over thar face. It's the funniest thang! Some of 'em like the shake. Some don't. Ain't too hard to tell which is which." The kind waitress laughed so hard that the milk sloshed over the side of the tin container she was holding in her hand waiting to hear what flavor to add.

"Strawberry, please," Bonnie replied, still trembling from her entrance to the soda shop, timidly glancing about.

In a booth near the front of the Apothecary sat the three elderly ladies. One had white hair permed in a tight bob. Bonnie recognized her as the angry woman who had barged in front of her. She was talking rather loudly.

"Oh great," boomed the voice of the rude woman. "Looks like we have us another outsider moving into Windy Garden. I'll bet she's a Yankee. I can't stand Yankees. They talk funny and you can't understand anything they say."

18

The other two ladies who looked like carbon copies of each other turned in their booth seat to take a gander at who the remarks were aimed at. It was not hard to discern that their stares were fixed on Bonnie.

Bonnie's eyes welled up with tears at the harsh words being spewed at her. There was no doubt she wasn't welcome.

But the waitress didn't miss a beat. The look on her face displayed how painfully aware she was of how uncomfortable Bonnie looked and felt; embarrassed that her own town folk would talk so unkindly, especially about a stranger. She quickly added, "Aw, they's nice folks, really. I know ya cain't tell right now but you'll get to know 'em better the more ya hang around."

Bonnie was not at all sure she wanted to get to know these people. But she liked this waitress a lot and desperately hoped there were more like her in Windy Garden.

Shaking off the harsh comments, she remembered Miz Jessie's words of old, "Some folk jus' hurt sa bad, they cain't hep hurtin' others. Don't let 'em get to ya. Hit's not 'bout you. Hit always 'bout somethin' else. Remember, chile, God puts folk in our paths to show us somethin.'"

Bonnie remembered the time she was made fun of at school by Matt Clary. Matt teased her about her handmade clothes and said, "Look at Bonnie today. She's got her hair up in braids and wearing those plain dresses her mama makes. Guess her daddy don't have enough money to buy her a real one from the store."

Bonnie was born with Miz Jessie by her mama's bedside. She was like part of the family. It was no easy task cooking and cleaning and watching over Bonnie and her two sisters and brother, while her parents worked their fields behind the house. Bonnie missed her something awful. Since moving to Windy Garden and being so far from home, she wondered if she would forget Miz Jessie and all her learnin' lessons. It worried her no end. Bonnie was glad for the timely reminder of the wisdom her Miz Jessie shared so long ago, that first impressions sometimes do *not* impress.

"By the way, you never did say. Are ya stayin' or passin' through?" the waitress asked from behind the soda counter.

Bonnie jolted back to the present. "Um, my husband Will and I just moved to Windy Garden a month ago. This is my first chance to meander around. Your downtown area is quite charming."

"Yeah, they redone the outsides of the buildin's just a yar ago. Sure did need sprucin' up. Walls were crackin', bricks missin' and people passin' through town didn't think any business was open or doin' nothin' so they just kep a truckin' down the road. The local yokels would stop by nows and a then but to tell ya the truth, it weren't a pretty sight to behold. 'Bout the only reason folks come in here was to git their medicine. This old stower was a sight. The roof leaked sa bad we thought about catchin' rain to save on the water bill!"

The way she said 'store' brought a giggle to Bonnie, once again remembering her Miz Jessie. "I've spent the morning exploring the town. A week ago, Will and I took a break from unpacking and had dinner at the old Edgewater Hotel across the street."

"Yeh, that's a big un. Covers half a block and is three stories tall. Big fer this little ole town. Then ya seen all them crystal door handles and clawfoot tubs?"

"Oh yes! We were given a tour."

"Them bedrooms are sa perty, especially the ones facing Main Street. I seen 'em when they finished up the remodelin.'"

Bonnie couldn't help but see the pride that sparkled in the waitress's eyes. "That was my favorite part! And the hand-sewn quilts on wrought iron beds. The old kerosene lanterns refurbished for electricity. Dry sinks on a lowboy dresser. Will said he remembered his grandfather's house in Alabama having items like that. Yes, it is something to be proud of. All the other storefronts look so lovely and inviting too. Surely business has picked up since the renovations. Seems to me anyway, with all the people in here today." She glanced around the café part of the Apothecary, seeing most of the tables and booths full of customers.

"Yes'm, that's the Lord's truth alright. They keep me sa busy and on my feet that I have to soak these tootsies ever night in hot water just to be able to come back the next mornin.'" A wide grin spread across her kind face hoping to dispel any discomfort Bonnie might be feeling. "When's the last time ya had a hand-dipped shake?"

"Oh my, it's been a long, long time. I guess it's been nearly two years now." The smile returned to Bonnie's face as she watched the ice cream scoop dig deep into the container.

She watched in delight as fresh strawberries were added with a tad of milk to the freshly scooped vanilla ice cream in the stainless steel container. The silver cup was lifted up under the green blender's spindle and the whir of the machine brought pleasant memories back from childhood days of sitting on a counter stool much like this one in the soda shop in Blodgett, Missouri.

The waitress finished blending the strawberry shake in the old fashioned green Hamilton Beach three stir milkshake machine and handed it to her.

"Best shake this side of the street! By the way, I'm Lucy. What's yer name?"

Taking a straw and inserting it into the thick strawberry shake, Bonnie watched it stand straight up in the air. "Bonnie, Bonnie McDaniel."

Sucking up a mouthful of this tantalizing drink made her mouth squeeze tight, like she was sucking a lemon. She drew back and said, "Wow, this is sure thick. And delicious! I will remember to come back here often."

Lucy picked up the glass tea pitcher and left to check on her customers, leaving Bonnie to enjoy her strawberry shake.

Remembering Miz Jessie's sweet wisdom brought comfort to her bewildered morning. Oh, how she missed that God-fearing woman. She had been afraid that leaving her home in Missouri with all the familiar faces would be more than she could bear. She was also fearful she would forget Miz Jessie. But not today!

Bonnie's thoughts were interrupted when a customer approached the cash register at the end of the counter to pay her tab. Lucy had returned from refilling drinks when her sweet voice drew Bonnie's attention.

"Well, Nettie, how was yer lunch?"

"You ask me that every time I come in here. And every time I give you the same answer. It was just ok. Now, how much do I owe you?"

So now I have a name for the woman who doesn't like Yankees, mused Bonnie.

"That will be $7.49, Nettie." Lucy said.

"You'd think Carl would give us seniors discounts. This store has been in his family for generations. The least he could do is help out the old folks around here." Nettie paid her bill and left.

Lucy did not seem fazed by the surly response from Nettie. She winked at Bonnie, picked up the coffee carafe and headed back to her customers.

Bonnie's gaze resumed at the surroundings of the quaint store, still sucking the thick shake with great pleasure. Under the mirror on the counter top were rows of vintage antique glasses stacked on plastic trays, some three trays high. There were no signs of plastic or foam cups and plates anywhere, only glass. There, next to the stainless steel containers with dippers for the various toppings for sundaes were vintage glass banana split boats. Each was shaped like a boat to hold the banana on each side of the dish and three scoops of ice cream in the middle.

Bonnie turned, sipping her shake, and noticed a shy elderly lady at a table behind her eating a banana split. The ice cream was not the soft-swirled kind but each scoop was hand-dipped, one of strawberry with real fresh strawberries on top, one scoop of chocolate ice cream with chocolate syrup cascading down the sides, and one scoop of vanilla with crushed pineapple oozing onto the banana in the bottom of the boat. To top it all off were dollops of whipped cream and a maraschino cherry perched atop each scoop of ice cream. And the best part of all was the chopped pecans sprinkled over the entire banana boat! A mouth watering treat if she ever saw one!

But the little lady sat quietly, her head down and shoulders slumped as though she didn't have a friend in the world. Bonnie's heart went out to her.

I wonder who that lady is, thought Bonnie. *Her face looks so sad and she is sitting all alone.* Bonnie looked around again. *No one else in here is sitting by themselves. Just her.*

She thought how, if her Miz Jessie were here, she would no doubt mosey over to the little lady and introduce herself, being the kind soul she was. If she were here. But Bonnie dared not speak to anyone else after the cold reception she had received earlier, when she had entered.

Bonnie watched Lucy attend to the other customers. Seems they knew not to ask her anything about the newcomer, because as she poured one old man his coffee, Lucy leaned down close to his ear and said so everyone could hear, "If ya wanna know more about this gal, go talk to her yerself."

Lucy turned and winked at Bonnie. Bonnie was so pleased that Lucy had come to her defense. *If I'm going to live in this town I sure hope the folks warm up to me real quick.*

Lucy returned and asked the shy lady if she needed anything else. The lady shook her head no and Lucy patted her shoulder saying she'd be right back. Bonnie finished her strawberry shake and thanked Lucy for her kindness while she paid her tab.

As she approached the door to exit, she wondered what was on the other side. She shuddered thinking of the 'Nettie lady' with the attitude. *I hope I don't run into her anytime soon, if at all!*

She gently opened the door and peered out, looking for the Nettie woman. She bravely walked back onto the streets of downtown Windy Garden. The train horn sounded, bringing back memories of trains and her far away childhood in Missouri.

In fact, whenever the high-pitched sound reached her ears, she was a child again, running along the tracks with the other children toward the oncoming train. Something about approaching trains was mesmerizing. They would run from wherever they were toward the sound, hoping to catch a glimpse of the powerful, majestic engine pulling behind it sometimes over a hundred cars. They knew because they counted each and every car that passed.

Standing here in her new town within 40 feet of the tracks, the thrill and excitement of the beast and its cargo still held the innocent fascination of her childhood. The determination and strength of the engine hinted there was a schedule to keep and a destination to achieve. Its huge black body displayed an ominous pride of years in use, as it slowly rolled out of town and gradually picked up speed.

An invisible hand pulled on hers as the train passed by. Miz Jessie's voice rang in her ears, "Now chile, don't ya be getting too close to them tracks, ya hear? They be fun to watch, but stay fer back. The good Lawd give ya some good cents, so spend it."

Bonnie laughed at the memories flooding her soul. Just then, her eye caught Nettie walking slowly up a hill toward the cemetery a block away.

3

Nettie's lunch did not sit well on her stomach as she walked home from the Apothecary. *"Every time I eat there my stomach ties in knots,"* she muttered aloud. But she knew it wasn't the food that upset her; it was her nerves. It had been a very trying day.

Why can't people get it together? Why am I always the one to have to set them straight? Mother was always meeting with the mayor or whoever would listen to get things fixed around this town. If she didn't do something about it, it never got done. It's now fallen on me to fill her shoes. I get so tired of this.

Nettie tripped over a crack in the sidewalk catching herself before she fell. *Oh, great! One more thing to address the city council about. Why, oh why, can't the maintenance crews keep these sidewalks fixed?*

Nothing was going to make Nettie happy today. She woke up in a sour mood, after stewing all night about what to say to the preacher. And her disposition had not changed all day.

Most days on her return trips from town she would stop and visit Henry's gravesite. This day was no exception. She needed to spout off to someone and Henry was her preferred audience.

Climbing the slight hill behind the church, she wiped the perspiration from her brow with a handkerchief from her purse. Brushing a leaf atop her husband's immaculately polished marker, she blew out an exasperated breath. "Henry, what a day this has been. If it wasn't for me, this town would go to hell in a hand basket. Great! There I go, saying things I got over saying a long time ago.

But this morning has me so upset. Wait til you hear what I've been through!" Suddenly, she felt as if Henry was standing beside her, looking right through her. It gave her pause. Her mouth drew up in a slight smile as she patted the top of his marker. "I know. I know. I remember how you would raise your left eyebrow and wink at me every time I spouted off bad words. Then you would say to me, 'Nettie, you're a smart woman. And downright pretty too. Try to make your words match the beauty inside of you. I know they're in there. Let them out, Dahlin, let them out.' She could still hear Henry's voice gently comforting her. He was the only person in her life, besides her father, who had that effect on her. The reflection made her forget her morning tirade. She began to relax, enjoying a sweet moment with the love of her life.

Interrupting her time with Henry, voices drifted up the hill. Nettie turned to see where they were coming from. She strained to look and saw Pastor Randy talking with one of the deacons in the parking lot. The lightness she felt in her soul a moment ago vanished. She was drawn back to why she had stopped by the cemetery in the first place.

Glaring at the scene below, memories of her meeting with Pastor Randy returned with a vengeance. Usually, when Nettie came to the gravesite to complain about one thing or another, she felt better having gotten the words out of her system. Whether alive or gone, Henry always had a way of calming her down. But this was one of those days she was determined not to be calmed down, by Henry or by anyone else.

"Well, would you look at that! There is the pastor joking around with Paul Grimes! Why, he acts as if what I told him this morning doesn't matter at all. And here I am, all upset! Since *I'm* still upset, you'd think he could act a little sorry for a couple of hours."

Turning back to Henry, she realized she had not told him what had roused the bees in her bonnet. "Henry, I was up most the night fretting over the sermons lately. They're like nothing I've heard before. I was so upset I could hardly eat or think. So I decided I needed to march myself down to the church and have a long chat with the man. And I did. I had to tell him how wrong his sermons have been lately. And they are, Henry. They are. I wish you had been at church yesterday. He had the gall to preach on loving ourselves. Can you imagine that? He said that we have to love ourselves before we can love others. Well, you know and I know that's a lot of holy baloney. And I pretty much told him so, too. Well," Nettie blew out a breath, "I picked up my purse to leave and he asked *me*, 'Do you know, really, *know* how much God loves you?'" Her voice cracked as she felt the sting of those words once again. "When we all get to heaven, we'll know God's love then, won't we, dear?" She felt justified spewing her anger and disappointment in her pastor to her beloved Henry. That justification, though, sat like sour milk on her stomach. An acrid taste rose in her mouth. She looked around for comfort. From anyone or anything. Something was not right. Something in Nettie's own words stirred an unrest within her. Her heart beat rapidly and her palms began to sweat. She steadied herself against Henry's gravestone. Taking deep breaths, she fanned herself with her handkerchief.

Calm down, Nettie, she said to herself. Quite unexpectedly, a breeze touched her cheek, giving relief. "Ooh. That feels better."

Maybe it was the quietness surrounding her. Maybe it was

remembering a fond memory just minutes ago. She didn't know why, but it had been painful to relate to her beloved the conversation she had earlier with her pastor.

Regaining her composure, Nettie decided to change the subject. It gave her the momentum to gain back at least a modicum of self control. Returning to her former tone she continued, "And guess what else? We have us another yankee moving to town. Before you know it, they'll be changing the name of our town to New York Garden. Why can't things stay the way they've always been? Why, there was a time we knew every person in Windy Garden." She wiped a smudge from around the H in his name on his gravestone with the handkerchief she had been waving over her face. "Well, my dear, I'm going home now. I think I'll sit on our porch and rest a spell. It's been a terrible, stressful day. Oh, how I miss you." She kissed her hand and placed the kiss atop Henry's gravestone, patted it lovingly, and left.

Nettie tucked her handkerchief back in her purse and snapped it shut. She draped it over her arm and headed down the hill. It wasn't easy going home to an empty house. She dreaded sitting alone on the front porch in her favorite rocker Henry had made for her fortieth birthday, brooding by herself. Henry always found creative ways to cheer her up. He was her loving companion and sweetest critic.

Ascending the front steps, she hesitated in front of the rocker that usually soothed her aching body and calmed her agitated spirit. She lovingly stroked the smooth, wooden spindles. Sighing, she turned and placed the key in the front door.

She wasn't sure if she wanted any cheering up just yet, or to be mad a while longer.

She decided to be mad.

Ida Mae Ledbetter noticed Nettie's angry tromp to the Apothecary. She wished there was time to find out what was troubling her best friend since the seventh grade, but she had a dental appointment in fifteen minutes. Ida Mae would have loved to have had an excuse to cancel her appointment, but a cracked tooth was a priority at the moment.

Ida Mae fretted over her friend often. Seems Nettie was constantly upset over one thing or another. She feared Nettie was growing more and more cantankerous.

When she reached the dentist's office, she sat down in the waiting room still thinking about Nettie. She was very aware that her friend was not happy with the sermons at church, given the disgruntled noises she heard each week. Sitting next to her in church service, it was hard not to miss. Only two weeks ago Ida Mae asked her why she was complaining so much about Pastor Randy and his sermons.

"Ida Mae, how in the world can you sit there and not know the pastor has changed his whole focus? He used to be so good. He'd preach each Sunday about what the congregation was doing wrong and tell them to repent! But ever since he returned from his sabbatical last summer, it's like he is ignoring all the sinning these people are doing. Instead, week after week he tells them how much God loves them. Surely he is aware it will make them go out and sin even more!"

"Have you talked with Randy about how you feel?" Ida Mae

asked.

"A few times. Right after church. But if this Sunday he continues on like he has, I'm going to march right into his office and set him straight again!"

Ida Mae wondered if that was why she was so upset just now. She had seen her friend come down the church steps, hesitate, then march over to the Apothecary. *Yes, that must be what happened. She must have met with Pastor Randy. I'll go over to Nettie's this afternoon. It's been a few days since I've seen her anyway.*

The dentist appointment took longer than Ida Mae had planned so she went home to rest a bit before going over to Nettie's. Her rest turned into a long nap. She woke at 4 pm. Groggy and sore, she went to the bathroom and looked into the mirror. The numbness in her mouth went all the way to her eye, over half her nose, and below her bottom lip. Attempting to smile she was horrified to see the right side of her face drooped and the other side lifted in a perfect smile.

I can't go out in public looking like this. Especially not to Nettie's. Guess I'll have to wait until tomorrow. She prayed for Nettie that night hoping she would be calmer by morning.

The numbness had worn off over night, bringing back her beautiful smile. Ida Mae dressed and headed over to Nettie's house. She knocked on the kitchen door. Nettie opened it wearing an apron and holding a dust cloth in her left hand. "Hello, Nettie."

"Come in. Come in," Nettie motioned. "What brings you over today?"

So much for chit-chat thought Ida Mae. "Oh nothing urgent. Just wanted to drop by for a visit. How have you been?" Ida Mae sat down at the kitchen table.

Nettie brought coffee over to the table with cups, saucers and spoons. "Oh, been my usual busy self. Dusting today. That young thing I hired to clean hasn't seen a dust cloth in her entire life. I don't know why I keep her."

"Is she still coming once a month?"

"Yes. She's due back next week and I intend to have a talk with her. She's not as good as she used to be." Nettie sipped on her coffee.

"Nettie, I remember when you hired her years ago that she came every week. And you were very pleased with her work. Could it be that dust accumulates over the month after she has cleaned? I know it does in my house. I clean and in a few days, there it is. Back again," laughed Ida Mae.

"Yes, well, that is *your* house. So what's the real reason you came by?"

As long as Ida Mae had known Nettie, she knew the gift of subtlety was not her strongest suit but she was used to her ways and loved her anyway. "I went to the dentist yesterday for this broken tooth. He numbed me so well that I couldn't breathe through half my nose or smile without half my face drooping. I wanted to come over after that appointment but my face felt like somebody else's." Ida Mae laughed thinking of her face in the mirror.

"I remember you telling me you broke that tooth last week. Why did you wait so long to go in?"

"Oh, you know how I hate going to the dentist. I put if off and put if off until the pain was more than I could bear. But I'm glad that's over. Well, for now. I have a temporary crown. The permanent one will come in in a few weeks so I have to go back for that."

The girls sipped their coffee in silence a few moments when Ida Mae cleared her throat and said, "I saw you on my way to the dentist yesterday. You looked upset. Are you alright?"

Nettie stared out the window and saw the new girl that was in the Apothecary, the Yankee, 'power walking' down the street. For some reason, it annoyed her to see her again.

Turning back to Ida Mae she said, "Remember, I told you last week that if Pastor Randy preached in the same direction he has of late, I was going to see him and set him straight. So I went."

"So, what did he say?" Ida Mae said, taking another sip of her coffee.

"I told him that if he keeps preaching like that I was sure others in the church would agree with me that he needs to go back to the way he was preaching before his trip. I just don't get it. Why would he preach that people can live in sin and God will just keep loving them anyway?"

A gasp escaped Ida Mae's mouth. "Oh Nettie, that is not *at all* what he is preaching. I'm sorry if you heard it that way. No, no. He is preaching on God's love and grace. Two things I really never understood growing up. I was taught that God would love us if we were good and did what He said to do. That He punishes us when we are bad and turns His back on us when we sin. All my life when I messed up, I thought He was angry with me and didn't want to hear my prayers if I didn't confess right away. That kept me bound in guilt and I kept condemning myself that I was this awful person. I did that all the time. I was so convinced of what

I had been taught to be truth, I was determined to never change my mind. But now, oh Nettie, I feel freer than ever in my life. I realize from what Pastor Randy has been saying that God loved me even before I gave my life to Him. Says so in Romans 5. And that I needed to realize what all Jesus had done for me. He took my sins on Himself and died for me so I wouldn't be held accountable for them anymore. What love! So now when I sin, I thank Him that He took my sin on Himself, a long time ago, and I fall more and more in love with Him and His sacrifice for me. That kind of love encourages me not to sin. It's just the opposite of being beat up all the time for everything I do wrong. Can you see what I'm saying?" Ida Mae looked lovingly into Nettie's eyes, searching for any sign of understanding.

Abruptly, Nettie began gathering the coffee cups and spoons and headed to the kitchen sink. She turned and faced Ida Mae. "No, quite frankly I don't. We need to be reminded of our sins. We need to be told when we do wrong so we can tell God how bad we've been. If people think they are already forgiven for everything before they ask, they'll keep on sinning."

Ida Mae stepped over to where Nettie was standing and lovingly touched her shoulder, "Nettie, my dearest friend since the seventh grade, God knows when we sin, before we tell him. And you and I both know when we mess up. We don't need someone telling us every week how bad we've been. We know we have. The question we have to ask ourselves is, 'Do I know how loved and forgiven I am?' Think about it. Ok? I'll go now. But give it some thought, alright?"

Ida Mae walked to the back door. Then turned. "It's always

good to spend time with you, Nettie. Thank you for the coffee. I really love you. Bye." With that, she left.

Nettie went to the front window and watched Ida Mae head for home. It saddened her that her friend was swallowing this bologna from the pulpit.

I will pray for you, my friend. You have been so deceived. I know what the Bible says and so do you. She walked away from the window and washed the coffee cups and set them on a dish towel to dry.

As a child, making friends did not come easy for Nettie. Most of the kids in her school were too poor or too undignified to be associated with. Or so her mother said.

Once in the seventh grade Nettie met a bubbly, sweet, vivacious girl her age named Ida Mae Astor. Ida Mae's parents had moved to Windy Garden from New York City. Nettie and Ida Mae hit it off right away. They sat next to each other in all their classes, ate lunch side by side, and arrived early each morning a few minutes before the bell rang to exchange stories of boys, and the latest fashions.

Nettie would go home and tell her mother all about Ida Mae. Ida Mae said this and Ida Mae said that. Ida Mae tells the funniest stories. Nettie observed her mother's expression reveal her pleasure to learn that the Astor family was from New York City. New York City was home to the rich and famous. It was her civic duty, after all, to welcome them to her fair city and introduce them to the members of various clubs and social functions that only those from prestigious backgrounds were allowed to attend. Rose would be the first to introduce the next wealthy resident of Windy Garden to the town's elite. Her status in the community was about to go up two notches.

"I'll call on Mrs. Astor tomorrow, Nettie. Do you know where she lives?"

"No, I haven't asked her. But I will tomorrow!" Nettie was so excited her mother approved of Ida Mae. Because in a short time, the two girls had bonded like glue.

The next day Nettie could hardly contain her enthusiasm. *I have a new friend! And mother approves! What could possibly be better?* When she reached the front steps of the school, she heard Ida Mae calling to her.

Fairly skipping up the steps, both girls squealed in delight, hugging each other. "Ida Mae, I have the best news! Mother is very happy I have a best friend. I have never had a best friend. But I am so glad it's you!"

The bell rang signaling them to their first class. They walked hand in hand down the hallway.

"Oh, I almost forgot!" Nettie exclaimed, as she abruptly stopped before entering the classroom.

"What is it?" asked Ida Mae.

"My mother would like to know where you live so she can meet your mother."

"Oh, goodness, for a moment there I thought something was wrong."

Ida Mae's shoulders dropped in relief. "I live outside town about two miles on Hilltop Park Road. I'm sure mother would love to meet your mother."

Nettie felt her face flush with the news. She recognized the name of that road. It was the poorest area in all of Windy Garden.

Ida Mae squeezed Nettie's hand and smiled, "We had better get in to class or we'll be marked tardy."

Nettie followed numbly behind. She felt as if her whole world was swallowed up in three words. *Hilltop Park Road. Oh no! What will mother think?* Nettie knew what mother would think. She would squelch this friendship like a bug. When Rose did not approve of Nettie's friends, she put a stop to any communication or contact. But this was the first true friend Nettie had ever acquired in her young life. *What am I going to do? I can't let mother spoil this friendship.* Determined to keep Ida Mae in her life, she fussed inside herself. *I won't! I won't let her spoil this friendship. Ida Mae is my best friend and very sweet. I don't care where she lives. I won't let her take away the only true friend I have ever had.*

Nettie set her books on the designated table in the foyer when she returned home from school. Her heart ached over the inevitable. *Maybe she will have forgotten all about Ida Mae's mother. I can hope, can't I?*

Nettie found her mother in the kitchen writing thank you notes to the hospital's fundraiser committee. She had written and rewritten these notes for days.

Nettie paused, took in a deep breath and entered the kitchen. "Hello, mother!" she chirped a little too exuberantly, "How was your day?"

Rose paused long enough to acknowledge her daughter's

presence, "Oh, fine, but busy. There's carrot cake in the pantry."

Good, Nettie thought, *she didn't ask.*

The temporary reprieve gave Nettie hope. There would be more time to figure this out. She walked over to the refrigerator, poured herself a glass of milk and cut a tiny piece of carrot cake to take to her room. "Well, I've got homework. I'll see you later." She moved quickly, trying not to spill the milk but anxious to avoid any further conversation with her mother.

The clock on the foyer wall struck three times, more loudly than usual, thought Nettie. Her punctual mother left the house at exactly 3:15 pm for the town hall. She would be leaving any minute.

She rushed to her room, shut the door, and breathed a sigh of relief. She sat down at her white antique desk decorated with pink roses and ivy vines to eat her snack. *So far, so good.* She stared at the carrot cake, her absolute favorite of all desserts. It was a family recipe handed down from her father's mother. Though she had never met her grandmother, she knew that if she had, she would have loved her. She must have been someone really special to be the mother of her loving father. Generational pictures hung in her room reminding her daily of her roots. Above her bed were tin plates and sepia tone pictures of her mother's ancestors. In each one, no one smiled. They looked to Nettie like standing corpses. No emotion whatsoever. Just blank stares.

Across the room on the far wall were her father's family pictures. His mother and father stood together holding hands, a gentle smiled tugged at their lips. Her favorite was a black and white photograph set in a field of dandelions, where they stood side by side. Something funny must have happened when the camera clicked, because grandfather Collins was laughing, while grandmother Collins put her hand to her lips to suppress a smile. It was an endearing picture to Nettie. Rose had mentioned several times how much she hated that picture. She always said, "The least they could have done was find someplace else for the picture instead of a field of weeds."

Nettie enjoyed rising in the mornings to the happy faces that seemed to wink at her, as she rose from her bed. She recalled a time when she was in the fourth grade, her mother angered her so much she ran to her room and turned her mother's family portraits to the wall. She didn't want anything to do with her mother or her mother's family. She made sure they were turned back before Rose found out about it. There would be a price to pay for her tirade. and her mother would make her pay dearly.

A knock on her door jolted her to her feet.

"Nettie, you left your school books downstairs. I brought them to you."

"Oh, I guess I forgot them." Nettie thought her mother had already left for the town hall. She opened her bedroom door, took her books and thanked her mother.

Quite abruptly, Rose turned back and said, "Did you find out where your little friend, um, what's her name, lives?"

Nettie froze. She was not ready to tell her, so she lied. "You mean Ida Mae? No mother, I completely forgot."

Pulling on her white gloves, Rose said, "I'm leaving now for the town hall meeting. And for heaven's sake, get that address tomorrow. The ladies tea is next week. This is very important. All right?"

"All right, mother." Nettie swallowed the lump in her throat and closed the door. The idea of losing her best friend brought her to tears. She threw herself on the bed crying softly into her pillow. *How am I going to get out of this? I have to think of something.* All afternoon and through dinner, Nettie fretted over her friendship with Ida Mae. Before her normal bedtime, she excused herself from the sitting room feigning a stomach ache. Her father raised an eyebrow in concern. Her mother simply said, "Good night." Nettie slept fitfully that night. She could not bear losing Ida Mae as a friend. She had to find a way.

Her mind raced all night jostling different scenarios of how to keep Ida Mae in her life. The clanging of milk bottles being delivered, before dawn, alerted her of the time. Nettie had not slept a wink. *Think, girl, think,* she said to herself. While brushing her hair at the dressing table, an idea popped into her mind. *Maybe if I talk to father!* The idea brought hope to her quivering lips. She jumped to her feet and picked up a hankie from her nightstand, wrapping it around her fingers over and over as she paced her room. *Oh yes, Father! He will help me!*

Nettie dressed and checked herself in the full length mirror. Taking in a deep breath, she tiptoed to the door. She wanted to catch Father before he left for work. Usually Mother did not come down to breakfast until he was finished with his second cup of coffee. *Surely that will be enough time to talk with him.*

Gingerly opening her bedroom door, she listened for any sound of her mother. She smelled the coffee brewing and heard the snap of the morning newspaper downstairs. Gently, she closed the door behind her and tiptoed down the stairs, avoiding the familiar creaks in the boards. She made it to the bottom without a sound. Glancing about for any sign of mother, she moved toward the dining room.

Sitting at the head of the table, holding the newspaper in front of him, was her beloved father. His black hair was combed neatly into place and could be seen above the paper. Nettie's shoulders lowered in temporary relief that her mother was still upstairs, but the butterflies in her stomach were about to take flight. She took in a deep breath and strode toward her father.

"Morning, Father."

The paper lowered. "Well, aren't we an early riser this morning. How's my Nettie girl today? Is your stomach better?"

"My stomach?"

"Yes, your stomach." Eyeing her above his glasses, he continued, "You said last night before you went to bed that your stomach ached."

Always caring. He didn't miss a thing where his Nettie was concerned. His smile melted her into a puddle of joy. "I am just fine, Father. It was nothing. Really. Maybe a little too much dessert?"

"Well, I'm mighty glad to hear it. What brings you down so early this morning?"

Here I go, she thought. *Be cool. Father knows you very well.* The pep talk to herself gave her the fortitude she needed.

"I...I...I thought I'd get up early and ask you something special."

"Well then. Why don't you sit down beside me and tell me what's on your pretty little mind." He dropped the newspaper to his lap and gave Nettie his full attention.

Nettie sat down in the adjacent chair and folded her hands in her lap, as all proper ladies do. "Ahem." She cleared her throat thinking of the right words to say. "Well, I've met this new friend at school. Her name is Ida Mae Astor. Father, she is the sweetest thing! We get along so well. I would really like you to meet her.

I wondered if I could bring her by your office after school today. Would that be all right?" Her eyes pleaded for understanding.

"Why, of course. I would very much like to meet your new friend. Ida Mae, you say? That is a very pretty name."

Nettie rushed to her father's side and hugged his neck, kissing his forehead as was her custom. She softly squealed in delight as her mother entered the room.

"Well, what is going on here?"

Nettie looked frantically at her father, her eyes wide as saucers.

Sensing his daughter's discomfort, he said, "Um, nothing, my dear. My daughter and I were just sharing a secret." He snapped his paper back into place, in an effort to ignore Rose's impending question.

Usually, no one dared speak to Rose until she had finished her second cup of coffee. It was first priority. Unless a secret was looming. She stopped pouring coffee into her favorite tea cup and returned to the dining room. "What secret? You know I don't like secrets in this house."

Samuel lowered the paper and laid it on the table, organizing it's contents before responding to his wife. Nettie saw him smile at the delay. "Rose, my dear, it won't be a secret anymore if we told you." He shot a quick wink at his daughter.

Rose tugged on her sleeves and smoothed her skirt. "I will find out one way or another. Mark my words." She turned toward the kitchen and left Nettie and her father alone in the dining room. Nettie blew out a sigh of relief.

"Come, Nettie, walk with me downtown a ways and you can continue on toward school." Samuel rose from his chair and walked to the foyer. Nettie followed. She slipped into her winter coat and picked up her books. Her father put on his coat, draped a scarf around his neck and set his favorite hat on his head. It was a gift from Nettie when she was nine years old. She saw her father admire it in the general store one day and later asked the clerk to hide it away for later.

Stepping through the front door, Nettie felt the cold breeze whip around her head and snuggled deeper into her coat. Daffodil bulbs were peeking through the light snow that had accumulated on the ground. Spring was just around the corner. As beautiful as that was, nothing was more special to Nettie than time alone with her father.

At the end of their walkway, Nettie heard her mother shouting from the porch, coffee cup in hand.

"Samuel!" Rose yelled. "Where do you think you are going? You haven't eaten breakfast yet. Samuel!"

Samuel raised his hand to wave over the top of his head but did not turn around. Nettie put her arm in triumph around her father's elbow. For the next few minutes, it would be just her and her father. She would memorize each second. They walked side by side down the street huddled together like one big coat.

"Nettie," Samuel said, patting her hand, "We will have to come up with a secret that will satisfy your mother's curiosity. Let me think. I know! Let's say we planned on stopping for a glazed donut at the Apothecary. In fact, let's do!" They crossed Main Street and entered the pharmacy, which was also a small diner. Inside, they sat at a booth near the window and ordered one cup of coffee, two glazed donuts and a glass of milk. The pharmacist's wife, Doris, who ran the diner, took their order. "Now, we must keep a straight face and play this out. I do love to tease your mother."

Tease mother? Nettie gulped. It sounded absurd. Nettie wouldn't think of teasing around with her mother! Though she did observe from time to time her father getting the best of Rose. "Of course, Father. And thank you for the donuts!" Biting into the freshly made glazed confection, she rolled her eyes in satisfaction. "I love you best, Father, you do know that, don't you?"

He blew on his coffee to cool it and looked out the large glass window onto Main Street. He spotted something moving near the train depot across the street. There it was again.

"What is it, Father? Do you see something?" Nettie looked out as well, searching for what had distracted her father.

"No, not something. Someone. Don't look now but your mother followed us and is ducking behind the depot spying on us. She cannot bear for us to keep something from her." He laughed so hard his coffee spilled onto the table.

"Should..should we ask her to join us?" Nettie's voice cracked asking something she really didn't mean.

"No. No. This is too much fun." Leaning forward on his elbows he said, "She will be coming by my office and peppering me with questions all day. I will play her game beautifully. Don't you worry. When she finds out donuts were the secret she will be furious." Doris appeared at his side and filled his coffee cup and left. He took another sip of the warm coffee. Placing it back on the table, he reached for Nettie's hand. "Don't you worry none. Her bark is worse than her bite." Looking her square in the face, he said, "She loves you, Nettie. You do know that, don't you?"

Nettie did not know that. But to assuage her father, she nodded in agreement. "Good girl. Now, you best be getting to school and I am late for the office."

They exited the Apothecary, hugged, and parted ways. Nettie fretted all the way to school about Ida Mae. She would put off telling her mother where she lived as long as she could. Sooner or later, she knew she would have to appeal to Father once more.

That afternoon Rose stopped by the bank where her important husband served as president. "Are you busy?"

He looked up from the paperwork covering his desk and heard the sugary sweet voice he knew so well. The only time she used that tone was when she wanted to squeeze something out of him. "I am. So what brings you by here?"

"I thought maybe we might have lunch, if you haven't already eaten."

Her flirtatious invitation tickled him. He studied her further and noticed she had changed outfits since that morning. She wore a sleek, tailored, scoop-necked olive green dress made of crepe. A felt, cloche hat with a shiny jeweled brooch adorned her head…a birthday gift from Samuel the year prior. She had never worn it before.

Walking to the tack board, he pointed to several papers. "See all this. I really have to finish the paperwork on the Jared House loan by tomorrow. The opening of the restaurant will be delayed if I don't finish on time, so I won't have time today." His schedule was not that tight, but he was enjoying playing the game.

"Samuel Collins, you have to eat something. It's not good for your body to go without food for too many hours. You didn't even eat breakfast this morning. Let's go to the Edgewater Hotel restaurant. Today's special is your favorite, prime rib." Her curiosity was dripping with sweetness.

"If you are trying to find out my little secret, I may as well tell you."

He stepped closer to his wife until they were almost nose to nose. *I can be just as clever as you my dear*, he chuckled to himself.

Removing her gaze from his probing eyes, she blurted, "I am not trying to find out your secret! I don't even believe you have a secret."

"Yes, my dear, I do. But if you are so desperate to know, I will take you up on your offer for lunch. You pay."

"Deal. So what's the big secret?" Rose was terrible at the game. But he gave her points for persistence.

He sat back down at his desk and leaned forward on his elbows. "Nettie and I snuck out for glazed donuts this morning."

"Glazed donuts? That's the big secret? Samuel, you are impossible. Forget lunch. I just lost my appetite!" She spun around with a flair and angrily slammed the office door.

"I guess that means no lunch, huh?" Samuel shouted to the closed door. He doubled over in laughter winning another game of Rose has to know.

Nettie's father was still working on the financing for the Jared house when two giggly girls entered his office.

"Well, what have we here? Could this be the famous Ida Mae?"

Ida Mae blushed at the compliment, curtsied and said, "Yes sir, I am Ida Mae Astor. Pleased to meet you."

Samuel rose and stood in front of the two girls leaning back against his desk. "Please, you don't have to curtsy to me. Nettie has spoken very highly of you. I feel I already know you. So, what do you girls have planned this brisk afternoon?"

Ida Mae explained that she had called her mother from school asking for permission to meet him. Mary Astor said she would meet her downtown at the Apothecary at 4:00. The girls were thrilled to have time together away from school.

Nettie jumped in, "We thought we would go over to the Apothecary for a chocolate milkshake." They both giggled and linked arms.

"Fine. Fine. That sounds like fun! If you girls don't mind, I would like to treat the two of you to the best chocolate milkshake you will find in Windy Garden." He reached into his pocket and handed Nettie fifty cents.

"Wow! Father this is way too much."

"I figured you might need some French fries to go along with the shake."

"Father, you are the best!" A hug and a kiss on the forehead from Nettie sent the two girls on their way. Samuel watched from the plate glass window facing Main Street and smiled, happy that his precious daughter had finally found a faithful friend.

Just before 4 p.m., Rose stormed into Samuel's office once again, slamming the door. "Do you have any idea who that Astor girl is? Do you?"

"Astor girl. I don't think I know the Astors." He was absorbed in the papers on the long wooden table across from his desk, unperturbed by the sudden entrance of his wife.

"Samuel! That friend of Nettie's. What's her name!"

"Oh, yes, of course. Sweet girl, that Ida Mae. What's the problem?" He was so wrapped up in his project, he did not have time to deal with trivial problems his wife was notorious for cooking up.

"When Nettie told me her last name was Astor and that her family moved here from New York City, I immediately began making plans to welcome them to the town." Pacing the room in dramatic style, she continued, "Imagine! A New York Astor moving to our small town of Windy Garden. I told all my friends about her mother. Why, I even set her a place at the ladies tea party for tomorrow, with a nameplate and everything!"

Stacking a row of papers and tapping them on the table to align them, Samuel asked, "All right. So, what is the problem?"

"I went to the school today to find out where Ida Mae lives and do you know what I discovered?" Samuel did not notice her foot tapping or her hands akimbo on her hips.

"No, I don't." Samuel was engrossed in his project not seeing the importance of this latest ranting of his wife.

"Samuel!" Her voice rose two decibels, as papers flew all over the floor.

"What?" he shouted back, stooping to pick up the mess she had created.

Pointing out the large plate glass window she railed, "They live in one of those broken down, dilapidated old shacks over on Hilltop Park Road. That's what!! They are poor, Samuel, poor. Well, I can tell you one thing. Our daughter is not going to hang out with the likes of her. Not while I'm still breathing. Nettie will not be influenced by some riff-raff from the wrong side of the tracks. Not to mention being the daughter of the most important and wealthy banker in town who has a certain level of propriety to maintain!"

Samuel rose to his full height and walked slowly over to Rose. He faced her squarely and said, "First of all, there is nothing wrong with poor people. And Nettie's little friend seems polite and respectful. And from what I can tell, she is a lovely young girl."

"You....you've met her? When?"

"Just a little while ago. They stopped in after school and are over at the Apothecary having a snack. With my blessing, I might add." Samuel held his ground, not moving an inch.

"Well, I'll put an end to this right now. I am going to march over there and pull my well-bred daughter out of there and demand she never speak to that...that... Ida Mae person again!" Rose turned but Samuel moved in front of her and blocked her way.

Samuel's ire rose to full throttle, a rare occurrence. "Rose Collins, you will do no such thing! I forbid it! Nettie has found a friend, her first real friend in her life and you will not interfere in their relationship. Do you hear me?"

Rose stumbled back a step at the tone and severity of Samuel's voice. Samuel did not back down. He knew he had made his point quite clear that on this issue, he would not yield.

Rose tugged on the bottom of her sweater and steadied herself.

Regaining her determination, she stepped toward him. With gritted teeth, she looked Samuel in the eye and said, "I most certainly hear you, Samuel Collins. Now move out of my way so I can retrieve my daughter from this embarrassing situation."

Samuel took her hand and lowered his voice, "Rose, I love you. With all my heart, I love you. But you will not break Nettie's heart." A long pause ensued. She started to pull away. "Go home, Rose. Go home." Suddenly, Samuel's energy drained completely from his body. He staggered over to his desk and sat down heavily.

Rose rushed to his side. "Samuel! Samuel! Are you all right?" She patted his hand in an effort to rouse him. There was no response. Realizing she needed help, she ran out the front door and screamed, "Help! Someone! Anyone! I need help!"

Doug Grimes, the town councilman, heard her cry and ran across the street to her. "What's wrong, Mrs. Collins?" She began to sway as if to faint. Doug put his arms around her shoulders to steady her.

Fear gripped Rose as she struggled to speak. She weakly pointed inside and said, "Samuel."

A crowd began to gather outside the bank. Doug guided Rose inside to check on Samuel. He found him limp in his chair and rushed over. Immediately, he felt for a pulse. "His pulse is weak. I have to find help." Doug hurried past Rose who stood with her trembling hands over her mouth.

By the time Doug reached the door, Sheriff Daniels entered. "What's all the commotion?"

Doug explained the call for help and that he needed Dr. Carter immediately. He wasn't sure what was wrong with Samuel but he did know he needed immediate medical attention.

"Dr. Carter is delivering a baby for Mrs. Sadler. I'll run and fetch Charlie." With that, the sheriff disappeared beyond the crowd.

Doug ran back to Samuel. The color had drained from his face and he was as pale as milk. He grew worried that his friend might be in real trouble. He loosened Samuel's tie and unbuttoned his shirt. Then removed his shoes to help with circulation.

The sheriff bolted into the Apothecary and found the pharmacist/part-time doctor, Charlie Hoover, at the pharmacy counter.

"Charlie, I need you! It's a medical emergency. It's Samuel Collins!"

"Find the doctor quick. I'm heading there now." Charlie grabbed his medical bag and hurried in the direction of the bank.

Hearing the shuffling of feet, Rose looked over to see Charlie rush in with his medical bag. "Step back, Rose, and let me have a look," Charlie ordered.

She rose to her feet and placed her arms around her waist.

Charlie took out a stethoscope and listened to Henry's heart, then took his pulse. With his fingers, he opened Henry's left eye and then his right.

Placing the stethoscope back in the bag he addressed Rose, "He's breathing a little better now. But his color is still pale. We need to get him to the hospital."

"Where....where is Dr. Carter? Someone get Dr. Carter! We have to get the doctor. Why is everyone standing around?!?"

"He's delivering a baby, Rose. I've already sent the sheriff for him. Just be calm. Remember, I am trained in medical practice too. I am doing the best I can."

Leaning over the patient, Charlie asked, "Samuel. Samuel, can you hear me?"

Samuel began to stir. He looked around as if to get his bearings. "I can hardly see. But I can make you out, Charlie. What are you doing? Playing doctor?"

His usual lightheartedness at every situation amused Charlie. "See, Rose, he is coming around. His sense of humor has returned. And look, his color is coming back." Charlie chuckled at his friend and said, "Now lie real still, buddy. We are going to get you to the hospital just as quick as we can. Dr. Carter is on his way."

Rose knelt again beside Samuel to see for herself he was rallying.

"Now, Rose. Don't go getting yourself in a tither. I will be fine." He reached up and stroked her cheek. She embraced his hand and held it to her chest.

Rose looked outside the large plate glass window in Samuel's office and saw more people gathering outside. She wished they would all go away and leave them alone.

Nettie and Ida Mae were enjoying their milkshakes when the sheriff ran into the Apothecary and Charlie ran out with him, holding his doctor bag. Most everyone in town knew Charlie was as much a doctor as Dr. Carter, who took care of everybody.

"I wonder where he is going?" Nettie pondered aloud.

"Who is he?" asked Ida Mae.

"He's the town pharmacist. He is also a doctor, sort of. He fills in when Dr. Carter is out on calls." Another slurp drew air from the almost empty glass tumbler.

"Where do you suppose he is going? There are lots of people right outside the window standing on the sidewalk," Ida Mae said leaning into the window for a better look.

Nettie's vantage point was hindered by her back to her father's office. She turned in her seat and looked out the window. It looked like they were gathering around the bank.

"Ida Mae, we've got to go. Come quick!" The girls jumped up and ran out the door of the Apothecary and fought their way through the crowd. When they reached the bank, Nettie plunged ahead and saw her father lying on the floor with her worried mother beside him.

"Father! Father! Are you all right?" Nettie knelt on the other side of him sobbing and taking his hand in hers.

Before her father could answer, Rose very calmly said, "Don't get so excited, Nettie. He will be fine. Now get up off the floor. You are getting your clothes dirty."

Nettie could not believe her mother would say such a thing at a time like this. Fury raged within her as she looked at her and said, "I will not! Father is hurting and I am going to stay right here with him!"

Rose started to protest when Samuel squeezed Nettie's hand and spoke softly, "My Nettie girl. Did you have a good time with your new friend?"

"Ye..Yes, Father. I did. What happened? Are you alright?" Tears formed in her eyes, falling freely, as if in defiance to her mother.

"Now, don't go worrying about me. I will be just fine. See, Dr. Carter has arrived. He will take good care of me." He patted her head and winked their secret wink.

Dr. Carter approached Samuel and ordered Rose out of his way, leaving Nettie the opportunity to stay by her father.

Nettie saw her mother open her mouth to protest but shut it when she saw the doctor take charge and call for the sheriff to bring in the stretcher.

Nettie looked around and saw the worried expressions on the faces of those who loved her father dearly. She weakly smiled a thank you, as she followed the stretcher out the door. Ida Mae was standing with her mother by the door and rushed to hug Nettie. "I'm so sorry, Nettie. Is he going to be okay?" Ida Mae sobbed.

"Oh Ida Mae. He has to be. He just has to!"

Immediately, there were more volunteers than necessary to help lift Samuel onto the stretcher. It was a short block to the town hospital. The townspeople carried Samuel Collins all the way.

4

The stretcher carrying her husband quickly disappeared behind two swinging doors inside the hospital's emergency care unit. Rose tried to push through behind the medical team, when a nurse stopped her and attempted to direct her back to the nurse's station. But Rose refused to move, and demanded to see the doctor. When the nurse informed her that the doctor was attending to her husband and would be out as soon as he could, Rose remained unmoved.

"Obviously, young lady, you do not know who I am. I am Samuel Collins' wife and I want to see the doctor and my husband. Now!"

The nurse did not show any signs of shock by this woman's behavior and calmly answered, "Mrs. Collins, I promise you that when the doctor is finished I will personally bring him to you. If you would be so kind as to have a seat over there, I'm sure you will not have to wait long." The nurse pointed to a room across the hall.

"I don't think so!" Rose responded indignantly, and headed for the closed doors. The nurse hurried after her. "Mrs. Collins, you cannot go in right now. Any interruptions might delay the doctor's evaluation of your husband's condition." She gently touched Rose's arm and met her gaze, "Please, come have a seat."

Rose strained to look through the darkened windows that led inside the emergency care area. She blinked back a solitary tear that threatened to flow down her cheek, and grudgingly followed the nurse back to the waiting room.

"I'll be back the minute I hear anything." Patting her shoulder, the nurse left.

Rose entered to see a room full of people. She recognized some of the people who had been outside the bank, now crowded into the small waiting room.

Instinctively, she felt put out by these people for invading her space. Every eye was on her. They were friends, business associates, and neighbors of Samuel. Doug, the town councilman, quickly rose and offered his seat to Rose, as did two other members of her church. She was stunned at the number of people there on behalf of her husband. A momentary feeling of shame washed over her for thinking badly about these people. But the feeling faded as quickly as it came. Sitting in the vacant seat, she just felt irritated that they would hang around. She had no use for these people invading her personal life. Business connections were fine, but this was far outside her comfort zone. She sighed and wished they would all go away.

Young Nettie was standing at the door with Ida Mae, and heard every word spoken in the hallway. When her mother brushed past her with the nurse, she never acknowledged that she had even seen her daughter. Nettie saw the hurt she was feeling reflected in her best friend's eyes. She slowly turned her gaze down the hallway for any sign of Dr. Carter or her father. She wanted to be as close to her father as they would allow. Glancing behind her, she marveled at all the people there. Every chair and wall space was filled, as well as much of the floor space in the middle of the room.

Nettie heard Ida Mae's mother speak to Rose, offering her help. She was embarrassed when her mother didn't even acknowledge the woman's presence. Mrs. Astor walked over to the coffee table and poured a cup of coffee. Returning with the coffee, she offered the cup to Nettie's mother. Rose waved her hand in dismissal. Nettie was alarmed at how rude her mother could be to strangers. Ida Mae noticed too, reached over and rubbed Nettie's arm and said, "It's alright, Nettie. Your mother is very upset right now. She is worried about your father. She's not thinking clearly."

Through gritted teeth, Nettie whispered, "I'm hurting too, Ida Mae. Didn't you see her brush past me as though I wasn't even here? And to treat your mother like that!"

Just then, the same nurse who left earlier returned and called, "Mrs. Collins?"

Rose stood, picked up her purse, and met the nurse halfway. Nettie hurried over and stood by her mother.

"The doctor will see you in a few minutes," said the sweet voice.

Rose seemed in a state of shock. She mechanically moved toward the doorway. Nettie touched the crook of her elbow and stood quietly, waiting with her mother. No one in the room moved or made a sound. Samuel's friends were anxious to hear the news as well.

Nettie trembled at the silence that followed. She didn't know what the doctor might say. "Oh, Lord, let it be good news," she whispered.

The doors opened and Dr. Carter stepped out. He made his way down the hallway and stopped in front of Nettie and her mother. "Mrs. Collins, let's sit down and talk about Samuel." He motioned her back into the room.

"No. I want to talk in the hallway. Not in there."

"That is quite acceptable. I understand." The doctor walked with her and Nettie over to the nurse's station and leaned his back against the high counter. Dark circles under his eyes indicated how tired he must be. "Well, Samuel has had a heart attack. A pretty severe one. I have him sedated so he can rest and recuperate from the intense pain he has experienced. I will keep him here tonight and then move him to a room tomorrow where you can visit. When he is able to go home, he will need lots of rest. I trust you will make sure that happens. Rose, I have to be honest with you. As a doctor, I am surprised he made it at all. As a friend and believer in Jesus Christ, I firmly believe God must have more for Samuel to do." Dr. Carter paused and wiped his brow with a handkerchief. Patting her hand, he added, "Rose, he will be fine." Then turning to Nettie he said, "Your father asked about you while I was examining him. He wanted to be sure you were alright and said to tell you he'll see you soon." His smile lit up the corridor.

Rose winced at the abrupt change of direction, but maintained her composure. "Can I see my husband now?"

"Sure, Rose. Come with me." Rose and the doctor turned and walked back toward darkened doors. Nettie began to follow as well when the doctor stopped and said, "I'm sorry, Nettie, but you are not old enough yet to go in. You will have to wait here." He patted her hair, smiled, and said, "But you can see him tomorrow, when he is in his room, ok?" Nettie sadly nodded. She watched her mother and the doctor disappear behind the double doors and felt very alone.

Why can't I see him? He is my father. I am twelve years old, not a baby anymore! She wanted so desperately to barge through those doors. She took a step forward when she heard the soft, sweet voice of Ida Mae behind her. "I know how hurt you must be, Nettie. But I'm afraid there is nothing you can do right now. Please. Come back to the waiting room." Ida Mae guided Nettie around the waist and into the room of anxious faces. She knew they were anticipating news of her father's condition.

Nettie was touched by the roomful of waiting people. She felt they had a right to know how her father was doing. Trembling, she addressed the gathered crowd. "Father had a very serious heart attack. Mother is with him now.

Dr. Carter said that he was surprised that he made it." Tears streamed down her face as she wiped them away with a lace handkerchief, and relayed what she knew. She brightened a little for the sake of those who had waited so long and said, "He also said that God must have more for father to do."

Smiles and sighs of relief bubbled forth at the good news. One by one, the town folks stood and began to chatter over Samuel's condition. Their beloved Samuel was going to pull through.

Rose's pastor, Tom, and his wife Emily were there. Tom asked if they would join him in prayer. Everyone gathered together in a large circle in the middle of the room. With heads bowed, Tom began. "Lord Jesus, we are so grateful to You that our Samuel is still with us. Thank You for watching over him and placing the right people around him to help in every way. Thank You that You are with him now and have been with him all along. Help him to feel Your presence and Your love while recuperating. We also pray for Rose and Nettie. They need You so much right now. Sometimes it seems like it's harder for those who wait. Open their hearts to receive Your love during this stressful time. And bless these kind folks who came out today for their dear friend. We are excited to see what You will do next in Samuel's life. Amen."

'Amens' filled the room as people hugged Nettie and said they would continue to pray for her and her family. Pastor Tom told Nettie he wanted to wait and see her mother before he left. They, along with Ida Mae's mother, stepped into the hallway, leaving Nettie and her best friend alone.

Nettie grabbed her friend in a hug and sobbed into her shoulder. "Oh, Ida Mae, father could have died. He could have died!" Nettie's heart broke at the thought of losing her father. She loved him with all her heart and could not imagine life without him. She lifted her head and looked at Ida Mae and said, "If anything happens to him, I don't know what I'll do. He loves me so much. And I love him too. If he was gone, it would only be mother and me. I couldn't bear that, Ida Mae. I just couldn't....."

"Nettie!" Her mother's voice interrupted, "Come along. It's time to go home." Her arms were crossed and her tone sharp as she glared at her daughter.

"I guess I had better go," Nettie whispered to Ida Mae. "Thank you for staying with me. And thank your mom for being here, too." She left and dutifully followed her mother out of the hospital doors. She did not want to leave. She wanted to see with her own eyes that her father was as the doctor described. It was not fair. What did age have to do with it anyway? Anger and despair replaced the atmosphere of love and hope only moments before, before the return of her mother. She was angry at the doctor for not letting her see her father, and angry at her mother for not caring that she was hurting too.

Nettie and her mother walked home and entered the house in silence. Rose hung the house keys on the wrought iron key holder near the door and went to the kitchen. She picked up the coffee pot and filled it with water. Then she opened the coffee can and scooped coffee into the strainer basket inside the pot. Nettie stood in the kitchen entrance and stared at her mother. It seemed to Nettie she must be invisible. Her mother had barely spoken to her since her father was taken to the hospital. No words that meant anything. The longer she watched, the madder she got.

"Why did you not insist that I see Father? You could have, you know?" Nettie approached the dinette set and placed her hands on the back of a chair, leaned forward, and waited for a response.

"What? What did you say?" Rose placed the lid on the coffee pot and lit the stove. "Were you saying something to me?"

"Mother!" shouted Nettie.

Rose banged the pot on the stove and turned to Nettie. "Why are you raising your voice to me! What is it you want?"

"I want you to see me, Mother! Really see me! I am hurting, too. I wanted to see father. But you don't care, do you, Mother?" Nettie was building to a rage. She had never dared speak so to her mother.

"Nettie, I will not have you speak to me in that tone of voice! I raised you better than that! Now go to your room and leave me be!" She turned back to adjust the burner on the stove.

Nettie stood her ground. "You have never cared how I felt. Never! All you have ever wanted out of me was to behave properly and not embarrass you in this precious little town. You care so much about what other people think about you, but you don't care what *I* think. Can you even see me Mother? Is it so much to ask that you love me? Father could have died, Mother. He could have died!"

Rose leaned into the kitchen counter, resting her palms on the edge with her back to Nettie and said, "Go to your room, Nettie. Now!"

Nettie stomped her foot and ran up the stairs, crying. She slammed her bedroom door and fell face down on her bed. She cried so hard, all energy drained from her body. Her father's heart attack weighed heavily upon her. She grabbed an afghan at the foot of her bed and covered up. Her sobbing exhausted her and she finally fell asleep. When she awoke, it was just getting dark. She sprang from her bed and looked outside her bedroom window. *Did Father really have a heart attack? Or did I dream it?* She rubbed her eyes and heard her mother's bedroom door shut. *It was real. Father is in the hospital. Why, oh why, didn't mother insist I see him?* The more she fretted over her own question, the more she knew the answer. *She doesn't care about me. She never has.*

Nettie opened her bedroom door and peeked out. She listened for signs of her mother stirring about. She looked down the hallway and saw a beam of light under her parent's bedroom door. *Mother must be in there.* Nettie tiptoed down the stairs, grabbed her coat and stepped out into the chilly evening. Wrapping her arms around her body, she scurried off to the hospital three blocks away. As she approached the nurse's station she was relieved no one was there. She continued on until she came to the familiar double set of doors on her right. She stood very still and stared at the doors that blocked her from her father. Trembling, she reached out and gently pushed on the door and felt it give. Pulling her hand back as if stung by a bee, she held her arm close to her chest. Her body shook in fear of getting caught. Glimpsing about, she dared reach out again, when a tap on her shoulder startled her. She jumped, suppressing a scream with her hand.

"Nettie. What are you doing here? I thought you left with your mother." It was Dr. Carter.

She grew frightened at the thought that he would send her home again without seeing her father. Quietly she sobbed, "Oh, Dr. Carter, I need to see Father. I need to see with my own eyes that he is alright."

The kind doctor pulled her into a grandfatherly hug and said, "All right, child, I'll take you in. But just this once." He led her through the double doors and over to her father. He was pale and had a breathing tube in his nose and tubes in his arm. She had never seen her father sick before. Nettie went to his side, afraid to touch him. Her fingers hovered above his arm.

"He is doing well, Nettie. He should be feeling no pain now." Nodding toward her father he said, "See how he is sleeping? Like a newborn baby." Dr. Carter reached for his chart at the foot of his bed and thumbed through the papers on the clipboard.

Nettie stepped closer, reaching out, her hand so close. But she was afraid to awaken him, lest she cause him further harm. Looking into her father's face, she memorized every detail. She was terrified she would return in the morning and he would be gone.

Dr. Carter touched her elbow and said, "Nettie, we have to go."

Hesitating, she leaned over closer and wished she could stay. She blew a kiss and winked at her father, as she turned to leave. It was their customary good-bye. She knew he could not see her, but sending the kiss gave her hope.

"Nettie girl," a soft voice called.

Nettie turned abruptly to see her father's eyes barely open and his hand raised slightly. She rushed back to his side. "Father! Father, I am so glad to see you. I have been so worried." She ever so gently rested her head on his shoulder. Samuel stroked her hair with his right hand and kissed the top of her head.

"Did you think I was going to leave my Nettie girl? Not a chance. I promise, I will be home soon and everything will be as it was."

Nettie raised her head to look at him. "Promise, promise?"

"I promise." He winked their secret wink and said, "Now, go home and look after your mother for me. Her schedule is all topsy-turvy and you know how she gets when that happens!" He smiled and motioned for her to go.

Nettie did not want to leave. She wanted to stay right there beside her father. And the last thing she wanted to do was go home to her mother. Nettie could not take her eyes off him as she walked out the doors and into the hallway. "Thank you, Dr. Carter for letting me see Father. Are you sure I can't stay? I'll be as quiet as a mouse. No one will know I'm even here." Her eyes pleaded with the kind doctor.

Dr. Carter patted her hand with his fingers and said, "I understand how you feel. But the nurses are with him every minute and are taking good care of him. Besides, you wouldn't want him worrying about you now, would you?"

Sniffing back more tears she answered. "No sir, I wouldn't."

"Now, don't you go telling anyone I let you in, ok? It will be our little secret. Now head home and try not to worry." Dr. Carter went back to his patients, leaving Nettie staring at the closed doors once again. She smiled at the thought of having two secrets in one day. One with her father and now one with Dr. Carter. She would keep his secret. Especially from mother.

She wished she could stay beside her father's side all night and watch over him, but she knew it was impossible. Breathing a heavy sigh, she turned and left the hospital. Walking home, Nettie felt like a ton of bricks had lifted from her shoulders. She had seen Father and he was going to be coming home soon. He promised.

Darkness had descended on Windy Garden. The gas street lights lit her path. She glanced upward and searched for the moon. It was a moonless night. All was peaceful and quiet. Even the mighty oak leaves were asleep in the calm. She turned the corner onto Depot Street, elated from seeing her father. Joy crept into her soul as she remembered the words of her father, "I will be home soon and everything will be as it was." He promised. And father never broke his promise.

Nettie stopped on the sidewalk in front of her home and stared at the huge Victorian house that looked especially cold this night. It looked lonely and sad without Father. He was the only reason she loved coming home every day. Without his presence, she felt alone and bereft of love.

A movement above caught her eye. Glancing up, she saw her mother standing in her bedroom window, holding the curtain back with her right hand, staring out. When the two locked eyes, she dropped the curtain.

Nettie sighed and walked to the front steps and sat down. She did not want to go in. She wanted to rewind time. Father would be well, sleeping in his bed down the hall from her. She would hear his soft whiffle of a snore and doze off into a restful night's sleep herself, knowing he was near. But time was not rewinding. Father had a heart attack and was in the hospital. It all seemed so surreal.

'What am I to do now? She asked herself. She did not want to go inside the cold, uncaring house. She wanted to go back to the hospital. She did not want to be here. Nettie remembered her father's words, "Take care of your mother." *So how in the world am I to do that? She doesn't need me. She doesn't want me.* Tears did not come this time. But what did come was the beginning of a hardened heart towards her mother. She had always hoped that one day her mother would love her...that they could become like other mothers and daughters, laughing together, hugging each other and doing the things she had seen other mothers and daughters do. It crushingly dawned on her that it would never happen.

Nettie looked around again, hearing only the rustle of her skirt, and resolved she would not hope for what would never be. Not ever again.

The following two years were filled with laughter and joy whenever Nettie was with her father. He still worked at the bank. But he had hired a secretary and a young apprentice to help out, which freed up his time to go home every afternoon and rest.

Every day after school, Nettie would run home and into her father's bedroom and tell him of her day. During the summer months, she would run to his office and walk him home. Sometimes they would stop off at the Apothecary for Nettie to get a hand-dipped milkshake. Samuel would enjoy a cup of coffee, listening intently to his daughter's cute ramblings about Ida Mae. His smile and attentiveness warmed her heart, as the coffee must have warmed his belly. Those were her favorite times.

At home, Rose did her duty for Samuel. She closed the draperies for his naps and did not allow noise in or near the house while he was resting.

One day, a dog dared bark out in front of the Collins home while Samuel was asleep. Rose hurriedly ran out on the porch trying to shoo the dog away but he kept on barking. She was so upset she ran inside and came back out with a pistol and shot at the dog. The neighbor, Carl, saw the whole thing and couldn't tell who was more surprised, Rose or the dog she missed. But she accomplished her purpose. The dog never returned.

On a cold, late winter day, Samuel called Rose into the bedroom. They sat on the settee facing each other. He took her hands in his and said, "Rose, my dear, I think I'll go see Dr. Carter in the morning. I feel some pains again. Only slightly, though."

Rose stiffened in fear. "Don't you think you ought to see him now?" He patted her hands and continued, "Now, we both know how bad the heart attack was before. This time it is not so intense. I think morning will be fine. I called you in to talk about some important things."

Rose pulled her hands from his and stood. "This is a silly

conversation. I don't want to hear another word. Why don't I fix you a bite to eat?" She started for the door when Samuel said, "Rose, wait. Please, come here beside me." He patted the settee. She turned and sat back down.

Rose leaned her head on his shoulder, afraid to look in his eyes.

Samuel stroked her shoulder length dark hair and said, "Darling, if anything should happen to me...."

She jerked up and spouted, "Nothing is going to happen to you!"

"Ok. Ok. Please. Just hear me out. I need to say these things to you now, because there may be a day, way in the future, you will need to remember what I have said. Will you hear me out?" He placed his hand under her chin and lifted her face.

She still refused to look him in the eye, keeping her eyes lowered. "Yes," Rose trembled.

"Alright. First of all, you will never have to worry about money. You have handled your family money and mine all these years, so you are well aware of what we have. What you do not know is that I have two secret accounts in the bank. One for you and one for Nettie."

Rose bristled, pretending to be offended and said, "Samuel, you know I have never liked secrets!"

"I know. I know. But this is a good secret. You alone have access to your account and when Nettie marries or turns eighteen she can access her account."

"Samuel, I could have just as well handled her account along with mine."

"Yes. I have no doubt of that. But I want Nettie to feel like she has something only from me. Something that will help her start her own life when she is old enough to marry or move out on her own. Do you understand?"

"I'm trying," she sniffed.

"Another thing, and this is the most important. I want you to promise right here, right now, that you will do nothing to interfere with Nettie and Ida Mae's friendship once I'm gone."

Rose bolted to her feet and paced in front of him. "Samuel, you know I have never approved of that relationship. That girl is not suitable for Nettie and you know it. I have kept my opinions to myself these last two years because of you." She paced in front of Samuel, thinking, *I'm glad he doesn't know how many times I have tried to squelch that friendship when he wasn't around.*

Samuel wearily rose and motioned his wife to come near. "Rose, this is very important to me. And important to Nettie too. I will not respect you if you interfere. Now, do you promise?"

Rose took her sweet time answering. "Alright, Samuel. If that is what you want, I will not interfere."

"Promise?"

Reluctantly giving in, Rose said, "I promise. But are you sure I shouldn't call Dr. Carter now? Samuel, if you're having pain again, I think we should call."

"Yes, I'm sure. If the pain gets worse, I'll let you call then, ok?"

"Well, alright. You will let me know?"

Samuel nodded. "I will let you know."

Rose took her famous stance, hands akimbo on her hips. "I'm going to keep a sharp eye on you, Samuel Collins. So don't go thinking you can be up here hurting and I won't notice."

Samuel laughed, "Oh, I have no doubt of that." He stepped up to her and placed his hand lovingly on her cheek, then added in a more serious tone, "Thank you, my dear, for understanding and allowing me this one little secret. Now. We will not speak of this again. I know how it upsets you. My hope was that we could talk over a nice romantic dinner. I would hold your hand and look deep in your eyes and remind you how very much I love you. And that you despise my game of secrets." He winked at his wife, who blushed.

"Oh, Samuel, you are such a tease." She placed her hand over his and felt the warmth. It had been a long time since she had allowed herself to feel his love. "Well, how about a small sandwich now? Surely, you are getting hungry."

"That would be nice. Thank you, Rose." He hugged her tightly and whispered in her ear, "Remember. I love you with all my heart. Always have. Always will."

Rose felt his love wrap around her, and briefly relaxed in his arms. He stroked her cheek once more and sat back down. Rose left and closed the bedroom door. She leaned against the door frame, feeling the fear creep back into her soul. *Samuel cannot die. I need him here with me. If he leaves me, I will be all alone.*

She rushed to the kitchen and reached inside the bread box. Tears ran swiftly down her cheeks. She cried for several minutes, leaning over the countertop. Wiping her tears on a dishcloth, she sat at the kitchen dinette and thought how this was the first time in her life she had openly wept.

And that was the last time she cried. Ever. Her beloved Samuel would not make it through the night.

5

"Bonnie!" "Bonnie!" Will yelled up the stairs the following Sunday morning. "You've got thirty minutes before we leave!"

"I know, I know," Bonnie yelled back, as she removed several sponge curlers from her hair.

My first visit to church in Windy Garden and my hair is a mess! My bangs are too long, and the ends are frizzy. I look like a cat fresh out of the dryer. She held up several strands of hair to the mirror in complaint. Dropping her hands to the sink and leaning forward, she resolved to fix at least part of the problem. Reaching into the vanity for a pair of scissors, she trembled thinking of the last time she trimmed her bangs. It took over a month to grow back the lopsided bangs that teased her unmercifully every day. Holding them in one hand, she raised the dreaded scissors in attempt to remedy the disheveled mess and look presentable at church. "I can't do this," she said to herself, "I best leave them be." Exasperated, she dropped the scissors back in the drawer. "Maybe there is a hair salon in town with a magician that can transform my hair into something easy to take care of." She turned her head one way then another, trying to imagine a hairstyle that would stun her husband. "Yes, I'll see what this town has to offer in beauticians tomorrow."

Bonnie had a habit of talking out loud to herself. Miz Jessie used to say she had "sa many words bouncin' round inside that perty li'l head that they kept spillin' out ever chance they got."

Oh, how I wish I was back home, Bonnie lamented. *I miss my mom and dad and gram so much I could cry. I even miss my sisters*

71

and brother. I miss my best friend, Shellie, too. She could always make me laugh when I needed it the most. Tears threatened to spill down her cheeks, while she tried applying foundation to her face. Leaning into the mirror with the mascara brush poised to make short eyelashes look longer, she began talking to herself again. *Oh, Miz Jessie, I wish you were here. You would have the words to comfort me and tell me everything is going to be alright.*

"Bonnie!"

The mascara brush slipped drawing a long black line from her cheek to her chin.

"What!!"

"Twenty minutes!"

Who does he think he is? The time warden? He does this every time we go anywhere.

Leaning closer into the mirror she saw the black streaks down her cheek. *"Look what a mess he made!"* She dipped her fingers in the cold cream and rubbed at the streak that matched her mood. By now her face was glowing red from scrubbing off all the mishaps due to the impatient calls from her husband.

She removed the remaining spongy curlers from her hair. Her mind raced with the prospect of visiting church for the first time since moving to Windy Garden. *Stop that,* she told herself. *You always get yourself in a tither when you think too much. Take a deep breath. You'll be fine.*

"Bonnie!"

She jumped at the sound of his voice and dropped the brush in the sink.

"What now?" she screamed back.

"Fifteen minutes!"

If he yells for me one more time... she said to herself through clenched teeth.

She picked up the brush, dried off the wet bristles and began furiously brushing the shoulder length frizzy hair with long strokes. *He is standing on my last nerve!*

Still holding the brush, she dropped her hands to her side and said, *I can't believe I'm this jumpy. I really hope I fit in here. I wouldn't want to embarrass Will or myself. I've met a few people. That Lucy at the Apothecary was a very kind soul. But that Nettie woman. What if there are more like her than Lucy? And what if she belongs to this church? No, no. That can't happen. There is a church on every corner. Maybe, just maybe, she's a Methodist or a Catholic. I know! She probably doesn't attend church at all. She didn't act like church folks I know back home. That's it!* Bonnie breathed a sigh of relief. *See girl. You are going to be just fine.*

But the more she mulled over the church visit in her mind, the more nervous she got. She set the hairbrush in the drawer and stared into the mirror, leaning against the sink. "Get a grip, Bonnie. You'll do just fine. Remember, Miz Jessie said it would take time to make friends. You're anxious and nervous for no reason. This is the first church you have visited since moving here. Give it a chance. Breathe, girl, breathe." She drew in great gulps of air in an attempt to calm down, only to break out in hiccups.

Holding her breath to ease the hiccups, memories of her childhood friend, Michele, bounced into her thinking between gulps of air. They were the same age and in the same grade at school. She called her Shellie for short. Not because she was short, which she was, but because the nickname Shellie rolled off the tongue much easier. Besides, southern folk either called you a name shorter than your birth name or called you by two names, like Ruth Ann or Billy Bob. Sometimes they would make up names that seemed to fit a person, like Stutter because little Timmy stuttered when he talked, or Red for the redheaded Frank down the street, or Toot because, well, anyone could guess that one. Either way, she liked the name Shellie best.

They took to likin' each other real quick after their first meeting at Sunday church, when they noticed each of them wore a handmade dress. It was true, Bonnie's parents did not have a lot of money, but she was always proud of the dresses her mother made. That is, until the teasing got to be too much. Miz Jessie used to tell Bonnie when she came home from school in tears, "Why, chile, ya got the purtiest dresses I ever did see. Yer mama can sure put together the nicest clothes. So there's nuthin' to be 'shamed of. Sides, no one in the whole world got's a dress like you. Hit's one of a kind." That was true, but Bonnie still dreamed of what it would be like to have a store bought dress, like the ones in the window at the JC Penney.

Spending time with Shellie was her favorite part of the day. They were as different as carrots and peas. Shellie was the adventuresome type. And Bonnie was content reading books or pretending to be a heroine she had read about. Some days, they would play tag, or jump in the creek, getting soaking wet. Yet they still found time to act out scenes in books Bonnie had read. Of course, Bonnie was always the good one. While Shellie had to be the villain or troublesome character. Seemed they fit into each other's world perfectly.

Most afternoons when they had finished their homework, Shellie would run from her house to Bonnie's and help her finish chores, so they could play while there was still daylight. They'd take off to the woods behind the house and play hide-n-seek among the poplar trees and majestic oaks and listen for each other's approaching footsteps crunching on the fallen leaves, then suddenly jump out from behind a hiding place and yell, "Tag! You're it." And the chase was on. Shellie beat Bonnie home most every time, but Bonnie did get in a victory now and again.

Often, they would arrive at Bonnie's house sweaty and giggly. Usually, Miz Jessie was there doing what Miz Jessie did best. Sitting in the creaky old rocker on the side porch shelling peas or snapping beans and fanning herself with her apron.

After running around for hours in the hot sun, they would be hungry for a snack. Miz Jessie would give them a tall glass of water and fruit, or sticks of carrots to munch on so they would 'not get their bellies too full afo' supper.' What they really would have liked more was a cookie or piece of homemade cake that Miz Jessie was famous for.

Munching unenthusiastically on their carrots, Miz Jessie raised an eyebrow, seemingly able to see inside their heads. "I knows ya wants a piece of that thar chocolate cake I done made, but hit will still be on the plate for ya for later on. So don't go a'sneakin a piece when ya don't think I'm not a'lookin." She sat back in her rocker and resumed with the shellin'.

"Miz Jessie? Why can't we have cake?" Bonnie begged. "We like cake!"

The poppin' of peas stopped as Miz Jessie drew a deep breath as though pondering Bonnie's question. "Well," she slowly drew out, "the way I sees hit, hit ain't good fer a body to have sweets when they been out a 'runnin and a 'sweatin. No, what a body needs is lots a good water from deep in the Lawd's earth. And fruit, healthy thangs like that."

"Aw, Miz Jessie, you always want us 'doin' the right thing.' Why can't we have cake when we want it once in a while?"

Jessie rocked back and forth and back and forth while the girls looked on, still hoping for a piece of cake. "Well, I believes that hit always be right ta do right. My mam taught me that when I was jus' a little 'un like you. Even when ya don't want ta do somethin' right, ya need ta do hit anyways. Hit always right ta do the right thang. You'll see when ya gits much older. Mmhm. But it all start with a piece of cake."

Bonnie and Shellie looked at each other like she had fallen off a turnip truck and banged her head. They didn't understand a word she said. All they knew was they wanted a piece of cake. Now!

"Well I'm just going to say it! There are times I just don't want to do the right thing!" Bonnie blurted out. She folded her arms across her chest to make her point.

Miz Jessie looked over the top of her glasses at Bonnie. The 'look' was enough to make Bonnie ashamed she had spoken so adamantly at her Miz Jessie.

She quickly apologized, "I'm sorry." Bonnie caught the twinkle of forgiveness in the eye of her most treasured confidant and smiled back.

"Miz Jessie," piped in Shellie, "Did you know me and Bonnie are the bestest of friends?" The girls giggled, bumping heads.

"Little 'uns, I thank I do, and thar ain't nothin' like a good friend, no sir, thar ain't. They's the best thang ta have, next to Jesus, of course. Ya talk and ya laugh with 'em like ya can no body else. Ya whisper yer deepest secrets to 'em and they don't tell, no, uhuhn, ne'er do they tell. And best of all, friends stick by ya no matter what and they believes the best about ya too. Yessiree, that's a good friend alright. And I gotta tell ya, they's mighty hard to come by. Uh-huh, they is."

The girls looked at each other and burst into spits of laughter. Miz Jessie rose from the rocking chair, smiled her big smile, and said, "Basides, ya better keep a really good friend for always, cause they know's too much about ya!" Laughing so hard her tummy jiggled up and down, she turned and walked into the kitchen, slamming the screen door that wap-wapped when it closed.

"She can be so funny," Shellie laughed.

"Yeah. But did ya notice we still didn't get any cake."

Shrugging their shoulders and linking arms, the two girls skipped to the woods and disappeared.

Will's booming voice broke the walk down memory lane. "Aren't you ready yet?"

"Just about!" Bonnie yelled back. *Men! It doesn't take them more than fifteen minutes to shower and get ready. Takes me a good hour. He knows that!*

She glanced back at the mirror one more time, applying lipstick. A smile lit up her face as she thought again of Shellie. Patting her lips with toilet paper, she spoke as if Shellie were in the room.

"Girlfriend, I miss you. But I am determined to make friends in this town. Today is the first day I will meet lots of people in one place. At church. *We* met in church and look how that turned out." Squaring her shoulders, Bonnie was determined to tackle her morning with a renewed sense of courage. Smoothing her skirt with her hands, she picked up her purse from the dresser, in a hurry to beat Will's voice from summoning her again.

Bonnie descended the stairs, looking for a compliment from Will who had one hand on the doorknob of the front door and his eyes glued to his wristwatch. "OK, let's go."

He held the door open for his wife without a comment. Bonnie was a little disappointed. She had noticed since the move that Will was working extremely long hours at his new job and several of his days off as well, paying very little attention to her. He was too distracted with being on time to notice her attempt to look beautiful. Settling in the car, Miz Jessie's voice came to mind. "Now 'member, Chile, yer Will, he gonna be a busy man on dis new job. He might even fergit things that be 'portant to ya. But love him through it, chile. Cause I ain't got a doubt in this world that he loves ya to pieces."

Will and Bonnie had driven by the Baptist church several times since moving to Windy Garden and noticed how it took up most of the block. The mere size was intimidating. Facing Main Street, the huge steepled church was one of the first buildings that could be seen entering town. Will parked in the east parking lot. Opening his wife's car door, he took her hand in his and led her up the concrete steps to the main entrance, where two sets of massive doors stood ready to greet the throngs entering the sacred building. Inside was a long, rectangular vestibule with two sets of doors leading into the main sanctuary. On each side were stairs leading to a balcony. They glanced inside the open doors on the main floor and saw three sections of pews divided by aisles. The podium at the far end was flanked by a massive organ on the right and a grand piano on the left. Behind the pulpit were huge organ pipes that rose above the baptismal pool to the ceiling of the second floor.

Will tugged on Bonnie's hand and to her delight, led her to the stairs leading to the balcony. They found seats on the front row overlooking the ground floor. After taking their seats, Bonnie leaned over the railing at the sanctuary below. The first thing that caught her eye were the massive stained glass windows on each side of the sanctuary. "Will, would you look at that! Aren't they beautiful!"

The sun was streaming through the windows and cast varied colors of light all around the room.

"Can you imagine what it took to hang those? They're huge!" Will commented. "I wonder if it took a crane to put them in place or if they were pulled up by hand."

Bonnie was not impressed with how they were hung. Her focus had shifted from the beautiful stained glass to the number of people entering the church building. Noises from the side doors to the sanctuary drew her attention as people were streaming in, most likely from Sunday School classes, she guessed. Never had she been in a church this big before. This was not at all the way her little country church looked back home. Nor Miz Jessie's, the way she told it.

"Lawdy, chile, ya ought to see our ole chuch! The buildin' is so old that the paint is the only thang holdin' up the boards. And the paint is a'peelin' like a ripe bananer. Inside, we sits on wooden benches that hurt yer beehind somethin' awful. There's a pianer in the front corner where Sara Bess sits, a playin' her heart out. I gits so tickled watchin' her backside bounce up and down on the pianer bench in time with the music.

"We ain't got those stained glass winders like the Metherdists do over yonder, but we do gots winders that crank open by hand in the summertime lettin' in a fresh breeze once in a while. And good ole Harvey from down at the Wiley Funeral Home give us some funeral fans. If it weren't for them fans, I could jus' melt aways on many a hot Sunday.

"And Lawdy Sue, we's a sangin' bunch. Yep, we love the sangin' part best. But don't ya go telling preacher Sam I said that. Sometimes I 'magine I see Jesus sittin' right in front of me listenin' like I be the only one in the whole room a'sangin'. And He jus a smiles at me. I get so 'cited that I feel like I been called to join the heavenly choir!

"Now the preachin' part is good, mind ya. Real good. Preacher Sam teaches us what the good book says fer' shore. He shouts it out sa loud that we cain't hep but hear it and hear it good.

"We shouts the 'amens' and the 'hallelujahs' so he knows we ain't a'sleepin'. Yeah, chuch is a great place to be, where there be other folks sangin' and learnin' about our Lawd together. Umhmm, it don't matter a hoot to the Lawd Jesus what yer chuch look like or if it got cushy seats for yer bee-hind, it jus matter where yer heart be. I'm jus' sayin.'"

Miz Jessie's words about church were right on. As Bonnie looked around this beautiful, lavish building, she was humbled at the real reason she was called to be there. To worship the One who loves her, to honor His presence in her life and to celebrate with those who love Him too.

Hearing the giggling and muted voices from women below, she noticed most of them were wearing dresses, although a few were in pantsuits, mostly paisley polyester pantsuits. She gulped and decided to wait a while longer before donning pants of her own. Yep, newcomers ought not to make themselves too comfortable at first. And polyester pantsuits were not on her list of fashionable clothing either, though it was the mid 80's and paisley was still in.

There were greeters at the doors and in the aisles passing out the church bulletins. One man walked up to where Bonnie and Will were seated and courteously welcomed them. But to Bonnie's dismay, they were the only people who volunteered to speak to them the entire service. During the 'greeting of visitors,' no one noticed them. They were invisible! This would just not do. She had come to make friends and find a best friend. *The folks in my church back home would never act this way!*

She decided it was up to her to do something about this. So she reached around those sitting next to them and introduced herself and Will, shaking hands, smiling, and even interrupting personal conversations.

"Hi, I'm Bonnie and this is my husband, Will. We have recently moved to Windy Garden and thought we'd visit your church and see how many friendly faces we could find."

Will rolled his eyes and sank back into his seat, holding the bulletin over his face.

Humph! Take that, she thought to herself. In church no less. The organ music began and it was time to settle in for the rest of the service. Bonnie glanced at the bulletin to see what the pastor's name was. Randy Gardner. She looked at the order of worship and noticed something missing. No sermon topic or order of worship listed. *Hmm*, she thought, *Interesting*. Maybe the sermon will be on welcoming strangers. They certainly needed to hear that!

As Bonnie sat down, something pointedly dawned on her. "Whatcha doing' girl? What be gotten into ya?" She realized how her focus had changed from worship to irritation. She could just imagine Miz Jessie sitting next to her, patting her hand.

"Why, Chile, whatcha thankin' here. Ya know it takes time ta make friends. They be jus' as much a stranger ta ya as you be ta them. But 'member, like I told ya many times afor, ya done give yer heart ta Jesus. That kind of inner 'tude is gone. Ya be new now. Ya be a child of God now, so member that 'younguns' of God respond with love."

Immediately, Bonnie was ashamed of herself. She felt the need to make things right. She excused herself from Will, telling him she would be right back. She slipped outside and inhaled a deep breath of clean mountain air as she spoke to God silently in her heart.

"Thank You, Lord, that I am not that person any more. I am

your child and you have given me your loving heart. Help me be the person you have saved me to be." Her silent prayer of the heart spoke deeply to her soul. She would try to remember that next Sunday if they returned to this church, or any other church for that matter.

Bonnie returned to the balcony to singing. It was a song she had never heard before, but she liked it. On the second chorus, she joined right in, happy she had settled her attitude with God. When they were seated, Will held Bonnie's hand. She felt a little conflicted. Was he holding it in love, or was he trying to keep her still?

The message was timely. It was a message on grace. The pastor spoke from his heart with only an occasional glance at his notes. He told how he had been raised in the law of the Word. Don't do this, don't do that, you ought to do this, you ought to do that, do this and do that.

"The ten commandments are good," he said. "They were to point out sin, but when Jesus came, He came to fulfill the law. Did ya'll know the word fulfill means to complete? He completed the law by grace. And grace is His unearned, unmerited favor. The law will not make you holy. But grace will! You do not have to do anything to get grace. It is something you cannot work hard enough for, pray hard enough for, behave hard enough to get. It is favor. A gift."

Bonnie liked what this pastor was saying. His words took her back to an image in her mind of Bonnie sitting next to Miz Jessie on the back porch step of their farmhouse in southeast Missouri.

"Ya ever gits tired of hearing "do this, don't do that, ya shoulda, ya shouldn't?" Bonnie shook her head up and down and rolled her eyes in agreement.

"I can tell ya I grew up on thatta one! Hit was a'pounded into my head over and over. Ya better behave. Ya needs ta not lie, Jessie. Be good so's you can go to heaven. Did ya confess all yer sins, ever one? Ya didn't miss any now, dids ya?

"I lived in that for many a yar. Believed hit was the gospel truth I did. Hit weren't til I was married that I heered from another preacher man that Jesus died for all my sins in the past, all the sins I dos today and all the sins I ain't thought ta do jus' yet.

"Cause if'n that ta be true, really true, then when I dos or when I says somethin' wrong, hit's already forgiven! Even before I ask the Lawd to forgives me. Ya know, a body's gotta chew on that for a spell.

"And I did jus' that. I gots my Bible out and I read and I read and I read. And one thang that struck me was this, chile. If'n God loved me afor' I loved Him, then He done knew all the bad thangs I did, all the bad thangs I'm a doin' now, and the bad thangs I'll do on downs the road. How can anybody love like that?

"I kept on a'readin' and a'readin' til I finally found out....only God can love like that! Only He can see our bad and love us anyway. Whatta ya think of that?"

Not expecting an answer, she continued her rocking. "Know what the preacher man said that was? He done called hit grace. Grace. I heered bout grace afor' but I ne'er could understand what hit mean. He said God give us favor. Favor we cain't earn. No matter how hards I trys or how hards I pray, I cain't get it. I jus' gots ta receive hit. Hit's mine. Hit's free!

"He say I don't have ta worry bout tryin' so hard ta be good and doin' the right thang. I jus' has ta believes right and then I gonna behave right. I has ta believe God love me. I has ta believe I am all forgiven. That He not be in heaven disappointed in me or waitin' til I say I'm sorry. Well, I can tell ya, that was a reverlation to me! Sounds too simple, don't hit, chile?"

Will elbowed Bonnie back to the sermon. The next words she heard were, "Right believing leads to right living. If you believe right, you will live right. It's pretty simplistic, isn't it?"

Bonnie's hand flew to mouth in excitement. *Why this is exactly what Miz Jessie said!* This was the teaching she was hungry for.

Interrupting her delight, Bonnie heard a noise and peered down from the balcony. She noticed several heads turn to the left. She strained to see where the noise had come from. It wasn't hard, even for a newcomer, to detect. The disgruntled remark came from the Nettie woman, sitting on the left, four rows back from the altar. Never had Bonnie heard anyone, other than a baby cry, make such a noise in church.

Groaning, Bonnie sat back heavily in her seat. *That woman goes to church here. Of course, she does. I saw her tromping across this church's parking lot last week.* Looking once more over the congregation, she saw the seats filled with people. *Must be over 300 in attendance today, she thought. I shouldn't have to run in to her too often with this many people around. Surely I can find a kindred spirit among all these people.* She settled back into her seat for the rest of the service. *Oh, Miz Jessie, you would love this church.*

She could imagine Miz Jessie chuckling over the message, agreeing with the pastor. She might even have chuckled over this Nettie character as well.

Walking to their car after church, Bonnie and Will noticed the oddest thing. There in the big parking lot of the church was a car parked 'catty-wampus.'

"Look, Will, at the parking angle of that car!"

Gazing on the old orange rusting Plymouth parked the wrong way, and halfway in the middle of the drive lane, they both chuckled. "There must be a story to this," Bonnie mused.

They had no choice but to wait and see who came out and claimed this bucket of bolts. Just a couple of minutes later, an elderly lady, all bent over from the shoulders came across the sidewalk to the parking area of the rusted car. She dug in her deep purse that looked more like a duffel bag, til she found the elusive keys. Once inside the car, she pulled the door shut and sat there, unmoving.

Will inched the car forward a little to see if he could squeeze by her. Suddenly, the brake lights lit. "I think she's starting to move now," Bonnie's unusually optimistic husband whispered.

Bonnie turned around in her seat and noticed there was a long line of cars waiting with them. No one was honking horns or trying to push the car out of the lane, so she figured they were used to whoever was in the car and knew to be patient or else park on the other side of the church.

Another thing she noticed was that those parked around this

lady had moved back to give her room to maneuver her way into the exit lane. So Will did the same.

Slowly, the rusted Plymouth began backing up. She managed to miss the other parked cars and inched her way to the east exit. Will pulled onto Cross Street behind her, heading in the same direction, and watched as the elderly lady straddled both lanes for five blocks and then turned onto a side street.

"I wonder if the lady lives down that street. The poor soul needs new glasses, or a chauffeur," Bonnie giggled.

"No, she needs her license taken away. She's dangerous. She almost took out the stop sign when she turned." Will had little patience for teenage or elderly drivers. Bonnie was sorely tempted to remind him he was once a teenage driver and would one day become an elderly driver himself. But she resisted the temptation. After all, it was Sunday.

"Where would you like to eat today, Bonnie?"

It didn't take Bonnie long to answer. "I saw a small diner that offered seafood over in Dillsboro. How about we give it a try?" Bonnie loved seafood. It was hard to find good seafood in the hills of North Carolina and Will was leery of seafood being transported so far.

"Uh, ok, if that's what you want." From his tone of voice, Bonnie could tell he was hoping she would change her mind. She didn't.

A few minutes later they pulled in front of Harry's Seafood and Grill. Will noticed the sign and groaned. "I don't think Harry and seafood go together," he remarked. But Bonnie wanted seafood and seafood she would get.

Harry's was crowded with all the 'after church' people. "Looks like the Methodists beat us to the restaurants today," Will grumbled. It took twenty minutes for them to be seated. Before the waitress arrived, a man at an adjacent table stood and walked over, "Say, didn't I see you in church this morning, the Baptist church in Windy Garden? My name is Bill Langford."

"Oh, hi. Yes, we were there. My name is Will McDaniel and this is my wife Bonnie." The two men shook hands. Bill nodded and smiled in Bonnie's direction.

"I'm so glad you chose our church to visit this morning. I sure hope to see you there again. I won't keep you from your lunch. It's very nice to meet you." He smiled and returned to his table.

"Seems like a friendly sort," Will said as he picked up the menu. They ordered their food and sat listening to conversations from tables close by. It wasn't hard to hear, since the place was so crowded. People were shouting to be heard above the din.

The table closest to Bonnie was so loud, she could hear someone complaining about the lady who owned the old rusted Plymouth outside church. Bonnie thought it must be the same Plymouth they saw while leaving.

"You'd think Marta owned the town the way she drives." said a man in a suit and tie. "I wonder how long the DMV will continue issuing her a driver's license? The law ought to make old people give up driving after 75, I say."

"And you don't dare say anything to her about it! She gets so riled when anyone talks about her driving," commented another.

Bonnie was beginning to feel downright sorry for this Marta. Church people weren't supposed to talk unkindly about one another. First Nettie, now these folks.

Bonnie felt sick at heart. She remembered Miz Jessie telling her how some folks jus' cain't say anything nice. "Someday," she said, "they may jus' be the person others be talkin' bout."

"Will, do you think everyone in this town is like this?"

Will tried to reassure her on the way home that not all people were mean- spirited, and it would take time to establish friendships. It wasn't all that comforting at the moment, though he meant well. Bonnie was sure there was a kindred spirit somewhere among those 300 people. Maybe even several 'someones' who would befriend her. Miz Jessie told her to be patient and wait. And maybe, just maybe, one of them would become her best friend.

Funny how Will said it would take time to find friends. As far as she knew, he hadn't had a close friend for as long as she knew him. Women and men differ where friends are concerned. Men need friends. They don't talk to them, but they need them.

6

"What is wrong with everybody?" Nettie pondered as she sat rigidly in her rocking chair on the front porch, watching neighbors pass by on the sidewalk.

She was still upset over the sermon messages she was hearing of late. Yesterday's sermon gave her a headache. It persisted when she went to bed and greeted her with throbbing temples when she awoke.

If Pastor Randy keeps telling people that they have been totally forgiven of their sins before they even ask, people will start living like the devil. Everybody knows that we aren't forgiven until we ask. And what's all this about grace? He preached two Sundays ago that we don't need to be reminded of how bad we are. He says we need to be reminded of who we are in Christ. So all he preaches lately is how much God loves us, how forgiven we are, and that we don't have to earn His blessings because we are already favored. Really? All my life I have been taught that if I do good, then I will receive good. And if I do bad, then bad is what I'll get. Plain and simple. I told Ida Mae a couple of days ago that she better start writing down her sins so she won't forget what she needs to confess, or else she'll get behind.

Nettie remembered her conversation with Ida Mae. "Nettie, beating the 'sheep' with the law has never worked this side of the cross. Jesus said we are saved by *grace*, not by the law. My eyes are being opened for the first time on how much I am loved by God and how he looks on me with favor, with grace. I don't have to do anything for it. It's a gift. He's not sitting up in heaven waiting for me to mess up so he can whack me on the head when I sin. Nettie, this is nothing new. It has been in the Bible all along. We've just never heard it taught so clearly before."

Poor Ida Mae. Our last pastor was here for twenty years and he sure knew how to keep his congregation from straying. He'd remind us how bad we'd been all week and then invite us to get right at the altar before we left church. Each Sunday he'd get up in the pulpit and let us have it! He didn't want us living in sin. He said guilt wasn't such a bad thing. It kept us from repeating the same sin over and over. Favor. Humph! Well, no one has ever done me any favors. Even God. It's all nonsense, just plain nonsense.

The more Nettie fussed in her heart, the harder she rocked. She leaned her head back and closed her eyes. She didn't even hear her good friend Ida Mae shout a greeting and wave as she walked by until it was too late to answer. *Probably a good thing, Nettie mumbled. I'm put out with her right now. Ida Mae has been swallowing everything the pastor says — hook, line and sinker. How could she be so gullible?*

Nettie's thoughts wandered away from the front porch. Far from the passersby. They drifted back to many years ago, when her Henry was still with her.

"Dahlin," Henry whispered into her ear as he surprised her in the kitchen preparing supper.

Nettie jumped as his breath touched her ear, dropping the potatoes and peeler in the sink.

"You scared the wits out of me, Henry Pegram! You know better than to come up behind me like that!"

"Didn't mean to alarm you, my sweet. Forgive your old man?"

Holding her around the waist and nuzzling his face next to hers, she knew she could not resist this handsome fellow she had loved for more than fifty years.

"Oh go on with ya," she giggled like a schoolgirl. "Course I forgive you, but you better be watching yourself, old man, or the neighbors will start talking about you sneaking up on old women."

Nettie loved it when Henry teased her. It was a quality she treasured in this gentle man. She turned to face him and Henry planted a firm, loving kiss on her lips that made her melt like ice. Tears formed in her eyes, threatening to spill over.

"What is it, dahlin?"

She always loved how he said 'dahlin' with that southern drawl.

She dropped her head in her hands and wept, unable to speak. Henry placed his hand under her chin and raised her face to meet his.

"Oh, my sweet Nettie. What is bothering you so?"

Nettie continued to weep. The tears that had been forbidden in her mother's house were encouraged by this loving man standing before her. There was no chastisement, no position of properness to be maintained. Henry allowed her to give in to her emotions. She loved him for it.

"A penny for your thoughts, dahlin. Remember, we promised the day we married that we would always be honest and share our feelings with each other, no matter what. No secrets. Remember?"

No secrets, she gulped.

Nettie wiped her tears with the hem of her apron as she lifted her head to look into his deep green eyes that had held her captive since high school. His hair was still full, though graying more each year, giving him a distinguished salt and pepper look. He kept in pretty good shape walking to his office in downtown Windy Garden, where he owned the town's oldest real estate office his grandfather started some 87 years before.

She looked painfully at the man she had reluctantly fallen in love with as a teen.

The pain of those memories jolted Nettie upright. She opened her eyes and felt the trembling of her hands. She looked down at the wrinkly, gnarled arthritic hands that reminded her again that age had crept up, stealing time and stealing her Henry. She rubbed her hands to relieve the pain and calm the shaking. She gazed about to see if anyone noticed her. No one was about.

Anger crept back into Nettie's heart as she slowly stood and walked inside. *Henry is gone. And I'm all alone. No children, no family, and very few friends. I wish I were dead.* As the front door closed behind her, her heart shut as well. Shut to the memories of the past, shut to the now. Shut to anything that reminded her of Henry. Shut to the secret she dared not face.

She spoke softly to the empty room, to the emptiness of her heart. *Love! I loved and look where it got me. I loved Henry so much I didn't want anyone else in our lives. All I wanted was the two of us. Henry wanted children. Lots of them. When he found out I could not give him the children he longed for, his love for me was greater than his desire for kids. Oh, how I wish I had done things differently.*

I wish I could go back and change the past. For Henry. For me. I can't bear this heartache any longer. Living without Henry is too hard. It's just too darn hard.

Deep despair and loneliness crept over Nettie like a glove fits over a hand. She felt as if she couldn't breathe, caught in a tight squeeze, unable to escape. Her life was filled with silent rooms, quiet where teasing once filled her lovely house, nights with no arms around her, and waking to another day with no one to say good morning to. No one to drink coffee with, no Henry to correct her when she stepped out of line. No one.

As Nettie ambled into the living room, she glanced around. The furniture she and Henry had painstakingly sought out and purchased four years before Henry grew sick seemed out of place. She no longer enjoyed its warmth and comfort.

Gingerly, she walked over to the front window and pulled the curtains aside, looking out at the street where neighbors dashed from one place to another. People going about the busyness of their lives just as she and Henry had. *Do these people ever give a thought that in the blink of an eye they could be right where I am? Do they know how lucky they are to have someone to come home to?*

With a heavy heart, she let the curtain fall back into place.

Nettie headed for the kitchen once again to prepare dinner. Dinner for one. But she still cooked for two. She turned the stove on, and then abruptly turned it off. Eating alone was the second worst time of the day.

"No! No! I won't give in to this. I have to be strong! I have always been strong. Snap out of it, Nettie!" she voiced aloud. She refused to lose control of her emotions. Letting go would force her to deal with her mistakes, her loss, her past, and her now.

Nettie went to bed before the sun disappeared. She reached for Henry's pillow and hugged it tight. "Oh, Henry, I miss you so much! There's so much about me you didn't know. So much I couldn't say. If I had told you the pain I bear, I feared you would have left me. Oh, my love, I wish I had told you."

7

Walking down Depot Street, Ida Mae waved at Nettie sitting on her front porch. She slowed her pace, looking at the unmoving figure in the rocking chair. Since her wave was not acknowledged, Ida Mae wondered if Nettie was still cross with her. It was the second time in a week this had happened. *Is she still mad at me? I haven't seen her this upset for quite a while. I wish she would tell me why she is so out of sorts.*

Ida Mae continued walking past Nettie's house. Her heart ached for her best friend. They had become bosom buddies when they were twelve years old, in the seventh grade, even though Rose was against it from the beginning. *I knew her mother was not fond of me. She made it very clear each time I was in her presence. She would roll her eyes, purse her lips and do everything she could to pull Nettie away from me. It was really bad the first couple of years, but after Nettie's father died, she seemed to back off and let us be. I am so glad she did. I love Nettie. I really do. I just wish there was something I could do to get back in her good graces.*

Ida Mae heard the sound of her own voice and stopped on the sidewalk. She realized she had passed her own house by a block. Retracing her steps, she made her way home. Unlocking the front door to her quaint little cottage-style house, she placed her keys in the bowl on the table near the door. Thinking again on her friend, she purposed in her heart to stop by Nettie's more often. *Maybe she needs me more now than ever. I guess I backed off when she began pushing me away. I shouldn't have done that. It's the opposite of what I should have done.*

She walked into her cozy living room. Ida Mae loved the warm and inviting feel her home exhibited. She tempered her love of bright colors for softer hues, which allowed the light from her many windows to give the room a feel of comfort and rest. Draped over the light blue checked sofa was her mother's hand-crocheted afghan. The walls were painted a soft yellow with white trim. Next to her mother's side table was a rocking chair Nettie's Henry had made for her as a birthday gift. It was smaller than Nettie's, but fit her perfectly. The living room flowed into an open kitchen with grey blue cabinets and a white cast iron sink with white porcelain countertops. Above the sink was a long shelf of varied potted plants in bloom.

She loved her little home. Her husband, Saul, built the house right after their honeymoon. The two had met at the North Georgia Academy in Dahlonega. Ida Mae was thrilled to be in college, and grateful her parents had eventually achieved some financial success in farming, which gave her the chance to attend. She was studying in the field of agriculture, planning to bring modern ideas to the farming community of Windy Garden. But before she was able to finish her degree, the Depression had begun to have a profound effect on the state of Georgia. She was financially unable to stay, so she packed her bags and returned home to help her family. Fortunately, Saul was able to stay on and continue his studies in engineering. What was needed was an industry that would survive the Great Depression in 1929. Saul's training and education catapulted him into a successful fabricated steel business. They eventually recovered from the Depression and became quite wealthy. But because of their modest lifestyle and humbleness of heart, the town of Windy Garden was never aware of just how affluent they had become.

Ida Mae moved over to the blue sofa and sat down heavily. She pulled a photo album from off the coffee table in front of her. Caressing the cover, she reverently opened it with the same care she might have used with a priceless china cup. It was her wedding album, her most prized possession. The first page was her handsome groom's picture taken on that day of days. He was standing on the steps of the Baptist Church, grinning from ear to ear. Weeks later, when she had first seen the photo, she asked him why he was grinning so. He smiled and deftly answered her.

"Well, I was about to become the luckiest man in the world with the most beautiful gal I had ever laid my eyes on!"

"Saul, you're just saying that. I know you guys were joking and teasing around. Now tell me, what were you really thinking?"

Saul raked a hand through his hair, grabbed her around the shoulders and said, "Well, if I wasn't thinking it, I should have been." To this day, she had never found out the truth of what gave him that peculiar smile.

Turning the page, she saw a photo of herself with Nettie, her matron of honor. Ida Mae was wearing a simple, satin white gown her mother had painstakingly made for her. It was modest in design, yet complemented her small frame. In her hair was a narrow band adorned with imitation pearls. She held a bouquet of sunflowers her sister had picked from their garden.

Ida Mae's mother offered to make Nettie's gown as well. But Rose had refused. She made it quite clear her daughter would not wear a handmade dress to any formal affair, much less a wedding.

So Nettie's blue satin gown with sequins and glitter was ordered from the Bloomingdale's store catalog in New York.

Ida Mae and her mother Mary had known Rose for years and were not all that surprised she would react this way.

Come the day of the wedding, Nettie appeared in the most stunning gown anyone from this sleepy little town had ever seen. The dress was as blue as the sky, with sequins glistening in the sun, a modest cut neckline and mid-calf length. No matter which way she turned, she sparkled.

"Oh, Nettie, you look beautiful! That gown is perfect for you!" Ida Mae was sincerely touched by the radiance of her friend.

"Oh, Ida Mae, I am so embarrassed. Mother always has to outdo everyone, even the bride on her own special day. I am so sorry!"

Ida Mae did not see the black and white gown in the photograph she held in her hands, but the gorgeous, elegant blue gown her best friend was wearing that illuminated her blond hair and fair complexion. She was truly beautiful.

Mary approached the two girls after the snap of the camera and gushed over the exquisite gown. "You look absolutely stunning, Nettie!"

Rose stepped into the fray and looked her daughter up and down. "The gown is beautiful, isn't it?" she said, fingering the neckline. "I picked it out myself. I'm so glad Bloomingdales had what I wanted."

Ida Mae and her mother looked at each other and winked. They both knew Rose was glowing with pride, adorning her daughter as the best dressed lady of 'that girl's' wedding. Rose was Rose. She would always be the proper, well-bred diva of Windy Garden. Ida Mae expected no more and no less from her. She was who she was.

Nothing seemed to dampen the spirits of the Astor ladies.

Her wedding day had been perfect. Gently placing Saul's photo back in the album, she heard familiar footsteps approaching the front door.

"Hi there, my lovely woman," her sweet husband called to her.

Ida Mae met him at the door, took his hat and coat, and hung it on the clothes tree. In her usual teasing Greta Garbo voice, she said, "Hi there, my gorgeous man." She reached up on tiptoes and kissed her darling on the cheek.

Seeing the photo album open on the table he asked, "Looking through pictures again? I'm surprised there are any images left, as much as you comb through them." His eyes narrowed as he walked over and picked up the picture of his wife and Nettie. "Something up with Nettie?" Her husband knew her well. When she became troubled about one thing or another, she would pull out pictures of old.

"Yes, I am afraid so," she sighed.

He reached for her hand and pulled her onto the sofa next to him. Stroking her hair, he gently pulled her to his chest. They spoke not a word. Nothing needed to be said. Only the embrace of love could soothe this moment.

8

Bonnie desperately needed a haircut. Her hair was getting shaggy and out of shape. She had not had it cut since leaving Blodgett almost three months ago. Struggling with her hair for church two Sundays ago convinced her she needed to find a hairdresser. And quick! What worried her was she had seen only one beauty shop in all of Windy Garden. It was located downtown on Main Street, just across from the cinema. Nothing was harder for a gal than finding a new hairdresser. But she had no other choices.

She drove down Main Street past the Apothecary and found the only parking spot to be in front of the movie cinema. A curved ticket office jutted out in the middle of the entrance. Old faded posters of classic movies were pasted onto the brick walls on either side of the ticket booth. The aging of the paper told of times long ago, where lovers would come to enjoy wholesome movies that brought tears to the eyes, and a renewal of true love that touched the souls of the still young at heart. Bonnie wondered if all they played were old classics. If so, she would be spending quite a lot of time and a lot of money there.

She looked around for the beauty salon and located it across the railroad tracks on the other side of the street. At that moment, the sound of an approaching train filled her ears. She stood quietly, waiting for the oncoming train to pass. It was always a joy to stand alongside the path while the beast of burden rumbled its way to another town with curious onlookers. She felt grateful for one thing, though. Will was at work. Trains had always held a certain boyish enchantment for him. He was fascinated by the powerful engines that pulled the train cars until they disappeared from sight. From their new home, they could hear each train winding its way from one end of Windy Garden to the other. Each time, her husband would stop whatever he was doing to catch the distant sound, and comment on its arrival. Which would annoy her beyond measure. Each time the train arrived, he told her, and every time it left, he told her. Every day he told her.

"Bonnie, a train is coming!" he'd say excitedly, as if it were the first train he had heard in his entire life.

"Yes, I know. I can hear it."

"I wonder how many cars it's pulling this time?"

"I really don't know."

"Sounds like a long one to me. I can still hear the train clacking on the tracks.....Think it might be a really long one?" Will said, gazing into the distance as if he could see it.

Good grief and a day, she mumbled to herself. *Enough is enough! Makes me want to go to the engineer's office and tell him to skip Windy Garden altogether.* She never voiced this out loud, but the look she gave him did. Still, it was of no use, since he never took his attention off the rumble and fading shriek of the whistle until it had completely left the area.

Once the train passed by, Bonnie crossed the street. She noticed for the first time, adjacent to the hair salon, a floral shop named Blooming Pretty. *What a cute name for a florist*, Bonnie thought. As she walked by, she stopped and noticed the window display was being changed by two robust women. They were redecorating from winter to summer, and they seemed unaware that their 'not so pretty' backsides were facing out, greeting all the passersby. She giggled at the sight of the faceless women and thought, *surely, they are not aware of the advertisement they are sending now!*

Several other stores flanked the Blooming Pretty, each in the original buildings of the mid-1800's with red brick fronts. Gazing up and down Main Street she felt like she should be donning an ankle length dress with button up shoes and a rather large flowing hat to crown her upswept hairdo. Now that was a scary thought!

She stood in front of the glass door leading into her future haircut, grasped the door handle and uttered a silent prayer. *Lord, help.*

A sweet southern accent greeted her. "Be with ya in a minute, sugah."

Bonnie thoroughly enjoyed the language of the south and loved hearing it often in Windy Garden.

After putting a towel around the wet hair of her client, the southern voice returned. "Hydie there, I'm Melissa. Did ya have an appointment?"

"Oh, no, I don't. I thought I'd drop in and see if you had an opening."

"No problem, no problem at all. Whatcha need today?"

"A haircut and set please."

"Samantha," Melissa shouted, "ya got a haircut and set here. How long ya think yer gonna be?"

"'Bout five minutes is all. Be right with ya."

Bonnie sat down in one of two chairs near the large plate glass window facing Main Street. She hoped to distract herself with a magazine in a vain effort to calm down.

"Hydie there, sweet thang! I'm Samantha. But you can call me Sam."

Bonnie dropped the magazine on the floor and looked up. "Uh, Hello. I'm Bonnie."

"A cut and style for ya today, right?"

"Yes. And please, not too short. Maybe just a quarter of an inch off the length." Placing the magazine back on the side table, she dutifully followed the hairdresser to her station. Back home, she had had the same stylist since high school, so this was a very scary situation. No gal likes a bad hair day.

Sam washed her hair in the basin, wrapped a towel around it and set the chair upright. Towel drying the wet hair, she asked Bonnie, "Are ya new to town? Don't think I ever seen ya round here before."

"Yes, my husband and I moved to Windy Garden a little over two months ago.

"Why, no wonder you need a haircut! Look at this!" Sam held up the ends of Bonnie's s hair and pulled it in front of her face. "Ya got some split ends going on here and fuzzy strands and Lawd knows what else."

If there was any time to bolt for the door, this was it. Bonnie leaned forward when the hairdresser pulled her shoulders back and said, "Now, if ya sit real still, I'll be done in no time a'tall. It's not really safe to be moving when a gal like me has scissors in her hand." She laughed loudly at her own humor. Sitting as still as a hen on her eggs, Bonnie opened one eye and looked around the salon. There were three other women getting their hair done. One was laid back in the chair getting her hair washed, and the other two she did not recognize. She was hoping for a familiar face. Lucy, maybe? The salon was quite small. Every conversation could be heard clearly. Bonnie grew alarmed as she became privy to the talebearers' stories flying faster than the clip of the scissors.

The first story began about a woman named Della. Within minutes Bonnie knew more about this woman than she ever cared to know. It seemed Della was in her mid-eighties, or at least that was the consensus of the wagging tongues. Della refused to divulge her age to anyone, according to a familiar voice. *Oh no, it can't be!* Bonnie leaned forward in her chair and saw Nettie in the beauty chair across the way with a cape around her neck.

The scuttle-butt, Nettie said, was that keeping her age a secret was Della's way of maintaining control over something in her life she didn't want anyone to know. Which Nettie considered selfish on the part of Della. The worst annoyance to these ladies was that Della tended to repeat herself over and over, ad nauseam. It seemed Della frequented the Apothecary and beauty shop often, leaving rolling eyes and dozing listeners in her wake.

"Nettie Pegram, what a gossiper you are!" declared a lady with tight tiny curlers in her hair. Indeed, this lady was addressing the very woman she had hoped to avoid.

"Now ya done it," came the voice over Bonnie's head.

Alarm registered all over Bonnie's face. "What? What did I do?"

"Well, when ya moved, I cut a piece shorter than the other."

Reaching behind her, Bonnie felt the hair on the back of her head.

Laughing, Samantha said, "I'm jus' funnin' with ya girl. Yer hair is just fine."

Bonnie could have throttled this woman. It was not funny to joke about your haircut in a new salon.

"Ida Mae, I am most certainly not a gossip! If it's true, it is not gossip!" Nettie was so smug she seemed to gain an inch in height as she walked in a stately manner over to the hair dryer.

"Nettie, I know you don't really mean it. You must be inhaling too many of those hair chemicals…..They've gone to your brain! You just can't help yourself." Ida Mae shook her head.

"Ida Mae, get over it. You've known me since the seventh grade. And you know fully well, I speak my mind, so stop fussing at me!"

"I'm sorry, Nettie, but you can be so exasperating at times," Ida Mae replied with a softer voice.

Bonnie gasped. She quickly noticed how this Ida Mae was not afraid of Nettie. She also noticed that no one else in the beauty shop seemed surprised. She had never known people who talked this way to each other, especially not in public.

It was embarrassing the way Nettie Pegram, a woman with an 'old lady' hairdo, carried on. Poor Della! Bonnie bet a dime to a dollar that if Della walked into the beauty shop this moment, compliments would fly!

"There ya are," said Sam as she turned Bonnie to the mirror. "How do ya like it?"

The gasp was discreet, but the look of horror on her face was not. Her hair was so short! She looked on the floor at all the hair that was on her head not fifteen minutes ago. She had been so engrossed in the mean-spirited gossip over Della that she forgot to pay attention to her own hairdresser.

I said take a quarter of an inch off the bottom, not leave a quarter of an inch! Bonnie fussed at herself for not paying attention.

"What is your name again?" Bonnie asked the young lady with the tree pruners.

"Samantha," she smiled, pleased with her work.

"I like the style very much, Samantha. But it is way too short for me. Short hair shows too much face on me." Bonnie tried to be kind and hide her disappointment.

"Oh girl, I think it looks lovely. And you have such a cute face, you need to show it off." Samantha tugged at the short bangs on Bonnie's forehead.

Bonnie pulled at the short strands hoping she could stretch them to a longer length. It was not working. When a haircut is too short, it seems to take longer than usual to grow back.

Managing a weak smile, Bonnie stepped out the door of the salon onto the relative peace of Main Street. As she glanced back to plant in her memory never to return to this place of business, she noticed the sign above the door, "Hair Buzz." Yep, no surprise there.

She kept thinking about Della. How could they talk about her like that? Bonnie's compassionate nature kicked in. She was beginning to like this elderly lady, even though she had never met her. If they could talk that unkindly about one of their own, she wondered what they were saying about *her* right now.

Bonnie reached up to feel the short strands all over her head. "I wonder how long this will take to grow out," she thought, as she wearily ambled in the direction of the Apothecary for a strawberry milkshake.

9

Doorbell! Bonnie had always loved the sound of doorbells. It meant she could stop doing whatever she was doing that she wasn't thrilled to be doing, and talk to someone.

Bonnie rushed to the front door, excited to see who might be dropping by. She opened it to find a petite, middle-aged lady standing on her welcome mat, holding a large pot of geraniums.

"Hi, I'm Kathy! I live down the street and have passed by your house several times, waiting for the right time to pop in and welcome you to the neighborhood. I decided this morning I could not wait another minute! I hope this is a good time to visit. I know how busy you must be, settling in."

My very first visitor! And bearing gifts, too! Bonnie was speechless and stumbled for words. "Oh! I'm pleased to meet you, Kathy! I'm Bonnie. Won't you come in? I am not busy at all and was so excited to hear the doorbell ring."

Embracing the potted plant in her hands, Kathy chirped, "I love flowers. Flowers of every kind. I thought you might like to have something colorful and blooming in your house. I was working in my garden this morning and it was so beautiful outside and the weather so perfect, I thought of you and gathered these geraniums from an area where they were taking over part of my flowerbed. I was hoping you'd like them, but not all people do." Kathy thrust the plant at Bonnie and added, "But be careful, I saw a wasp around this plant earlier, but I think it's gone now."

She talked so fast Bonnie blinked several times trying to keep up with her. Gingerly taking the geranium from Kathy's outstretched hands, she held it at arm's length. Bonnie's eyes grew wide searching for the elusive wasp that might not have left the plant after all. Looking back at her new neighbor, she smiled. "Oh! Thank you! Would you like to come in? I could make you some iced tea and we can chat a bit." Instead of carrying the plant into the living room, she placed it on a table inside the front door, planning in her mind a quick exit from a potential outbreak of killer wasps. After all, she did not want to offend her very first visitor. And a chipper one at that!

Kathy stepped inside. "I'd love to! I can't stay long, though. I'm going to the grocery store for bread and tea bags. I'm having a tea party next Monday morning at my house and wanted to invite you to come. I'm a 'tea party gal.' I used to belong to a group of tea loving ladies years ago, before moving to Windy Garden and decided to start a get-together of my own. I invite every lady I can think of. I provide hats and gloves and dainty spoons. Bob and I live in a close-knit neighborhood and I am in charge of block parties too. Every so often, though, I can't resist a good tea party with the girls. I sure hope you can come!"

"Oh, I wish I could, but next Monday is my husband's day off, and we have plans. Maybe another time?" Bonnie held her breath, hoping she had not offended her.

"Oh, a day with the hubby! Don't you think about me for one second. You go have a lovely day with that man of yours! I'll let you know when the next party is."

Bonnie smiled in relief. Kathy followed her into the kitchen. Her eyes widened at the view of apple trees out back, framed by the kitchen window. Inching forward for a closer look, she exclaimed, "Well! I believe God painted this gorgeous scene entirely by hand, don't you? Your apple orchard is nestled safely in the shadow of those gorgeous mountains that seem to touch the face of God." Turning, she noticed the sunroom with its large windows, which offered an even more beautiful view of the small orchard. "Could we sit out here where we can enjoy your lovely view?"

"Of course," Bonnie replied with a smile. Carrying the pitcher of tea and two glasses, Bonnie followed behind the energetic woman who had already picked out her seat. To Bonnie's amusement, Kathy was making herself right at home.

"I absolutely love back porches. I spend most of my free time on my own. I don't have quite the view you have, but it is lovely all the same. From there I can see our nine bird feeders, two bird baths, and, oh yes, we have three finch feeders. Our backyard looks like a bird retreat. Teehee!"

Kathy's charm and exuberance were an unexpected blessing for Bonnie. Feeling unwelcome by the few she had come across in Windy Garden, she wondered if she would ever fit in. Her hopes soared listening to Kathy express herself. As Kathy talked, Bonnie's heart was warmed by her presence.

Kathy told her that she and her husband belonged to the First Baptist Church downtown. "It's the one with the big steeple on top, situated on the corner of Main Street and Cross Street, that most people mistake for the city hall or hospital. Countless times people pull up to the steps of the church office looking for the emergency room."

"I can see now why people might think that. Will and I visited there the last two Sundays."

"You did?" Kathy said, astonished. "I wish I had seen you. I always make a point to welcome newcomers. Usually I'm all over the sanctuary during greeting time."

"Well, we sat in the balcony our first time."

"So that's why I didn't see you! Girl, I will find you the next time, you can count on that."

Bonnie watched Kathy's eyes roam over her backyard. The smile on her face and the twinkle in her eyes shone with such pleasure that Bonnie had to look too.

Taking a sip of tea, Kathy asked, "So, tell me about yourself. How long have you been married?

"Will and I have been married for three years. He works as a manager at the new entertainment park, in their wardrobe and costume department. It's about to open real soon, just south of here."

"From what I've been told, it's going to be a huge complex of rides and shows and all kinds of music," Kathy chimed in. "Sounds really fun. But from the rumors and gossip, I've heard not everyone is very excited about it. People around these parts like their small town atmosphere and quiet streets. Hard to tell what a mega-business like that will do to stir things up."

Bonnie hadn't thought about that. All she cared was that Will had a job. A good one that could provide for their future children someday. *Children*, she thought.

Kathy interrupted her thoughts. "Say, we have a ladies Bible study that meets each Thursday morning at 9am in the basement of the church sanctuary. Why don't you come with me sometime?

Our pastor's wife teaches the class and she is wonderful. I have learned more there than any other class I have attended. And I can tell you, I've been to lots! Who knows, you might just like the church and become one of us! Oh, look at the redbird! I love watching the birds flit from one feeder to another. Did you know that they have one mate for life?"

Kathy was an encyclopedia of information. She seemed genuine and down to earth, and Bonnie liked her. A little chatty and excitable, but easy to warm up to.

Seemingly picking up on Bonnie's thoughts, Kathy said, "Oh, I do hope I'm not overwhelming you. Bob says I have this inane tendency to carry on. I just get so excited sometimes! I sure hope I am not scaring you off. I do tend to be quite chatty. And I wanted to meet you right away!"

Bonnie wondered in amusement how a hyperactive stranger bearing a giant pot of geraniums with a wasp lurking inside could possibly overwhelm someone. She smiled at the humorous thought.

"You are my very first visitor in my home, and I like you! And no, I didn't know that cardinals had one mate for life. They are my favorite bird. Maybe because they are so colorful. And, maybe, because I am a Missouri girl and a baseball fan!"

"You were born in Missouri?"

"Yes! I was raised on a farm in a small town in southeast Missouri."

"You were? I was raised in Michigan in the city. But I have always wondered what it would be like to be raised on a farm."

Bonnie refilled their tea glasses from the pitcher on the coffee table.

"Look again!"

Bonnie followed Kathy's pointing finger to the praying hands bird feeder under the oak tree. Sure enough, two redbirds, a male and a female, were perched on each hand, pecking at the black sunflower seeds in the palm. "Another redbird! Two this time!" Only one other person in her life got this excited over redbirds and that was Bonnie's dad. He was a St. Louis Cardinal baseball fan and loved watching 'his birds' play too.

Kathy bubbled with excitement, "Goodness me! That reminds me of the Bible story about Joseph. You're familiar with that one, right, Bonnie? Bonnie nodded her head in agreement while sipping her tea.

"His father had given him a very special coat of many colors. And his brothers hated him for it. Guess they were jealous and felt their father favored their younger brother. So the older brothers conspired together to get rid of him and threw him in a pit. Can you imagine! Those boys sat down beside that pit and ate lunch. And there was poor little Joseph down in the hole, wondering what was going on. After a while, a caravan came by and the brothers sold him. What a story of betrayal. But you know what? I think God's plan was greater than the brother's plan. Joseph would one day become a great man who would save his family from famine. Oh, there I go again, rattling on. I just have so much to say in so little time. Teehee."

Kathy looked at the time, and jumped to her feet. "I need to get my little tushy to town and pick up the vegetables Bob wants to cook for dinner. She picked up her purse and keys and headed for the front door, with Bonnie in tow. "I'm so glad you were home this morning, Bonnie. I had such a good time. And now I can add you to my list of friends."

A friend! Bonnie registered this in her heart. *My first Windy Garden friend, other than Lucy, I guess.* "Thank you for dropping by, Kathy. And thank you for the geranium. I am going to move it to the sunroom where I can enjoy it's coat of many colors!"

Kathy giggled. "I like that! Bye now!" She fairly ran to her car, hopped in, and waved enthusiastically.

Bonnie turned and re-entered the house, closing the door behind her. Spotting the geranium, she glanced inside. No sign of a wasp. Gently, she picked up the geranium and stepped back in satisfaction. She had not seen any wasps loose in the house, but she wasn't going to take any chances. It was a beautiful plant and she hoped she could keep it alive. Will said she could kill a cactus. Not many people can kill a cactus. But Bonnie was determined to keep her very first gift in Windy Garden alive and thriving. Placing the plant on a table on her back deck until she could be absolutely sure there were no wasps lurking inside, she turned and went back in the house.

Walking to the kitchen, Bonnie realized she was suddenly tired. She glanced at the kitchen clock. It was only noon, which was an odd time to be tired. The day had just begun. She ambled to the living room with the sparse 'early Salvation Army' furniture; a term her mother used good-naturedly to tease Bonnie about her decorating style. A framed picture of a little boy sitting under a tree caught her attention. She picked it up. It was a wedding gift she had been moving from wall to wall before Kathy had arrived, in an effort to figure out where to hang it. Too tired to deal with it, she set the picture against the wall. Wearily, she eased herself onto the couch. Within moments she fell fast asleep. She slept for almost two hours. When she awoke, she was shocked she had nodded off. She felt her head. No fever. Was she coming down with something?

Bonnie looked again at the picture against the wall near the staircase. She had been trying for weeks to get her home organized and eliminate the endless stack of boxes. Climbing the stairs to the bathroom, she washed her face, and soon felt more refreshed than she had in months. Bonnie smiled into the mirror as her hopes soared. Another friend! And *a talkative one at that!*

10

Bonnie and Will attended First Baptist the following week. They were led to a Sunday School class, where the ages ranged from seventy to one foot out of the grave. It had to be the oldest age group of the entire Sunday School assembly. As they entered the room, they saw at least twenty-five men and women attending in their Sunday finery, all talking to one another, mostly about someone else.

They eased themselves into the back row of chairs, listening to conversations buzzing around them. Bonnie whispered to Will, "Surely, someone has made a mistake placing us here." Will nodded and whispered back, "I'm sure somebody will notice us and send us to the proper age class."

As they waited, Bonnie was reminded of Miz Jessie telling her how she felt in the grocery stores back home. Some folks seemed to pay her no never mind, like she was invisible. That was how Bonnie felt. Invisible and unwanted.

An elderly man, fat as a stuffed bull and as old as dirt, stepped to the front of the class. His sparse graying hair had receded, leaving only a grey band circling from ear to ear. His eyeglasses looked as thick as coke bottle bottoms. "Now ya'll stop yer yammerin'. I studied real hard this mornin' for almost an hour to get through this lesson. So listen up!"

A hush settled over the room like a cloud over a picnic.

Bonnie leaned toward Will to make a remark, but Will touched her arm and said out of the corner of his mouth, "I know what you're thinking. Don't say a word. We will be out of here within the hour."

Bonnie sat back and grabbed Will's hand for support, just in time to see the teacher peering over the rim of his glasses. "I see we got us some visitors. Hey, there! My name is Clyde Williams and I'm the teacher of this here class. Been the teacher in this same room for some thirty-five years, right Maddie?" He motioned toward a plump little woman with grey hair that curled into a tight bun sitting on the first row.

"Yes, I believe that is right," she timidly responded without looking around at the new couple. She stared straight ahead, her eyes following the teacher as he moved.

"That must be his wife," Bonnie whispered again, without turning her head.

"Yeah, I been teaching right here in this very room all that time and I can tell ya there is no one in this church that knows his Bible better than me. Nope, not even the preacher. I spend nears an hour ever' Sunday mornin' in the Good Book so's this here group can hear the Word of the Lord. These folk here rely on me to tell 'em what the Word says. And so's ya know, I don't like question askin.' Askin' questions just confuses ever'one. Welcome to the Freedom Class!"

Bonnie looked at Will and sighed. "Freedom Class? Freedom from what?" Bonnie mumbled, smiling back at the teacher with that fake kind of smile that people plaster on their faces when they don't want to reveal what they're really thinking.

Mr. Williams continued. "Let's pray. Thank You, Lord, for makin' me teach each Sunday. If it weren't for you makin' me, I surely wouldn't. These people sittin' here this mornin' have been out all week, sinnin' something awful. So I ask that ya don't strike 'em dead befor' I give em the message I studied so hard on this mornin'. They don't mean to sin. They just cain't help themselves. So I ask ya, Lord Jesus, to set 'em straight. Amen." Most of the people in the room gave a hearty, "AMEN!"

Bonnie strained to open her eyes, fearful of being caught in a state of shock in the house of the Lord. Or was it a side room off the house of the Lord. Or could it be the outhouse of the house of the Lord. Discomfort settled in on her like a dense fog. It was not about to lift any time soon.

Bonnie had never heard praying like that before. As a matter of fact, she had never met a fella like this Clyde Williams before either.

"Ya'll might want to grab hold of yer seats cause this lesson will shake you to yer socks, or pantyhose as the case might be." Clyde laughed at himself for effect.

Bonnie did not find it the least bit amusing. Pursing her lips and settling back into her chair, she folded her arms, not sure what to expect next.

"Open yer bibles to the book of James, chapter 2, verse 17. Hurry up now. Got it? Ok. James says, 'even so faith, if it hath not works, is dead, being alone.' He means that if ya don't serve the church, then yer *dead!*" If any of you yahoos are not on a church committee or helpin' with the little kids in the nursery or parkin' cars for the old folks, then yer dead. Says so right here in this Good Book." He had his Bible in one hand and slapped it with the other to drive his point home. He hit the book so hard everyone jumped in their seats!

"So," he paused and pointed to each person, "any of you here ain't serving this church, then yer plain ole' dead."

Clyde dropped his Bible on the stand before him for emphasis, slipped his thumbs through the suspenders holding up his pants, and walked up and down before the class.

"I have served this church for nigh forty years. I began the first day I joined this here church volunteerin' to park cars for old folks. Then I joined the Men of the Night patrollin' the parking lot on Wednesday and Sunday nights for kids up to no good. After that, I starting teachin' the Freedom Class and I became deacon to make sure the preacher didn't start tryin' to put new ideas in our heads. Been through five preachers. Seen em come. Seen em go. I been here the whole time. And I plan to stay here and keep on servin' til the day I up and die."

Bonnie shook her head. She noted how proud he seemed of his accomplishments in the church by how he puffed his chest out like a rooster. It reminded her of early mornings on the farm when the rooster would perch atop the hen house and announce sunrise.

"For you newcomers, we do prayer requests at the end of class, so no one takes too much time away from my teachin'. Now. Anyone got any prayer requests?"

A lady in a green paisley pantsuit stood and said, "We need to pray for Richard Farley. He was told this week he has cancer."

Bonnie gripped Will's hand harder, hearing the sympathetic moans filling the air as Clyde took up the challenge.

"Ok, let's pray. Lord, we know You know Richard Farley's got the cancer, since it was You who give it to him. So we pray that You do what You will. If it be Yer will that he be with You, then take him. If it be Yer will that he stay here longer, then make him well. Amen."

Another hearty "AMEN!" resounded throughout the room.

Bonnie sat dumbfounded. Will didn't seem to be breathing. In all her short life she had never heard teaching and praying like this before, certainly not in their church back home. Too afraid to move, lest her facial expression reveal her dismay, Bonnie's eyes followed the people as they began to leave the classroom. Exiting in numbness toward the door, Bonnie fumed. She was so upset, her jaw clinched and her shoulders tensed.

Will could easily read her body language. Leaning in to her ear, he whispered, "I know what you're thinking. We'll discuss this later. For Pete's sake, don't say anything right now."

But for Bonnie not to say anything required an act of God. And that very Sunday morning, a miracle took place. She held her tongue. But she chewed on that absurd lesson throughout the church service. It didn't spill out her lips until she shut the car door after the sermon. "Did you hear what I heard in Sunday School? What was that self-righteous man thinking? Has he ever really read the Bible? Oh, it was all I could do to sit there and endure that man's crazy thinking. And to pray like that for the poor man with cancer. I can't believe a loving God would 'give' anyone cancer. Cancer is a bad thing. And God can do nothing bad! What was that all about?" Bonnie leaned back hard against her seat and blew out a loud breath.

Will knew he would have to diffuse the moment or he would hear about this for the rest of the day. Turning to face her, he said,

"Now, Bonnie, I'm sure not all the Sunday School teachers are like that in this church. There must be some really good ones somewhere. We'll just visit other classes until we find one with sound teaching. Besides, it could have been worse."

"Yeah, you're right. I guess the lesson could have been worse," she admitted, "there could have been swarms of bees stinging our faces for a solid hour, or a tsunami could have drowned us all in seconds. Yeah, it could have been a lot worse."

"You say the silliest things. I love it when you just blurt out what you're thinking. That was so funny!"

Bonnie had to agree. It was a funny comment, but sad too, as she thought how the preacher might not be aware of what was being taught behind closed doors. She had never heard that you didn't have faith unless you were serving on church committees or parking old people's cars. This Clyde fellow looked like he had been teaching since the Civil War, and he could not seem to be able to get out of the bondage of the Old Testament to freedom in Christ in the New Testament.

Waiting for Will to start the car, she recalled quite vividly her Miz Jessie saying, "Sunday School teachers tend ta stay in their positions 'til the day they up and die.' It be a lifelong thang. Old age, memory loss, or teched' in the head, ain't an excuse for a teacher to quit. Which might make some thank that bein' off in the head was required for the job anyway. I don't hold to that at 'tal. Well, I'm jus a sayin."

Bonnie's mind raced faster than a hummingbird's wings. "And that prayer, Will! It sounded so sanctimonious. Not only that, but praying for God's will like that made it sound as though it gave

those praying an excuse to not have to believe one way or the other. That way, if the person was made well, then the response would be Hallelujah! And if the person died, then they could say, Hallelujah, it must have been God's will. Freedom Class, indeed!" Bonnie harrumphed. "That Clyde fella does not know the first thing about freedom." She knew precious little herself, but she was embracing the grace of God and was determined, along with her husband, not to go back to that type of teaching again.

Bonnie missed her church back home. She missed the lively discussions she had with Miz Jessie. Two days before they left Missouri, Miz Jessie shared a Bible verse with her and Will. She had brought her Bible along so she could quote what she wanted to say, word by word. "Younguns, I am going to miss ya somethin' awful. But I knows the Lawd gots big plans for ya. I jus knows ya gonna do really fine. I ain't got a goin' away gift for ya, but I do gots this." She opened the well-worn Bible she was holding in her wrinkled hands. Reading slowly and deliberately she said, "The Good Book says in Galatians, 'See to hit that you are ne'er taken to a yoke of bondage, for hit was for freedom that Christ set you free.' One day, chillun, this here verse will pop back into yer heart and hit will explain itself to ya. I am gonna pray ever day for ya, ever day." She reached out for Bonnie and embraced her in a big Jessie hug.

She wished at this moment she could run over to Miz Jessie's house beyond the woods and tell her about the Sunday school lesson this morning.

Bonnie was seeing a lot of bondage in the people here in Windy Garden. Bondage to hurt, disappointment, grief, loneliness, even

122

tradition. She felt like she had grown up in another world, one that was hemmed in a bubble of protection. She could not understand how that kind of pain had made itself at home in Windy Garden.

What kind of wind has blown through this town that has created such a place of bondage? she wondered. Miz Jessie used to say, 'some folk has this need to control everone, so theys don't have to face whatever be wrong in their own life. Others hold their hurts sa tight inside they feel they jus' gonna fall apart if they give it to Jesus, and still, some are lonely or angry 'bout one thing or 'nuther, feelin stuck, stuck in a life they cain't seem to change. Yeah, them folk don't know that Jesus came and set 'em free! Free from the hurts, free from the pain and anger, free from control. Maybe, jus' maybe, one day they learn there be a whole lot more to know than what they think they know.

11

Going to the grocery store in Windy Garden had become an unexpected challenge for Bonnie. Never had she imagined going grocery shopping could be such a difficult chore.

There were two small local stores close to downtown, and one new chain store not too far away. It was Friday, and Bonnie decided to stop at one of the local stores to buy fresh fruit and vegetables for the weekend. She entered the store and picked up a basket to gather her items.

The owner quickly approached her and introduced himself. "Hey there, welcome to Gus' Produce. I'm Gus."

"Hello. My name is Bonnie." Glancing about the store, she saw rows and rows of handcrafted tables, waist-high, filled with vegetables and fruit. Watermelons were piled high in cardboard boxes by the door. Herbs hung in clusters along the wall, tied with strings. "My, you sure have some pretty produce. Prettier than I've seen for a while."

His appraising looked suggested she was a newcomer to town and asked, "Well, little gal, where do ya plan on gittin' yer food from? That big monster out on the highway? What they got ain't real food." He stood his ground waiting for an answer.

Bonnie's grip on the little basket in her hands tightened. "Um, well, to tell you the truth, I did visit the megastore when we first moved here, but I thought maybe I would try to shop more local, since the other one is three miles away. I'm just checking out all the possibilities."

One might have thought she'd slapped him in the face. His cheeks grew beet red and Bonnie believed she saw steam coming out of his ears. Of course, that could have been her imagination.

He said, "Lookee here, young lady, if yer gonna move to this town then ya support the locos. Ya hear?"

'Locos' indeed, Bonnie thought to herself. *I wonder if he really understands what he is saying.* But yep, she got his message loud and clear.

Attempting to lighten the conversation, Bonnie asked, "Say, do you attend the Baptist Church over on Cross Street?"

The puzzled Gus looked at her as if to say, *what business is it of yours?* "No, I ain't a Baptist, I'm a Metherdist and proud of it!" He poked his thumbs through his overalls and flashed a toothless grin, rocking back and forth on his heels.

That could be good, I guess, thought Bonnie. *I was beginning to think most of the cranky people went to the Baptist Church.*

"Oh, ok. Well, I think I'll check out your tomatoes and onions. Nice to meet you." She scurried off in the opposite direction.

After purchasing her needed items, Bonnie left Gus' Produce. She sat down on a bench outside the door. She took a moment to reflect on the people she had met in Windy Garden since the move. Some of these people were not quite the friendly sort she grew up around in southeast Missouri. The Lucys, Kathys and Sues here were plentiful back home. And at this moment, she sorely missed them. But the Netties and Gus's were a strange lot. Bonnie shook her head as if to clear away the images.

Rising, she walked the block to her car parked outside the cinema. She placed her veggies in the car and shut the door. Turning, she stared at the old movie house. Instantly, she was five years old. Her mom and gram had often taken Bonnie to the movies at their little downtown theatre. The concession lady there was a lot like Lucy in the Apothecary. She would smile and talk to you like she'd known you your whole life.

But even in her hometown of Blodgett, a few exceptions stood out in her mind. A gulp formed in Bonnie's throat, as one particular instance bounced into her memory. Just down the street there had been a small mercantile on the corner, where three dirt roads converged. A man named Bubba Banks was the owner. Gus reminded her of Mr. Banks.

Bubba was as round as he was tall, and sat on a stool near the cash register all day long. Bonnie would never forget the day she first met Mr. Banks. She was visiting her Aunt Virginia who lived real close to the downtown area. Her mama had sent her to Bubba's only a block away to get a loaf of bread. It was perfectly safe for young children to wander from their own yards back then, since everyone knew everyone. All the parents kept watch on each other's kids as well as their own.

Bonnie walked the one block to the store. When she crossed the threshold, a bell suspended over the door alerted the owner someone had entered his place of business.

To Bonnie's right sat a man on a stool that looked eight feet tall and eight feet wide! To the eyes of this little child, anyway. She froze in her tracks at how huge the man was. He had a lollipop in his mouth with the white stick hanging out over his lips. Removing the lollipop, he leaned forward with his chubby hands on his knees and said, "Ain't you Verna's daughter?"

Trembling, she answered, "Ye..Yes sir."

Bonnie wondered how he could have known that! She was so scared she thought she might burst out crying.

The man with the lollipop laughed so hard his big belly shook. He slapped his knee and said, "Well girl, I coulda been yer daddy!"

Shocked and scared, she turned and ran back out the door. Without the bread. Crying, she ran straight home to her mama, who stood at the kitchen sink peeling potatoes.

Hearing her daughter's cry, she dropped the potato peeler and knelt to face her hysterical child. "What happened? Why are you so upset? Are you all right? Where is the bread?"

Mama's sisters, Aunt Mary and Aunt Virginia, rushed into the room, hearing the cries as well.

"That man…that man… man at the store said…." Bonnie began crying again, her body trembling with fear trying to find the words to describe the fat man with the lollipop.

"What man? What did he say?" Her Mama held her at arm's length, searching her face for anything that would explain the look of sheer terror on her daughter's tear-streaked face.

"That man at the store said….he said he could have been my daddy!" She broke down in tears again, as her mama held her to her breast, relieved that it was not something worse.

Mama wiped Bonnie's tears with the dish towel and smoothed the hair from her face. Whispering she said, "Bonnie, honey, he was just a boy in school who liked me. That's all. There is no way that Bubba Banks could ever, ever have been your daddy! I'm sure he was just teasing you. I'll speak to him about this, you can count on that!"

Even at five years of age Bonnie knew a scary man when she saw one and this 'loco' grocery man scared her so bad, she imagined herself twenty years down the road sitting on a stool with fat thighs.

A car horn sounded, drawing Bonnie back to why she came downtown to begin with. She needed a cucumber, but was so rattled she just wanted to go home. Pulling out of her parking space, she saw a sign on the next block, Walter's Groceries. She had to wonder what kind of 'loco' operated that one as well. "Who knows," she mumbled under her breath. "Could be some close relative to Gus." Her dinner salad would have no cucumbers on it tonight.

12

Two weeks later, Bonnie was growing tired of being stuck in the house, unpacking box after box. Slumping into the worn Early American chair her mother had given her, she sighed. "I am not in the mood today to figure out what goes where." Looking about her mis-matched hand-me-down furniture, Bonnie decided what she needed most was lunch. Running upstairs, she quickly changed clothes and walked briskly in the direction of the Apothecary. Entering the diner, Bonnie noticed the banana split lady eating lunch. She was the same lady Bonnie was drawn to on her very first visit to the sweet little cafe. Something about this little lady tugged at Bonnie. Finding an empty table next to her, Bonnie took a seat.

She couldn't help but notice the sadness that permeated the lady's eyes, yet her lips parted into the sweetest smile when Lucy approached her table to fill her tea glass. "Alice, ya not real hungry today? Ya hardly touched yer food," Lucy said as she poured iced tea into the glass. Lucy was not only the best waitress in town, she was caring and attentive.

Timidly, Alice moved her napkin from her lap to the table and set it beside her plate. "I guess I don't feel much like eating today."

"I'll fetch ya a box to put yer sandwich in and ya can take it with ya and eat it later. Maybe ya feel up to finishing it at home, ok?" The lady smiled at Lucy and looked back at her plate. As Lucy walked away, she glanced at Bonnie and shrugged her shoulders, as if to say it was a perfectly normal exchange between the two women.

Bonnie's heart went out to the lady named Alice. Forgetting she was a stranger, Bonnie picked up her purse and went over to meet this lady with the sad face. Will often said that his wife never met a stranger.

"Hi," Bonnie spoke softly, so as not to frighten her, "I'm Bonnie. I'm new to town and thought I would come over and meet you."

Alice looked up and smiled. "Oh! That is so sweet of you. My, you are a pretty young thing. I'm Alice Barker. Please, have a seat." She motioned for Bonnie to sit at the chair adjacent to her.

"Thank you." Bonnie pulled out the red plastic-covered chair and sat down. Air squeezed out of a hole in the seat cushion, making a sound like a natural body function that properly-bred ladies would never allow to 'eek' out of them, especially in public. Her face turned beet red as she looked at Alice to see if she too had heard the sound. By the giggle in the lady's voice and the dainty little hand over her mouth, she had. Seeing the blush in her cheeks, Bonnie burst out laughing. She leaned into Alice and whispered, "You do know that wasn't me, don't you?"

At that very moment she was about to learn that Alice was truly a southern lady, a genteel sort, brought up with decorum and style, yet balanced with charm.

Clearing her throat in an attempt to regain her composure, she gently tapped Bonnie's hand with her fingers and said, "Young lady, I can tell you with all honesty that I heard nothing short of old worn-out chair seats, well past their prime, in dire need of repair." Alice removed her fingers and properly folded them on the edge of the table. Leaning slightly forward she whispered, "I may have been brought up a lady, but I know an embarrassing moment when

I see one. And you my dear, have made my day!"

Her giggle reminded Bonnie of her Gram. Some sounds and voices from childhood rise to the surface of our memories like bubbles in a bathtub, bursting with nostalgia at just the right time. Gram's laugh was sweet and genuine, like Alice's. Homesickness threatened to steal this moment, but was quickly squelched when Alice said, "Young lady, I have been coming to the Apothecary since I could eat with a spoon, and I don't recall a time when someone as young as you wanted to sit with an old lady like me. I daresay most young people miss out on a great opportunity to learn from our experience. I guess they are too wrapped up in their 'now' to pay much attention."

"You remind me so much of my Gram. Her face would light up when us grandkids would tease her, and listen to her childhood stories, or spend time cooking with her in the kitchen. I do miss her."

"Is she very far away?"

"Yes, she is 500 miles away in southeast Missouri with my parents, two sisters and brother. It's such a long drive. But Will and I hope to be able to go home for Christmas, if he can get off work then. Do you have family close by?"

Bonnie saw a cloud pass over Alice's face and regretted asking. She thought about changing the subject, when Alice spoke.

"I have a granddaughter in California. Talk about a long way off. I miss her too."

Bonnie wasn't sure how long they sat there getting acquainted before Lucy returned with a box for Alice's leftovers. "I see ya met our Alice, Bonnie. Isn't she a darlin?"

"A darling and a lady and a new friend of mine, I hope. We were just doing our very best to impress each other and I think, if I do say so myself, we fooled each other nicely!"

Alice laughed, not a dainty chuckle like before, but a full belly laugh that brought smiles to both Lucy and Bonnie's face.

"Alice, it does me good to hear ya laugh. This Bonnie must be a good influence on ya." Lucy patted Alice's shoulder and stepped over to the next booth to take another customer's order.

Alice's shoulders relaxed. It seemed to Bonnie that Alice had completely forgotten how melancholy she had been just minutes before.

Looking at the Coca-Cola clock on the wall above the jukebox, Bonnie said, "I'm sorry, Miss Alice, but I have to leave. I've got a few errands to run. But I can't tell you what a joy it has been to meet you! I do hope to see you again and real soon too. Oh, do you mind if I call you Miss Alice?"

"Not at all! I haven't been called Miss in.....well, let me put it this way, since Japan surrendered the war! I like it! And the pleasure was all mine. If you drop in again, I am here at this same table every Tuesday and Friday at 11:30 for lunch. Do drop by and join me when you can." There was that smile again that lit her up like a Christmas tree.

"It will be my pleasure! Bye." Bonnie went to the counter to pay for lunch. She also paid for Miss Alice's. While Lucy rang up the bill, she leaned over and said, "Thank ya for taking time to meet our sweet Alice. She's a very lonely woman and gets depressed easily. It did her good to laugh. And it was very sweet of ya to sit with her too. I knew I liked ya the first day ya come in here. Have a great day, sugah!"

Looking back at Miss Alice, it dawned on Bonnie why she had not noticed her before. She rarely came to the Apothecary on Tuesdays. And the Fridays she did come would have been a little earlier. Bonnie made a mental note to come back and spend time with this sweet lady who needed a friend to laugh with. And Bonnie needed to enjoy fond memories of home without crying.

As she stepped out of the Apothecary, a light breeze blew Bonnie's hair into her face. "Ah, a refreshing wind." She sniffed the clean mountain air and strolled down the street.

After running several errands around town, Bonnie had a few minutes to waste. She decided to sit on the town swing and reflect on her visit with Miss Alice. In that short span of time, she had learned her new friend was a widow of many years and lived alone. She had one granddaughter living way out in California whom she did not see as often as she would like. But Bonnie could tell she was crazy about her precious Elizabeth. Miss Alice also attended the First Baptist Church and was very active, as long as she could get there. She lived several blocks away, and driving at her age had become more difficult. Sometimes friends would pick her up and take her to Bible studies and senior adult functions.

Bonnie rose from the swing and walked to the Bloomin' Pretty to purchase a single small rose with baby's breath to place on her dining room table that evening. Roses were a symbol of love, and despite a few unfortunate first impressions, she was slowly falling in love with the people of Windy Garden. She loved compassionate Lucy, the energetic Kathy, the quiet Miss Alice, and yes, she was somehow even beginning to love the unapproachable Miss Nettie.

13

Miss Alice left the Apothecary, stopping to rest on the town swing. She thought of her sweet Elizabeth and wondered when she would come again. It had been a little over six months since her last visit and she missed her darling granddaughter.

Her thoughts wandered back to the day when she received the dreadful call that her daughter was in a serious car accident in California on Interstate 5 while driving home from work. A man in a black pickup truck had had a heart attack, and rear ended her compact car. She lost control and ran head-on into the guardrail, her car bursting into flames. She died before reaching the hospital. "My baby. My precious Carolyn. I miss you so. I wish I could have been there to hold you in my arms one last time. I am so lonely without you. All I have left is our Elizabeth."

Her grief was palpable. She looked about. No one was nearby to hear her words of despair. The only movement that caught her eye was the young Bonnie she had met earlier at the Apothecary. Her new acquaintance was now leaving the Blooming Pretty with a red rose peeking out of the green florist paper. *What a sweet girl. She reminds me so much of my Carolyn.*

Alice could hear the sound of a train in the distance. She rose from the swing and walked slowly across the street to her home, only two houses down on the right, behind the Hair Buzz. She opened the front door and stooped to pick up the mail that had been deposited through the slot in the door. *Bills, only bills. There is not even one piece of junk mail,* thought Alice. *It's the same every day.* She let out a heavy sigh and tossed the mail on the coffee table in the living room. Placing her purse beside the mail, she sat down heavily on the Queen Anne chair that faced the large plate glass window. She watched a loud mockingbird land on the bird feeder underneath the oak tree alongside her front walk. Closing her eyes, she savored the chatter of the mockingbird. A respite from her own introspection. Then she opened her eyes, no longer hearing the sound of the bird, and felt alone once more. *The doctors gave me a year to live six months ago. I wish the good Lord would give me a restful sleep tonight and not awaken me in the morning. But there is one thing I wish would happen first. I'd love to see my Elizabeth one more time. I know it's very expensive for her to fly here from so far away. Although she calls me every day and wants to come desperately, I understand the lack of funds to make the trip.*

Alice rose from her chair and walked into the kitchen. She filled a small watering can with water. It was the first Wednesday of the month, which meant it was African violet day. Gently lifting the velvety leaves, she poured water around the base of the plant. Her wooden stand held eight potted violet plants. Each a different color. Her friends commented to her often that they had never seen such beautiful violets.

The sun shone through her bay window onto her large variety of plants. Several of them began as sprigs from older plants that she and her husband had grown together. They had carefully cut a leaf with its stem from each plant. Alice would use small scissors to cut the stems at a 45 degree angle, about an inch from the leaf. Her husband would then place each cutting in the center of a very small pot, filled loosely with peat moss and vermiculite. Alice would lightly water the soil, being careful not to get the leaves wet. Fred had even made a wooden plant stand for this very purpose. It was small enough to handle eight tiny plants. They placed the new shoots on the stand in the living room where they could watch then grow. It was a labor of love, one she even shared with her granddaughter. Elizabeth had a sprig from each violet, and told her grandmother on the phone that they were thriving beautifully.

Before dressing for bed, Alice went to check the locks on the doors. Assured she was secure for the night, she turned from the front door and noticed an envelope which had slipped underneath the door mat, it's edge peeking out. She stooped to retrieve it from its hiding place. In the living room, she turned on the light and sat in her favorite wooden rocker with ruffled chair pads. Turning the envelope over, she did not see a return address. *This is odd*, she thought. It was addressed to Mrs. Alice Barker, with her correct address. *Well, that's me, alright.* Then she noticed there was no stamp. *Now this is going from odd to strange,* she thought, with her hand to her mouth. *It's handwritten to me; not typed. But how did this get through the mail with no stamp?* Puzzled, she turned the envelope over and over, studying it thoroughly. *Now this is a mystery*, she giggled to herself. *Guess it's time for me to solve it by opening it up.*

Hesitating, she sat back and stared for the longest time at the strange letter she held in her hands. She loved getting mail, but this was definitely not typical. In fact, she hadn't received personal mail since her birthday, three months ago. *Hmm, maybe I'll wait until the morning to open it. It will prolong the suspense and give me something to look forward to.* Placing the letter in her housecoat pocket, she shuffled off to bed. As was her custom every night, she laid her housecoat on the opposite side of where she slept. Ever since her Fred had died, she didn't have to make his side of the bed because she only slept on her side, never uncovering his pillow at all. Reaching for the nightstand lamp, she switched it off. Settling beneath the covers, she prayed. "Lord, thank You for this day you made. The weather was nice. The birds still came for their food. And I have food for tomorrow. And thank You for lifting my spirits by the odd letter. It is the strangest thing! Imagine! A letter under my door mat that I didn't notice earlier. I wanted to rip it open right away, but thinking on it, I decided to keep the mystery going for a while. It may be hard for me to fall asleep, Lord, thinking about the letter, but please help me not lose rest tonight. My body aches so, when I don't sleep well. Thank you, Lord. Amen."

Fluffing her pillow under her head she added, "And Lord. Please wake me in the morning!"

14

Bonnie called Kathy the following Thursday morning and asked if she could ride with her to the Bible study.

"Of course!" Kathy replied. "I'm so glad you asked. I will pick you up in the morning at 8:30 sharp. You will meet lots of women who are as sweet as pie!"

"Thank you, Kathy. I am looking forward to it." Bonnie was excited about becoming a part of a group of women digging into the Word of God. She had attended small Bible studies back home in her little church where maybe only five or six women attended. They were mostly older than Bonnie and a little on the boring lecture style.

Kathy arrived the next morning and honked the horn. Bonnie pulled back the curtain and waved out the window. She grabbed her Bible and purse and hurried to the waiting car. "Good morning, Kathy. It's real pretty outside today."

"It is a gorgeous morning, isn't it? The sun is shining, the mountains are clear and the car is in reverse!" Kathy backed out in one swift movement and hit the pedal. Off they sped in a blur, with Bonnie holding onto the armrest for dear life.

"You're not going to believe what I did this morning! My little eyes fluttered open and reminded me that it was Thursday and you were going with me to Bible study. I didn't want to be late so I jumped out of bed and hurried to the kitchen. I filled the kettle with water for hot tea and slid a cinnamon roll into the oven to warm, while I rushed to get dressed. I spent a half hour in the Word sipping my tea and nibbling my roll as I do most every morning. Then went to the bathroom to fix my hair and put on makeup. I just knew I'd be late. I went in to kiss Bob goodbye when he glanced at the clock and said, "For heaven's sake, Kathy, it's only 4:00 a.m!"

"Well, no wonder it is so dark outside," I said. "He just groaned his morning groan and went back to sleep. I was fully dressed and ready to leave but had hours to wait. So I made another cup of tea and another cinnamon roll and sat down in the sunroom to watch the stars wink at me. You know they do that, don't you? If you sit real still, they will twinkle just for you."

Bonnie smiled at this lady who had more energy than a windmill in a tornado. Miz Jessie used to say that about *her!* But she liked this Kathy very much. Arriving at the church parking lot in record time, Bonnie saw several ladies entering the doors to the sanctuary.

"We meet in the basement," Kathy said, shutting the car door. Descending the stairs, a hallway opened to their left. They followed a lady with a tote full of what looked like a Bible and several legal-size notepads. Pockets on the outside were filled with pens, a variety of colored pencils, and a ruler. Bonnie gulped. *What have I gotten myself into?* But it was too late to back out now.

The hallway opened up into a large room with rows and rows of tables that faced huge blackboards on the wall stretching from one end of the room to the other. In the back of the room through a doorway was a long narrow kitchen. Several women had arrived earlier and were clustered in small groups, laughing and sharing cute stories about their kids. Kathy motioned Bonnie over to the front row of tables. Bonnie shook her head, clutching her Bible tightly to her chest. She did not want to sit up close this soon.

Kathy motioned to the second row. Again Bonnie shook her head. Then Kathy moved to the back row. Bonnie came up beside her and whispered, "Thank you, Kathy. I'd feel a little funny sitting up so close to the front today."

"I'm sorry, kiddo. I should have thought about that. This is just fine." They set their Bibles and purses down on the table in front of their seats.

"Debbie! Good morning! Come here. I have someone for you to meet," Kathy shouted across the room. Bonnie cringed.

The Debbie lady smiled and walked over to where Kathy and Bonnie stood. "Debbie, this is my new friend, Bonnie McDaniel. Bonnie, this is Debbie McLaren."

"So happy to meet you, Bonnie. How nice, another Mac. Welcome to our group of chattering women." The three glanced around the room and laughed. "I think you will love this Bible study." She placed her hand on Bonnie's arm and said, "It may seem a bit overwhelming at first; it was for me, but hang in there. After a few weeks, it will all start to make sense."

"Thanks," Bonnie said, timidly.

"You'll do just fine." she said reassuringly, and headed in the direction of the kitchen.

Kathy hustled Bonnie off to meet the others. She must have met thirty women in thirty seconds! *Sure hope it doesn't take me long to learn their names. After all, there is only one of me to remember, and dozens of them.*

"It's 9:00, ladies, let's get started. Please take your seats," came the announcement from the front of the room.

"That's our leader, Sue Gardner. She's the pastor's wife and very sweet." Kathy and Bonnie took their seats along with the rest of the women.

Just before prayer began, Bonnie flinched to see Nettie Pegram and the twin sisters from the Apothecary enter and take their seats in the back row near the kitchen. Her stomach began fluttering when she heard Nettie tell the other two ladies where to sit.

Sue waited patiently for the latecomers to settle down. "Let's pray." After the amen, Bonnie watched the teacher's eyes fall on hers. "I see we have a new student in attendance. Welcome! I am so glad you have decided to come this morning. My name is Sue Gardner. I don't want to embarrass you, but if you would like, could you introduce yourself to everyone?"

Nettie softly grumbled, "We don't have time for this."

Bonnie heard the snide remark. And so did Kathy, who jumped to her feet and said, "This is Bonnie McDaniel. She lives down the street from me on Fullers Road. I think she's a little nervous this morning. But I can tell you she is a wonderful young lady! I visited her a few weeks ago in her lovely home and invited her to our Bible study." Kathy leaned over to Bonnie and whispered, "Oh dear, maybe I shouldn't have mentioned where you live."

To ease Kathy's concern, she whispered back, "It's fine, Kathy. I don't mind."

"As I was saying," Kathy excitedly continued, "This is Bonnie McDaniel. Oh, I said that already. Teehee! She moved here from Missouri. You know, the 'show me' state. She has a husband named Will. And well, here she is!" Kathy beamed at her newfound friend, proud to be the first one to formally introduce her to the ladies of the church.

"We are very pleased to meet you, Bonnie," Sue responded. "And don't think you have to know all our names at once. That will come in time if you decide to continue with us. Let me tell you a little about what we are learning. This type of study teaches you to study the Bible for yourself. It is called an inductive study. We start by recognizing the most obvious truths of the Word and working our way into the more obscure passages. It's kind of like putting a puzzle together. You start with the obvious pieces, the corners and edges. Then fill in the center with the less obvious pieces. I hope you will enjoy all the little nuggets you get from studying God's Word with us. It can seem a little intimidating at first, but I think you'll get the hang of it before too long."

Bonnie thought it was very kind of the teacher to explain the type of Bible study she was teaching. She hoped she could keep up.

Sue asked that everyone open their Bibles to Philippians, chapter three.

Bonnie sat the entire morning with her mouth agape as they went deep into the Scriptures and seemingly dug 'to China,' expounding on Paul's journey to Philippi. Sue wrote words on the blackboard in English as well as Hebrew and Greek. In fact, she used the entire board!

What in the world have I gotten myself into? She had attended a few Bible studies before in her church back home, but had never experienced anything like this. Her head was bursting with so much information that she grew a headache. Her temples pounded and she thought there was no way she could be a part of this. The archaeological dig into Philippians was overwhelming!

After the lesson concluded, Kathy drove her home, talking all the way. Bonnie heard nothing coherent as they drove into her driveway. She was truly overcome with the wealth of information given this morning and no place to put it. She determined the best thing to do was to just chuck it all and take an aspirin. She stepped out of the car and thanked Kathy for picking her up and taking her home.

"My pleasure! Want me to pick you up next week? I can, you know. I pass right by your house."

"Right now, Kathy, I am so tired I can hardly think. But thank you for the offer. Can I call you?"

"Of course! Well, go inside and make a cup of hot tea and relax. I will see you around. Bye!"

Bonnie watched Kathy back into the road. The horn honked, and with a wave, Kathy headed in the same direction they had just come from.

Wonder why she is going back to town? Oh, I'm too exhausted to even think about it. Dragging herself wearily into the house, she dropped her study material and Bible on the dining room table. It was quiet inside and she relished being home, where she did not have to talk to or hear anyone speak. Dropping her tired young body on the sofa in the sunroom, she closed her eyes and bemoaned the fact that those women were miles ahead of her. *They really know their Bible! How can they know that much? I never knew there were that many questions to be asked and answers to be found. Back home the preachers said the Bible was full of mysteries that no one could solve.* At least that is what she thought they had said.

Bonnie wasn't sure she wanted to go back again. But her desire to make friends would prove to outweigh the headache and confusion.

The very next week Bonnie drove herself to class. Once again she sat in the back row, as close to the door as she could, just in case she needed to escape this room of vast, mind boggling questions. In Greek no less.

But Bonnie stuck with it, and week after week, things became more clear. She was learning the value of 'context.' By taking a verse and seeing it in light of the chapter, and then seeing that chapter in light of the book, and the book in light of the whole counsel of the Word of God, it made more sense. Still, she had missed the introduction part of the class that included the basics of the study and had jumped right smack dab in the middle. No wonder she felt lost at times. But Bonnie had to admit it was the most intriguing study she had ever encountered. It gave her a hunger to know more. Maybe if she could just grasp what she could each time, she could start putting all this information into perspective.

Before she left, Sue gave her a workbook on Philippians and told her to take her time catching up on the lessons she had missed. "Just take in what you can. Remember, God is your teacher." Having the workbook helped tremendously.

Bonnie flipped through the pages. She was sure the workbook would help her catch up to the rest of the ladies. Slipping it into her tote bag, she smiled. *Not only am I gaining knowledge and understanding of the Bible, I am also gaining new friends.* Bonnie was beginning to feel comfortable around these ladies, even those who attended other churches.

Bonnie would eventually learn why this particular group of

women were somewhat different than those she had met upstairs in the sanctuary. Most of them were not natives, nor were they even related to the town's original population. They were transplants, just like her! It was then that she realized that this is where she would most likely fit in... with those like herself who were not born and raised here. In fact, not all of them were Baptist. Several attended other churches. There were two Methodists, one Presbyterian, one Catholic, one from a non-denominational church, and two charismatics. Funny thing, no one seemed to care. All they seemed interested in was getting to know the Lord better through His word. Bonnie liked that! She remembered Miz Jessie told her once that the best place to be was "with women folk who love Jesus. No matter what chuch' they goes to."

During a break in the session, Bonnie was reminded of the day she had asked Jesus into her heart, at the tender age of ten in southeast Missouri. Miz Jessie talked with her that day and shared what it meant for Jesus to live in her heart.

You see, Miz Jessie was goodness wrapped up in *love*. Not just any old kind of love, but a forever love, a love that came from her deep faith in God. It was hard to understand that kind of love. Even Bonnie's mama said so. It wasn't the love that's seen readily in folks, even good church going folks. No, hers was a love everyone wanted.

"Miz Jessie?" she asked, her voice full of concern. "How come you can love like you do? Ya love so good, even to that mean ole Mr. Goolsby who treats ya so bad. I don't like him."

Bonnie sat down on the bottom porch step, reached over and pulled a blade of grass from its root, twiddling it between her fingers.

Being around Miz Jessie made Bonnie feel bad for thinking

mean thoughts. For example, at school, Bonnie tried hard to love Freckles Joe, but she just couldn't do it. Those freckles clumped together in a huge mass on his nose and cheeks that made him look downright silly. She laughed every time she saw him. Why, just last week she had asked him if he ever tried to connect the dots!

Miz Jessie was sitting on the back porch snapping beans into a big bowl. Rocking back and forth in that old wooden rocker Bonnie's grandma used to sit on in the evenings, she hummed. She was always humming something. But Bonnie was too engrossed in the 'twitterin'' of her own thinkin' to listen.

"Whatcha mean, little un?"

Taking the blade of grass from her mouth, Bonnie ventured, "What I mean is, you seem so content, you don't seem to worry none. You love everybody the same, though I can't understand how. I been sneakin' off sometimes, watching you and I saw you take some hot soup over yonder to Mr. Goolsby, and he's meaner than a snake. But you, you were humming with a glow on your face, haulin' that soup in your big heavy cast iron pot up the lane to his house like you was takin' it to the Preseedent of these United States."

Seemed like when Bonnie was around Miz Jessie, she talked like Miz Jessie. Bonnie stayed right still, too embarrassed to look Miz Jessie in the face.

"Come here, chile."

Bonnie stepped up on the porch and sat cross-legged in front of Miz Jessie's rocker, which had stopped. Miz Jessie leaned forward with her arms outstretched, as far as her plump middle allowed, beckoning Bonnie to place her hand in hers. She stroked Bonnie's hair with her other hand. After a moment, she smiled and leaned back into the rocker.

Bonnie's eyes were glued on her mentor and friend.

"Ya know, chile, I was so much like you when I weren't much older than you are rights now. I didn't know how some folk could be so kind and so lovin' all the time either. I saw my own mam feedin' no good people who jus' wanted somethin' for nuthin.' Yet, she fed 'em anyways. It made me downright mad, it did. I'd tell her that those folk was jus' usin' her.

"My mam knew how to love good, I can tell ya that. But me? Not me. I wanted to love like mam but I was too mad at those folk to care."

A troubled look crossed Miz Jessie's face. It did not escape Bonnie's notice.

"Miz Jessie, are you alright? Ya look like ya could cry." Bonnie leaned forward with her hands on Jessie's knees, about to cry herself.

"I'm fine, chile. I'm fine." She looked endearingly at her Bonnie girl.

"I knew they'd be a day when we might have this little chat. Though, I gotta say, it gonna be mighty hard to say what I gotta say. Cause I'm perty embarrassed 'bout it."

Bonnie didn't know what to say to that! She sat back again with a concerned look on her face, yet eager to hear more.

Jessie sensed her discomfort and spoke, "Little un, I hadn't always known how to love right. In fact, I was quite the rascal growin' up. Seemed I bounced from rascal to angel all in the same day."

Bonnie's hand covered her loud gasp in disbelief.

"Not only that, but I even sassed my own mam quite often."

"No!" Bonnie whispered. She could not imagine her Miz Jessie even being a child, much less sassing her mama.

"Ya see, Bonnie, when I was a little un myself, I tried real hard to be good. My mam and pap were good folk. And I wanted to be good folk too. I would git up each day and say to myself, "Jessie, you be good today and mind your mam and pap. Do good things. Say nice things. And don't go gettin' into no trouble.

"But hard as I tried, most days I would mess up sa bad I didn't know when I started and when I ended. I even learned how to swear words I done heered other kids use and mam would hear me and give me a lickin'. She'd tell me how sad she be I wadn't using my tongue for speakin' good instead of evil.

"Then the time came when I started really spoutin' off to my mam. I made sure Pap weren't near cause lawdy Sue, he would whoop me a good un if he heered me mouthin' mam! He didn't take no disrespectin.'"

Miz Jessie looked at Bonnie, making sure she listening. She was.

Picking up on her tale, she continued, "Well, the meetin' of judgment come a knockin' on the door. One day Pap walked into the kitchen when my mouth was a' runnin' out of control."

"Well! What we gots here?" boomed my pap's voice. It sounded like thunder bouncing off the walls. "Julia, what this be comin' outta our daughter? Who does she think she be?"

Then pap turned and stared at me as though the devil was standing right beside me. "Daughter!" he yelled.

Bonnie jumped.

"When I heared him shout, 'Daughter!' in that booming tone

of voice, I knew I was in trouble fer shore', deep, deep trouble."

"Whatcha gots to say fer yerself?" Pap's eyes bored into mine like a hot cattle prod. He didn't even blink. His hands were on his hips and bent forward like Old man Zeke, staring me down."

"Who's old man Zeke?" Bonnie asked in anticipation.

Miz Jessie chuckled, "Old man Zeke was a deecon in our chuch and was bent over lookin' at the ground for as long as I knowed him."

"Anyways, I done realized I was in for a lickin'. From Pap. There weren't nothin' worse than crossin' my Pap. My mind started racin', trying to figger a way out of this.

"I thought I had come up with the perfect answer.

"Well Pap, she and me jus' not gettin' along lately. She always on me for somethin' or 'nuther," I said with a boldness that surprised mam and pap. But it weren't no boldness a'tall. It was jus' plain fact, far as I was concerned."

Miz Jessie was fully in her story now. And so was Bonnie.

"I figgered that pap would now turn on mam. I stood there real sure of myself thankin' I done won this a'one. But pap didn't move, he didn't even bat an eye. His eyes never left mine."

"Daughter," he said real loud agin, "I best not be hearin' that kind of talk EVER come outta yer mouth agin' or so hep me, you'll be sorry for the day ya learned to talk! You will not be disrespectin' yer mam!"

"Mam started to cry, wipin' her tears with her apron. She ne'er cried much, especially in front of me. Guilt rose up in me sa fast, I thought I was goin' to throw up. I made mam cry. I was so 'shamed of myself. Mam left the kitchen weepin' while I stood there feelin' awful bad. I dared a look at my pap. All he had to do was nod his head at me that I best be gittin' to my room. And quick like! I ran straight away, hearin' his voice behind me. "And ain't gonna be no supper for ya, ya back talkin' youngun!"

"I hurried to my bedroom and shut the door, breathin' hard and leanin' against it. I could still hear the sobs of my mam through the walls. "How could I do such a terrible thang to her?" I asked myself over and over. I threw my sorry body on the bed and cried for a long time. Later I could smell supper cookin' and hoped mam would come git me and all would be well. But....she didn't come."

"Oh Miz Jessie, yer pap made ya go to bed without eating? That sounds so mean."

"Well, no supper makes a growin' sassy girl mighty hungry. Late that night, my stomach was growlin' to be fed. I wadn't sure I should try to sneak a snack but my empty tummy talked louder than my fear. So, I tiptoed past my folks' bedroom door and seen pap sound asleep in the bed. I snuck into the kitchen, not makin' a sound. Gently, I rolled open the bread box when I heered mam's voice. It sounded a long ways off. The voice come from the back porch! So I eased myself to the screen door leadin' to the porch and saw mam sittin' in the straight back chair talkin' to someone. Who was she talkin' to? Couldn't be pap. I seen him sleepin' in the bed. Now who could she be a talkin' to in the middle of the night?"

"Who was your mama talkin' to? A ghost? The wind?" Bonnie's eyes were wide as saucers.

"Well, I wiz wunderin' that myself, chile! I leaned against the doorframe to hear what she was sayin'. Soft and clear, mam spoke, 'Oh, Jesus, what do I do? I be the baddest mam in the world. Look at my poor baby. She becomin' someone I don't know. Oh sweet Jesus, give me my girl back. She really be sweet and kind. Maybe she jus' goin' through a spell. She don't mean what she say, really she don't. Forgive her, Lawd. And hep me hep her. I been a'prayin' and a'prayin' fer her since she grow'd in my belly. She jus' don't know how much she be loved. Pap and I love her so much. But You! You love her more than we ever could. Someday, maybe soon, she will see Yer love and want it for herself. Then she become the lovin' girl I know is in there somewheres. She jus' havin' a hard time rights now.'

"My mam sighed real deep, starin' out into the dark of night at the fireflies talkin' to each other with their blinkin' and winkin.' Mam had high hopes fer me. She knew if I could jus' see how much God loved me, I would be a different chile.

"I stepped back into the darkness of the kitchen to head back to bed when I heered mam again. 'I jus' know ya got yer lovin' hand on my Jessie to become someone who folks will come from hither and yonder to see, cause yer love will shine sa bright. I knows she will. Thank ya for listenin' dear Jesus. Amen and amen.' Mam wrapped her shawl around her wide shoulders, sittin' straight as a board in the old wooden chair on a cool, dark night, lit only by a fingernail of a moon."

Jessie's voice rose as she related, "I ran fast back to my room, quiet as a mouse and jumped into my bed. Tuckin' the covers under my chin, I cried fer hours and hours into my piller. I finally cried myself to sleep.

"The next morning, I found mam on the back porch, sittin' in the same straight back chair. I wondered if she had been there all night. I walked ever so slow in front of her. I couldn't look her in the face, I was too 'shamed. So I stood there tremblin' and cryin' and confessed, 'Mam, I am so bad! Why am I so bad? I'm sorry, Mam. I wish I could be good and lovin' like you. I try and try but I jus' cain't!' I fell in mam's lap in a heap of tears. Mam dried my tears with her apron and lifted my face to hers. I couldn't believe what I saw!"

"What did you see?" Bonnie asked with alarm. She was sitting on pins and needles to know more. Miz Jessie always had a way of capturing her attention with her storytellin.'

"No, chile. I seen the sweetest look on her face I ever did see. Then…..she smiled….and heavens to Betsy, I thought mam would float right out of that chair into heaven like a angel I seen in pictures! Her face glowed with a ring of light round 'bout, and when she spoke, her words sounded like a song."

Bonnie was on her knees now, leaning on Jessie's lap, eyes wide with wonder.

"'Chile, of mine," my mam said, 'I have waited fer this day since you was born. Ya not small or a baby no mor.' Ya becomin' quite grown up. There be some thangs fer babies, some thangs fer kids in the middle of their growin' time, and some thangs ain't ready til a body ripe to hear. You, baby, are in the middle of yer growin' time. It be time to put away baby thankin' and start thankin' more grown up like.'

"I liked it when she done said I weren't a baby no more," Jessie smiled.

"I'd been wantin' to be more grown up for a while. But that day I was. Mam said so.

"Today, Jessie," mam continued, 'ya gonna hear where real love come from. It cain't come from inside ya by yerself, no matter how hards ya try. It can only come from the Lawd. He be love. It is what he be. He cain't be nuthin' else. He gotta be what he is or he ain't God.

"Ya see, Jessie, when ya open yerself up to the one who made ya, bigger than me or pap, ya begins to see thangs different like. Ya begins to see like Jesus. And when ya see what he sees, ya begins to see the good in folk. Even them that was mean to ya. Ya start to see that somewhere they been hurt too and so they hurt others.

"And ya begin to feel changed insides yerself too, like ya be meetin' yerself for the very first time,' my mam told me. 'Ya been tryin' and tryin' to fill a big hole in yer heart by bein' good and doin' good, but no matter how hards ya tried, it never got filled up.

"Jessie girl, when I was yer age, before I opened my heart up to Jesus, I thought God was mad at me ever time I did somethin' or said somethin' wrong. But when I seen how much he loved me, even in my bad, I wadn't the same no more. I had a new heart, filled with love he done give me. He hadn't been mad at me all along. He was jus' waitin' fer me to see His love. Ya see, most folk don't know God loves 'em. They really don't. They knows how to be good chuch' folk, do chuch' folk stuff, and even try to love the best they knows how, but insides, they knows somethin' ain't right.

'Jessie, yer ne'er gonna know love til ya know how much ya be loved. Mostly by God. Then he teach ya how to love right. Baby, do ya understand any of this?' my mam asked me.

"Bonnie, everthang mam said sounded real good, but I shook my head 'no.'

'Well, the first thang ya need to do, Jessie, is ask the Lawd to come into yer heart and give ya the love he has been wantin' to give ya for a long time.'

"I told her, 'But I prayed like that a long while back, mam.'

"Well, then, what kind of change did ya see? Did ya see God lovin' on ya? Did ya love others like ya saw him lovin' ya?"

"Now that was the big question, Bonnie girl. As I thought really hard on it, I didn't see that kind of love comin' to me or goin' out of me. So I told mam so."

'Then Jessie,' she says, 'when yer ready to be open to that, pray again. This time ya will know if yer heart be ready to take to his love. It will be mighty eveedent, that's fer shor.'

Bonnie looked askew at Miz Jessie and asked, "Well, Miz Jessie, all I can say is, you must have prayed an awful lot sometime along the way. 'Cause you love like crazy!" Both enjoyed a hearty laugh together.

"Yes, chile, I did, right there and then. I prayed with mam and opened my heart to the love of Jesus. I cain't tell ya what it looked like, but there was nary a doubt somethin' broke insides me. Then somethin' really big filled that hole mam spoke of."

"Was it Jesus?"

"It was. I seen love like I ne'er had before. I saw me like I ne'er seen me a'for too. Then I beguns to see folk like I ne'er seen 'em. I seen us all with new eyes. Jesus' eyes."

Bonnie's face scrunched in a deeply introspective way. Miz Jessie resumed rockin' and snappin' beans.

"Miz Jessie?" Bonnie asked.

"Yes, chile?"

"I want to love like you. Can you show me how?"

"It's quite simple, little un. Talk to God. Tell him how hard you've tried and failed. Tell him ya know ya do and say thangs ya ought not to. Then ask him to show ya' how much he love ya.' It will change yer life." Jessie smiled.

"Can we do it now, like you did with yer mam?"

"We shore' can." Right then, Bonnie prayed the words Miz Jessie said. When she was done, she asked, "How long does it take to work?"

Jessie stopped what she was doing and cupped Bonnie's face in her hand. "Well, little un, what's happenin' in yer heart right now?"

Bonnie paused for the longest time before she answered. Her scrunched up forehead relaxed as she said, "Well, I think it might be sayin' that I can't love other folks right til I know how much God loves me."

"That be right."

"Well, I feel like I may be startin' all over." Bonnie giggled into her hands.

"I'd say startin' at the beginnin' is a good place to start."

Slowly, Bonnie rose to her feet. She smiled at her dear friend and turned to leave. At the bottom of the porch steps, she stopped and turned. "Miz Jessie, does this mean I have to like Freckles Joe?" And off she skipped.

15

Sunday morning after church let out, Bonnie and Will headed for their car. Under a tree in the shade nearby was Miss Alice, holding her Bible close to her chest with her purse under her arm. "Hey, Miss Alice!" Bonnie made a beeline for her new friend, with Will in tow. "Will, this is the lady I told you about at the Apothecary. Miss Alice, this is my husband, Will."

Alice extended her frail hand and Will shook it lightly. "Nice to meet you, young man. I want you to know that even after one visit, I have fallen in love with your sweet wife."

"Why, thank you, ma'am. She is a prize! And quite frankly, I am not at all surprised that she invaded your space. You see, this little gal doesn't know a stranger."

The three laughed at Will's evaluation of their meeting. "Oh, Bonnie, there's Doug. I need to speak with him. Miss Alice, it was a pleasure to meet you."

"Don't mind him, he's such a tease," Bonnie said, watching Will walk away.

Alice glanced over at Will and said to Bonnie, "Meeting a young man with manners is quite the catch. I like him!"

"Me too! Well, how are you doing today, Miss Alice?"

"I have been under this tree waiting for you. I was hoping you were at church this morning. Come closer."

The mystery in her voice intrigued Bonnie as she took a step forward. "This sounds secretive," she smiled.

"I have something exciting I have been waiting to tell you for weeks!"

Bonnie was surprised at the surge of energy and liveliness of her new friend.

"For weeks? Why, Miss Alice, I wish I had known. I would have come right over!"

"Well, I didn't have your phone number, so I couldn't call. But over my many, many years I have learned that sometimes waiting heightens the excitement."

"Now you have me on pins and needles! What is this all about?" Bonnie pressed.

"Well, when I got home after our lunch at the Apothecary, I make it a point to check the mail. You see, in my house, the mail comes through a slot in the door and falls on the floor. I picked up that day's mail and there were only bills, which is quite normal these days." Her voice dropped with a hint of sadness.

Bonnie reached for her hand and held it warmly.

"Anyway," she said, shaking off the impending melancholy, "that night I was preparing for bed when I checked the locks on the doors as I do every night. When I went to the front door, I glanced down and there was an envelope barely peeking out from under the doormat. I bent over and picked it up. It was a strange looking envelope. It had my name and address on it, but no return address. It was handwritten, not typed. And what really alarmed me was that there was no stamp. I said, 'Alice, how can mail be delivered with no stamp on it?' I do that a lot. Ask myself things. Anyway, that had me stumped." Her eyes were wide as saucers.

Bonnie opened her mouth to say something when her husband returned.

"I'm hungry. Let's get a bit to eat. Miss Alice, would you like to come have lunch with us?" Will asked.

Bonnie slapped his arm playfully. "Will, you have the lousiest timing! Miss Alice is telling me about an envelope she got in the mail weeks ago. And you interrupted her. Go on, Miss Alice. I am so intrigued. What did you do next?"

Before Miss Alice could answer, Will stepped over to Alice's side and said, "Aren't you hungry? I am! And look, there is no one left in the parking lot. We may have to eat the crumbs from the table of the Methodists if we don't leave soon."

Alice laughed so hard she leaned against his side and said, "Bonnie, dear, we need to feed this man. I will finish my story at the restaurant." Linking her arm through Will's, she followed him to the car. Bonnie stood there, mouth gaping. Then she realized that these two might just leave her in the parking lot if she didn't hurry and jump in the car.

After settling Alice in the back seat, Bonnie sat up front with Will. Exasperated at the delay, she turned around in the car and asked with a hopeful smile, "Miss Alice, why don't you finish your story on the ride?"

A mischievous grin appeared on the old lady's face. Will winked at Miss Alice in the rearview mirror and Bonnie slumped back in her seat.

Will drove to Maryland Fried Chicken about a mile down the highway. Inside, they ordered their food and took a seat in a booth. Bonnie was chomping at the bit to hear about Alice's letter.

"Miss Alice, please! Don't keep me in suspense any longer," she pleaded.

Will leaned forward with his elbows on the table, cupping his chin. "Yes, I agree."

Alice loved the attention. She reached into her purse and pulled out the long envelope. It showed wear from all the times she must have opened and reopened it. "Well. Remember me telling you that I was locking the doors for the night when I noticed a letter peeking out from under the front door mat?"

Bonnie nodded.

Smiling, she leaned forward as well. "It was the strangest thing! When I discovered the letter, I carried it to the living room as though it were a treasure map." She looked at the couple and saw their eyes wide with suspense. "So I sat down in my chair and thought about ripping it open. But the more I thought about it, I couldn't bring myself to do it. I said to myself, 'Alice, you haven't had mail like this in….well, forever! Why don't you hang on to it for a while. So I did! I didn't open it until after breakfast the next morning." She paused for effect.

"And! And what did the letter say?" Bonnie interjected excitedly.

"Well, let me read it to you." Alice slowly opened the envelope and took the letter from inside. She smoothed the paper on her lap, then held it in front of her. "It is addressed to Mrs. Alice Barker…"

"Is this table 7? I have a liver basket for?" Will held up his hand. Handing it to Will, the chicken lady continued, "And a shrimp basket for?"

Bonnie grabbed the two remaining baskets. "Thank you, I've got it."

The lady left. Bonnie shoved Alice's basket in front of her. "What lousy timing! Go on. Read the letter."

"Don't you think we ought to bless our food first?" Will asked.

"Bless the food? Oh, alright." Bonnie groaned. But don't go blessing every person in Windy Garden. Make it quick."

The threesome closed their eyes as Will asked the blessing. He kept it short.

"Ok, Miss Alice, you can continue," Bonnie said, looking over at Alice chewing a mouthful of shrimp.

Pointing to her mouth, Alice chewed her bite, then swallowed. "I'm sorry, I absolutely love fried shrimp. I just couldn't wait."

"Bonnie, why don't you let Miss Alice eat her food while it's still hot?" Will looked pleadingly.

"Wait! I've waited for hours!" Bonnie exaggerated. Then she felt embarrassed at the outburst and apologized. "I'm sorry, Miss Alice. But I love intrigue. Go ahead and eat. But we are not leaving this place until Miss Alice reads the letter," she said, glancing at Will.

Alice smiled and thanked Bonnie.

It was hard to make small talk when such a looming mystery hung over their heads. Alice talked about the sermon. Will talked about his latest project at work. Bonnie did not volunteer anything except an occasional nod.

Bonnie watched Alice eat her last bite. "Ok, Miss Alice, it's time. Please, please, please read the letter," she begged.

Alice wiped her hands on the towelette beside her basket. Then picking up the letter once again, she began, "It is addressed to Mrs. Alice Barker."

Bonnie groaned and dropped her head.

Alice read on.

Dear Alice,

I do not believe we have ever met, but I am an army friend of your husband, Fred. We served as medics in the same unit together in France during World War II. I haven't seen Fred since the end of the war, but have been trying to locate him ever since. I don't know if he ever told you, but Fred and I were crawling out to wounded soldiers on the battlefield in Normandy. Fred carried a man on his back to safety while under heavy artillery fire. I was behind him carrying another man who had been shot in the right side of his head. Before reaching safety, my leg was severely injured when I was hit by shrapnel. Down I went with the man I was trying to save. I lost consciousness. I woke up two days later in a hospital. The fragments shattered my left leg. I kept asking about the man I carried, but no one could tell me whether he survived or not. When the doctor arrived to examine me, I asked again about the man. The doctor said that your Fred had run back onto the field and saved us both. The two men we went after survived and were headed stateside to U.S. hospitals. That evening, Fred came to see me. He talked with me for two hours, joking and laughing, making me feel whole again. He did not mention saving me or the other men, but I couldn't help but cry before him. I thanked him over and over for saving my life. But all your humble Fred said was, "You would have done the same thing for me." Alice, when I was finally able to learn where you are located, I was told Fred had passed on a few years ago. I am so sorry. I wish I had found him earlier. But now that I have an address, I would like to come see you and have you meet my wife. If you would call me at the phone number at the bottom of the page, I will come to you as soon as possible, if you don't mind.

My kindest and fondest wishes,

Vern Waller.

No one moved or said anything. Alice folded the letter and replaced it back in the envelope. Resting it on her lap, she sighed.

Will spoke first. "Alice, that is amazing. You must have been so blessed to receive that letter. Did you know that your husband saved this man's life?"

"No. Fred never liked to talk about the war."

Bonnie reached across the table and offered her hand. Alice raised her dainty hand and placed it in Bonnie's. "Miss Alice, that letter is priceless. Are you going to meet the man?"

"I already did."

"You did?!?" Bonnie asked incredulously.

"Yes. I called that morning and he caught a plane the next week. He brought his dear wife, Louise, with him. Vern came to the door with a walker, his wife beside him. I was so excited to see them. He introduced himself again. Then his wife. "I want you to meet my wife, Louise, my love of 62 years." We had a delightful visit. They were the kindest couple I have ever met. We talked for hours about Fred, the war, their lives. I was so glad they wanted to talk about Fred. It's funny really, most folks don't like bringing up someone who is gone. I guess they think it's too uncomfortable to talk about them. But Vern talked about him so kindly, that I could picture my sweet man sitting right beside me. Vern told me so many things about him I didn't know. It was a meeting that I will remember forever."

"Oh, it is a lovely story," Bonnie said.

"And that's not all!" Alice said with enthusiasm. The earlier sadness of the war and Henry's passing vanished with Alice's burst of energy.

"That's not all?" Will repeated.

"No. There's more."

"Well, tell us!" Bonnie said cheerfully.

"Well, before they left, Vern handed me another envelope." Alice reached into her purse once again, pulling out a second envelope.

"Have you opened it yet?" Will asked.

"Why, land's sake, yes! Louise insisted I open it immediately. Which I did!" Slipping her hand inside, she pulled out a check. Smiling, she turned the check to face Will and Bonnie.

Leaning in, the couple's eyes grew wide.

"$10,000!" Bonnie squealed into her hand.

"$10,000," Will mouthed.

Alice laughed at their response. "Yes," she whispered, "$10,000. Vern said that he wanted to thank Fred for saving his life. Because of Fred, he was able to continue to provide for his family, his sweet Louise and five children. And well, evidently, he has provided quite well, from what he told me. When I saw the check, I reacted like you. I told him I could not accept such a generous gift. But he insisted. 'You must! It is a blessing from God to me. And now a blessing from me to you. Please do not rob me of a blessing.'" Alice giggled, placing the check into her purse.

"I knew right away what I was going to do. I plan to use the blessing for my Elizabeth to fly out to see me more and I am going to California as well!" She beamed with joy. Her face looked years younger, the relief evident. "As a matter of fact, I leave tomorrow. I cannot wait to hug my precious Elizabeth and hold my great granddaughter in my arms."

Tears came to Bonnie's eyes over her friend's happiness and

good fortune. And if she wasn't mistaken, she saw Will get a little misty as well.

Miss Alice left the following week for California. She wrote Bonnie often, telling her how precious her great granddaughter was. Bonnie missed her at the Apothecary. In her last letter, Alice did not indicate when she would return.

Reading how happy her friend was being reunited with family made Bonnie reflect on how much she missed her own family back in Missouri. With each letter, Bonnie's heart ached. She ached for her parents, her Gram, Miz Jessie. She missed her sisters and brother. She missed being home.

Bonnie placed her hand over her empty womb and ached for a child that was not there. A child she and Will had been trying to conceive for four years.

Maybe it was time to see a doctor.

16

Sue presented the lessons with clarity and excitement. It was obvious she spent many hours preparing and praying over the lessons each week. Her heart was tender and compassionate toward her students and Bonnie loved her from the start.

This was Bonnie's third month in Bible study and she felt like she was getting the hang of it. Delving deep into the Scriptures, Bonnie could see herself walking alongside the apostle Paul on his journey to Philippi, or sitting with her knees pulled to her chest on the hillside, listening to Jesus deliver the Sermon on the Mount. She was there, drawn into the history and heart of the New Testament. It was not hard to imagine.

Bonnie felt a peace wash over her each time the name of Jesus was mentioned. Each week in Bible study, a memory from her past would flood her soul. The Bible took on a life that echoed Miz Jessie's tellin's. Bonnie knew for sure she was in the right place. Right here in Windy Garden. Right here in this church.

Most of the women in the class were glued to their Bibles, delving deep, seemingly enjoying their personal revelations as much as Bonnie. Yet, there were still the inevitable know-it-alls. Myrtle, Melva Jane and Nettie tended to speak too often and rarely allowed for other points of view. Some of the ladies would even head to the kitchen for a drink or go potty when the trio began their personal takes on the Bible. They seemed more content to cause disruption than learn truth. It seemed to Bonnie that their challenging questions were directed personally at Sue. She admired the way Sue handled them with grace and love.

Why is it that some people get so set in what they think to be true that they will not even consider they might be wrong, or at the very least may not have all the truth? I can't imagine ever getting to the point where I know everything!

Again her Miz Jessie came to mind. "Folk who are a pain in the patootie are most likely in pain. My sister in the Lawd, she always be tryin' to get her two cents in. No matter where she be, she think she know best. I keep tellin' her she done spent them two cents. That it be time to earn some more cents by listenin' and by learnin'. Whoee, she would give me a look that would melt a rock." Bonnie enjoyed her flashbacks with Miz Jessie. They helped change her perspective at times like this.

Class ended and Bonnie gathered her Bible and notebooks and placed them in her satchel when Kathy approached.

"Hi Bonnie! Wasn't that a great lesson? My head is so full I think I'm going to burst with joy! I'm also bursting with hunger. I'm going to lunch at the Apothecary. Want to come along? I hope you don't have anything planned. I am so hungry I could eat two hamburgers, three orders of fries and down it with a large chocolate milkshake!"

Bonnie looked up and down at the petite body standing before her and wondered how anyone so small could eat so much. "Oh Kathy, I'm sorry, but I have to finish a project I'm working on for the Fall Festival celebration. How about another time? I'd love to sit and chat over lunch sometime. Maybe next Thursday?"

"Oh, sure, that will be fine. It will give me something to look forward to. I do love anticipations. Don't you? And thank you for reminding me about the celebration. I promised two pies. Bob will make his favorites, a pecan pie and a chocolate pie, which means he'll probably buy them back. Teehee."

"Sounds like it will be a fun day. Maybe I'll see you around town during the festivities. Bye, Kathy."

"Bye, Bonnie."

Kathy's tummy rumbled with hunger so loudly she could hear it herself. *Gee, I must be hungrier than I thought. I wonder who else is still here I could ask to go to lunch with me?*

She looked around the room. There were only a few ladies left and each one of them had children in the nursery, so she knew they would most likely be heading home.

She picked up her Bible and headed for the stairs when the ladies bathroom door opened. Nettie Pegram stepped out. "Hey Nettie, I'm headed over to the Apothecary for lunch. Would you like to go with me? I'm starved." Kathy asked as she approached her.

"Lunch? No. My plan is to go home and fix a tuna sandwich. And maybe cut up an apple with peanut butter." Nettie started for the stairs.

That was not enough to dissuade perky Kathy. "I have an idea! Why don't you come with me and we'll share a tuna sandwich at the Apothecary? They make the best tuna around! Besides, you wouldn't want to eat lunch alone, now would you? I can't stand eating alone. It's no fun and I usually grab something quick like a piece of cake or chips, neither of which is a good choice."

Nettie paused, thinking to herself how she didn't like to eat alone either. But she was not about to admit that openly. In no mood to go home to an empty house, she gave in. "I guess so, but I get the pickle."

Kathy picked up on the seriousness of her tone about the pickle. There would be no doubt who would eat the pickle.

"Ok, let's go!" Kathy said.

Stopping to put their Bibles in Kathy's car, they continued across the parking lot and onto Main Street. Kathy talked nonstop all the way from the church basement to the Apothecary, where Lucy greeted them with a smile.

"Have a seat girls and I'll be right with ya!"

"I like Lucy. She is always so cheerful!" Kathy said.

"Humph," replied Nettie. "She's just doing her job."

Nettie picked out a booth near the back of the room. "Drafts bother me. I like tables away from the door. Last winter, Jake Spears came in and stood in the doorway what seemed like forever, letting all that cold air smother the warmth in here. And I let him know too. I said, 'Jake, what's the matter with you? Are you trying to freeze us all to death? I've got goose bumps on my goose bumps.' Well, he shut the door real quick."

Kathy slid into the booth across from Nettie and said, "I can understand how the cold might bother you. It does me too. Most times I bring a sweater wherever I go. My husband, Bob, says I must have been born in a meat freezer. Teehee."

Kathy's 'teehee' drew a frown on Nettie's brow, but Kathy did not notice.

"Ok girls, would ya like a menu or I can tell ya what our specials are today?" Lucy held two menus under her arm just in case.

Kathy jumped right in, "Oh, we have already decided. We would like to share a tuna sandwich. And could you put the pickle on Nettie's plate, please? And I'll have potato salad, a side order of fruit and another scoop of tuna on my plate."

Lucy began writing.

Nettie quickly added, "I want wheat bread toasted, not burnt and not moist. And I'll have iced tea, no sugar and no lemon."

Kathy agreed. "Me too, but sugar in the tea please. I have a sweet tooth." Lucy was used to Nettie's curtness and said sweetly, "I'll get your teas and be right back."

Kathy placed her elbows on the table and leaned in slightly. "I love tea. All kinds of tea! But my favorite is hot Earl Grey. Quite often I have tea parties in my home. I invite neighbors and friends and we all dress up in our best attire. I supply the hats and gloves since most ladies don't wear them anymore. My mother was a hot tea gal, too, and a stickler for fashion. She used to say that a proper lady keeps as much skin covered as possible to stay above reproach. Teehee! Isn't that the most old fashioned thing you've ever heard? But I loved my mother dearly for raising me with manners and tea etiquette."

Nettie bristled at the mention of Kathy's mother. Just the mention of the word 'mother' sent chills up her spine as her shoulders shook off the comment.

"Say, Nettie, would you like to join us sometime? We have so much fun. It's nice to know that there are still some well-bred southern ladies around." Kathy was all smiles.

"I don't do teas." Nettie pulled her purse onto her lap, snapped open the latch, pulled out a hankie and placed it up her long sleeve.

Kathy noticed and just had to comment. "Oh my! I haven't seen anyone do that with a hankie since before mother died. She refused to use tissues. She would have a clean hankie ready at the first itch of her nose. She would take her hanky from her sleeve, dab her nose and tuck it back under her sleeve. What a memory! I do miss her."

Nettie thought she should say something. "I'm sure your mother was a proper lady."

This amused Kathy. "Oh, she was! She made sure I was wearing clean underwear everyday. She would say, 'Kathy, you never know when you may be taken to the hospital and I would be mortified if you were wearing soiled panties.' Mother was one for keeping yourself clean."

The tea arrived. Kathy added more sugar before taking her first sip. "Nettie, tell me about your mother."

Nettie had no desire to talk about her mother to anyone at any time. "I don't talk about my mother." She snapped her purse shut and set it on the booth beside her.

"Oh, I'm sorry. Then we'll talk about something else. I know! Bible study. I love our Thursday morning Bible studies. Sue has taught me so much. I was raised Catholic, you know, and I love the ritual side of Catholicism, but I have never been taught the Bible. When I go home and do my quiet time, I can look up Hebrew and Greek words and get my socks blown off! There is so much more meaning to words than I ever thought before. I just love it!"

Nettie waited for Kathy to wind down and said, "I've been in church my whole life and I already know what I believe and no one is going to change what I believe." She sipped her tea hoping this discussion would end or change to something more generic.

It didn't.

"I was raised in church too. But think of all the things Jesus did for us that we haven't begun to scratch the surface of. Like when he healed the woman with the bleeding issue. She bled for 12 years. It was against the law for anyone who was bleeding or had any other oozing of body fluids to be in public. She knew she could be arrested if she was caught disobeying the law. But she didn't care. She knew that if she could just touch the hem of Jesus' garment, she would be healed. And she was! The woman was convinced that Jesus was who He said he was. Oh, Nettie, to be so sure of Jesus being our Healer like she was. I want that kind of faith! I want to know that I can charge through the crowd of unbelief and be healed." She thrust her hand forward to illustrate her point. Kathy bubbled with excitement talking about Jesus.

"I know I talk too much. But I can't help myself. I have so much inside my head that it keeps spilling out my lips before I can contain it. My mother used to call me chatty Kathy. After the famous doll you know."

Why, oh why did I accept this lunch invitation with the most talkative woman I have ever met in my entire life. Here we are at lunch and the conversation has bounced all over the place from panties and hankies to bleeding women, Jesus and mothers. If the food doesn't hurry up and get here, I'll make an excuse I have a headache and go home. This is pure torture.

"Nettie, Nettie, are you alright?" Kathy asked, leaning further across the table and patting her hand.

Nettie roused from her ruminating. "What? What? What did you say?"

"I said, I hope Lucy remembers your pickle." Kathy glanced toward the kitchen, "Oh look! Here she comes now!"

Lunch arrived and on each plate Lucy had placed a half tuna sandwich on wheat bread, toasted, not moist, and a pickle. Lucy set a separate place beside Kathy that held a scoop of potato salad, a small bowl of mixed fruit and another scoop of tuna. Kathy immediately noticed the pickle. "Oh! Thank you, Lucy, for giving us both a pickle. I do love dills. You are so sweet. Teehee."

"Enjoy, ladies. If you need anything, just give me a holler, ok?" Lucy hurried off to a customer at the cash register.

The food had arrived too soon for Nettie to make her exit. She sighed heavily and picked up her tuna sandwich and took a bite.

"Oh! Nettie, let's give thanks first. Ok?"

Nettie placed her sandwich back on the plate, folded her hands in her lap and bowed her head.

"Oh most gracious heavenly Father, thank You for loving us. Thank you for sending Your Son to take away all our sins. Thank You for our wonderful Bible study time together. Thank you for this lunch. Thank You for our sweet Lucy. And thank you for my friend, Nettie. Teehee and amen!"

If she tee-hees one more time, I'm going to have to stuff this pickle in her mouth, Nettie inwardly groaned.

"Well, I'm starved and this looks delicious, as always. I love the tuna here better than anywhere. Bob makes a good tuna sandwich too. Did I tell you he is a great cook? I like that he is. But I would never tell him I like the tuna here better. I wouldn't want to hurt his feelings. Don't you think this tuna is divine?"

Kathy's constant smile and exuberant personality were exhausting to Nettie. Sitting in the seat opposite her was a woman with the energy of ten people.

"The tuna is alright. I've had better." Nettie was still pondering the earlier inquiry about her mother. She was rapidly losing her appetite. Not only that, but her mother raised her to keep conversation at the table to a minimum.

"I heard you like to travel and have been to many places and eaten several varieties of foods. Oh, that would be a grand adventure! To see and experience different cultures. When Bob and I save the money, we plan to do a little traveling too. Maybe the New England states or overseas to Ireland. My family hails from Ireland. Yes! That's where I would like to go first." She was almost finished with her sandwich before Nettie finished her second bite.

Nettie set her tea glass down a little too hard and asked, "What makes you think I've traveled a lot?" She did not like being the focus of gossip even though she had no qualms about doing so herself.

Kathy did not catch the offense. "Ida Mae mentioned in Bible study a while ago that you had taken a trip to England. Jolly ole England. I have always wanted to see Westminster Abbey, the Tower of London, Big Ben. I've mentioned to Bob on several occasions that if we ever get the chance to go to London, I'd like to eat at an old bistro in the heart of the city. Sit under a table with an umbrella for shade and watch little mopeds buzz by the busy street. I love old things. Old artifacts too. When I was in college, I majored in archaeology. I went on a few digs, but not overseas. Now wouldn't that be fun? Digging for bones in Egypt, or for heroes of the Trojan

War, or bullets and shell casings from World War II in England, and my favorite of all, Jerusalem. It would be most fascinating to be part of a dig near Masada or the Dead Sea."

The mention of a London bistro transported Nettie back to England in her mind. She could see the very bistro where her Henry had taken her, with its quaint surroundings, and she could hear his distinct voice asking the waiter for a table outside with an umbrella. The waiter had directed them to a small round table with two chairs right next to a black wrought iron fence separating the pub from the sidewalk. A white linen tablecloth was draped over the café table, with a red rose in a crystal vase.

"Charming," Henry said, "Simply charming, my dear." His try at a British accent was hilarious. Earlier when he had tipped the hotel footman, he said, "Cheerio, my good man. It's off to lunch for crumpets and tea."

Nettie cherished the memory of her beloved's laughter. An involuntary smile appeared on her face.

Kathy's giggle brought her back to the present. "I'm so glad you joined me today. I had asked Bonnie earlier, but she had something to finish for the Fall Festival celebration. Yum! Yum! I do love this tuna." And with that, she ate her last bite.

Lucy appeared and refilled their tea. Kathy looked over and noticed Nettie was not quite finished with her sandwich. Which meant she could talk a little longer. "I'm going to begin a quilt next month in my home. I am inviting ladies who would like to help me with it. We will be making several for cancer patients. They can curl up in them while they recuperate and know that loving hands and hearts went into every stitch. Would you be interested in participating?"

Nettie wasn't sure she wanted to get involved with this talkative teehee lady. But it wouldn't look good for her image to not help a worthy cause. "I'll think about it."

"Wonderful! When I have a starting date, I'll let you know. It will probably be in the winter after the busy holidays. That will give you plenty of time to check your calendar. Bob said he would make lunch and desserts for us. Did I tell you he is a fantastic cook? Instead of being a chef, he sells cars for a living. I keep telling him he ought to apply at local restaurants and see if they'll hire him. But he says he doesn't want to work nights, even though he does now, teehee, and he enjoys cooking so much he doesn't want to spoil the fun by making it a career." Kathy saw Lucy deliver a large slice of chocolate cake to the adjacent table. "Oh, look! Chocolate cake. Let's splurge and have dessert!"

"No thank you. This was enough for me. I think I'll head home. Here is my half of the tab. Do you mind paying for me? I am tired and need to rest a spell." She held out the money to Kathy.

"Oh, no, this is my treat. Please take your money. I can drive you home if you like. Besides, you left your bible in my car. And you're right, dessert is too much for the waistline. Especially mine! Teehee. I'll go pay and meet you at the door." Kathy rushed off so quickly, Nettie did not have time to protest. She set down a tip for Lucy. She didn't know how much Kathy might tip but she did not want to be known as a poor tipper in this small town.

Kathy drove Nettie home, chatting all the way. Stepping out of the car, Nettie thanked Kathy for lunch. As she reached the back door she could still hear Kathy talking through the open window as she drove away.

Closing the door behind her, she set her Bible on the kitchen counter. Fatigued by her morning out, she dropped into her favorite chair in the living room and closed her eyes.

"'Teehee,' who says that anymore? If she said it once, she said it a dozen times. Her poor husband must have the patience of Job. Reminder Nettie....no more lunches with Kathy."

17

Two months after her last haircut, Bonnie realized that she would have to endure the Hair Buzz for a while until she could locate another salon. She couldn't forget her first visit, when she'd needed a strawberry shake on the rocks by the time it was all over.

Reclining in the chair while her stylist washed her hair, she heard voices from the front of the shop.

"Here come the birds," announced Julie Ann, owner of the Hair Buzz. Groans floated heavily throughout the salon, as though a storm was brewing and was about to hit.

"The birds? What birds?" Bonnie asked Samantha as she towel dried her hair.

"Oh," Sam grimaced, "that would be Nettie, Melva Jane, and Melva's twin sister Myrtle coming for their hair appointments." Her sigh spoke volumes.

"They come swooping in here every week wagging their tongues and making everyone uncomfortable. They're like three magpies perched on a telephone wire listening in on personal conversations, spreading what they think they know all over town."

Bonnie closed her eyes and imagined a tornado approaching in the form of three old ladies… ladies notorious for wearing the town thin with their gossip and haughty attitudes.

"Morning, Mrs. Pegram. Morning, Melva Jane. Morning, Myrtle," said Julie Ann cheerfully when the three ladies entered the salon.

"Humph, fine morning this is," announced Myrtle. "I'm just

fit to be tied. Nothing's gone right all day. And it's only 10 a.m."
Myrtle hung her shawl on the coat rack next to the door and turned
her wide body around, slowly continuing her tirade. "I woke up
with a crick in my neck, burnt the toast in the oven, and Melva Jane
here took her sweet time getting dressed. Then strolled all the way
here as if she had all the time in the world."

"Oh, Myrtle, stop your yammerin'. I got ready as fast as I could.
For the record, you were the last one putting your shoes on. And
if you'd not stop and gripe about everything in our path, we'd get
here on time," Melva Jane said, defending herself.

"Don't you go getting on your high horse, sister. Every time
we go anywhere, you're always the last one out the door."

"For Pete's sake, you two, stop with the bickering. Can't go
anywhere with you two ninnies. Now behave yourselves, and sit
down!" Nettie was definitely in charge of these birds because sit,
they did.

Julie Ann finished with Sue, the preacher's wife, and turned to
Nettie. "Ok, Mrs. Pegram, hop in the chair and let's get started."

"Be right there." Nettie took her sweet time hanging up her
sweater next to Melva Jane's wrap, and picked out a magazine to
look at while her hair was being fixed. She seemed in no hurry.

Sue stopped to greet Myrtle and Melva Jane with a smile. "Good
morning, ladies. God sure has given us a beautiful day to enjoy,
hasn't He?"

"Yes, ma'am," replied Myrtle. "He sure has. Melva Jane was
just saying the same thing a few minutes ago. Right, sister?"

Melva Jane glared at her sister for telling such an untruth. Her
furrowed brow wanted so bad to tell her. And right here in front

of the preacher's wife, to boot! "I did! I was saying the same thing when I noticed the sun shining and nary a cloud in the sky," she lied.

Sue turned to Nettie. "Hello, Nettie. It's good to see you. Last night you came to mind and I prayed for you. Are you doing alright?" Sue had a big heart and a genuine compassion for the members of their church.

"I'm fine. But thanks for your prayers."

Sue smiled at Nettie. "I'm so glad to hear that." Turning, she left the beauty shop. The bell jingling on the door.

Nettie jumped at the sound of the bell jingling. "Julie Ann, do you have to have that bell on the door? Every time it opens with someone coming or going, it rings. And besides, it interrupts important conversations."

"To tell you the truth, Nettie, we enjoy the bell. I put it up the first day Donut Queen opened down the street so we would know when the delivery boy brought our donuts each morning. If there wasn't a bell, we would miss the invitation to eat 'em while they're hot! Besides, it also lets us know when customers arrive."

Samantha lifted Bonnie to a sitting position and asked how she wanted her hair done. "Oh, just a trim. Not too short, please. And what do you think of a few layers? I need my hair easy to manage on busy days."

"Not a problem. Got just the thang. Sit back and relax and I'll be done in a jiffy," Samantha exclaimed, a little too eager.

Relax was the last thing Bonnie would do in this hair salon. *And for Pete's sake, take your time,* she prayed to the Lord of hairdressers.

"Well, lookee there! Ole Mr. Spears strutting down the street like he owns it," Myrtle shouted for all to hear. "Lookee, Melva Jane, look who's coming. You once took a shining to him in school, remember? I know you remember. And here he is, plain as day." It was obvious to everyone she was clearly hinting for a fight.

"What? That ole coot! What's wrong with you this morning, Myrtle, you step on a pebble on the way over here?"

"You did! You had a crush on Bernie so bad that you used to follow him home from school hiding behind trees so he wouldn't see you. Now don't you go saying any different. I remember that well."

"Sometimes, Myrtle, I wish you weren't my sister. You have a big mouth and a twisted memory. You sure know how to embarrass me, you know that? I'm ashamed of a God-fearing woman like you talking like this! You been visiting that sorry brother of ours? Every time you go see the lazy thing you come back with his lousy attitude."

"Me! Me? You sit there judging me? And leave Roger out of this! He's never liked you anyway, ever since you glued his foot to his head in the fifth grade! And I'm old enough to talk any way I want. I don't need you telling me what to say and what not to say!"

The hair dressers had a hard time getting their comb through the twins' hair as both ladies kept jerking their heads around to fuss with each other.

"Good grief and a day, you two," interrupted Nettie. "I got a mind to call your kids and get them to put you both in the loony bin! Now hush up."

The 'birds' stopped their rude bickering, and began telling their hairdressers the proper way to manage their hair.

Samantha leaned over and whispered in Bonnie's ear, "They do this every week. Come in here fussin' with each other and tellin' the gals here how to do their hair. They been doin' this for over thirty-some years. As if their hairdressers don't know what they want."

Bonnie stared at the twins in disbelief, not uttering a word.

"I remember Bernie from school. He was friends with my Henry," Nettie said looking out the window. "He was a good fellow, he was, until he met Connie. Yeah, she was no good for him. She never did speak to me or most people at church. They usually sat in the very back so they could get away fast at the end of service. I never did like that woman." Slapping the magazine shut on her lap, she fumed.

"Me neither," Myrtle agreed.

"I liked her," chimed in Melva Jane. "When my James passed on, she brought over the most delicious coconut cake I ever did eat! I always wanted her recipe but she upped and died before I could get it. Guess she took it to her grave." Leaning forward to look out the window, the countenance on her face changed. "Come to think of it, I don't like her anymore. She could have given me that cake recipe months before she died. Now I've gone and made myself mad! Myrtle this all your fault!" she said, slapping the arm of the chair.

"You gals are giving me a headache," Nettie muttered under her breath.

"What? Did you say something, Nettie?" Melva Jane asked.

"No. I didn't say anything."

Mr. Spears had disappeared out of sight and the gossip ended.

Bonnie was stunned. Such gossip! And mean gossip, too. She felt sorry for this Mr. Spears fellow. Her heart went out to him. She wondered, *Could he possibly know the nasty gossip buzzing about him here? Surely not! No wonder his wife got out of church fast! She must have been anxious to get away from these sour faced, tongue-wagging women.*

Turning to face Samantha, she quietly asked, "How long has Mr. Spear's wife been gone?"

"Well, let me think. I guess it's been close to six months."

Oh my, only six months. How can these women be so cruel? she thought. Bonnie's face flushed with embarrassment, at such terrible and hurtful gossip. *How do these women sleep at night?*

Bonnie was beginning to wonder if she had made a mistake moving to Windy Garden. She had never heard such nasty talk before. Growing up around Miz Jessie and her own kinfolk had protected her from such mean nonsense. She was not too happy with this town right now.

Once again, Miz Jessie's words echoed from the back porch where she was shelling peas. "When folks says mean thangs 'bout other folk, just 'member, Chile, hurtin' people hurt people. I don't know why theys' do, they jus' do. And maybe, jus' maybe, when you grow up, you gonna be one to help 'em not hurt sa much. You can show 'em how much God loves 'em. Mmhmm. Jus' maybe you be the one." Words of wisdom seemed to come easy for Miz Jessie when she was shellin' peas. And she shelled many a pea, she did.

Refusing to accept Miz Jessie's words, Bonnie began to hope that she would never have to say anything whatsoever to any of these 'birds.' Their tongues were sharper than a viper's.

"Here ya are, honey." Samantha turned Bonnie to the mirror.

Surprisingly, Bonnie was pleased with what she saw. It was pretty close to what she had envisioned when she entered the salon. *Maybe the Hair Buzz will work out for me after all.* She paid Samantha and left, the bell jingling on the door. Lucky for her, she left before the 'birds.' They were still carrying on about anyone who dared cross in front of the window. It was more than she could bear.

Nettie left the Hair Buzz ahead of Melva Jane and Myrtle. She was in no mood for their continued bickering. Many times she stepped into the middle of their arguments. The hour getting her hair done seemed to go on forever. And now she had a headache.

She walked to the town swing and sat down. The swing had a bronze plaque fastened to the top that read "dedicated to the memory of Samuel Pegram." Nettie ran her hand along the smooth plaque and remembered her father.

"Where is the birthday girl?" father called from the doorway, returning home from work. Nettie squealed and ran to the sound of her father's voice.

"Father! You're home!" She jumped into his arms and hugged his neck.

"Where is my baby girl? I don't see her anywhere." He looked about the foyer, teasing Nettie.

Nettie placed her hands on his cheeks and turned him to face her. "Here I am, daddy. Right here."

"No, I don't see my baby."

"But father, I am right here! Can't you see me?" She placed her hands on his cheeks and pulled his head toward her.

Looking her over, her father said, "This can't be my baby. This must be my little girl who is turning five today. I don't see a baby." He tickled her belly and set her down.

"Oh daddy, you are so funny. And I am five! And guess what? Mother ordered my birthday cake with white icing. It is so pretty. And there are five candles in the middle."

"Well then, let's go see this cake." Father took Nettie's hand and followed her to the kitchen. Nettie skipped alongside her father.

"About time you got home. Dinner is getting cold. Sit down so we can eat." Mother motioned to the table which held three place settings of china, gold eating utensils, a white tablecloth with three tapered candles set perfectly in the center of the table.

"Let me wash up and I'll be right back." Father tossled Nettie's hair and headed for the small bathroom in the foyer.

Nettie looked at the dining room table where her cake had been only minutes before, but did not see it anywhere. "Mother, where is my birthday cake? It was right here on the dining room table a few minutes ago."

"I put it in the kitchen while we eat dinner. It looked so gaudy alongside our dinnerware."

Nettie glanced in the kitchen to see her cake next to the dirty dishes in the sink. Her heart sank into her shoes. It was obvious her birthday was not important to her mother.

Father returned from the washroom and looked about the table.

"Where is our five-year-old's birthday cake?"

"It's in the kitchen until after we eat. Sit down, Samuel, our food is cooling down." Mother motioned toward his chair.

"Hmm. Something seems to be missing," he said looking about the table. "Oh, this just won't do." He marched into the kitchen and found the birthday cake with white icing and placed it beside his plate. Then reached over and grabbed the three candlesticks and removed them to the buffet. As if presiding over a banquet, he picked up the cake and set it smack dab in the middle, highlighting the importance of the occasion.

A gasp escaped his wife's mouth. But before she could protest, her father said, "Now, this looks like a birthday table! Don't you think so, mother?" His slightly reprimanding tone elicited a reluctant positive response from Rose.

"Um, yes. I suppose it does."

A smile returned to Nettie's face. Once again, Father had come to the rescue. He always had.

Memories of Nettie's father brought tears to her eyes. As her hand stroked the plaque on the swing, Nettie felt comforted knowing that her father loved her deeply. After he died, she became a project of her mother. Missing her father, she could not resist the strong will her mother had over her. Over time, Nettie built a wall around her heart. She didn't know how to let anyone in without being hurt. She couldn't understand why her father loved her mother so much. Without father around to take up for her, Rose did her best to control Nettie's life. Love got lost over time. For both of them.

It wasn't until Henry entered her life that she was able to see what love looked like. Again.

Brushing off the sadness, Nettie whispered, "Oh Father, how I miss you. Why didn't I turn out more like you?" She realized her vulnerability was showing and rose from the swing to head home. She glanced over the sidewalks of Main Street and saw the newcomer heading into the Apothecary. *Why do I keep encountering that girl? And why does she irritate me so? Seems everywhere I go, she's there.*

Main Street was beginning to buzz with movement and voices. The activity drew Nettie's attention. She looked about. Laughter rang in the air. Couples were holding hands. A husband's soft kiss gently landed on a wife's cheek. A baby in a stroller kicked his feet wildly enjoying the ride.

All the town excitement did not warm Nettie's heart. In fact, it broke it. Loneliness gripped her. She wearily walked home. Each step felt like a concrete block was tied to her legs. Her thoughts muddled into a heavy sigh. She was not only lonely for a soft kiss from Henry… She was lonely for true friends, genuine friends that didn't just hang around for her money or influence. She wanted to be loved like her father, like Henry. There would be no love today. Maybe never.

Bonnie sat at the window of the Apothecary, sipping her strawberry shake when she saw Nettie walk in front of the Apothecary and cross the street.

Her heart broke as she took in the sight of this hurting woman. Miz Jessie had taught her long ago to look for the signs. 'Slumpin' shoulders, slow steps, no lights on in them eyes, a sadness to the lips, and no one payin' no never mind to.' Miz Jessie said she knew what that felt like.

Most folks, around where Bonnie grew up ignored Miz Jessie, or as she used to say, "paid no never mind to." She seemed invisible to the world unless someone wanted something from her like cooking, cleaning, washing babies, tending gardens, canning, milking cows, gathering eggs, washing clothes, and hanging them on a clothesline.

And Miz Jessie would do just as she was told, with no complaining. She hummed, she sang, but she never complained. Not even when she was told she couldn't be paid to come help for a while. A sad longing came across her face as she heard the words spoken by Bonnie's mama one day.

All Miz Jessie could utter was "yes, ma'am," "I sures do understand, ma'am," and "don't forgit your Jessie, ma'am." She walked away slowly, as if each step had aged her in just a few minutes time. Her head was facing the ground and even from the back, Bonnie knew that tears were puddlin' in her eyes. Heartbroken to leave for sure, but also painfully aware that there'd be no extra money to feed and care for her own young'uns.

Bonnie's mama and daddy always told Miz Jessie she could take from the garden any vegetables she needed for her own family, and milk from the cows and eggs from the chickens. But Miz Jessie never touched any of those for her own brood. She wouldn't take from anyone anything unless she really, desperately needed it. Someday she might.

Her short, round body with a wide behind looked shorter and wider that day. Her apron lifted to dry the tears she did not want Bonnie to see.

Most days when she left Bonnie's house at the end of a long day, she would head home, tend her own small garden, cook dinner, clean the dishes, wash those babies of hers and then rock and sing each one to sleep.

Bonnie followed Miz Jessie every chance she got. She would sneak out after her chores were done and run over a half mile to the woods by the creek and hear laughter before she even reached Miz Jessie's land. A favorite tree hid Bonnie from view as she dared peek at such a private moment.

Jessie had two boys and three girls. Their faces would light up when they saw their mam come home, listening real hard for her sweet hum as she neared their humble abode. It was obvious they adored their mam.

James, the oldest, was twelve and tall, like his Pappy. He was in charge while mam was gone, and the children obeyed James like he was their pappy.

Miriam was eleven and hovered over the little ones like a hen over her baby chicks.

Matthew was nine, going on ten, and helped James with all the man's work around their little farm.

The yard was clean as a whistle and the small barn kept so neat that "ya could've eat off the floor out there." Even the hen pens were orderly and cleaned daily. There was no slack where those two boys were concerned.

Miriam watched over Sarah who was five and Rachel, age four.

They made sure the house was clean, as much as children could, helped in the garden when mam came home, and kept the clothes clean and smelling 'fresh as rain' as their mam liked to say.

The school age children would pack their own lunches each morning and tend to Sarah and Rachel before heading off for the better part of the day. Before they left, Miz Jessie's sister, Rosie, who lived up and over the hill came to watch the two smallest kids til the older children returned home from school.

Their pappy worked hard in the fields nearby for stingy folk, who paid their hired help 'dirt cheap' for grueling, calloused and 'sweat of the brow' labor. He brought in precious little money for the time and effort he expended in the fields, but there was never any comparison between his earnings and mam's. Each week they would both drop their earnings in a Mason jar and set it on the mantle over the fireplace for all to see. Mam would gather the children together after Sunday singin' and preachin' and tell the children they all earned that thar money, ever penny, that the good Lawd provided each and ever day.

"The good Lord don't take much likin' to a lazy one. No sirree, He say ya don't work, ya don't eat!" Pappy would say with a grin.

Squeals of laughter and hugs would abound in this precious home each Sunday as mam and pappy spent the day lovin' on each child as though this was the only day there ever was.

One day, Miz Jessie told Bonnie about her childhood. She said growing up along the mighty Mississippi River in in the 1920's was a hard and strenuous life. Jessie's family grew up poorer than poor. Her daddy loaded boats along the river. The docks were a very dangerous place to work, especially for those of color. Every dollar was stretched, wrung out, and squeezed. There was no room for waste.

Miz Jessie told her that they had to make use of everything. Even the peelins' from the vegetables had a purpose. Miz Jessie's mam would boil onion skins and put the juice in a canning jar which she'd use for flavorin.' And tater skins were used to treat bruises and sprains. The potato itself was used to help treat tummy ulcers and arthritis. They worked hard for what they had and were a proud people. They were very protective of what little was theirs. It was all they had.

When they moved to the valley of southeast Missouri, they had to rely on the land for most of their support.

"The best part of them high hills, nearst the Mississippi, was when the fiddlers and the banjo men began a playin.' The sound would move up the hollers and over them thar ridges. Many a time it be a foot stompin' tune. Other times it be kinda soft and perty. We lived for them times of rest and fun," Miz Jessie would say with a faraway look in her eyes.

"And ole man Zeke! He could spin a yarn. He could tell a story that would keep ya up all night sceered to close yer eyes."

Rural mountain folk had a language all their own back then. It was viewed as an ignorant language to the educated, but to Jessie's family and friends it was a language of the heart. Born and bred through suffering. That's why Miz Jessie wanted Bonnie to speak correct English and not be thought 'ignereent' like her.

They were a proud people, family people. People who took care of their own and each other. Even amidst the prejudice and hatred in their parts, they had to use every resource of the land to survive, and made sure they gave back to the land for future generations.

Bonnie learned many valuable lessons from Miz Jessie. Practical lessons, safety lessons, and most importantly, lessons of the heart. Unbeknownst to Bonnie at the time, the lessons of her past would impact not only her life, but the lives of those around her. Even Miss Nettie's.

18

Bonnie felt so blessed after prayer time with Diane, Sharon and Kathy. She felt the presence of God in a way she had only felt with her Miz Jessie. The girls had begun meeting a week ago on Wednesday mornings to pray for their pastor, their families, the sick, the sad and lonely, and those looking to God for big answers. Sitting motionless after the "Amen," Bonnie was too caught up in the sweetness of their time together to hear Kathy talking to her.

"Girl, where are you? You seemed so far away."

"I think she drifted somewhere we all would like to go, right, Bonnie?" Sharon's soft voice was not such a jolt as Kathy's. But their love and concern was always welcome.

"Oh! I'm sorry. I was just lost in the presence of the Spirit. Did ya'll feel it? It was so comforting, so exciting! I believe God heard every word we prayed today."

Diane had been standing near the door to the room, Bible in hand and purse slung over her shoulder, when she jumped into the conversation. "I felt it too! I was just not sure y'all did."

"When we began praying, I felt God listening, really listening." Sharon smiled. "I wish this feeling would last beyond a few moments. Sometimes when I pray on my own, I feel like my prayers evaporate before they hit the ceiling."

"Me too!" Kathy exclaimed, her eyes sparkling. "These last two weeks praying together has changed my prayer life. But a lot of times when I am home in prayer, I feel like even Brendle isn't impressed."

"Who's Brendle?" Bonnie asked.

"Brendle's my little Shih Tzu. She's the cutest thing. I'm afraid we have spoiled her something awful. Since Bob and I can't have children, I guess the pooch has become our 'first born.' Teehee!"

"You crack me up, Kat!" Bonnie laughed, picking up her Bible and notepad. "Thanks, girls, our time together has made my day. I really wish I didn't have to go home."

"Well, let's not go home! Let's get some lunch at the Apothecary, ok?" Bonnie had heard that Diane was always one to plan get-togethers and was ready to eat twenty-four hours a day.

"I wish I could, but I gotta get back to work." Sharon sounded sad. "But you girls go on and have fun. Maybe some day I won't have to work and will be able to go with you." With that she picked up her Bible and headed back upstairs to her office.

"I sure wish Sharon could come with us," Diane sighed.

"Well, I wish I could go too," perky Kathy added. "I've got too much on my plate today. Why don't you two go on and then you can miss me and Sharon! Then it won't seem like Sharon's missing all by herself! I gotta go to the dry cleaners, pick up some dog food for Brendle, and Bob wants me to go by Gus's for some asparagus and oranges for supper. He's planning something yummy to make tonight and since I don't like to cook anyway, I'd go to the moon for supplies if he asked me! Teehee! Doesn't that sound fun?"

Kathy was a trip. She was so energetic and funny that they couldn't help but laugh at her exuberant way of expressing herself.

"Guess it's just you and me, kid," Diane smiled at Bonnie.

"Sure. Let's go! I'm too pumped to go home. Besides, I've wanted to have lunch with you for some time now."

As they walked into the Apothecary, Diane noticed how crowded it was. "Lucy, you sure are busy for a Wednesday. What's happening? An Episcopal gathering of some sort?' she laughed.

"Nah, cain't rightly say. Folks been comin' in here since 7 this mornin' and not been much of a break in the bunch yet. I did hear that there was a revival down at the Methodist Church startin' tonight. Think maybe they're fillin' their tummies for a long-winded preacher?" Laughing at herself, Lucy sloshed water over the side of the pitcher she held in her hand. "Let me look around and see what I can find for ya. Oh, wait. I got a table emptyin' now, so if ya wait a sec, I'll go clear it for ya." Lucy scampered off where four women had scooted out of the booth at the far end of the diner.

Bonnie and Diane followed Lucy and stood behind her as she cleared the dirty dishes and wiped the table clean.

"Hey ya go." Lucy smiled and handed them menus. "I'll be right back for yer order."

Sitting across from each other in the booth, Diane and Bonnie's attention was drawn to the table beside them. They could see their pastor's wife Sue sitting very still, flushed with embarrassment, or so her cheeks indicated. The other woman, her back to them, was clearly upset. By the tone of the voice, there was no mistaking who it belonged to. Nettie Pegram. They could tell something was amiss, as Lucy was assuring them she would take care of whatever had Nettie so peeved.

Unable to stop herself, Diane stood up and walked over to Sue's table. "Well, hi there, Sue! Nettie! How are you two this afternoon?"

Before Sue could utter a sound, Nettie jumped right in. "Diane, be careful what you order in this place. I just found a lipstick mark on my water glass!" She held the glass up to illustrate her point.

"Oh, I'm sure it was an oversight. Lucy will take care of it for you."

"Oversight! It wasn't an oversight. It was pure carelessness. I have come here for years and never have I experienced such a lack of cleanliness. It is not acceptable, that is what it is!" Nettie's face was red with rage.

"Well, Nettie, you made a very important point." Diane's smile was as sweet as her voice.

Bonnie listened to her friend's words and saw a smug look appear on Nettie's face. Holding her breath, she waited to see what would happen next.

"You said you have been eating here for years," Diane continued. "That is quite a compliment for the Apothecary. In all those years you must have been pleased with the service to come back so many times. And now, one time you find a dirty glass. You did right in calling Lucy's attention to it. And she's taking care of it. The Apothecary's reputation is still in tact, don't you think?"

Nettie did not respond. She sat there quietly as Diane turned to Sue and said, "Sue, what did you order for lunch? I was thinking of the chicken salad. Sounds light and healthy to me."

Sue gave her a gracious smile. "Yes, I did order the chicken salad sandwich. I am sure we will both be very pleased."

"Yes ma'am, we will. Well, have a great lunch, girls. See you at church." With a smile and a wave, Diane returned to the booth where Bonnie was sitting.

"That was amazing! You left Miss Nettie speechless," Bonnie whispered, leaning forward on her elbows.

"Aw, Nettie is harmless. Really. Her bark is worse than her bite. She's become a bitter, lonely woman since her Henry died. Not that she was always nice. She had an edge to her before Henry got sick, but once she lost him she grew much worse. It's really sad, though."

Still whispering, Bonnie told Diane about her first encounter with Nettie. Nettie had left an indelible first impression on Bonnie. It was not a happy one.

Bonnie opened the menu before her and said, "I remember back home Miz Jessie telling me how some people don't make very good first impressions on others."

"Miss Jessie? I don't think I've heard you mention her before," Diane said.

"Oh. I'm sorry. I thought I had. Well, Miz Jessie was always around. She was Miz with a 'z.' In fact, she was there the day I was born in a little farmhouse in southeast Missouri. Back then, when you didn't have money for a hospital, your kids were born at home. Miz Jessie's loving hands caught me as I took my first breath. Since mama had to help daddy a lot in the fields, Miz Jessie would come over and cook and clean and take care of me. Later she would take care of my two sisters and brother as well. Seemed she was always there. She was like a part of the family, really. And we all loved her dearly. She taught me so much about Jesus. And people too. Maybe I can tell it to you like she said it to me." Bonnie giggled.

A smile spread across Diane's face. "Now that's a giggle with a memory attached, I can tell. I do it quite often, myself. Spill the beans, girl."

Bonnie took a deep breath, pulled out her little girl southern drawl and said, "When ya meet folk for the furst time, leave a good taste in their mouths. 'Cause they will 'member that furst meetin' and judge ya by it. Tho' they ought not be a judgin',' they's do. So watch yoself. Folk are watchin' ya close like, to see if ya be what ya say ya be.' I had to quit talking like that when I was around seven years old. Mama and Miz Jessie didn't want me 'talkin' igneerent like."

Both girls burst out laughing.

Bonnie looked out the window. "Miz Jessie would love our prayer time. Her love of Jesus was so real. She couldn't walk without talking of Jesus. I learned so many things from her and they seem to come flooding back to my mind quite often. Now 'that' is the kind of faith I want." Bonnie smiled at the memory.

"Sounds like a very godly woman to me," Diane sighed, looking around the Apothecary. "Not many of those around much anymore."

Bonnie looked over at Nettie and wished there was something she could do or say to help bring Nettie some joy in her life. "Diane, can I share something with you?"

"Of course."

"Seems everywhere I go in this town, I encounter Miss Nettie one way or another. And to be truthful with you, I don't know why. I can't imagine what, if anything, I could do to be a friend to her. Maybe I shouldn't even try. She doesn't seem to want or need anyone."

The sandwiches arrived and Lucy filled the tea glasses. Diane mixed her tea with water, half and half. Stirring her drink, she said, "Bonnie, I have known Nettie a long time. She is a hard one. But I can't help but think under all those layers of ornery is a soul crying to be free. Free of what, I don't know. Maybe Nettie isn't even sure what that is. But I keep praying for her." Setting her spoon aside, she looked Bonnie squarely in the face. "If you feel God leading you into her life, you know you have to step in, don't you?"

Bonnie nodded slowly. She looked once more at Nettie and pleaded in her heart for God to show her why she kept being thrust into Nettie's space.

Bonnie followed Diane's glance over to Sue's table. They both saw Nettie pull an oversized calculator from her purse. Nettie began punching numbers into the machine, then said loudly, as if Sue were deaf, "Here's what you owe, plus half the tip."

Diane blew out a puff of air. "I wish, just once, Nettie would pay for Sue's lunch. She has more money than anyone in this town. And our pastor is on such a humble salary." Seemingly embarrassed, Diane turned back to Bonnie. "I'm sorry, Bonnie. That came out too quick. Sometimes I speak before I think. Please forgive me."

"It's alright," Bonnie said. "I am very good at that myself."

Hearing chairs scrape the floor, the girls turned and saw Nettie and Sue rise to leave. Sue looked over, with a smile and a wave, as she followed Nettie to the cash register.

Diane and Bonnie finished their lunch with a bit of small talk, and then paid their bill. Once they were out on the street, Diane gave Bonnie a generous hug, and headed for her car.

Bonnie opened her car door and sat behind the wheel. Heavily in thought, she knew without a doubt that Nettie would become a part of her world. How, she did not know. But she could not look away. It was a frightening prospect. Rubbing her temples, she realized she had grown a headache.

19

Will and Bonnie visited two other Sunday School classes over the next several weeks, and felt at ease in a class taught by Tilly Albright. She was delightful! Her spirit was sweet as sugar and she seemed genuinely in love with the Lord. She taught from the heart and welcomed questions. If she did not know the answer to a question, she admitted she didn't. But she always said she would do her best to look it up and report back the next week.

Teasingly she'd say, "If I can't find your answer, then I'll be honest and tell you I don't know, or that it's a mystery." She'd giggle at herself, along with the rest of the class, who seemed to feel the same way as Bonnie.

Her lesson this week was on the grace of God. She taught that when we accept Christ into our hearts, we are "a new person." The old has passed away, the new has come. That on the cross, Jesus paid a huge price for our sins. They are gone, totally forgiven. And because we are forgiven, we are not condemned when we sin, but we are reminded by the Holy Spirit of who we are in Christ. Knowing that sets us free from condemnation, by others or by ourselves.

Tilly's love for the Word of God was contagious. Bonnie leaned forward in her seat, not wanting to miss a word. "We all have learned very well how to condemn ourselves," she began. "To feel guilty. To feel ashamed. Unworthy. We beat ourselves up all the time, don't we? No one can do that better than we can. But there are those around us who feel it their duty to point out our sins. The Bible says Jesus came to set us free. Free from guilt, from condemnation.

Jesus paid a huge price for our freedom. Let's learn to accept the love behind that sacrifice." Tilly was a breath of fresh air.

Bonnie leaned over to Will and told him she sensed the atmosphere in the room was infused with a lightness, a feeling of burdens being lifted. It felt like a safe place to be. It was the same feeling she felt alongside Miz Jessie's 'learnin' lessons.'

As a child and teen, she had struggled to believe that the God of all creation loved her. Little Bonnie from 'podunk' Missouri. Not that she was a terrible, ornery kid growing up. No, not at all. She was a pretty good kid and was loved by her dad and mom, her Gram, and by Miz Jessie. But she had always felt such guilt when she did wrong. A guilt that had never let her be free of the hurt she caused, no matter how small. Where that came from, she didn't know. But it was there. Over the years it kept her from allowing God's love to penetrate that guilt.

She grew tired of beating herself up every time she said a hurtful thing or was rude to her parents. Feeling that way always made her feel unloved. But one day Miz Jessie asked her why she was so irritable all the time. "Chile, ya jus' not yerself these weeks. What be troublin' ya?"

"Oh, Miz Jessie, I feel guilty over everything. I feel bad when I say the wrong thing or when I don't say the right thing. I feel guilty when I think bad thoughts, then I feel bad when I don't think the right thoughts. Oh, I am so tired of feeling. Seems I can't do or say anything right anymore."

Miz Jessie stopped the rocker and eased over to the side porch step where Bonnie was sitting, arms wrapped around her legs. "Chile, give me a hand." Bonnie stood and helped lower Miz Jessie onto the top step. She knew she would have to help her back up.

"Whooee and a day! These legs jus' don't wanna bend like they used ta." Fanning herself with her apron, she looked over at Bonnie. "Tell me, youngun, why did Jesus die fer yer sins?"

Bonnie stared straight ahead, out beyond the fields, far away from herself. Sitting still as a rock, Miz Jessie waited. Humming.

Bonnie listened to the sound of Miz Jessie's soothing hum and a tear escaped her eye. Wiping it away, she answered, "He died to take away my sin."

"Yes, yes, He shorely did. So if he took 'em away, why are ya playin' 'em over and over in yer perty lil' head all the time?"

Bonnie turned and faced her dear friend. "You mean, you mean," she sputtered, "that all this time I have been feeling bad about myself for something that is not even there!"

"Umhm, coulds be," came the gentle reply.

Bonnie chewed on that for a minute, looking at the sky, then back over to Miz Jessie. "Well, for goodness sake! I have been wasting so much time and energy for nothing!"

Laughing a deep belly laugh, Miz Jessie said, "Ya surely have! Ya might be only twelve yar old but over many a yar to come, ya will see that when ya hurt someone, tell 'em yer sorry and thank the good Lawd for already forgivin' ya, even before ya done it. And then, walk away from hit, knowin' He give ya what ya don't deserve. He done give ya grace! Ya didn't deserve hit, but he give it to ya anyways, because He love ya. Then ya go on and pass hit ta others. 'Fore long ya be livin' in freedom and grace. Yer gonna find hit a lot more fun! Umhm."

Now, as Bonnie sat in Tilly's class, the soothing voice of her

Sunday School teacher stirred Bonnie's heart. She felt like she did that day on the step with Miz Jessie. She was being set free. She had tried to practice the grace she knew since leaving her hometown, but found it particularly hard here in Windy Garden. No one prepared her for the kind of folks she would meet here. She didn't get it right all the time, but she was trying. For the moment, she was thrilled to be a part of Tilly's Sunday school class. Now *this* was a freedom class! Not at all like the teaching she had heard by another teacher a few weeks ago. She still shuddered when she passed Clyde's classroom down the hall.

Bonnie was impressed with the simplicity of the lessons Tilly taught. It wasn't really all that hard to understand. God's love was simple. And Tilly's excitement was contagious! Her closeness to the Almighty gave her hope. A hope that she could have a deeply personal, intimate relationship with the One who created her.

She couldn't help but think about the close earthly relationships she had experienced in her life. Her mama and daddy loved her dearly. Her Gram was her first tie to the Lord. Miz Jessie built on that love, sharing Jesus with her in a simple, childlike manner. And Will. She loved her Will deeply. He was her world. She was getting to know him better, day by day, year by year, as they spent time together, walking through a few tough patches and celebrating the victories they experienced along the way.

It must be the same with God. There must be a deep desire to want to know Him day by day, year by year, walking through the hard times together and celebrating the joys that bring hope. Bonnie liked that! She really wanted to know God. Really know Him. Not just about Him.

A deeper quest began that day. Her hunger to know was profound. And it was fueled in *this* class, in this moment in time. She felt sure God would give opportunities to deepen her understanding, as she listened and studied God's Word.

She began looking forward to church each week and the sermons that inspired her. She and Will met several friendly couples, which pleased her immensely. Miz Jessie said it would take time. And she was right.

Will and Bonnie walked to the sanctuary after Sunday school dismissed. They sat up close, fourth row from the front on the right side, on the ground floor. The praise music enhanced Bonnie's worship time. She could hardly wait for the message. Only ten minutes into his message, grunts and groans emanated from the left side and close to the front of the sanctuary. She closed her eyes, wondering if it was the same woman voicing her disagreement.

Sitting behind her was her Sunday School teacher, Tilly, who must have heard the disgruntled woman as well. Tilly spoke in a quiet whisper that only Bonnie could hear. She overheard Tilly pray quietly, "I need to pump up my prayers for our Nettie, Lord. She must be having a difficult day."

Bonnie realized she should pray for this woman as well.

At the end of the service, Bonnie saw several church members leaving the sanctuary in the opposite direction of Nettie Pegram. To her, it looked like they were trying to avoid a train wreck. Bonnie excused herself from her husband to go to the restroom. As she left, she saw Will approach a man she thought she recognized, but she couldn't quite make the connection. When she returned, Will was still talking to the same fellow. Before she had time to ponder much longer, the man introduced himself. "You must be Bonnie. I'm Don Sadler. Will has been telling me about you. It is so nice to finally meet you."

Bonnie shot a curious look at Will, wondering what he had told this man about her. Shaking off the thought, it dawned on Bonnie where she had seen him. "Oh, I think I've seen you in the Sunday School class we attend. Nice to meet you, Don."

Don directed his attention back to Will, talking about an upcoming men's event at the church, when Bonnie felt someone bump into her.

Turning to apologize for something she had not done, her eyes widened.

"If you people wouldn't hang out in the aisle, a body could get through," the woman grumbled.

"Oh, I'm so sorry, ma'am." Bonnie apologized. Here she was face to face with the angry woman. Again. Her voice shook as she introduced herself, "Oh, hi. I don't think we've met. My name is Bonnie. Bonnie McDaniel."

"I'm Nettie Pegram and you...."

Bonnie watched as Nettie's eyes glazed over, and her body began to shake. She stood transfixed for what seemed like minutes, unable to move. Suddenly, she swooned and Bonnie caught her elbow.

"Are you all right, ma'am? Here, let me help you sit down. You are shaking all over!"

Nettie reached for the pew next to her, feeling Bonnie's arms supporting her as she sat. Bonnie picked up a church bulletin that had been left on the seat and began waving it in front of Nettie's face to cool her down. Color began to slowly come back into the older woman's face.

Hearing the commotion, Will, Don and the pastor rushed over. Pastor Randy knelt down beside Nettie and patted her hand. Speaking softly, he asked, "Nettie, what's wrong? Do you need to go to the hospital?"

Nettie tried to rise, but felt weak and settled back onto the pew.

"Take it easy, Nettie," Randy said, "just rest for a few minutes. You'll be ok. Tell me, how are you are feeling?"

Nettie slowly roused herself, embarrassed by all the attention and spoke. "I am fine, no need for all the fuss." She forced herself onto her unsteady feet and once again stood tall and regal. "I need to go home and rest, is all."

Bonnie touched her elbow and offered, "Let us drive you home. If you have a car, Will can drive it for you."

"She walks to church and only lives a couple of blocks away," Pastor Randy replied. He gave Nettie a worried look. "I can drive you home, if you like."

Nettie looked from Randy to Bonnie and back. "This…. Bonnie girl asked first. She can take me home."

Randy nodded, more worried than before. Never once had he known Nettie to welcome strangers, much less allow them to drive her home.

Bonnie focused solely on Nettie. Gently guiding her down the aisle to the exit door in the vestibule, she led her out the church doors, followed by Will.

Once outside, Will opened the back door of their car and Nettie eased herself in. Before he closed the door, Nettie leaned out and huffed, "I am so glad everyone has departed. I would have been mortified if anyone had seen me like that."

Will closed the door and looked at Bonnie. "Don't you think she needs to see a doctor?"

"Yes, I do." said Bonnie. "We'll ask her again when we get her home."

They drove down Depot Street three blocks when Nettie pointed to a stately white Victorian house. "There it is on the left. Park around the back," Nettie said.

Once Nettie was settled in her living room, Bonnie asked if she was sure she didn't need to go to the emergency room. Nettie replied flatly, "No. I got a little dizzy is all. Happens quite often. Go on home. I think I'll take a little nap." She stretched out on the sofa and Bonnie covered her with an afghan that was draped over the back of a nearby chair.

"Miss Nettie, can I make you something to eat? Maybe a sandwich and a glass of tea?"

Nettie bolted upright. "Why do you call me *Miss* Nettie? Everyone else calls me *Mrs.* Pegram or Nettie!"

Bonnie winced and took a step back. "Oh, I didn't mean to offend you, ma'am. It's just that I was raised to respect my elders. Our Miz Jessie back home taught me that if I address older people saying Miss with their first name, it fostered a closer relationship without all the formality."

"Well, no one has called me 'Miss' since before I was married."

Nettie's reputation had proceeded her and Bonnie had no desire to get on her bad side, so she smiled sweetly and said, "It's ok. I'll call you Mrs. Pegram."

"Manners. Hm. Well, it's refreshing to see someone so young

with manners. And you have me curious, young lady, who this Miz Jessie might be. But I'm too tired right now for idle chat. I just want to rest." Nettie settled back down onto the sofa.

Bonnie smiled at the thought of Miz Jessie. She would love to share how precious Miz Jessie was in her life but knew this was not the right time.

"All right, Mrs. Pegram, we'll let you rest, but I am leaving my phone number for you in case you need anything. We can be back in only a few minutes time. Will, would you write our phone number down please?" Bonnie asked.

Will wrote their phone number on the church bulletin from his pocket and set it on the coffee table.

Then Nettie motioned with her finger for Bonnie to come closer. In a moment of vulnerability, she whispered to Bonnie and said, "You may call me Miss Nettie if you like."

Bonnie knew it was a concession, and she would take it. "All right, 'Miss Nettie.' Have a restful afternoon. If you need us, please call."

After Will and Bonnie left, the stillness was too loud for Nettie. She heard the rustle of leaves in the trees and the beautifully carved oak clock ticking in the hallway.

"Henry. My Henry. What have I done? What have I done to you?"

Nettie closed her eyes trying to shut out the past she had covered up for so long. *Why, oh why, did this Bonnie have to come to Windy Garden?*

"I wonder how Nettie is feeling this morning?" Bonnie asked Will over breakfast.

"I don't know," replied Will, focusing on a report he had brought home from work the night before.

"I couldn't stop thinking about her all night long. When she had her spell in church, I thought she was going to pass out. Do you think she has a heart condition? Or maybe breathing problems? You don't think she's diabetic, do you?"

"You never know."

"Will! Are you listening to one word I am saying?"

"Oh, uh, yes, I'm listening."

"Then what did I say?"

"You said you were worried about the lady who fainted in church yesterday?"

"Will, did you see anyone faint in church yesterday?"

"No. Didn't you say someone fainted?"

"Good grief, Will. I'm trying to tell you how worried I am that Nettie Pegram might really be sick. I mean, her face went pale as milk. And her breathing was so shallow, I thought she might stop breathing altogether. Maybe I will pay her a visit this morning."

Will did not respond.

"Will!" Bonnie shouted.

Paper went flying all over the kitchen table. "Now look what you've done," Will scolded. "It will take me hours to put these back in order." Will knelt and picked up the scattered reports, wiping the butter off the edge of the summary page.

"Me! Me?! Sometimes Will.....oh never mind." Bonnie stormed out of the kitchen and slammed the door. She sat on the porch swing where she usually went when she was upset or needing a good cry.

Moments later, Will came out to join her. "Bonnie, I am so sorry I wasn't listening to you. Would you like to tell me again what has you so upset?"

"No!"

"You said something about the lady we took home after church, didn't you?"

"Yes. I said I was thinking of visiting her."

"Oh. I think that's a great idea."

I could have said I was going to drink poison and he would have thought it was a good idea. Men!

Will went back inside and came out a few minutes later with his briefcase in hand. "Are we ok? I don't like it when you're mad at me."

His handsome face was too cute to resist. "Of course, we're ok." Bonnie rose and threw her arms around his neck.

"I'm glad." Will kissed her tenderly, patted her cheek and headed to their car. He honked the horn and waved as he backed out the driveway, his traditional goodbye. Bonnie stood and waved until he was out of sight. Walking back to the door, she could not get her mind off Nettie. Miz Jessie always said that if God puts someone heavily on your heart, then it must be for a mighty special reason. Bonnie was not too thrilled that this 'someone' was Nettie Pegram.

Bonnie went inside and dressed in her navy jogging pants, white tank top, and matching navy jacket. She sat on the front porch stoop, laced her walking shoes, and then headed in the direction of Nettie's house. She loved walking. Especially here in the mountains. The leaves were changing colors high along the mountaintops and the air was crisp with the first hints of autumn. The valleys looked as though their hard work for the season had ended. It was tough to choose where to place her focus. The mountains or the valley. Regardless, it was a great way to get familiar with her surroundings, as well as the town. The walk took her past old barns that were falling apart, chimneys standing alone that were once part of a house, farmhouses in need of repair, horses and cows in large, open fields, and acres and acres of farmland. *There's a story there*, she said to herself, as she stopped from time to time to take a closer look at the old barns and empty houses. *A family once lived there*, she pondered. *Wonder what took place within those four walls.* Whenever she noticed abandoned dwellings, she repeated the same thought in her mind.

The countryside invigorated Bonnie during her walks. It reminded her of home. She shielded her eyes from the bright morning sun, and surveyed the fall crops that were already planted in the ground. Cabbage and spinach were topping the mounded rows with leafy stems reaching up to six inches. Rows and rows of carrots and onions filled acre after acre. To her right was an apple orchard that lay like carpet in the valley, and ascended halfway up the mountain. Acres and acres of apple trees stood proud, as if waiting for the right time, when an anxious hand would reach into its boughs and pull the fruit of its labor, enjoying the taste of its offering.

Once Bonnie reached town, the community melded into close

neighborhoods, businesses, churches, criss-crossing streets, and lots of shady trees. Bonnie noticed something new each time she made her trek into town. She entered from the east and headed up Depot Street to Miss Nettie's. She was not as nervous as yesterday, but still felt intimidated to be going back to the home of the most cantankerous woman she had ever met.

Towering old oak trees lined the sidewalks of Depot Street. They stretched the entire three blocks overhanging the street, like a canopy of leaves. Period homes stood proud on each side. Most could be traced back to the late 1800's, a bit of history Bonnie had learned from her tour of the old Edgewater Hotel. It was a gorgeous sight!

Coming up on the right, Bonnie once again saw Mrs. Pegram's home, the spacious two story white Victorian home with filigree trim and three fireplace stacks. It took up half the block. A large wrap around porch started on the left front side and stretched clear around the back to the right. Flowering fall mums hung in baskets over the railings, bringing color to the stark white of the paint. Everything was immaculate. Standing at the edge of the sidewalk, Bonnie wondered if a lonely leaf would ever dare fall into into the yard of Nettie Pegram. She placed her foot tremulously on the walkway leading to the front steps. Her nervousness had returned and her shoulders tightened. She heard a noise and stopped. Looking up, she saw Miss Nettie sitting in a rocker on the front porch.

"Well, are you going to come up or stand there staring all day?"

Bonnie stood frozen to the spot. "Oh, uh, good morning Miss Nettie. I thought I'd come by and see how you are feeling today."

"Well, if you've come to visit, then come on up. I don't like having conversations where I have to shout to talk. C'mon now."

"Yes, ma'am." Bonnie walked up the steps to the porch. Her eyes locked onto the handsome rocking chair that had caught her eye the day before, when she had dropped Nettie off from church. What a lovely rocker you have! I don't think I've seen one quite like it. The old rockers we had back home were quite rickety and old. But this one! Oh my!" Bonnie looked admiringly at the wooden rocker Nettie was sitting in.

Nettie rubbed her hands over the smooth wood of the armrests and said, "My Henry made this for me many years ago. It is my most prized piece of furniture." She looked away as though recalling a memory.

"I can see why. It is quite unique. May I sit?" Bonnie motioned to another rocker alongside Nettie's.

"Of course, where are my manners? Sit."

"I see you are feeling much better today. I'm glad."

"When you get to be my age, feeling better is a matter of what aches the least. But thank you for saying so."

Bonnie saw Nettie glance at her out the corner of her eye and their eyes locked for a brief moment. Suddenly feeling more comfortable, Bonnie settled back into her rocker. Bonnie loved rockers. Ever since she was a little girl, her Gram would rise early in the morning and sit on the side porch in the high back rocker with an afghan over her shoulders and a Bible in her lap. She could still hear the sound of Gram's special chair creaking the boards beneath its wobbly rockers.

She glanced about at the beautiful surroundings in Nettie's front yard. A bluebird lighted on the edge of a bird bath in the center of a blooming flower bed. It was overflowing with orange asters, yellow sunflowers, purple impatiens, petunias and autumn snowflake. It made a brilliant display of color.

The bluebird dipped his head and drank from the cool clear water, then hopped right in, flapping his brilliant blue wings which glistened in the sunlight. After a few moments of silence, Nettie asked, "How far away do you live? I didn't see a car pull up. Did you walk here?"

Bonnie felt pleased Nettie was asking a personal question instead of impersonal chats about the weather or what-not. "Oh, I live about two miles away, over on Fullers Street. I love to be out in the sunshine and today is such a perfect day for a walk."

"Bonnie…" Nettie began.

Bonnie spoke at the same time, "Miss Nettie, I was just thinking…..Oh, I'm sorry. You were saying?"

"No. No. Go ahead with what you were about to say."

"Well, I was thinking about back home where I grew up. My mom, and my Gram, and Miz Jessie would spend most of their time on our side porch where three rockers and a straight back chair welcomed their tired bodies in the afternoon. We lived on a good-sized farm. It was hard work running a farm! Gardens had to be tended, canning took place from early summer to mid fall, eggs had to be gathered from the chicken coop, our four cows had to be milked every day, and all our food was good ole' southern cooking. It wasn't anything as grand as your home. Not near as lovely or big. But it was home. Miz Jessie used to say, "Home is where ya feels the best. Hit be the place where ya lay yer head at night and sleep like a baby. Hit smells good from the kitchen. Not likely to 'tract much 'tention cept flies and varmits. But I can tell ya home is home. Uh-huh, hit is."

Bonnie giggled and looked at Nettie. "That Miz Jessie could sure tell it like it is. Isn't that funny? When I think of Miz Jessie, I start talking like her. If she had heard me just then, she would take me to task for that! There's just something about being here in Windy Garden that pulls up my roots."

Catching her attention, Bonnie saw a young mother pushing a baby in a stroller in front of Nettie's house. Bonnie leaned forward.

Before reaching the front walk, the baby began to cry. Instinctively, the mother stopped and picked up the child, bouncing it from side to side. Soon the baby hushed. Turning back to Miss Nettie, she noticed her focus on the child as well. "I hope one day God will bless me with a child. We have been trying since we were married, but no luck so far." Her voice held a tinge of sadness. She saw Nettie lower her head and wondered if she had any children. She had not thought to ask before.

"Miss Nettie?"

Nettie's head raised but she did not make eye contact with her visitor.

"Yes?" she responded quietly.

"I was wondering. Do you have any children? I never thought to ask, but…"

"No!" Nettie answered sharply.

Bonnie was startled by the harsh reply. She thought she was making headway with her. She didn't anticipate such a snappish answer.

Bonnie turned and refocused on the mother leaving with her

child. Bonnie felt terrible. Both for herself and for Miss Nettie. *Did they just not want children? Or maybe.....maybe she couldn't have any!* The anxious thought bounced in her head like a ping-pong ball. *What....what if I can't have children? No. No. That can't be what's wrong. All I have ever wanted in my life was to be married and have kids. It's been my lifelong dream.* She felt like cold water had been thrown in her face. Shaking her head sadly, she rose from her chair. "I think I need to run along."

Before Bonnie reached the steps, Nettie finally spoke. "You mentioned this 'Miz Jessie' before. Who is she? The hired help?"

Bonnie wanted to go home. Her emotions were reeling within her. About to burst into tears, she took a deep breath and willed them not to flow. Turning, she walked back to the porch railing and leaned against it. "Oh no. Not at all. She's like part of the family. She has been around as long as I've been alive. She watched over me and my two sisters and brother while daddy and mama worked in the fields. Miz Jessie handled most of the house chores. And Miz Jessie was, well, she was the one who told me all about Jesus. Her and my Gram. She felt it was her God-given chore to make sure I knew how much He loved me. She had to cook, clean, bake, and still found time to straighten me out. Yes ma'am, she made sure I didn't grow up a heathen."

Nettie groaned the same groan she emitted in church. Bonnie took this as a cue to leave. Relieved, she pushed off the railing, faced Miss Nettie and said, "Well, I best be heading home. I've taken way too much of your time. But I am really glad you are feeling better. See you Sunday in church."

And with that, Bonnie left. She rushed back home. She knew

if she didn't hurry, she would burst into tears right there on the sidewalk. Trying to reject the horrible thought that threatened to destroy her dreams, she rushed into the house and broke into heavy sobs. Throwing herself on the sofa, she cried until she had exhausted herself and fell asleep.

Bonnie's exuberant personality and laugh had caught Nettie off guard. She watched Bonnie disappear out of sight. Then she leaned her head back on the rocker and allowed herself to drift back...back to the last time she had genuinely felt laughter.

On sunny, calm days she made it her ritual to wait on the porch for Henry to return home from work. She cherished his usual greeting. Ascending the porch steps, he would invariably stop alongside her and wrap his arms around her shoulders and hug her tight. This particular day in her memory, he held something behind his back. Then springing them out in surprise, he beamed, "Impatiens for my impatient wife!"

"You have a twisted sense of humor, Henry," Nettie said, trying to sound offended. She laughed in spite of herself and admired the flowers.

"I love it when you laugh, my love," Henry commented as he sat in the rocker next to her.

"Henry, you are such a tease."

"You can't fool me, my Nettie dahlin.' You can't help but love me, and my wit."

Nettie smiled at the memory and how it made her feel light and happy. Only in her memories could she find such laughter and love.

She opened her eyes and felt a shiver. Ever since the episode in church, she felt uncomfortable around this Bonnie. She had hoped she might never encounter the likes of her again. But there was something about this girl that intrigued her. And frightened her.

Winds of change were coming. She could feel it in her bones. She stood, looking about. Wrapping her arms around her bodice, as though cold, she sensed a foreboding chill. Fear gripped her.

20

The following Saturday was a beautiful, slightly warm day with not a cloud in the sky. Bonnie stood at the sink admiring the apple orchards behind the house and the gorgeous weather beckoning her outside. She washed the last breakfast dish and decided to ask her hubby to take her on a ride up into the mountains. Maybe even get in a short hike. Drying her hands on the dish towel and looking around at her immaculate kitchen, she went to find Will.

"Will!" she called, walking down the hallway. "Will!" she called again, approaching their bedroom.

"I'm in here!" came the voice of her love.

Hearing his voice always brought a smile to her lips. She loved his days off work where they could spend time together, whether it was working around the house or taking short trips. Today was a day trip kind of day.

Stepping into the bedroom, Bonnie stopped and stared. There before her was her husband, sitting on the floor of the walk-in closet with a multitude of hangers all around him. "What? What are you doing?" she shrieked.

"I'm sorting hangers. Have you ever noticed how many different kinds of hangers we have?" He looked up at her holding a white plastic hanger in his left hand and a wire one in the other.

"No," she giggled. "I have not given it a thought one way or the other."

"Our closet is a mess. There were hangers facing the wrong direction, broken ones hanging loose, and look at this." He held

218

a wooden hanger up to emphasize his point. "The metal part is bent and puts creases in my dress pants. I can't believe you haven't noticed." Will pointed to the hanging rods where not a single item of clothing hung.

Bonnie's eyes grew wide. "Will, where are all the clothes?"

"I took everything out of the closet and laid it on the bed."

Bonnie glanced around and sure enough, all their hanging clothes were lying across the bed. Admittedly, she had to give her husband credit for placing them so neatly. Stepping back she said, "Will, I was going to ask you…"

"I'm kind of busy with this project right now. It shouldn't take me too long," he smiled.

A thought popped into Bonnie's mind. She sat down in front of Will and said, "It will go much faster if I help. What can I do?" She was thinking if they finished his 'project' together there would still be time for a long ride.

"I don't need your help. Sorry, honey, but you wouldn't understand my method. See. Over here I have a stack of plastic hangers, all sorted by color. And over here is another pile of wire hangers." His face beamed with pride over his organization skills. "And those over there have a paper roll on the bottom and that pile beside you are the broken ones that I plan to get rid of."

Bonnie smiled weakly, too overcome with all the descriptions of hangers.

"Oh! And see!" his arms spread wide, "all the hanger loops are facing the same direction!"

She knew she had married a man who loved order. But this was taking it too far. She rose to her feet and looked down at the busy man absorbed with clothes hangers. Shaking her head, she left the room.

An hour later, Will found his wife cleaning out the refrigerator. "Come with me! I want you to see the closet."

Bonnie wiped the last shelf and replaced the final items, and then followed her husband back to the bedroom.

Will opened the closet door and stepped in, spreading his hands wide. "Well, what do you think?"

Seeing the clothes hung neatly in the closet, Bonnie smiled. "You've done a fantastic job!"

Touching the rod, he explained what he had accomplished. "See, the white plastic ones hold dress shirts, the blue ones hold everyday shirts, the green ones are for your dainty things and the wire hangers hold less delicate items. I have a bag full of bent hangers that are going to the trash."

Seeing the joy on his face was endearing, and she let her earlier upset fade away. "It looks great! Good job, honey! Now that you've finished, I thought we could go for a ride today. It is so pretty outside. We could head toward the Nantahala mountains and maybe take a short hike."

"But I'm not done."

"What do you mean you're not done?"

"Well, I'm almost done."

Almost! What does he mean, almost? If he thinks I am going to figure out what hanger to use for what when I do the laundry, he is nuts! "What do you mean, almost?"

"Now I'm going to color-coordinate the clothes. I'll put all the white colors together, and the blues, and the greens and so forth.

Yours on your side and mine on my side." He quickly began moving clothes around to illustrate his point.

Bonnie disappeared into the kitchen and cut a large slice of brownie. It was all she could do not to add ice cream.

21

Ida Mae called Nettie after a fitful night's sleep and invited her
to meet for coffee the next morning at the Apothecary. "Nettie,
good morning! I was wondering if you'd like to join me for a cup
of coffee tomorrow. I don't have much to do then and thought we
could have a little girl time."

Nettie used to like 'girl time,' but lately she viewed it as a waste
of time. However, something pulled at her and she relented. "Just
a minute. Let me check my schedule." Nettie knew she have didn't
anything on the calendar but wanted Ida Mae to think she had to
fit her in. "I checked. I can make it."

"Good! Good! How about 7 a.m? Does that sound ok or is it
too early?"

"No, 7 is fine. I am usually up by 5 o'clock anyway. Any particular
reason you want to meet?" Her tone carried a hint of suspicion.

Ida Mae had tried her best to mask her concern over Nettie, but
they both knew each other too well. "No, not really. It has been far
too long since we've been able to get together. So, I thought, what
the heck, let's have coffee."

Her laughter over the phone reminded Nettie of how close
they used to be. Like sisters. And since Nettie was an only child,
Ida Mae had filled the void of siblings. *What has happened to us?*
Nettie wondered. Little did she know Ida Mae was asking herself
the same question.

"You're right. It has been quite a while. I'll meet you at 7 sharp."

Ida Mae could hardly contain her excitement over Nettie's

acceptance. "Thanks, Nettie. I'll see you in the morning." She held the receiver in her hand for a few moments, contemplating what they would talk about that would be safe topics and not rile her friend even more than she was. Randy's sermons were out. And she sure didn't want to talk about generic things like the weather or how many apples went into a Dutch apple pie. She decided to leave it in the hands of the Lord and pray for the best.

Ida Mae was standing outside the door of the Apothecary waiting for Nettie. She was early and didn't want to start off on the wrong foot by being late. The air was crisp and clean. She inhaled the fragrance of the roses beginning to open in the flower pots that lined the clock tower. She admired how proud the town council was of Windy Garden. Every effort was made to display spring, summer and fall flowers, each attended with great care. Enjoying her beautiful surroundings. she heard a voice call out to her.

"Ida Mae! Oh, Ida Mae!"

Looking across the street near the Blooming Pretty was Kathy waving her hands in the air.

"Hi, Kathy!" Ida Mae waved back.

"Wait right there. I'm coming your way!" Kathy was especially perky this morning, but Ida Mae didn't mind one bit. She liked Kathy.

Out of breath from sprinting across Main Street, Kathy fairly jumped the curb and embraced Ida Mae in a big hug. "I haven't seen you in a week or two. How are you doing?"

"I'm fine. And you?"

"Oh my, I am as fine as peaches in the summer. Teehee!"

"I'm glad to hear that," Ida Mae smiled.

"Are you coming to the Apothecary for breakfast?" Kathy asked.

"Well, sort of. I'm meeting Nettie here in a few minutes for coffee."

"Oh, well, if you'd like, the two of you can join me. I am bursting at the seams to tell someone all about my beautiful flowers that are showering me with color! I was telling Bob this morning about each one. I had to follow him out to his car when he left for work to tell him we had ten purple bearded lilies in bloom. As he was backing out the driveway, I shouted, "And the lilies of the valley have multiplied like rabbits!" I don't think he heard me though because I saw his car window up. Teehee!"

Ida Mae loved this girl's spunk. She was lively and attentive to even the smallest of God's creation. "Oh. I'm sorry Kathy, but Nettie and I haven't had the opportunity to get together in the longest time. We will be catching up on so many things. Maybe another time?"

"Of course! You gals have fun. And don't forget to order Sandra's breakfast muffins with your coffee. They are the best!" Kathy stepped around Ida Mae and saw Nettie approaching. "Look, Ida Mae, there's Nettie now! Good morning, Nettie!" Kathy jumped up and down, hoping Nettie could see her. She did.

Ida Mae saw the rolling of eyes from her friend. She hoped Kathy did not. She had noticed several times that people had a tendency to avoid this sweet gal. But Kathy was not one to be easily offended. She seemed to always see the good side of people. One more hug around the neck and Kathy turned and entered the Apothecary.

By then, Nettie was at Ida Mae's side. With a sneer she asked, "She's not joining us, is she?"

"No, silly. It's just you and me today. Let's go inside."

They found a booth Nettie picked out far from Kathy. Lucy appeared and greeted them with her usual southern charm. "Hydie, ladies. Would you like some coffee?"

"Yes," they both said.

"Let's splurge and get a pastry to go with our coffee. Lucy, I'd like a blueberry muffin to go with mine. How about you, Nettie?"

"Oh, well, if you are, I might as well too. Do you have any of Sandra's apple cinnamon muffins?"

"I shor' do. Both are good choices. Would ya like me to warm 'em up a bit?"

"Yes, I would like that," said Nettie. With a nod from Ida Mae, Lucy disappeared. It was now just the two of them. Ida Mae was not sure what to say next. The air hung heavy waiting for someone to dispel the tension.

Nettie spoke first. "Looks like we're supposed to have good weather for a few days."

Ida Mae inwardly groaned but kept her composure. "Yes, I've heard that too." She picked a napkin from the napkin holder and placed it in her lap. Looking up, she noticed Nettie staring out the window. "You see something out there, Nettie?"

"Yes. It's that new girl in town. She's always showing up no matter where I am. Just seems odd to me."

Ida Mae looked out too. Seeing the girl, she said, "Oh, Bonnie. She seems such a sweet young thing. Have you met her?"

"Yes. But I see her everywhere. Just seems odd."

Lucy arrived with the coffee. Ida Mae was grateful for the interruption.

"The muffins will be out shortly, gals. I got 'em wrapped in foil in the oven. Shouldn't take but a minute or two." I'll have 'em here before the warm lets out." With a smile, she turned and left.

Leaning to Nettie, Ida Mae fairly whispered, "Isn't she the loveliest thing? She is the main reason I come here so often. When I feel a little low, her sweet smile gives me a reason to perk up."

Glancing over at Lucy refilling empty coffee cups, Nettie said, "Yes, she is very good at what she does. I like that my coffee never gets cold. She does seem to know the right time when I need a refill. I like that about her." She sipped her coffee and, holding it in her hands, added, "And the coffee is always the right temperature."

Wow, thought Ida Mae, *a rare compliment. We are off to a good start.*

"Ida Mae, I've never known you to get down that often. Is something wrong?"

"Well, not today!" Ida Mae smiled over the rim of her cup. "I just meant that I do have moody days from time to time and seeing someone cheerful and caring bolsters my mood and before I know it I have forgotten what has gotten me down."

The muffins arrived, warm and smelling good. "Mmm, they both smell so delicious. I am so glad Lucy talked Carl into bringing Sandra's baked goods in here. I'll bet her oven hardly cools. The last time Saul and I came here together, we had the coconut cake. I was so glad Connie bequeathed the recipe to Sandra before she passed on. Everyone wanted that recipe! Even me!"

Ah, so Connie did leave her recipe here. I thought so from the taste of the coconut cake before. Won't Melva Jane be shocked when she hears this. Nettie felt a sadistic glee from this bit of information. She took a satisfying bite of her muffin, pleased with her choice. "I'm glad I chose the apple cinnamon. It is very delicious. How do you like yours?"

Ida Mae felt her heart leap with joy. Nettie seemed to be settling in to their time together. She had not felt this close to her friend in a very long time. "Mine is too! Next time I'll have to try yours."

Nettie picked up her knife, wiped it clean with a napkin, and cut a small piece. "Here, try it now." She slipped the piece of muffin onto Ida Mae's plate.

Ida Mae took a sip of coffee to clean her palate, then tasted the apple cinnamon muffin. "Oh my! I see why you chose that one. It is delicious!"

Memories of old flooded Ida Mae's mind. Times when she and Nettie would frequent the Apothecary and share milkshakes and French fries.

"Nettie, do you remember the time back in junior high school when we would come here after school? I don't think I will ever forget the day we drank two milkshakes each and were so sick we couldn't go to school the next day. Remember?"

"Yes, I do." She smiled briefly, then added, "Mother scolded me for being foolish and immature."

"I remember! Wasn't that after you had thrown up on her shoes?"

They both giggled like two schoolgirls. "It certainly was. And you know what? She shrieked so loud that I do believe the windows creaked."

Ida Mae put her hand on Nettie's. "We sure had fun back in those days, didn't we?"

"Yes, we did. I forget sometimes all the silly things we did together."

That familiar young smile she was accustomed to from their childhood days was something Ida Mae had not seen in years. It warmed her heart to see her friend relax and enjoy being together again.

"And remember when we went on a double date together? You and Henry and me and Saul?"

"I think I do. Didn't we go to the movies? We saw.....we saw, I don't remember the movie, do you?"

"I remember it starred Mary Pickford. It was a silent film. Oh, what was the name? Oh, Oh, I remember! Heart of the Hills!"

"That's it! And I believe that was the night my Henry and your Saul mimicked the whole thing. We kept elbowing them and asking them to stop, but they kept on silently mouthing the words."

Ida Mae's face lit up. "I do remember. We laughed so hard we had to go to the ladies room during intermission to reapply facial powder where our tears washed it away. Oh, Nettie, those were the days."

The two women talked on and on about old times and how often they double-dated to the movies and took walks around the lake. They did not notice an hour had passed and yet their coffee was still warm and full.

As Ida Mae reached for her coffee cup, she glanced at her watch. "Oh, my goodness. We have been here for an hour. This has been so much fun, Nettie. I am so glad we made the time to get together.

We will have to do this more often!" Setting her cup back on the table she said, "I hate to run, but I told Saul I would meet him to pick out new curtains for the living room."

Nettie looked at her watch. "I can't believe the time either. Amazing how time flies. When you get your new curtains, call me. I'd love to see them."

More than pleased with this morning's outcome, Ida Mae scooted out of the booth and looked down at Nettie. "I have had the best time walking down memory lane, my dear, dear friend. Thank you for meeting me today. With a peck on the cheek, she left Nettie to their memories.

Nettie watched Ida Mae cross the street to the church parking lot where Saul was waiting. When he caught sight of his wife, he grinned. *Just like Henry used to do,* she sighed. Nettie gathered her purse to leave, when out of the blue she heard a familiar sound. It was coming from the jukebox. The music eased her back into her seat. *I know this tune.* As well as she knew her Henry, she knew this song.

Henry sang it to her while walking home after they left the cotillion. Their first real date. She closed her eyes and leaned her head back. Softly humming along with the music, she could hear his lovely tenor voice, *"Why do I do just as you say, why must I just give you your way, why do I sigh, why don't I try to forget....it must have been that something lovers call fate, kept me saying I had to wait, I saw them all, just couldn't fall til we met..........It had to be you, it had to be you, I've wandered around, finally found somebody who, could make me be true, could make me be blue, and even be glad, just to be glad, thinking of you...."*

229

His voice in her memory was as clear as her own. He sang it quite often, often enough that it became 'their song.' She would pretend to be embarrassed when he cleared his throat to sing, but she knew better. He had revealed to her that he had had a crush on her even while she rejected his presence in their high school life.

She was so glad she had married Henry. Even though her mother set up the cotillion date, she was determined to prove her mother wrong. But as fate would have it, she eventually fell in love with her handsome and talented pursuer.

She thought back on how it all came about. An arranged date. Her refusal to cooperate. Wanting to defy her mother more than wanting to date Henry. The walk around the lake. The cotillion. The persistent Henry. Then giving in.

When Nettie was sixteen she became infatuated with a very handsome fellow named Michael who attended the same high school. Because Michael was being raised on the 'other side of the tracks,' Rose refused to allow Nettie to date this boy of so-called ill repute. Nettie did her best to convince her mother that Michael was a very kind and caring boy.

Her mother raised her voice in anger. "Nettie! I will hear nothing more about this boy. He is not good enough for you. I have spent sixteen years of my life raising you for better than this and I will not allow you to throw your life away on that boy. And I don't want to hear another word about it!"

Nettie was deeply hurt that her mother would not trust her judgment in boys. Michael had asked her to meet him at the

Apothecary after school for a milkshake, for crying out loud. It wasn't a real date. Besides, she was only sixteen. She was not thinking of marrying him.

Nettie wished with all her heart that her father was still alive. He died when she was in the ninth grade. Fourteen was terribly young to lose a father. Especially her father. He understood her and loved her deeply. They were always teasing and laughing together. She missed his secret wink that made her feel secure whenever her mother was upset about one thing or another.

After he died, Rose took charge and raised her daughter to look and act her position. She taught Nettie how to be firmly decisive, standing against anyone who would challenge her opinions, lest the town suffer from the lack of Collins wisdom. Stand up straight. Hair up, never down around the shoulders. I*t was a sign of a loose woman,* her mother would say. Never let anyone see you lacking confidence, even if you are unsure of yourself. You are a Collins. Act like one.

From that point on Rose arranged all of Nettie's dates, to which Nettie complied as the obedient daughter of Rose Collins. Besides, protesting never got her anywhere since her father died. Rose was very particular who she spent time with and what young man would be suitable for her daughter. The only exception to her harsh stance of whom she kept company with was Nettie's best friend, Ida Mae. Rose kept her promise to Samuel before he died that she would not interfere with the relationship the two girls had formed. It galled her to no end. But she would not break her word.

Rose had to plan fast. The cotillion was in three weeks and she had not yet decided which young man in Windy Garden was suitable enough to escort her daughter to the dance. An idea popped into her head. But she would have to hurry. She finished dressing, sent Nettie on her way to school, and left the house without breakfast. She walked the two blocks to town and entered the Windy Garden Real Estate office. Jeffrey Pegram was the owner of the only real estate company in town. His father had founded the business almost 25 years ago and it had been in the family ever since. Jeffrey was chairman of the town council, on the board of directors for the bank, and president of the rotary club. Rose could not have been more pleased.

"Good morning, Jeffrey." Rose said as she sauntered into his office, removing her gloves.

"Good morning, Rose," he said, shaking her hand. "What brings you out so early today? Is there something I can do for you?"

Rose took a seat across the desk from Jeffrey. "Well, as a matter of fact, you can."

Jeffrey took his seat behind the desk and placed his folded hands on top. "I will do my best."

Rose jumped right in. "The cotillion is in three weeks and I was wondering if your Henry would like the honor of escorting my daughter, Nettie, to the dance." She looked at him as if it were a done deal.

Jeffrey was stunned. Here, sitting across from him was the most brazen woman he had ever seen. He had known her for years. Her reputation was well known in Windy Garden as the town queen. Jeffrey despised social elitism. Therefore, he rarely attended social gatherings that included only the rich and prominent members of Windy Garden and excluded the middle class and poor. He was a man of principles and raised his children to be loving and giving to those in need, making no distinction between the poor and those with means.

Henry was his oldest child and possessed a heart like his father. Jeffrey was not about to *arrange* a date for his son.

"Mrs. Collins, I am quite surprised that you would request such a thing. However, Henry is eighteen and mature enough to choose his own dates. If you would like, I can ask him to drop by your house and discuss the offer, but do not be taken aback if he chooses otherwise."

It was quite obvious by the inflamed cheeks and hard stare on Rose's face that she took offense at his response.

"Mr. Pegram! Are you suggesting that I would stoop so low as to beg a date for my daughter!" She was on her feet staring at the man behind the desk.

Jeffrey rose, realizing he had sounded harsher then he had intended. "Please, Mrs. Pegram, please sit down. I am sorry if offended you. It was not my intention." Rose sat. "I only meant to say that if Henry so chooses to date your daughter, it is up to him. Now, if you have decided to change your mind about Henry, then we can forget the whole thing."

Rose looked down at her hands, quite flustered. She thought this would be an easy request. After all, it was *her* daughter she was talking about. She did not want any disgrace to fall upon her shoulders if Nettie went to the dance with someone less suitable. Thinking fast and hard, she could not come up with another viable option for Nettie. And she did not want it to be known that the son of the only real estate company in town refused her daughter. She would just have to take that chance.

Rose held her head high regaining her usual superior facade and said, "I would like it very much if Henry would come by this afternoon. Tell him to be there at 3:15 sharp. I don't want Nettie home when we talk." She stood to leave.

Jeffrey rose as well and escorted her to the door. "I will ask Henry. But again, please do not be upset if he is not agreeable to your suggestion. But he has been raised properly and will be at your house precisely at 3:15." Rose nodded in assent.

Before she left the office, Jeffrey added, "And Mrs. Collins, if this does not work out as you desire, it will be just between us, I assure you."

"Thank you," Rose said, as she stepped onto the downtown street of Windy Garden. *I must get home and make sure everything is as it should be when he comes calling. He cannot refuse. He cannot!*

"Hello, Father!" Henry said, shaking his hand. Henry adored his father. Every day after school he stopped by his father's office to spend a few moments talking and laughing over their ups and downs of the day. They were extremely close.

"Henry, my boy, how was school today?"

"Oh you know, go to classes, eat lunch, eye the girls, go back to class and then the best part of the day....I come see you."

Jeffrey laughed. It was their normal banter that endeared this son to his heart. "Well, I just have to ask. What girls are catching your eyes these days? Any one girl in particular?" He lit his favorite pipe and the sweet smell of pipe tobacco filled the air.

Henry's face changed color at the mention of one *particular girl*. "As a matter of fact, there is." He leaned forward on his father's desk and continued, "Remember me talking lately about a girl that is very beautiful but doesn't give me the time of day?" He chuckled at his own words.

"Yes, I do. Mind me asking who this pretty and elusive girl is?" Jeffrey leaned forward as well, wanting in on the secret. Making an important decision like this is what Jeffrey had been praying for all these years. That his boys would prayerfully search for girls that have the same values and beliefs his children had.

Henry stood and paced the floor before he answered. "Well, father, I wanted to be sure before I said anything to you. I have prayed really hard about this. I don't know why, but my heart has fallen hard for..." He stopped, turned to face his dad and said, "Nettie Collins."

Jeffrey's chair fell back hard against the paneled wall. Henry ran to him, "Father, are you alright?" Panic gripped him as he helped his father to his feet.

Embarrassed that he reacted so strongly to Henry's news, he hoped Henry did not connect his fall with the mention of Nettie Collins. "Um, yes, yes, I am fine."

Henry helped his father into his upright chair and scrutinized his appearance. "You look pale. Should I call the doctor?"

"No. No," Jeffrey responded good-naturedly. "This chair has been feeling out of balance lately. I think I'll get your brother to look at it later."

Henry breathed a sigh of relief. His brother, Charles, was very handy with woodwork. He promised himself to follow up with Charles to make sure father never falls again. Picking up his father's pipe from off the floor and handing it to him, he sat down on the edge of the desk and asked again, "Dad, are you sure you're ok?"

Jeffrey tapped the tobacco down that was left in the pipe and relit it. He was stalling for time, not sure how to proceed with the direction of this conversation. He cleared his throat and shakily said, "Well, now that I have embarrassed myself in front of my son, tell me again about this young girl."

Henry's face lit up like a street light in the dark. Excitement filled his entire body as he jumped from the desk and ran his hand through his thick black hair. He had waited for the right moment to tell his father about Nettie. And now the moment presented itself. He could not contain himself any longer.

"I can't say when I started feeling this way, Dad, but over the last year I have not been able to keep my mind off of her. She is so beautiful. Her hair is like wavy silk flax and her eyes sparkle when she laughs. But I do have to say, I don't see her smile very often. I've often wondered why. Well, anyway, I wait to catch a glimpse of her changing classrooms every day. I speak to her at least once a day and tease her about one thing or another. But honestly, she doesn't pay one bit of attention to me. But I think in time she will." Henry wasn't in the room. He was off in dream land somewhere with Nettie finally acknowledging he even existed.

Jeffrey didn't know what to make of this as he heard the wall clock strike three times. Quickly, his thoughts flickered back to the earlier visit from Rose Collins. "Um, Henry, there is something quite funny I need to tell you. But before I do, I need to ask. You are talking about Rose and Samuel's daughter, Nettie, right?"

"Yes, that's her! I know her father died when she was in the ninth grade and I've heard her mother seems a little difficult to bear but I really believe God wants me to pursue a date with her."

Jeffrey could not resist the smile and determination he saw in his son's eyes. He would have to trust his son. Mostly he would have to trust his God even more. "Well then, I may just have some welcome news for you. Early this morning Rose Collins came to see me."

Henry straightened at the name of Nettie's mother. He rushed back to his father's side. "She did? What did she want?"

"She came by to see if you would like the honor of escorting her daughter to the cotillion in a few weeks." Jeffrey waited for Henry to hear the haughtiness in Rose's request. Henry's face revealed otherwise.

"Really? Really? She asked if I would…..Oh Father, this is great news. This means Nettie must know that her mother is asking me."

Jeffrey did not want to burst his son's bubble, but he shared what he thought. "Henry, I don't think Nettie knows anything about this. Mrs. Pegram asked if you would take her. I said I'd ask you but that you are free to choose whomever you would like to date. That it was entirely up to you."

"Do I want to? Of course I want to! This is an answer to my prayers!"

Jeffrey looked again at the clock and said, "If you are really sure about this, Mrs. Collins would like to see you in five minutes at her house."

Henry looked over at the clock to confirm the time. "Then I had better hurry." Henry jumped up, ran around the desk, and hugged his father's neck and said, "I'd best not be late." And off he went.

Jeffrey sighed and leaned back into his chair. He didn't know what to think of the daughter, but he knew what he thought about the mother. Putting this in God's hands was the only thing he could think to do at this point. He rose and watched through the plate glass window as his son sprinted hurriedly across Main Street.

Looking to heaven, he implored, "Lord, he seems so sure that this is from You. I have to trust that he is hearing you correctly. But I have to say, I'm not sure of this. Not sure at all. So, help me to be there for my Henry if she breaks his heart."

Rose doubted her earlier resolve and fretted about the house since her visit with Jeffrey Pegram. *What was I thinking? All I accomplished this morning was to embarrass myself in front of a very important man in town. I hope he has not changed his mind after I left. After all, it is Nettie, my daughter, whose reputation is at stake here. The boy must come. He must! And he had better be on time.*

Random thoughts of how to redeem herself with Jeffrey Pegram played in her mind. She must not lose her respectability, nor her esteemed position. Had she made a foolish mistake? She hoped she'd find out shortly. The clock in the hall chimed three times.

Rose walked to the kitchen and poured herself a cup of coffee. Coffee always calmed her nerves. She sat down at the formal dining room table and sniffed the tantalizing aroma of the rich brew. As she lifted the cup to her lips, the doorbell rang. Her hands trembled and coffee spilled down the sides of the cup, little droplets falling on the sleeves of her blouse. She quickly wiped at the spots with her napkin. The doorbell rang again. She found herself rushing to the door, swiping at the spills, regaining her stately composure.

She opened the door to a young man who was the spitting image of his father. She had seen him often over the years at festivals and town activities but kept her circle tight with those she could sway.

"Mrs. Collins, my name is Henry Pegram. My father said you came to see him this morning."

Rose stared at him. Handsome and well-mannered too. "Yes, yes. Come in."

Henry followed her to a sitting room off the front entrance. High windows with sheer curtains allowed sunlight to warm the room. Rose prided herself on the number of windows she insisted upon when Samuel added this room to the original house where she could entertain her friends.

After a prolonged silence, she spoke. "Yes, well, let me get straight to the point. My daughter, Nettie, she…..um, you do know Nettie from school, don't you?" She hadn't thought before whether or not the two knew each other or had even met.

"Oh, yes," Henry exclaimed, a little too exuberantly. He dropped his head and fumbled with his collar. Shyly he said, "What I mean is, yes ma'am, we know each other from school."

Rose pointed to a Queen Anne chair next to the window. Henry obliged and sat. She took a seat across from him in her favorite red velvet-covered high back chair.

"Well, alright then. As I was saying to your father, the cotillion is in a few weeks and I thought you might want the honor of escorting Nettie to the dance."

Henry thought this was an amazing coincidence. He wanted to ask Nettie to go with him to the dance but she wouldn't even acknowledge his presence in school, much less consider an invitation to the cotillion. Or so he thought. *So Nettie must know!*

"Mrs. Collins, since Nettie is agreeable. So am I!" He smiled excitedly at the possibility that Nettie was just being coy with him, and that she and her mother had planned this all along.

"Young man. Nettie knows nothing about this. I feel it is my responsibility as her mother to make sure she only sees boys worthy of her stature. The Collins name founded this town and I aim to see that no disgrace falls upon it. Do I make myself clear?" Her stern look pinned Henry to his chair.

"Oh, yes. Yes ma'am." He struggled to hide his disappointment that Nettie knew nothing of her mother's invitation.

Rose stood and walked toward the front door. A deflated Henry followed.

Just as Rose opened the door, Henry turned and asked, "Mrs. Collins, I think it would be helpful if I could spend a little bit of time getting to know Nettie before the dance. I was thinking maybe next Saturday I could take her to dinner. Or we could take a stroll and talk."

"Very well, then." Rose said. "Be here Saturday promptly at 2:00. You will be dressed appropriately and bring your best manners with you. And I expect you to behave in a way that will not bring shame on this family."

"Mrs. Collins, I assure you that no harm will come to Nettie.

I will treat her as if she were a cherished treasure. And thank you for asking me."

At the sound of the door closing, Henry jumped the five steps that led up to the house and skipped down the sidewalk, whistling a tune his father taught him when he was a child. He turned and headed back in the direction of his father's office. But with each step, his elation waned. On one hand, he was excited about having a date with the girl of his dreams. On the other, he could not shake the feeling that Nettie might not be as agreeable as her mother.

Nettie heard someone whistling as she approached the side street to her house. She looked about but saw no one. She entered her house and hung her shawl on the peg near the front door. "Mother, I'm home." She had started up the steps to her bedroom when Rose called her into the sitting room.

"Nettie, come here."

Nettie did not like spending time with her mother. The shorter the contact, the better. But it was easier to appease her mother than to rebel. She walked over to the sitting room and stood inside the doorframe. "Mother, I have lots of homework. Is there something you want?"

Rose stiffened at Nettie's curt response. "Yes. There is. Sit down over there." Rose realized she needed to temper her demeanor or all her plans might fall like a tower of cards.

Nettie reluctantly sat and stared at her mother.

"Nettie, I have good news for you. The cotillion is in a few weeks and I have found a very nice, young man to escort you there. Isn't that wonderful?"

Nettie cocked her head and shockingly said, "What? You what? You arranged a date for me to the cotillion? Did you not consider I might not want to go to the cotillion? Or that I could pick my own date? After all, I am 18!" Nettie's shock registered all over her body. "And really, mother, I can just imagine whom you might have picked." Too late for appeasing her mother.

Rose bolted upright. "Child, you will never speak to me like that again! And yes, I arranged a date for you. He is from a very respected family and he is going to escort you to the cotillion!"

Nettie was used to her mother's tirades but she knew when to give in and when not to. This might be a time to give in. "Alright mother, who is it?" she sighed.

Rose stood with her palms together, proud of her decision. Her plan would work. She would not be embarrassed. Henry had agreed. So all was well in Windy Garden and the Collins home. "That's better. It's Jeffrey Pegram's son, Henry."

"Henry Pegram?" Nettie stood to her feet and paced. Henry was handsome and charming. She'd admit to that. "Henry Pegram?" she asked again, aghast. In school, Nettie did not like how he saw through her and challenged her snobbishness. She was used to having her way, even at the expense of others. Her mother had taught her well. Nettie didn't give him the time of day. She decided she was not pleased at all with her mother's choice. And yet, she relented.

"Ok, mother, at least it is only for one night." With a heavy sigh, she started to her room.

"Um, well, not exactly," Rose called after her.

Nettie turned. "What exactly do you mean, not exactly?" She pinned her with a stare.

Rose had to think fast or her whole plan would go up in smoke. She walked up to Nettie and said as convincingly as she could, "Henry has asked to take you to dinner next Saturday. I have agreed. He will be here at 2 pm." She patted her daughter awkwardly on the shoulder and made a hasty retreat.

Nettie stood there like a statue and thought of having two dates with the boy she avoided most. "*Two dates?* I have to endure *two dates* with him? Grrr." She pounded each foot on the stairs to voice her disapproval loudly. She shut her bedroom door, flopped on the bed, and mumbled, "I will be the laughingstock of my friends. I have purposely shunned Henry. All my friends know. Only Ida Mae thinks he is good-looking and I should be nicer to him. Two dates! These next few weeks had better fly by so I can get this over with." She didn't know if her mother could hear her complaining or not, but this time she didn't care.

Saturday's outing fell short of Nettie's idea of a perfect date. Henry surprised Nettie by taking her an hour's drive away for a walk around Mirror Lake. Nettie was not impressed. Her idea of a date was eating at a five-star restaurant in the nearby city of Highlands.

Nettie had dressed in a long, flowing purple linen dress with ivory lace which fit her long, slim body nicely. Her high heels were not suitable for the sandy beach, which she removed with reluctance to satisfy Henry's impulsiveness. The wind blew her hair out of the carefully knotted bun. She reached up, pulled the bobby pins and let her hair fall over her shoulders. She would not fight the wind and keep a bun.

Strolling around the lake, Henry spoke. "Nettie, you look beautiful. I really like your hair hanging loose around your shoulders, instead of tied up on your head. It flows softly with the breeze, accentuating your beautiful face and eyes." He stopped, turned, and gently tucked a strand of hair behind her ear.

"Henry James! Never has anyone taken such liberties! I am far from beautiful, and you know it." Nettie strode ahead of Henry, continuing along the shoreline. He ran to catch up with her.

"I see what I see, Nettie," Henry whispered as he leaned into her ear, "and I like what I see."

Nettie flushed for the first time in her life at a compliment that seemed more genuine than the water lapping at her feet. She had to wonder why she had avoided this handsome young man for so long. Conflicted, she did not want her mother to be right about him. *Oh what am I supposed to feel? He seems nice enough. But mother being right? Well, I'll have to wait it out and see.*

They walked on in silence, enjoying the warmth of the sun on their shoulders and the sound of an occasional fish splashing nearby. Henry dared slip his hand into hers and surprisingly, she did not protest.

Henry spotted a concession stand near a parking area. They ordered hot dogs with all the toppings and soft drinks. Nearby, a dock extended over the lake with benches on each side. To Henry, it served as a romantic place to eat their lunch. This lake walk and lunch were a far cry from the date she had envisioned. Initially, anyway. She had hoped for white tablecloths and silverware.

"Henry, I have to admit I was very cross with you for bringing me here. I dressed for a more elegant date and here we are at the lake eating hot dogs!" Her polite laughter brought a smile to Henry's lips.

"I thought if we were going to the cotillion together, we might as well get to know each other better."

A fish jumped in the water and left a rippling splash that caught Henry's attention. "Look, Nettie! Did you see that?"

"It's just a silly ole fish," she said, continuing to eat her hot dog.

"No, no, it's not just a silly ole fish. It's you!"

"Me! Henry James Pegram, how can you compare me to a fish!" Her indignation rose as Henry placed his hand on her shoulder.

"No, I meant no offense. Not at all. I have been watching you at school for quite some time. When I come up to you and make silly remarks, you walk away from me, not realizing the ripple you have made in my life. That fish is you. And the water is me. When I come around you, you jump away, leaving me with a greater desire to capture your heart."

Nettie froze. No one had ever said anything so kind, so sweet to her, other than her father.

"I….I don't know what to say," Nettie stuttered.

"You don't need to say anything. I wanted you to know up front how I feel about you. Actually, I can't believe I said it on a first date!"

"It's not a first date. It's hot dogs and a lake."

Henry laughed at her observation.

They both sat in silence, watching the sun's rays twinkle diamonds on the surface of the water.

Breaking the quiet, Henry softly spoke, "I understand if you don't want to go with me to the dance. I shouldn't have said what I did so soon. But, Nettie," he turned to face her, "I am smitten with you. I have been for some time. I will not hold you to going with me to the cotillion if you'd rather not." He could tell she was struggling for a response. "Are you ready for me to take you home?" he asked.

She nodded.

Rising, they threw their lunch remains in the trash can at the entrance to the pier. Slowly walking along the shore in the direction of the car, Nettie said, "Henry, I would like very much if you would escort me to the cotillion." She smiled into his handsome face.

Henry was thrilled that she accepted. It took a lot of man power to control the exuberance he felt, but he did. "My honor." He picked up her hand and kissed it gently.

They walked hand in hand back to the car and returned to Windy Garden.

Henry had been the perfect gentleman on their 'lake date.' Nettie was quite surprised that a date arranged by her mother could turn out to be so romantic and promising. She had hoped it would turn out to be a disaster so she could throw it in her mother's face. But it wasn't.

She had waited expectantly for the goodbye kiss at her doorstep, but it did not happen. Henry stroked her cheek and said, "I'll pick you up an hour before the cotillion. Thank you for coming with me today." He smiled and left.

His hand on her cheek had sent sent chills up her arm. She felt the goosebumps and watched him leave until he was out of sight.

Once inside, she ran like a little girl up to her room to change clothes. She donned a pale yellow silk and cotton ankle-length dress with a point Chelsea lace- trimmed collar. A powder blue sash belt adorned her hip. She sat at her dressing table, giggling at her day. As was customary, she pulled her hair into a bun. Before knotting the bun, she looked at herself from different angles.

"He likes my hair loose," she smiled, and ruffled her hair with her fingers. Never had a compliment felt so good. Staring at the mirror, she thought she did look kind of pretty. She left her hair down and went to meet her mother in the kitchen.

"Mother, surprisingly, I had a really good time with Henry today. We went to the lake and walked for what seemed hours. I'm really looking forward to the cotillion now."

Rose was making her usual grocery list at the kitchen dinette when she turned and looked at Nettie. "Nettie, why are you wearing your hair like that? Go upstairs and make yourself presentable. Long hair shouts 'I'm easy.' A bun is more respectable and practical. Go on now. And don't be late for dinner."

Nettie turned away from her mother so she would not see the hurt in her eyes. It was as if all energy drained from her body as she wearily climbed the stairs to her room, threw herself on her bed, and sobbed. She had hoped her mother would be pleased that the date she had arranged for her was a success.

She returned for dinner at six o'clock sharp. With her hair in a bun and not a strand out of place.

22

As Bonnie descended the stairs to the church basement for her weekly ladies Bible study, she could hear talking in the hallway. A familiar voice rose above the others. Approaching the huddled foursome, it was evident by the tone of their voices that there was a disagreement among them. Scooting around them to avoid being sucked into the vortex of the storm, Bonnie hugged the wall, taking care not to make eye contact.

"Good grief, Melva Jane, anybody knows that chartreuse and rose pink do not go together. You ought to get your vision checked. I've been on the committee for bathroom paint since Sherwin Williams borrowed money from my grandfather. Besides, didn't you tell me once that you are color blind?"

"Nettie Pegram, I know colors just as well as you do. And I am not color blind! This is a committee of *four*. Not a committee of one. We all have a say in the ladies bathroom colors. Right, Myrtle?"

Myrtle looked uncomfortable being stuck in the middle of her twin sister and Nettie.

Squeezing past the four women, Bonnie excused herself and eased around the gathered storm when Nettie stopped her.

"You. Bonnie, girl. Come over here and give us your objective opinion. We're discussing the paint colors for the ladies' bathroom. There is a small sitting area before entering the lavatories. I'm sure you've seen it. I think it should be painted deep mauve, and the bathroom walls a deep pink. Don't be shy now. Speak up! Let's hear what you think."

Bonnie dutifully obeyed and stopped. She looked from one lady to the other and saw faces that seemed to reflect their own opinions that were not being considered. This Nettie woman had placed her in a terribly embarrassing situation. She did not want to be drawn into a contest of opposing opinions, especially being the new kid in the church.

"I'm sure that all of you have wonderful ideas on the matter and I can't wait to see what you will agree to. Sorry, but I'm late to class."

Bonnie smiled and turned away quickly, feeling the stares penetrate her back. Her smile was genuine since she envisioned in her mind Miz Jessie guiding her wise words. "Chile, some things be yer business and if they be, then listen to all sides afore deciding what be best. If it ain't yer business, then don't git in it! Some folks gots to be part of everthin.' They think the chuch gonna up and die if they don't run it. But the chuch is God's chuch. It belong to Him. Uhuh, that's what I'm a sayin.'"

Jessie laid that one on her one Saturday morning when her mama asked her to help carry some cleaning supplies to Jessie's church. On the foot of the steps leading to the sanctuary stood several women arguing over choir robes. What color they should be. What kind of collars. No collars. Should there be a cape. No cape. Pockets. No pockets. Yes, pockets for hankies are a *must*.

As Bonnie and Miz Jessie approached the fussing gaggle, Miz Jessie grabbed Bonnie's hand and whispered sideways, "Now Chile, jus' keep walkin' straight into the chuch. Don't mind those women up there. They sure as rain gonna ask me what I thinks. I ain't on that committee, don't wanna be on that committee and don't care if they sings in their chuch dresses or pajamers. Long as the good Lawd knows we be praisin' Him, no matter whats we wear, I'm happy as a lark."

Miz Jessie marched up the steps with Bonnie's hand in her right and cleaning supplies in her left. Sure as rain, a tall, skinny woman with her hair braided into a bun stepped in Miz Jessie's way and said, "Jessie, you got some good sense to ya. What color choir robes ought we be gettin'?"

The silence was so loud that even the wind stopped blowing and the birds stopped chirping. Seemed all of creation hushed at this most important decision of all time.

Jessie looked at the assembled group, smiled her Miz Jessie smile, and said, "Well, Sadie…." She paused for dramatic affect. "Well, this be how I sees it, it ain't any of my business. And I don't think the good Lawd give a hoot or a holler what ya be wearin.' We's could be in the garden of Eden with nary a fig leaf sangin' our hearts out and He wouldn't care a bit. It's da heart He hear."

Hands on her hips, Sadie answered, "Well I suwanee, Jessie. It's just a robe. Cain't ya jus' pick a color?"

Jessie rolled her eyes, lifted her hand to the Lawd, then politely entered the church with Bonnie in tow.

"Miz Jessie, that was so funny!" Bonnie whispered out of earshot.

"I guess it was at that, lil un," Jessie laughed. "I jus' thinks that some folk get so wrapped up in doin' for the Lawd, that they forgets why they do what they do. Hit's all about Him. Uhuh, it is."

Bonnie snapped back to the sound of her Bible teacher asking everyone to be seated. *Whew! That was a close one,* she muttered to herself. *Miz Jessie is right. Sometimes the workings of the church becomes more important than worshipping God.* "*I'm jus' a sayin,*" she giggled to herself.

23

Nettie walked home frustrated with the paint committee and the bickering among them. After much discussion and debate, no decision was made. The grounds committee was waiting for an answer so they could purchase the paint and schedule the men of the church for a clean-up day.

She fumed as she walked, swinging her purse wildly. *Those people couldn't even decide on what brand of toilet paper to buy if given the choice. Oh, what is this world coming to? I could tell them, alright. Northern is two-ply and soft on the toosh. How hard is that? And don't they know how important it is to choose the right wall colors? The devil will take up residence between the commodes and the sinks if the walls are painted those ridiculous colors they want. Why, Myrtle had the gall to suggest, "Why don't we choose black for the men's room. Seems appropriate,* Nettie mocked. *"Good grief and a day, Myrtle! Black!"*

She was still talking to herself when she approached her house. *A decision has to be made soon and I'm going to do it. I'll just have to call Carl myself and tell him the colors I chose. Mauve and rose pink for the ladies and camel tan for the walls and chocolate brown trim for the men's. There! Done and done!*

Arriving at her back door, she heard her phone ringing. Quickly unlocking the door and entering the kitchen, she set her purse on the kitchen counter and picked up the receiver. "Hello?"

"Nettie, this is Cindy. The paint committee is still here at the church. I slipped away to call you. How about a compromise? You can have your rose pink walls and Melva Jane can have her grey trim? I think grey trim with the rose pink is a great idea. And you were right about the chartreuse. It was an odd combination. Surely, we can all agree to disagree and still make everyone happy. Picking paint colors must be a challenge for Melva Jane. I was over at her house the other day and all her walls are white!" Cindy laughed, trying to break the tension hanging heavily over the phone line. "What do you say, Nettie? A compromise?"

Nettie looked around at her own white walls and grunted. "Cindy, I appreciate your call. But I have already decided to call Carl and tell him to paint the entire ladies sitting area and bathroom rose pink with mauve trim and the men's room camel tan with chocolate brown trim. I've developed a migraine dealing with this and am making a final decision. But thank you for your input."

"But Nettie, you can't do that. The decision is to be made by the committee. We haven't even voted yet."

"Cindy, it is quite apparent that this committee will never reach an agreement that will pass a vote and since I am chairwoman of the committee, I have decided this has taken long enough. Now, if you don't mind I'm going to hang up, call Carl, take an aspirin and lie down. Good-bye." The click of the phone satisfied Nettie with her bold ruling. *I need to get this over with*, Nettie mumbled as she dialed Carl's number. "Hello, Carl? This is Nettie Pegram. I am calling to tell you the decision has been made on the paint colors for the men's and ladies bathrooms at church."

She began describing, in detail, the colors for each and how he should go about painting the walls and trim. "And don't leave any drips or you'll just have to redo the entire project. Thanks, Carl,

I've got to go. Good-bye."

Once again, Nettie got in the last word before the dial tone reset. It was her way. She had mastered the art of control and wielded it with great satisfaction.

Grabbing the bottle of aspirin, she downed two in one gulp. Then moved to the recliner to rest. Before she could shut her eyes, the doorbell rang. Grudgingly, she moseyed to the front door. Pulling back the lace curtains, she saw the three other paint committee members standing on the other side of the door.

Good grief! The nerve of them coming here. If I wanted to discuss this further, I would have called another meeting. Nettie's temples throbbed as she opened the door and stepped onto the porch as Melva Jane began her tirade of being left out of a vote. Myrtle merely nodded in agreement.

Cindy, who had only been a member of the church for five years, jumped in to play peacemaker. "Now girls, we all know that a committee has shared responsibilities in decision making and that it is proper to have a vote on the issue. So, let's calm down and try to get along. I'm sure we can come to some sort of agreement." She looked pleadingly at each one.

But Melva Jane was not finished. "Nettie, you just have to have your way all the time, don't you? Well, for once, you will not. We are going to vote and that is that!"

Exasperated and out of patience, Nettie grudgingly acquiesced. "Fine! Let's vote. But may I remind you, Melva Jane, who financed your down payment on your house when your husband couldn't save two cents to save his life."

Looking to her left at Myrtle, she said, "And who helped pay hospital bills for your Hudson when he had an appendix operation and never asked for a dime in return?"

Looking at Cindy, she stopped there, since she had nothing on her.

The intimidation continued. "Fine, let's vote," Nettie urged. "All those in favor of rose pink walls and mauve trim for the ladies' room and camel tan with chocolate brown for the men's room, say aye."

An embarrassed gasp escaped Melva Jane's lips. Without making eye contact with her two companions, she dropped her head. Myrtle squeezed her hand gently and the two replied together in a whispered tone, "Aye."

"All those opposed?"

"Nay," said Cindy, who saw the deck stacked before her, but voted her conscience anyway.

"The 'ayes' have it!" Nettie proclaimed. "Now if you girls will excuse me, I have a splitting headache."

"You know something, Nettie?" Melva Jane said meekly, yet pointedly. "You have become your mother."

Nettie's jaw dropped. But before she could respond, Melva Jane and Myrtle had descended the steps. The silence was deafening. Cindy looked at Nettie, shook her head and followed the ladies to the sidewalk.

Turning to go inside, she overheard Cindy stop the twins and ask, "How could you girls give in to that? She bullied you into going along with her."

"Nettie always gets her way. She always has and always will. Her family has helped lots of people in this town over decades and no one will challenge her. For all practical purposes her family has owned this town from its beginnings. She shared publicly what once was very private. I feel totally humiliated. Let's go home. I can't deal with this anymore."

Nettie saw Melva Jane's shoulders slump as the three women walked out of sight. Entering her house, she turned and slammed the door. She paused and for a brief moment regretted what she had said. Slowly, she walked over to the window and parted the curtain. The girls had disappeared down the street. Before dropping the curtain in place, she noticed the Bonnie girl standing beside an oak tree at the edge of her property.

What is she doing there? Is she eavesdropping on us? I have a mind to march out there and give her a piece of my mind! But her headache grew in intensity and she gave in to the recliner instead.

Bonnie was shocked at the loud exchange between these God-fearing women of the church. After Bible study, she had changed into her walking clothes and set off for her daily exercise. Her shoelace had slipped out of its knot and she bent to tie it when she heard the loud voices. She did not mean to overhear anything so dreadful.

Stooped over her shoe, Bonnie looked at the house and saw Nettie drop the curtain back in place. *Oh no, she saw me! I didn't intend to overhear anything! I just felt I should not approach and embarrass anyone. Well, that didn't work! Oh, what do I do now? I was beginning to make strides with Miss Nettie and now....well, now I'm not sure what will happen next.*

Continuing on with her walk, she felt sad for Miss Nettie and the other three women as well. It sounded like longtime relationships had just been shattered. Along with her hope of befriending Miss Nettie. It quickly turned into a sad day all around. The only thing that seemed powerful enough to break the spell of these foolish exchanges was a hand-dipped strawberry shake. Picking up her pace, she headed downtown.

24

Two days later, Nettie dodged rain drops on her way to Henry's grave. She felt drained of all energy since last Thursdays unpleasant showdown with the paint committee. She almost chose to stay home and not visit Henry, but in five years she had not missed a single Saturday. Since she always carried cleaning supplies to the cemetery, she drove the short three blocks to Henry's resting place.

Opening the trunk, she lifted out her usual paraphernalia and closed the lid. Carrying an umbrella was awkward at best, with one hand holding a bucket, and the other balancing a stool.

When she approached Henry's marker, she placed the stool in position, set the bucket down and tried to hold the umbrella over her Friday hairdo. She greeted Henry with a weak smile. "It's Saturday, my dear." She stared at Henry's name for a long time. Sitting on the stool she pondered what to say. She wanted to talk with him about last Thursday but she wasn't quite sure how to begin. She desperately needed Henry's ear. She sighed, painfully aware how she had been a much more pleasant person when Henry was alive. He seemed to find the good in her. Good she could not seem to see in herself.

Drawing a deep breath, she mustered the courage and plunged in. "What is happening to people around here, Henry? I have to let this out or I'll burst! Remember when I told you I was on the paint committee at church? Well, those looney twins just came up with the most outlandish color choices you have ever heard of. If I told you, you would think they had gone completely mad. Anyway, you know how particular I am about how the church looks. I could not in all good conscience let them paint the bathrooms those hideous color combinations they suggested. If I had let them have their way, the whole church would blame me for how awful they looked. Black, Henry! They wanted to paint the men's room black!"

Nettie arched her back working out the kinks. She regretted not placing a bench on this very spot a long time ago but thought better of it since she would be positioned right over Henry's chest. Straightening, she continued, "They were so upset over our meeting Thursday morning, they marched over to my house and yelled at me. When I told them I had gone ahead and called Carl to begin the painting without a vote, they were furious. And get this! Melva Jane accused me of becoming my mother. It was the final insult. I am nothing like mother! She was controlling, manipulative, and unloving. When Melva Jane said that, she cut me to the quick. And she's supposed to be my friend. Why would she attack me like that? I AM NOT MY MOTHER!!" Nettie had worked herself into a frenzy. She would not, *could not* believe she was anything like Rose.

"Well, if she can accuse me of something so malicious as that, then she is not my friend. How dare she? How dare she, Henry!" The rain was beginning to let up. She picked up the polishing cloth from the bucket and rubbed the headstone, harder than she ever had before. "I will never speak to her again for as long as I live!" Being compared to her mother infuriated her.

Standing to inspect her work on the headstone, she felt satisfied. "There. It's done. And I'm so glad the rain stopped." She lovingly patted the headstone, and with a deep sigh said, "I do wish you were here. I miss you. I know I was not very affectionate but honestly, Henry, if you'd come back, I'd let you hold me more. Kiss me more. Tease me more. I'd lean on your strong shoulder and shut out this pathetic world."

Gathering up the supplies, she walked away. Reaching her car, she slipped the cleaning items into her trunk. Hearing the lid snap shut, she felt a sudden chill. She sensed the finality of something valuable. The realization that she was cutting off her closest friends caused a shudder to seize her. She wrapped her arms around herself, warding off the invisible cold. A foreboding overshadowed her, a sense of dread, as she slipped into the driver's seat and slowly headed home.

Walking up the sidewalk toward the church, Pastor Randy heard a familiar voice. He stopped and followed the voice, coming from the cemetery. There sat Nettie, on a stool in front of Henry's grave. He was well aware of her weekly Saturday visits to the gravesite and wished there was something he could do to help her be free of whatever kept her upset with everyone. Before Henry died, Nettie was condescendingly polite, yet enjoyable to be around on her good days. He knew, too, that Henry's loving influence on her life contributed to her change of demeanor. But after Henry died, Nettie regressed. She reverted back to the behavior of her upbringing, or so he was told by her best friend, Ida Mae, who loved Nettie dearly and was concerned for her health and state of mind.

Instead of stopping and interrupting Nettie, Randy continued on toward the church. He prayed as he walked, and asked God for direction. He knew she was unhappy with his sermons of late and would welcome the opportunity to talk with her once again in private, in an effort to help her understand that the love Henry had for her was a love he received from his relationship with God.

Fond memories flooded his senses as he remembered the times he and Henry would sneak away from work to go fishing. They kept their fishing poles in their offices and when one called the other, they quickly grabbed their poles and hurried off to the Tuckasegee River. They would stand on the bank and talk while watching the bobbers for any sign of a strike. Most of their conversations centered on Jesus. Randy remembered a particular conversation one day that would begin a change in his life. One that would affect Randy personally, as well as his ministry.

"Pastor, I was wondering something." Henry's eyes gazed about at the mountains surrounding the lake.

"Wondering what?" Randy answered.

"Well, I've been thinking on this for some time and have never been sure it is something I should ask."

"Henry, you can ask me anything. I think highly of you and your walk with God. Not to mention your friendship."

Henry smiled and set his pole on the bank where he could keep an eye on it if a fish struck his line. He turned and faced Randy. Gathering his thoughts, he cleared his throat and said, "Thank you for your kind words, Pastor. It means a lot coming from you. I don't mean any offense in what I am about to ask, though. I'm just curious."

Randy set his pole down as well. The men sat down on the ground settling in for the curious question.

"I enjoy your preaching very much. I do. I was just wondering why you mention so little of Jesus' love. Mostly I hear how we don't behave right and what we should do about it." Henry plucked a blade of grass and ran it through his fingers. "I guess it seems to me that if we could really embrace how much God loves us, our behavior would not be such an issue."

Randy leaned back on his hands and said, "I have to say I didn't expect that particular question!" He laughed, putting Henry at ease. Pondering the puzzling question, he glanced at the lake, wondering how to respond. Turning to Henry he said, "Well, I don't think anyone has ever asked me that before. I…I…." He stopped and stared ahead at the lake, uneasy about looking Henry in the eye. What was making him so uncomfortable? Glancing over briefly, he observed Henry pulling his pipe from his fishing tackle box and lighting it with a match. *Always the gracious Henry,* he smiled.

Silence prevailed. Moments that shook Randy to the core of his faith. *Is it true I mention so little of Jesus' love?*

Just then, Henry's line tugged. He jumped to his feet and grabbed his rod. A fish jumped out of the water and gave Henry a fight. "Pastor, look! I have a bite!"

Randy barely noticed his excitement. He was gazing into the heavens, looking for an answer to this most crushing question.

Henry pulled the fish to shore and proudly scooped it up with his fishing net. It was a good sized trout. Big enough to keep and have for supper. Nettie would not be pleased one bit. She detested the smell of fish in her house. She would pretend to be upset when he walked into the kitchen holding a dripping wet fish in his hands. She would snatch it from him, throw it in the sink and say, "Oh

Henry, what am I going to do with you?" He placed the fish in his fishing basket and looked over at Randy. He saw tears running down the man's face. Henry felt as though he had terribly offended his pastor and friend. He walked over to him and put his hand on his shoulder. "Pastor, I believe I owe you an apology. I am very sorry if I have upset you. It was not a fair question."

Randy rose to his feet and wiped the tears with the back of his hand. "No, no, please do not apologize. I have always valued your insight. I believe this is a question I will need to chew on for a while. In fact, I think you may have hit on the very thing that I have struggled with for quite some time. Thank you for drawing it to my attention." Randy's gaze fell on the wiggling fish basket. "You caught a fish!"

"Yep. It's a trout, probably sixteen inches. But my tale will be that it is two foot!!" They laughed and slapped each other on the back. It was time to leave and head back to work. Henry was elated over the fish, but secretly concerned he may have hurt his dear friend.

Randy left more subdued than when he had arrived. Henry's question rattled him to the core of his faith. He had known Henry to be a tender and compassionate man, gracious and loving. Randy held him in the highest regard and secretly envied his simple faith. Posing the question the way he did, Randy was forced to face a conundrum he had struggled with for years. Had he come face to face with the very issue he had so desperately avoided all these years? If so, his life and ministry would change. And change did not come easily to Baptists.

It took almost two years for the truth of that question to finally penetrate Randy's heart. That day with Henry began a journey that would eventually lead to a profound mountain experience that would set him free. Free from trying to earn God's love, free from constantly reminding his congregation of their sins and the need for them to do something to make it right. Free to experience all that Jesus had done for him at the cross and to share it with his flock. A freedom he wished Nettie could now embrace.

Arriving at the steps to the church, Randy looked over and saw Nettie gathering her supplies. He thought of rushing over to help, but thought better of it. The last time he offered to help, she made it quite clear that time with her Henry was only for the two of them. He could hear her voice traveling across the parking lot. He had to smile. She must not know how her voice travels when she is there. He could usually hear every word. *Wouldn't she be mortified?* he chuckled, closing the door behind him.

25

Fall had finally arrived! It was Bonnie's favorite season of the year. She had looked forward to this day for months.

Saturday morning brought an excitement to the air as the townspeople of Windy Garden prepared to celebrate their biggest festival of the year. The anticipation of autumn lifted the spirits of those who had tired of the hot summer weather. Fall crops were at their peak and fragrant apples filled the air with dreams of apple pies, apple cobbler, applesauce and apple butter. Women had been busy sterilizing mason jars, pulling large pots out of storage, crock pots at the ready to can the various apple recipes. It was also time to break out the sweaters and scarves.

Anticipating her first fall celebration in her new town, Bonnie woke early. The ladies of the Baptist Church had planned a large booth with crafts, baked goods, and crocheted doilies, hats, and blankets. All donations were going to the Children's Home. Bonnie's contribution was a rag quilt she had made from donated old clothes. She was proud of her accomplishment. Will asked her why she would make something so tacky.

"It's not tacky. It's creative," Bonnie countered.

"Let's just hope that thing sells, so we don't have to bring it back home," laughed Will. Obviously, he was not at all impressed with Bonnie's project. He was well aware sewing was not her strong talent. The truth was she had no talent for sewing whatsoever. Period. Finishing his coffee, he hugged her shoulders in what Bonnie thought was a slightly patronizing gesture.

I'll show him. This lovely quilt will sell fast! She held it up for one last look, pleased with the many colors and varied fabrics. *Yep, it's real purty.* Even Miz Jessie would be proud of her efforts. Bonnie remembered a sewing project assigned in home economics class in the eighth grade. All the students were to make an apron. The teacher handed out instructions and sent the joyful students home to find fabric. Bonnie couldn't wait to get home and tell her mother.

"Mama!" she yelled as the screen door wap-wapped behind her.

Miz Jessie was peeling apples at the kitchen sink. Bonnie looked around and asked, "Where's mama?"

Before Miz Jessie could answer, Bonnie's mom Verna appeared in the doorway. "What is it, Bonnie? I could hear you clear across the house."

"Oh, I couldn't wait to tell you. I have to make an apron for home economics class. I need fabric. Do you have any I could use? I can't wait to get started this afternoon!" Her voice escalated with each word.

"Let's go have a look." Her mother went to the bedroom, the young Bonnie in tow, pulled a box from under her bed, and sat on the floor. The two searched through a myriad of fabrics, and found a leftover piece with a green gingham pattern. "How about this one?" She held it up before Bonnie.

"Mama! That's the fabric you used to make my bedroom curtains. I can't use that! Everyone will know."

"Who knows what your room curtains look like, except Shellie?"

"Well…well," Bonnie struggled to come up with anyone else. "They would know. I just know they would." Her face fell at the thought of her apron looking like a curtain.

"Do you have any instructions that tell how much fabric you need?" her mother asked.

"Yes I do!" Bonnie jumped up and ran to the kitchen table where she had deposited her backpack from school. She rummaged through the disorganized bag and pulled out the instruction sheet her teacher had handed out. She ran back to her mother and handed it to her. Reading the paper, Verna said, "It says here that you need a half yard of fabric." Looking again in the box, she found another piece that might work. "How about this one? I made you a dress from this last year."

"Oh mama, don't you have anything else? I wore that dress so much last year that Matt McClary teased me all the way up to Christmas." Bonnie sat back on her heels and groaned.

"I'm sorry, honey, but it's all we have."

"Can't we buy a piece of new fabric?" Bonnie pleaded.

"No, honey, I'm afraid we can't. Not just now. Harvest is coming in but the money hasn't. We have to watch our spending very closely right now." Verna patted Bonnie's hand, hoping she'd understand.

"Oh, I just don't know what to do." Bonnie's bottom lip quivered.

"Tell you what," mother began, "Why, don't you make a mutli-colored apron? You can use a little of all of them!"

Bonnie's hopes soared. "That's a great idea! No one else could possibly have one like it! Thank you, mama!!" Bonnie leaped over and hugged her mother almost knocking her backwards.

"Can we start now?"

Looking at the instructions once more, Verna said, "Well, it says here the sewing must be done in class, all except the handwork. So you won't be able to make it at home."

Disappointed, Bonnie said, "Ok then." They spent the next few minutes pulling out different fabrics that Bonnie liked and put them in a small paper bag for her to take to school the next day.

Bonnie tossed and turned all night long. She was so excited over the sewing project that she slept with the bag of fabric at her feet. The next morning, she bounded into class to show the teacher her fabric. She dumped its contents on the teacher's desk. Smiling and proud, she said, "Look at all the pretty colors! I can't wait to get started. Do we begin sewing today?"

Not wanting to break the spirit of this bubbly young girl, but knowing she had no choice, the teacher said, "Bonnie, these are beautiful colors. They really are." She fingered the small pieces. "But we just don't have the time to sew all these pieces together and then make an apron in the time allowed for this class. I'm afraid you will have to bring in one piece that is large enough. I'm sorry." She placed her hand on Bonnie's slouched shoulders.

"But, but, the only piece we have big enough is leftover curtain fabric," she whispered so no one else could hear.

The teacher whispered back, "That will be fine, Bonnie. It will be our little secret."

Bonnie reluctantly returned the next day with the green checkered gingham. She cut her fabric. The edges were crooked. Her scissors tore at the fabric instead of cutting smoothly. It was an ugly beginning. She then proceeded to sew the front to the back with no opening. Holding it up, tears ran down her cheeks. She noticed the other student's aprons had openings. Before class ended they had to make the band long enough for tie strings. Bonnie's rolled and curled.

When the other kids left for their next class, Bonnie put her head on her sewing table and cried. The teacher knew the reason for the tears and approached her unhappy little protege. "Bonnie, let me look at your apron." Examining each piece she said, "This is not so bad. It can be fixed. Tell you what. Take it home and redo the whole project. I grade on effort, not looks. You are doing just fine."

Bonnie wiped her tears with her sleeve and thanked her teacher. She sulked all day over the dumb project that she wished she had never started. Once home, she pulled the pitiful apron from her backpack and laid it on the kitchen table. Her mother and Miz Jessie stared wordlessly.

"Bonnie, what happened?" her mother asked, holding back her laughter, hand over her mouth.

"I... I don't know! I followed the instructions. But look at this. It's a mess!" She dropped into a dining table chair and blew the bangs off her face.

Verna hurried out of the room and came back with her sewing basket. Miz Jessie was still staring at the green checkered gingham, wondering what it was.

"Here, Bonnie, start ripping out all the seams. We'll start over."

Mama's smile encouraged Bonnie and gave her a glimmer of hope. She picked up the seam ripper and proceeded, picking out the thread. With each rip, the fabric frayed.

"Wait, wait," said her mama reaching for the seam ripper, "like this." Showing Bonnie the proper way to remove the thread without fraying the delicate edges, she pulled the thread through without effort. Mama reached over and set the sewing machine on the table before them. "Now, let's sew." Bonnie watched her mother sew the seams with ease.

"Oh, that is so pretty," exclaimed Bonnie.

Next, her mama cut a new piece of fabric for the band. She placed the folded piece under the needle and sewed the edges shut. "Now, it is inside out. You have to pull it through, so the seam is hidden inside." Miz Jessie handed Bonnie a wooden spoon and Bonnie pushed and pushed until she could grab the end. Before long, there were two finished pieces on the table, ready to be put together.

"I don't think I will ever get the hang of this. Sewing is just not my thing." Bonnie wished she had the skills her mother had.

"It takes practice. Lots of practice."

"Well I can tell you this. I am glad this project is done. But I still think I will be laughed at in school. Can I go see if Shellie can come over?"

"Sure," her mama said, "Go have some fun."

Bonnie kissed her mother's cheeks and waved at Miz Jessie. Before the screen door finished wap-wapping, the two ladies burst out laughing. They couldn't contain it any longer.

Bonnie heard the laughter, stopped, looked back and shrugged her shoulders. *Well I better get used to that,* she sighed.

The next day Bonnie took her finished project to school. She handed it to her teacher who was very impressed. "Why, Bonnie, this is lovely!" She told her teacher that she did very little sewing, that her mother put most of it together. Confessing eased the guilt of her ineptness.

"What did you learn, Bonnie?"

Stammering, Bonnie answered, "That I don't want to sew anything else for the rest of my life!"

Looking down at the rag quilt folded over her arm for the auction, Bonnie remembered how generous her home economics teacher was in giving her a "B" for the apron. "If she could see my quilt, I'm sure she would give me an "A!"

By nine o'clock in the morning, downtown Windy Garden was buzzing with excitement. Main Street was closed on each end to allow unhindered access and safety to the many people who would mill around the displays. Covered booths and open tables revealed the hard work of the folks who spent months preparing for this occasion. Mr. Spears had a knife-sharpening table, the Apothecary had two long tables with hamburgers and hot dogs ready for the grill. The auction area was huge! It was situated at the end of Main Street with rows and rows of chairs, under a huge white tent. Inside, a raised platform with a preacher-like podium stood ready for the auctioneer. A megaphone stood ready for action on the stand.

The auction was to begin promptly at noon. Every participant was to have their items registered and in place. The sewn items were to be suspended on clothesline that was strung around the entire tent. Ladies from several churches and organizations lined up to sign the forms and drop off their treasures. Bonnie stood in line with her patchwork rag quilt, caressing the fabric as though it were a prized pet. When it was her turn, she gently draped it over her spot on the line. A man with a clipboard tagged her quilt with her name and donation cause. She read the card with pleasure. *Bonnie McDaniel, First Baptist Church of Windy Garden, to benefit the Baptist Children's Home.* Other volunteers helped the older ladies hang theirs.

Bonnie stepped back a distance to admire her quilt hanging proudly next to a gorgeous hand-crafted wedding ring quilt. Looking back and forth between the two, her knees grew weak. She thought she might lose her breakfast. The other quilt was amazing! *Maybe if I step back even farther, it will look at lot better*, she thought. Taking two steps backwards, she bumped into someone. "Oh, excuse me," she said, turning around.

"You need to be more careful with this many people milling around, Bonnie."

"Oh, Miss Nettie, I am so sorry, I didn't see you. I was looking at all the beautiful quilts up for auction." Her gaze settled back on the display of quilts.

"Yes, they are very nice. I never liked to sew, myself. But I do know there is a lot of work in them. It's beyond me why someone would want to put that much work into a project just to give it away."

Bonnie was barely listening, staring at her quilt that looked so out of place among the other beautiful creations.

"Oh my!" Nettie gasped, her hand on her throat.

"What? What's wrong?" Bonnie asked in concern.

"Would you look at that one, third from the right? It is the most hideous thing I have ever seen! Who in their right mind would display something like that for charity? Surely, it's a joke."

Bonnie's eyes welled with tears as she excused herself and turned to see Will standing only a few feet from her. She ran into his arms. He led her outside the tent and found a private space near the street.

"Nettie, how could you?" came a familiar voice to Nettie's right.

Turning, Nettie saw a horrified look on Ida Mae's face. "What? What are you talking about?"

Ida Mae moved slowly over to the rag quilt and reached for the card hanging on the edge. She turned it to face Nettie.

Nettie took a step closer, leaning forward. Startled, she stepped back. "But....but I didn't know."

Ida Mae saw Nettie's face turn ashen and spoke softly, "It doesn't matter. You should have held your thoughts to yourself." Ida Mae turned before Nettie could respond and left the tent.

Stepping forward again and reaching with trembling hands, she turned the card over once more. *Bonnie McDaniel*, read the card. She gasped with a hand to her throat. *Oh my! I didn't mean to hurt the girl. I really didn't.*

Nettie hurriedly left the auction tent. Finding the town swing with her father's name on it, she sat down heavily. *Oh, why do I say these things? Why, father?*

Will had led Bonnie to an old oak tree across the street from the auction and said, "I heard what she said, Bonnie, and I am so sorry. I feel like I have let you down too. I didn't realize how much this meant to you. I really am sorry."

Will walked his wife back to the empty tent and looked again at the quilt his wife had made out of love. Cocking his head this way and that he said, "From this distance, it looks really good."

Bonnie shook her head and added, "Yeah. And it will look a whole lot better from the depot, too."

Will kissed her. "Let's go see what the festival has to offer. It might cheer you up."

Together they walked among the rows and rows of canning displays, wood turning and log splitting demonstrations, cotton candy and funnel cake vendors, kid tables, apple sellers and so much more. Bonnie was mulling over the idea of withdrawing her quilt from the auction, when Kathy came up beside her, bubbling over the exhibits at the festival. Will excused himself to visit the gun display one row over. Slipping away, he winked at his wife.

The two girls chatted for several minutes, when a loud voice announced that the judging for the quilt auction would begin in fifteen minutes.

Oh no, Bonnie said to herself, *I was hoping to sneak back into the tent and retrieve my quilt before the auction.* Dropping her head, she knew it was too late.

"I had better find Bob," Kathy said. "He has already bought back his pies and put them in the car. Teehee! I'm sure he will want to be at the auction. See you later, girl." Kathy waved and disappeared in the crowd.

Bonnie looked around for Will, but couldn't see him anywhere. Sighing and highly embarrassed, she grudgingly walked in the direction of the auction tent. Most of the seats were filled with people. There was no way she would be able to retrieve her quilt now and leave without drawing attention to herself. She stood in desperation at the back of the auction tent. A few minutes later the auctioneer stepped onto the platform and picked up the megaphone. Cheers sounded. And the auction began.

The wedding quilt next to Bonnie's was the first to be sold, The church secretary bought it for her soon to be daughter-in-law for $100. Each one quickly sold, while hers hung pitifully alone. She sat heavily in a vacant chair and wished she could disappear.

Finally, the auctioneer pointed to Bonnie's quilt. He did not mention her name as he did the others, but announced, "This quilt is in a category all its own. So, the committee has decided that it will be sold in a silent auction. If anyone would like to bid on this quilt, come forward and fill out a form with the amount you propose and drop it in this bucket. We will announce the winner in 30 minutes." A wooden box with a slit in the top was placed on the auctioneer table. Several people laughed and stood to leave.

Bonnie watched as one by one, the people left the tent, leaving only a few seated up front. She never saw anyone go forward. Never had she been so embarrassed. With a heavy heart, she stepped outside the tent. She hoped to find Will quickly. Once on Main Street, she meandered through the crowds, when a hand touched her arm. It was Will.

"Where have you been? I've been looking for you." Searching her face, he said, "You look upset. Are you not feeling well, honey?"

"My tummy is a little upset, that's all."

"Has the auction started yet?" Will asked.

Rolling her eyes, she said, "Will, it started a half hour ago."

"Oh. I'm sorry. I didn't hear the announcement. How did it go?"

"Can we go home? I can tell you about it on the way."

"Bonnie what's the matter? How did it go with your quilt?"

Sighing, Bonnie recanted the selling of the other quilts.

"And yours?" Will pressed.

"Mine is up for a silent auction in a few minutes."

The disappointment was not hard to detect. "Well, let's wait for that, ok? I'm sure it will do well for the children's home. Let get some lunch, ok?"

"No one went forward to place an offer in the box. It's not going to sell. I am so humiliated."

"You don't know that. It might sell. C'mon, it's the fall festival. Let's try to enjoy the rest of the day," he pleaded.

Bonnie shrugged her shoulders and Will led her to the Pete's BBQ and Grill trailer and purchased two BBQ sandwiches and drinks. They sat down at a table off to the side. Will gulped down his sandwich. Bonnie did not touch hers.

"Honey, please. You need to eat something."

"I can't eat. I just want to sneak that quilt out of there and go home."

"Then can I have your sandwich? They're really good."

Bonnie pushed her plate over to Will.

"SILENT AUCTION BEGINS IN FIVE MINUTES," came the voice again. Bonnie jumped.

Will finished his last bite and grabbed Bonnie's hand. "See! Five minutes. Let's go." Will led his reluctant wife into the tent. He started toward the front row of chairs, when Bonnie pulled back on his hand.

"No, Will. I don't want to sit up front. Let's sit in the back. I want to be able to slip out quietly." She found two seats in the very last row and sat down. Will followed, looking over the heads of the people in front.

To Bonnie's dismay, the tent was once again full of people, no doubt to see who would be foolish enough to buy her wretched quilt.

Will looked around and saw the auctioneer pick up the megaphone.

"The auction is about to begin."

Bonnie crossed her arms and looked up where her rag quilt was hanging. It was gone! *Where did it go? Maybe the judges took it down, after looking it over more carefully, embarrassed by the poor quality. Oh, I wish I had never made the dumb thing.*

"Attention. Attention, please." The laughter and talk subsided and the auction tent slowly grew quiet. Bonnie was sure they were talking and laughing about her. She could still hear her mama and Miz Jessie laughing over the high school apron. And added to that, Miss Nettie's harsh but honest words ringing loudly in her ears.

"Thank you for coming to the silent auction. As you can tell, the quilt is no longer hanging before you. I'm sure you are wondering where it is. Let me explain. Earlier this morning we had a request for a silent auction on this one item. The person making this request asked for it to be sold with anonymous bids to which the auctioneers agreed. The quilt sold and the highest bidder took it home immediately. Not only that but it was the highest selling quilt of the day. We would like to thank all the quilters for their hard work and dedication to a wonderful cause."

Bonnie was shocked. Her quilt sold for more than all those exquisitely hand crafted quilts? *There must be some mistake*, she thought.

"For all of you waiting to hear, the rag quilt sold for...." He hesitated, drawing out the announcement, "... for $300!"

The room exploded in applause. A few commented in Bonnie's hearing how that horribly stitched, unevenly seamed quilt could have sold for more than theirs. She was stunned. She inched herself taller in her seat. Will hugged her and whispered, "See! It sold! And made more money than any of the others. Congratulations!"

Bonnie didn't know what to say. Kathy ran over and hugged Bonnie tight. "I am so excited for you! I didn't know they did silent auctions here. But girl, I am so proud of you!" Will nodded at Bob and the couple left.

Bonnie's stomach miraculously calmed down. She asked Will to buy her another bbq sandwich with fries and a coke. She even shared a funnel cake with her sweet husband.

"I can't believe it! Who would do such a thing? I know it was the ugliest one there. It looked so terrible next to those professional looking quilts hanging all around it. You were right, babe, it was tacky!" Bonnie laughed. "But I am so glad it made money for the children's home."

Will put his arm around his wife and said, "Whoa there! I remember I had to apologize for saying that a little while ago."

"I know," she giggled, "but it was. I just didn't want to admit it. Still, I wonder who bought it."

26

One week later, after the town's excitement over the fall festival subsided, Nettie rose from bed, made a strong cup of coffee, and sat at the dining room table. Normally, she put the coffee on the stove, went back to her bedroom and dressed for the day. She was taught to be prepared upon rising, lest someone drop by unexpectedly. This was not to be a normal day.

Sipping her coffee slowly, she sighed. She looked about her spacious home and felt like a stranger. The house was empty without Henry. She remembered how she used to have friends and Henry's clients over for brunch quite often. The aroma of quiche in the oven and the beautifully arranged table settings adorned her dining room. Fresh flowers from her garden graced the center of the table, emitting the fragrance of her favorite Irish Elegance Rose bush. It was a fond memory.

Nettie walked back to the kitchen and refilled her coffee cup, catching a glimpse of her reflection in the glass window above the sink. Her hands traced the lines on her face. She remarked on how she had changed. "You used to be quite attractive. At least my Henry thought so. What has happened to you?" She mindlessly wandered into the living room and looked around. She did not want to be in this empty room alone. So she opened the front door and stepped onto her porch. Thoughts of yesterday flooded her with sadness. Nothing had changed overnight. She sighed in absolute resignation that life was meaningless and worthless without Henry.

Sauntering over to her rocker, she stroked the back with her hand. It was her most prized possession in all the world. She sat down and sank back into its familiar grooves. Setting her coffee cup on the side table, she leaned back and ignored the world, lost in her own grief, lost in despair.

She had not heard from Melva Jane and Myrtle in over two weeks, ever since the episode on paint colors. The silence added to her misery and loneliness.

Bonnie got an early start to the morning. She had no time to waste. She was meeting with Sue, the pastor's wife, at 8 a.m. at the church and maybe having an early lunch. She did not want to be late. Miz Jessie used to say being late was 'plumb rude.' Leaving a little early, Bonnie decided to reverse her usual route to change things up a bit. She passed cows grazing in the fields, old barns and broken down silos. Past the depot and onto the downtown street of Windy Garden, she noticed how beautifully serene it was this time of morning. No one about. No noise, except for birds chirping merrily in the trees. Main Street was quiet and peaceful. The sun was just beginning to break the sky and a cloud hung low obscuring the distant mountains. She turned down Depot Street and caught a stirring to her left. She stopped to catch her breath and sip water from the container hanging around her waist. Placing the container back in its awkward holder, she saw Nettie sitting in her rocker on the front porch. Bonnie waved. There was no response.

Maybe she didn't see me. She took a few steps closer and softly called her name. "Miss Nettie?" Still no response. Bonnie grew concerned. She stepped a little closer. "Miss Nettie, are you alright?"

The rocker stopped and slowly Nettie's head pulled forward. She looked completely drained of energy. Bonnie watched her carefully, noting how she seemed disoriented and unfamiliar with her surroundings. Nettie removed her glasses and rubbed her eyes. Her hands moved along the arms of the chair. After rubbing her eyes once more, she replaced her glasses, dropped her hands to her lap and became still.

By now, Bonnie had reached the bottom step leading to the porch. With her hand on the rail, she leaned forward and asked again, more quietly this time, "Miss Nettie, are you alright?"

Nettie turned and glanced in Bonnie's direction, but there was no recognition in her eyes that she had even seen Bonnie. Closing her eyes once again, she rested back against the rocker.

Peeking around the porch post, Bonnie noticed Nettie was still in her nightclothes. She looked as if she had just risen from bed. Her hair had not been brushed and she wore slippers on her feet. "Miss Nettie is sitting outside with her nightclothes on!" Bonnie gasped. Never had she seen this puritanical lady without being properly dressed and every hair in place. The prim Nettie Pegram would never want anyone seeing her like this. Something was drastically wrong. *Oh my! I need to get help. What should I do? Should I run to the church and get Pastor Randy? He won't be in for a couple of hours. Or should I slip inside and call for a doctor? But I don't know a doctor here in this town yet. Oh Lord, what can I do?*

Bonnie eased herself onto the porch deck and sat down on the railing, not saying a word, just sitting and waiting, hoping to be of some help or comfort to this woman who puzzled her at every turn.

She knew from prior confrontations and talks that Miss Nettie might be hurting something awful. Miz Jessie often said that 'some folk hurt sa bad inside they shut out everone and everthang. They jus' cain't seem to let anyone in. It be a sad thang to behold. It surely tis.'

Nettie stirred and rolled her head. She rubbed her eyes again and looked about. She looked over to her right and saw Bonnie. "What…what are you doing here?" she asked in a daze.

"I was walking by and called your name several times, but you never answered. I thought something might be wrong. I just wanted to be near you, if you needed me."

Nettie groaned and sat back into the rocker. Wearily, she said, "Go home, Bonnie. Go home."

Never had she heard Nettie speak like this. Bonnie's internal alarm rang again. She knew she should not leave her alone. Not like this. Why… she didn't know. She just knew. "If it is alright with you, I'd like to stay here beside you. I thought you might need a friend this morning."

"Friend! Friend!" Nettie bolted upright. An unexpected surge of energy burst through her body. "I don't need a friend or anyone. Just leave me alone and let me die!" She leaned back and closed her eyes once again.

Bonnie could hardly believe her ears. *Is she saying what I think she is saying? No, that can't be true. She must be upset and talking out of her head. Has to be. She is usually so self-assured, so in control. What could possibly have gotten her this upset? Oh, if someone would just walk down the street. I could ask them to call for help.* Bonnie looked up the street one way and back the other.

The sun was rising, but no one was about.

I don't know what to do. I can't leave her alone. I'm so afraid for her. Maybe if I sit here real quiet, she will wake up as her old self.

Within minutes, Bonnie heard Nettie's breathing ease. Without moving her body, Bonnie turned her head to see Nettie sleeping, fitfully but soundly. Bonnie's legs cramped from sitting in the same position for so long, her legs dangling over the railing.

She wasn't sure how long she had been there but needed to change positions. She moved her hips to allow feeling back in her legs. A soft snort alerted her than Nettie was stirring.

Stretching her arms and looking down, Nettie's eyes widened. She looked around and pushed to her feet. Her gaze traveled down to the nightgown and slippers, and she gasped. Folding her arms across her bodice, she bolted for the door. Not seeing Bonnie, she almost tripped over her. The shock of someone there infuriated Nettie. Startled, she yelled, "Why in the name of heaven are you still here?"

Bonnie grasped for words that stuck in her throat.

"I thought I told you to go home! Now go!" she said, pointing the way out.

Bonnie stood up, blocking her way to go inside. She reached for her hand and said, "Miss Nettie, I am worried about you. I didn't know if you were having a stroke or a heart attack or what! I will not leave you alone until I am sure you will be alright." She noticed a slight softening in Nettie's face and for a brief moment Nettie hesitated. Jumping at the opening, she said, "Please, Miss Nettie, sit down. I know something is wrong. I'd like to help."

Nettie stiffened, regaining her veneer. "There is nothing wrong and I don't need your help. Just go home."

"I will sit here all day if I have to, but I am not leaving," Bonnie replied firmly.

Nettie grumbled and walked to the door. She reached for the knob and said, "If you insist on staying, allow me to put on some clothes." She grudgingly gave in to Bonnie's refusal to leave and stepped into the house.

Sending a fervent prayer to God, Bonnie pleaded for God's help. *I don't know what to do, Lord. I don't know what to say. Please help me be the friend Miss Nettie needs so desperately right now. I am so scared for her. She sounds like she is on the verge of giving up.* She waited and waited, pacing back and forth.

Once inside, Nettie walked to her bedroom and sat on the edge of the bed. She could not believe that this Bonnie girl had seen her in such a state.

Staring at the blank wall, Nettie felt bereft of feeling. Slowly, she stood and walked into the bathroom. Staring at the mirror, she sighed. "Why can't people just leave me alone?" She bent over the sink and splashed water on her face, then dried with a towel. Looking up, she felt conflicted. On one hand, she wanted to die and be free of this wretched life. But on the other, she was baffled by Bonnie's continued presence.

With every hair in place and appropriate clothes, Nettie went back in the living room and pulled the curtain slightly aside. Seeing Bonnie, she blew out a deep breath, "Oh good grief, she is still here." Dropping the curtain, she shrugged her shoulders and muttered, "I guess I had better go out there or she'll never leave. And then what would the neighbors think?"

Even though she had dressed and fixed her hair, Nettie still felt exhausted. She had only enough energy to walk back out and sit in her chair.

Bonnie heard the door open and out stepped Miss Nettie, fully dressed and every hair in place. The determined look on the woman's face alerted Bonnie that the fight was not over yet.

"Bonnie, you can leave now. I will be fine, " Nettie said as she sat down.

"Miss Nettie, you are not fine. You have had me so worried. You were so distraught when I came. And the things you said. Well, I'm very concerned over something you mentioned."

Seeing neighbors begin to stir in the neighborhood and not wanting to draw attention, Nettie quietly responded. "There's no need for you to worry. I told you, I am fine."

"But I am worried! You said something that disturbed me greatly." Not seeing any visible reaction from Nettie, Bonnie continued. "I'm sure you were just talking out of your head. I mean, you couldn't possibly…" Bonnie saw no signs of regret or embarrassment over her earlier statement. Feeling like she had no right to confront Miss Nettie, she forged ahead anyway. "If you are not willing to admit it was a crazy thing to say then, I will just have to say it. Earlier you said you wanted me to go home and" …. Bonnie struggled with the words that wounded her spirit to even think of uttering……"You said to go home and let you die." It came out in a low whisper. Those were probably the most heart-wrenching words that Bonnie had ever spoken in her entire life. She bit down on her lip to stop the trembling. "Can you see how concerned I am about you?" A tear rolled down Bonnie's cheek.

"You mustn't be. Sometimes people say things they don't mean." Nettie refused to look at Bonnie and stared straight into the yard.

Bonnie was shocked at the lack of emotion. "Did you mean it?" Bonnie dared ask.

Nettie shifted her weight in the rocker, clearly uncomfortable with where this conversation was going.

"Miss Nettie, answer me. Did you mean it?" Bonnie said forcefully.

"Yes! Yes I meant it!" she growled.

The shock of those words jolted Bonnie to her soul. She had not expected an admission. She was sure she would hear a denial or a lie. She suddenly realized she wasn't as prepared as she thought she would be.

Frozen in fear and concern, Bonnie waited.

Slowly and methodically, Nettie began to speak. "Bonnie, you cannot possibly understand how terrible it is to live without Henry. You cannot fathom the loneliness that exists in my house. I eat alone. I sleep alone. I get up every morning with no one to talk to. I drink my coffee alone. I walk through my days alone. And at the end of the day, I come home alone."

Bonnie had to admit to herself that she could not understand that kind of loneliness. She had Will and the love of her family back home. It must be awful to feel that alone. "Miss Nettie, you are right. I don't know how you feel. And I am so sorry you have to walk the rest of your journey without your Henry. I wish there was something I could say to......" Bonnie paused. Something from long ago jumped into her mind. It was Miz Jessie!

While Bonnie tried to remember the conversation from long ago, Nettie took in a long breath. "There is nothing you can say. There is nothing anyone can say. Now, please go," she pleaded sadly.

Lord, is this memory what you want me to share with her now? Will she even listen? I don't know what else to do. If it can help her, I will try. Please help me remember it all.

"Before I go, may I share something with you Miz Jessie told me when I was about....oh about....twelve years old, I think. Please?"

"Just be quick about it." Nettie's expression had not changed the entire morning. She was clearly still distraught. Bonnie had never seen her like this. It was most disturbing.

"Thank you, Miss Nettie. I will try to be brief. If you don't mind, I'll try to remember it as close to her own tellin' as I can."

Nettie's jaw tightened and her rocking resumed.

Bonnie took a seat in the rocker adjacent to Miss Nettie and began slowly. "As I remember it, I was real sad when my grandfather passed away. My Gram was devastated. She ambled around the house going from room to room with seemingly no purpose. She would sit on the back porch for hours staring into space. I would try to talk with her, but it was as if she didn't even know I was there. Other times, she would force a smile for me, but I knew it wasn't a real smile. Our family was very worried about her. It was like she had built a wall around herself. She thought grandpa's love was gone. But it wasn't. It was still there. It was in the memories, and the pictures, and in all of us."

"So one day, I asked Miz Jessie, What can I do to help my Gram? She is so lost without Grandpa."

"Miz Jessie was sitting in the rickety old rocker on the back porch with a bowl of potatoes in her lap. Anyway, she looked at me sitting on the top step of the porch and said, "Chile, I do's understand what ya sayin'. I do. My gramammy went through the same thang. After her husband done died, she jus' 'bout dried up. She'd put on a happy face and try to fool everone that she was happy but we's all knew better. The twinkle was gone in her eyes. Gone somewhere. Finally, one day, a stranger come into her life, while she was a sittin' on the bench in town waitin' on my mam to finish her food shoppin'. This cute little thang of a girl come up and sat right down aside her.

"She was a youngun for shor. Maybe she be ten, maybe, she said. Well, Grandmammy said that spunky young thang walked right up and plunked her behind on the bench next to her and started talkin' like a magpie. She swung her skinny, little legs back and forth and back and forth under the bench. Then, finally, she stared gramammy dead in the eyes and with a serious look said, "I don't think I ever seen anyone look as old as you! How old ya be anyways? If ya be a 100, I most likely gonna believe ya." Her eyes grew wide as she looked over and behind and up and down my gramammy. Well, let me tell ya, gramammy said her tongue tied in knots sa tight, she thought she might swoller the whole thang! *"Someone needs to take that youngun out behind the wood shed for a good lickin' for bein' so smart aleck like,"* she said ever time she retold the story.

"Gramammy looked that chile up and down and back and forth, from her wiry hair to her muddy feet and burst out a laughin'. She laughed and laughed without saying a word. Said the little upstart reached over and hugged her round shakin' belly. When the girl sat back up gramammy said, "Don't' think I ever seen you a'fore. Where ya come from?"

"Oh me and daddy come to town to get some feed for my Aunt Jenny's cows. We live over the river in 'Hio."

"Well, what made ya think to come over here by me?"

"Ya looked so sad. Like ya lost yer best friend." She looked down at her muddy feet. "Aw, I didn't mean nothin' by what I said." Her orange caked feet resumed kickin' back and forth. "My daddy says I talk ta much anyhow and speak my mind a'fore my brain can shut it up. But when I saw ya lookin' so sad and all, I jus' thought ya needed someone here 'sides ya. Ya looked jus' like my grama looked after my grapppy went to live with Jesus, that's all. Her face got real old, real quick cause she stopped laughin.' She stopped bein' happy too. And in one month, she upped and went to Jesus. My mam said she died of a broken heart. She told me the Good Book says 'as a man think in his heart, so is he.' Grama thought she was no good to no body. Mam said she been lied to by the devil. She could have done sa many thangs. Hepin' people, givin' to em that needs her, and showin' people what Jesus look like. And when it her turn to see grappy agin, she could go with a happy face." Leaning closer, she said, "Ya know somethin'? You gots that same look on yer face, like my grama."

"Pausing a bit, the little girl asked, "Ya lose someone like grama? You ain't gonna die of a broken heart too, are ya?"

"Gramammy's face grew sad agin. She pondered the question for quite a spell. She had thought of givin' up, she hurt sa bad. She couldn't find no good reason to stay bahind. She had poured all

her lovin' into her man and it hurt somethin' awful.

"Gramammy said, the chile stopped swingin' her legs, leaned over and put her muddy caked hands on each side of her face, looked her squar' in the face and asked agin, "Ya ain't gonna die of a broken heart too, are ya?"

"Gramammy said she wished the child would jus' go away.

But seein' somethin' in that chile's face, told her what she been a missin.' Hope. She weren't seein' no hope.

"Thinkin' on the girl's young wisdom, she knew she wanted to git real busy pourin' her life into somethin' else 'sides waitin' ta die. She would do hit for the Lawd Jesus. She would do hit for granpappy.

"She patted the little girl's hand, smiled and said, "No chile, I ain't gonna die of a broken heart. Not anymore. I'm plannin' ta die of a happy heart."

"Good, cause ya really don't look 100 a'tall. I was jus' teasin' ya. Ya don't look a day over 90!"

"Gramammy lived another 15 yar fo' she passed on. She was 102. She was a good cook and made a mess o'meals for hurtin' friends and neighbors. She even taught me how to cook! She told us kids lots and lots of stories we never heard a'for.' And wooee, she could make the purtiest quilt blankies for newborn babies. Granmammy 'membered that young un, she did. Cause ever day, she'd look in the mirror to see if her face looked old. She had lots of wrinkles, yep she did, but ya know what? I don't think she ever saw 'em. She saw herself as young as a new pup, a wrinkled one mind ya, but spry as a pup ta the end."

"Remember that there Bible verse, chile? 'As a man think in

his heart, so is he.' Well, Gramammy had been thinkin' herself sad. And sad she were. But she begun thinkin' herself well and well she was!"

Bonnie finished her story and looked over at Nettie. Surprisingly, she was looking back at her too.

"I like your Miz Jessie, Bonnie. I believe my Henry would have liked her too." Nettie sat upright, hands in her lap.

Bonnie felt the atmosphere changing. Nettie was not quite as agitated as before. She spoke softer and her demeanor relaxed.

"Miss Nettie, I know nothing can fill the void of Mr. Henry being gone. But something CAN fill the time and the loneliness. Like thinking of others and what you can offer them. Think about why you are still here. God is not finished with you yet!"

Leaning into the side table, Bonnie said, "I was so excited several weeks back when Pastor Randy taught on God's love and grace. He said what Miz Jessie had told me when I was in my teens. She said, "Sweet Chile, whene'er ya feelin' down and sad and go to thankin' no one loves ya, and thar ain't no reason to go on, 'member this...... God always loves ya. He never stops lovin' ya. He cain't. Because He is love. He gotta be who He gotta be. He cain't be no different. And when ya do thangs ya ought not do, He gives ya grace. Grace is givin' ya somethin' ya don't deserve."

Bonnie saw Nettie bristle. But she continued on. "She said to me, 'Member when you didn't understand yer daddy not whippin' ya when ya sassed yer mama? And when ya broke yer Gram's favorite mixin' bowl and didn't own up to hit? She found out ya done hit and told ya she weren't mad, jus' disappointed ya didn't tell her yerself?"

"Yeah, I felt terrible about those things," I said. "I thought daddy was going to whup me for sure. But he didn't. And my Gram wasn't mad at all. It made me feel real bad that I wasn't being punished."

Looking at Nettie, Bonnie said, "Miz Jessie told me those times were all grace. I didn't get what I deserved. I got love instead. And after that, I never wanted to disappoint my Gram or dad again. Miz Jessie said that God calls it grace."

"Grace," Nettie whispered.

Bonnie gave Nettie room for that to sink in. After a minute or two, she reached for Nettie's hand and said, "I'll bet you haven't eaten this morning. Can I get you something to eat? A sandwich maybe?"

Nettie slowly nodded. Bonnie patted her hand in reassurance that she would be right back. She stopped in the doorway and looked back. Nettie was rocking, her hands relaxed in her lap. *Thank You, Lord, that Miss Nettie is going to be alright. I was so worried about her. Help her to see Your grace and love in her own life.*

Shortly, Bonnie returned with a sandwich and a glass of tea. Nettie nibbled slowly, looking at Bonnie every once in a while. "Thank you, Bonnie," was all she said.

It had been an extremely stressful morning for both of them. Bonnie felt drained of all energy and sat back in her rocker, relieved that Nettie was more alert and talking.

The neighborhood began stirring with life. Some leaving in cars, others walking about. A few bent over flower beds pulling intruders from around their beautiful roses and mums. A light breeze fluttered the leaves on the old oak trees that canopied the street. The cooler temperature heralded the beginning of fall.

Breathing in the fresh air, Bonnie was pleased with the change that was coming. Hopefully, a wind of change was entering Nettie's heart as well.

A soft voice broke the stillness. "Bonnie."

Returning her focus to Nettie, she replied, "Yes?"

Shaking her head, she said, "I don't know what has gotten into me lately. One minute, I wish I was dead and didn't have to feel the loneliness and anger anymore. And the next minute, I wish I knew why I was still here. I've been so unhappy most of my life. I really haven't known love. Not really. My mother never loved me. Even as a child, I kept hoping she would, but she never did."

Bonnie gasped. She felt her heart plummet to her toes. She could not imagine a mother not loving her child!

Hearing Bonnie's gasp, Nettie said, "It's true, Bonnie. It is really true. As a child, I kept thinking I had done something terribly wrong that caused her to dislike me so. It wasn't until I was married that I realized her obsessive need to control my life and all those around us. I have often wondered if she didn't know how to love. Maybe she never received love from her parents. Like me, maybe she built a wall around herself too. A wall of self-protection. A wall where no one could hurt her if she let love in."

Bonnie could not fathom a wall like that. She had always had the love of her family, friends, Miz Jessie, and now Will. She wanted to cry for Miss Nettie.

"Now don't go thinking that I didn't crack that wall a bit for love to creep in. I did. I knew the love of my father until he died, when I was fourteen. It was very painful to lose him at that age. After that, mother took over my life, and love was no longer in the picture. I always missed it. But after time, the wall grew higher. It wasn't until Henry came into the picture that I gave in to love once again. I was a changed person. His love opened me up to a world I had never known."

Bonnie nodded, listening intently.

"Now, don't get me wrong, Bonnie. I still had some mighty strong bricks in that wall. Bricks that even Henry couldn't topple." She smiled at the mention of her husband. "I was much more pleasant to be around when Henry was alive. He would take me on dates nearly every week. And the twins, Melva Jane and Myrtle, would invite us over for dinner with their husbands quite often. Ida Mae and I spent lots of time together too. We'd go shopping and have lunches at the Apothecary. Sometimes we would treat ourselves to brunch at the Edgewater Hotel."

Bonnie saw Nettie's expression change. The grief that was there earlier had returned and settled over her body like a limp rag. She looked weak again.

"But when my Henry got sick, I prayed and prayed that God would let him live. I went to the church and promised God anything if He would let Henry be by my side for many more years. But it didn't happen. Henry died. I became so angry. Angry at Henry for leaving me. Angry at God for taking him away. That is when I knew God didn't care about me. The only true love of my life and God takes him away. I vowed never to give in to love again. It hurt too much. So I built the wall higher and stronger than I ever had before."

Being a good listener was an attribute Bonnie learned from her Gram. Her attentive silence gave Nettie the freedom to open her heart. She made no sound, nor offered advice.

Nettie continued as though she were talking to the wind, "For the last five years, I have been utterly miserable. Over that time, I have forgotten what love looked like." Nettie leaned cautiously toward Bonnie and whispered in a fragile voice, "Until you came along."

The shock on Bonnie's face would have stopped a train. "Me?"

"It's true. I was not happy you moved to Windy Garden. At first I didn't know why. I just was. Each time you stopped by to visit or share your Miz Jessie with me, I pushed you away. I couldn't bear to be around you. All that time you reached out to me, I backed further and further away. I backed so far away that I pushed everyone else away too. I alienated myself from all my friends. Ida Mae. Melva Jane and Myrtle. The pastor. I didn't want anyone to get too close. Caring, loving, hurt too much. My wall of protection would have cracked. I would have had to face why I am the way I am. The loneliness I felt losing Henry was only compounded by the distance I've put between my friends and me. I thought I was alone after Henry left, but now, after losing everyone else....."

A solitary tear ran down the cheek of the woman sitting next to Bonnie. A bitter, lonely woman confessing her pain, for all practical purposes, to a stranger.

Leaning back in her chair, Nettie's voice cracked. "This morning, I awoke empty. Empty of spirit. Empty of hope. Empty of friends. Empty of love. I could see no way out. All I saw was loneliness and despair. I truly wanted to die."

The two women did not look at each other. They simply stared into the yard, oblivious of any motion around them, whether it be the birds that landed on the feeders, or the curious looks from passersby. Several minutes passed. "Bonnie, would you mind refilling my tea?"

"Of course." Bonnie said and stood.

"And please. Make yourself something to eat and drink too. I don't like eating alone."

"Thank you. I will." Smiling, Bonnie entered the house and headed for the kitchen. Her heart warmed at this latest vulnerability and openness that was taking place between the two of them. She opened the refrigerator door and refilled Nettie's tea. Seeing a bowl of fruit, she set it on the counter. Reaching for two bowls, she scooped fruit into each one. She noticed the bread box next to the toaster and pulled out two thick pieces of bread. Opening the refrigerator once more, she found a small container of pimento cheese. *Oh, I love pimento cheese!* Slathering a generous helping on her bread, she cut it in two. Next, she poured herself a glass of tea. Looking around, she found a serving tray and placed all the items on it. Careful not to spill anything, she went to the front door. Balancing the tray, she pushed the door open with her foot. She set the tray on the side table between the two chairs and sat down.

Discreetly studying Miss Nettie's face, she was pleased to see her cheeks regain their color. "I thought you might enjoy some fruit, so I fixed us both some. And I couldn't resist a pimento cheese sandwich!"

Nettie looked at the tray of food and up at Bonnie. Her eyes revealed her recognition of a very large sandwich overflowing with cheese. Picking up her glass of iced tea, she took a sip. "I've been thinking since you went inside. Your Miz Jessie told you that you don't lose the love of one who has died before you?"

"Yes, ma'am," Bonnie mumbled through a mouth full of cheese. Swallowing her rather large bite, she said, "I'm sorry. That was a mouthful, wasn't it?" Wiping her mouth with a napkin she answered, "Yes, that's what she said. She said that love is forever. That it has no end. Because true love is from God. And He is forever."

"Hmm," muttered Nettie. "So love doesn't end. But does it change?"

"Oh boy, does it ever!" As soon as the words spilled into the air, Bonnie saw Nettie's body stiffen.

"What do you mean? Does love get weaker? Has my love for Henry and his love for me ended?" The rocker stopped and Nettie looked anxiously at Bonnie.

Setting her unfinished sandwich back on the plate in her lap, Bonnie explained. "Oh my, no! Miz Jessie says that it only gets bigger and better! She said it this way......"Why chile, love ain't a'tall what it ort ta be on this here earth. It be weak and fickle-like. It change with da wind. But in heaven! It be perfect! And even more than we can even make up in our 'maginations. Basides, if'n our love is a God love, then it goes on and on and on." Bonnie looked at Nettie to see if she was understanding.

"So, Henry's love for me came from God?" She tapped her fingers on the rocking chair arm, her mind reeling before Bonnie.

"Well, all I know is what the Bible says. It says, 'love is of God.'"

"Ohhh," came the drawn out reply.

"I guess that's why people call the Bible 'the good book!'" Bonnie laughed and picked up her sandwich.

"Why have I never heard this before? I have been in church

most of my life and this is all new to me. I thought that once you died, you stopped loving." It seemed Nettie was talking to herself more than Bonnie.

"I can see why you might think that. But Miz Jessie told me that most folk never hear it because mostly what they hear from preachers is what all they've been doing wrong. And when the focus is on the wrong, we don't hear what is right about God. She said that if we would believe that He loves us, then we would be able to love like he loves. I don't think I'm explaining that quite right."

Bonnie finished her sandwich and offered Nettie her fruit. It was waved off in dismissal, but accompanied with a slight smile in the refusal. Bonnie picked up her own fruit bowl and began to eat. All the emotional stress of the last couple of hours had made her hungry. She savored every bite.

After finishing her tea, Bonnie spoke. "Are you ok, Miss Nettie?"

With eyes closed, Nettie said, "You know, Bonnie. I believe God put you in my path to help me face some things I have refused to deal with for many years. You and your Miz Jessie. I think I am finally beginning to see that. I am sorry I have been so rude to you. I hardly offer apologies, Bonnie. Mother said it was a sign of weakness. But I truly am sorry."

The vulnerability that emanated from Nettie moved Bonnie deeply. "Oh Miss Nettie, I was never offended. Not really. Miz Jessie used to say 'always look bahind the eyes, youngun. That whar' the truth be.' I kept looking, like she said. And I have to admit too, that at first I tried to avoid you."

"I'm sorry if I made you feel that way, Bonnie. Can you ever forgive me?"

"To be honest with you, I forgave you a long time ago."

"Your Miz Jessie teach you that too?"

"Yes, ma'am!" she beamed proudly.

Contentedly rocking, Nettie said thoughtfully, "I would have loved to have had a Miz Jessie in my growing up years. Thank you, Bonnie, for coming to my aid today. I don't know what would have happened if you had not." Rising to her feet once more, she stood in front of Bonnie. "I do appreciate your friendship."

Bonnie heard the chimes on the far end of the porch sing a soft tune. She felt a change coming. Jumping to her feet, she threw her arms around her new friend's neck and hugged her tight. Whispering, she said, "I'm glad we're friends."

Bonnie pulled back, alarmed. "Oh no! I'm terribly late for my meeting with the pastor's wife. She's probably really upset with me now."

Nettie held her by the shoulders, looked her in the eye and said, "I do believe your Miz Jessie might have said, 'She ain't gonna be mad. Not if she love ya.'"

The endearing smile warmed Bonnie's heart. Before her stood a totally different woman than the woman she first met outside the Apothecary her first day in downtown Windy Garden. A woman whose life had been rocked by love. She couldn't help but wonder what would come next. "I'm sorry to rush off like this, but I really should try to find her and apologize." Hesitating, she cleared her throat and asked, "Are you going to be alright?"

"Yes. I am now. Go. Run along."

Bonnie began to leave when she saw the tray with plates and cups. "Here, I'll take this inside first."

Reaching for the tray, Nettie put her hand on Bonnie's arm, stopping her. "Don't worry about that. I'll take it in. You go on and meet with Sue."

Tears welled up in Bonnie's eyes before she reached the steps. She turned and ran back into Nettie's arms. Kissing her on the cheek, she ran down the steps and turned toward town, waving enthusiastically.

Nettie picked up the tray. Stopping at the door, she looked down the street. "My, how different things look." The slight breeze tinkled the chimes once again. Nettie chuckled, "Of course, it does. Real love changes things."

27

That night, Nettie took a shower and dressed for bed. She felt more refreshed than she had since before Henry got sick. The day had been emotionally draining, but she was too wound up to sleep. Winding the alarm clock, she looked over to Henry's side of the bed and saw his Bible on the nightstand. She smiled, thinking of how many times she had dusted that old Bible cover while cleaning the bedroom. She walked over and ran her hands tenderly over the leather case that held a well-worn Bible with torn seams. Reaching down, she picked up the sacred book and carried it back to her side of the bed. She slipped beneath the covers, plumping up several pillows behind her. Leaning back, she settled in and opened the cherished treasure in her hands.

The zipper sounded so familiar. Most nights before going to sleep, Henry would unzip the cover and read for at least an hour. She smiled at the memory. Laying it open in her lap, she noticed papers askew. Along the sides of the case were pockets full of notes and miscellaneous clippings. She felt as if she were intruding into his personal space, but was amused at the silly thought. Never before had she cared to peek into this most private place.

Sighing, she leaned her head back, patted his pillow and quietly spoke to Henry as if he were there. "I remember you spending hours and hours making notes in your Bible and writing your Sunday school lessons on the dining room table. I used to be quite jealous of all that time taken away from me. In fact, I believe I made comments about it often." Looking back at the book which lay open before her she said, "But seeing this in my hands, I can't wait to hear your voice jump off the pages."

Flipping to the book of I John, Nettie began reading. She read not only the Scripture, but every notation in the columns that Henry had penned himself. When she reached the fourth chapter, verse 8, she bolted upright. She read it again. The third time, she read it aloud. "The one who does not love, does not know God, for God is love." Her hand rose to her throat. "Oh, my." She frantically searched to see if her beloved had written anything in the margin alongside this verse. He had.

Pulling the Bible closer to her eyes, she read Henry's handwritten side note, "I pray today for my Nettie. Open her heart to Your love, Lord, so she can truly see mine."

Nettie placed her hand over the verse and looked up. "What did you mean Henry? I knew you loved me. I don't understand." Shaking her head, she tried to comprehend the meaning of such a request. "Henry, what were you saying?" she voiced aloud. Setting the Bible aside, she threw back the covers and padded to the kitchen. She opened the refrigerator and pulled out the milk. Pouring a small amount of the milk into a saucepan, she heated it on the stove. She was stunned at Henry's words. Stirring the milk, she placed her finger in the warm liquid to test the temperature. Satisfied, she poured it into a coffee mug. Carefully carrying the cup to the table, she sat down. Nettie couldn't imagine that Henry would ever have questioned whether she knew the depth of his love for her.

"It was a silly thing to write," she said, as she sipped her milk.

Standing with her cup in hand, she paced the living room floor. Her earlier conversation with Bonnie entered her mind. "Could it all be that simple? Maybe what I have been doing all my life is living by so many rules that I couldn't find any freedom in them. I was so bound by them that I could not see love."

The words of the little girl with the muddy feet rushed back into her mind. "Hope. She weren't seein' no hope." This thought coupled with Henry's notes caused her hands to tremble and her heart to race. *"Love is of God. Help my Nettie to see how much she is loved."*

Nettie dropped her cup, spilling milk across the wide plank floors.

"Oh Henry, I think I am beginning to understand! I finally get what you were trying to say. You knew I could not *see* love. You knew I needed to know the One who *is* love in order to be able *to* love.

Hope. Love. Two words that had baffled Nettie throughout her entire life. But two things she desperately needed this very night.

Ignoring the spilt milk, Nettie rushed back to the bedroom and picked up Henry's Bible. She read the verse and her husband's notes again.

Pulling out the remainder of Henry's Sunday school notes hidden inside the Bible cover pockets, Nettie read every one. "How did I miss this all these years?"

She leaned back against her pillows, hugging the notes to her breast. Sorrow filled her soul for all the time she had wasted in bondage to a hardened heart. It had robbed her of the only thing she had always wanted. Love.

Setting the Bible aside, she knew what she must do. But in order to do that, she needed to talk with her loving man. "Henry, tomorrow I must tell you something very important. Actually, two somethings. But for now, I must sleep on it. If I can." She glanced at the wind-up clock. It read 3:30.

Nettie headed back into the living room and retrieved the cup from the floor. She then went to the kitchen for a damp cloth to clean up the mess she had made. "Oh, there are so many mendings that I must attend to," she said, wringing out the dish rag. "I don't know if I have the courage to do what I must do, but with God's help, I must try."

Nettie slept fitfully, if at all. She turned and glanced at the alarm clock. 6:00 a.m. Squeezing her eyes tight, she knew this would be the day she had been dreading for a long, long time. She trembled at the task before her. Rising from the bed, she went to the bathroom and washed her face. She reached for the hand towel and dried her hands. Staring into the mirror, she spoke to herself. "Nettie, the most important fence to mend now is with your Henry. It is time. You can do this." Drying the water from her face, she placed the towel back in its holder and brushed her teeth. She turned and opened the closet door. She knew exactly the outfit she would choose. She slipped into her favorite grey skirt, light pink blouse and grey blazer that Henry had picked out for her the week before their 50th anniversary. She wanted to look especially nice today. Nettie walked into the kitchen and made a pot of coffee. She knew she had better eat a little something before heading to the cemetery. Her stomach had a habit of growing queasy whenever she faced stressful situations. Buttering a piece of toast and cutting up an apple, she wasn't sure she could swallow a single bite. She managed to hold down half the toast, three small slices of apple and drank her cup of coffee. She was a jumble of nerves.

Glancing at the clock on the stove, she saw it was already 7:00 a.m. "Maybe if I go early, no one will be about and I can have time with Henry completely alone." She grabbed her purse, jacket, and car keys, and left.

Pulling up to the entrance of the cemetery, she hesitated. Her shaky courage waned and she thought she might get sick. Inhaling a deep breath, she opened the car door. Walking to the back of the car, she opened the trunk and retrieved her stool. In an effort to remain calm, she squared her shoulders and started up the slight hill. Each step shouted for her to turn around and go home. But Nettie knew if she did not follow through with her reckoning this cool morning, she would not ever have the strength or determination to set herself free.

Approaching Henry's marker, she felt like a stranger. Looking down at his name, she softly called out to him. "Henry... I'm here." Setting her stool in place, she sat down. She wanted to reach out and touch his name, but felt ashamed to even be sitting before him.

Where do I begin? she asked herself. *There is so much to say.*

Boldly reaching forward, she felt the dips and curves in the engraving with her fingers. "Henry. My Henry. I have been so lost without you. All those years you put up with my persnickety ways and loved me anyway. It must have been terribly difficult for you, though it never showed." Nettie saw a smudge on the "Y" in his name. Reaching into the pocket of her jacket, she pulled out a handkerchief, spit on it and rubbed the blemish. "Such an ugly mark on such a godly man's name," she said, rubbing harder. Removing the smudge, she sat back.

"That soiled spot is me, Henry. I am afraid I have been a blemish on your good name. I have let anger and my need to control keep me from embracing love. Especially your love. I hurt you. I know that now. Oh, Henry! What have I done? I...I ...I should have trusted your love. Why, oh why, didn't I?" Her words slurred through tears that spilled down her cheeks. Her hands trembled in fear for what she knew she must say.

Sitting back onto the stool, she slowly drew another breath of courage. Blurting it out in a hurry, lest she change her mind, she began, "I...I have to tell you something. Something I have held inside me for a very long time. Something I am terribly, horribly ashamed of. I should have come to you at the very beginning. I should have trusted....you....us. I'm glad you can't hate me where you are now for what I am about to say.

Her grief was palpable. Her shoulders heaved with emotion. "Henry. Just after our third anniversary, I began feeling dizzy and nauseous, so I made a doctor appointment. You and I both thought it might be the flu. I asked mother to go with me to the doctor and bring me home since I was feeling so weak. You had offered but I insisted you didn't need to miss work. I didn't want you getting sick too. Truthfully, I thought if mother got sick, it would keep her home and away from me for a few days." A slight smirk lifted her eyebrow but quickly subsided. "I discovered I was with child. When Dr. Carter gave me the news that I was expecting, I was so excited. I knew you wanted children. You talked about it all the time. I wanted to rush to your office and tell you straightaway. But

I felt so sick.

"After the appointment, mother urged me to go home with her for a cup of tea, even though I didn't feel like it. 'Tea is good for anything that ails you,' she used to say. But tea was not what she had in mind. The door had barely shut when she spun around and told me that a baby would mess up my perfectly good life. That you would give all your time and attention to the baby and not to me. She told me I would not have the energy to properly take care of a child and the community and the church, as well as attend to you. That afternoon mother convinced me that we should do something about this. We should do away with the problem and not tell anyone, especially you. When I got home, you called to check on me and I told you it was the flu. I lied. Then a few days later, mother and I went away for a week together. Remember? The truth is.... we went away to.......to take care of the problem."

Sobbing, she reached out to steady herself against the stone. "Henry, she had me so convinced it was the right thing to do. Mother was always so seemingly right. She contacted a doctor she knew just over the border in Tennessee. When we got there, I was shaking all over. But in a short time, it was over. The baby .... was gone. I kept telling myself that maybe later would be a better time for a child in our lives. Maybe another year or two. But without my knowledge, mother paid the doctor to make sure I could never get pregnant again. I never knew that until later.

"The next year, I was determined to give you the child you longed for. I regretted ever 'doing away with the problem.' After several months of trying, nothing happened, so I went to see Dr. Carter. That's when he told me I could never conceive a child again. My womb had been altered. Hearing the news, I was sure mother had something to do with it. So I went to her house and confronted her. She confessed what she had done and said it was for my own good. My own good?!? She didn't even blink an eye telling me. She said I'd get over it in time. I never have.

"When she made that 'choice' for me, which should have been mine, I knew she thought father loved me more than her. It wasn't true. But she must have thought so. That could have been why she felt she had to do what she did. That was the final betrayal. I knew her to be a mean-spirited and controlling woman but I never would have imagined she would go so far. I hated mother after that. I rarely spoke to her again. Over the years you tried so hard for me to make peace with her. I feigned trying to pacify you. If only you knew, you might have understood why I could not. She had ruined my life! Or so I believed. Even back then, I couldn't tell you what I had done or what mother had done to me. I feared if you had known the truth, you would have hated me for it. I couldn't take that chance."

Pulling out a handkerchief she kept inside her sleeve, she dabbed at her forehead, now wet with perspiration, and drew in a deep breath. Waving the cloth before her face to cool her body down, she felt the already intense morning sun on her back.

Gathering all her remaining strength, she plunged ahead. "There's something else I must say. Remember that new girl who moved to Windy Garden last year who I said was a Yankee? Well, I figured out why I was so upset over her moving here. Her name is Bonnie. You see, when I was a child, Father gave me the most beautiful porcelain doll on my fifth birthday that I named Bonnie.

She kept me company when I was all alone, comforted me when I was sick, 'listened' to all my complaining about mother, and slept by my side each night. I knew that someday if I had a little girl, she would be named Bonnie."

Nettie felt exhausted confessing the dark shadows of her soul. Sins she had buried long ago. Secrets she had held so close. They were supposed to remain buried. Forever. Not to be resurrected. She had never imagined in her wildest dreams, or nightmares, that she would ever expose them to anyone, especially Henry.

Nettie fell from the stool to her knees and pressed her head against the granite stone. "Henry, I have made such a horrible mess of my life. I am so sorry for not giving you the children you so desperately wanted. So very, very sorry. I should have had more faith in your love for me. I am painfully aware how full our lives could have been, if only I had known what real love is. God's love. Your love. There would have been children we could have cherished together and grandchildren to dote on. I could be telling them how wonderful their grandfather is. Oh, how much we missed. All, because of me." Nettie's tears were uncontrollable. Waves of exhaustion threatened to sap her of all energy. Sitting back on her heels, she realized she had more to confess.

She paused wearily, then pressed on. "My life has been such a mess. I'm beginning to see myself as never before. For most of my life, I blamed mother for everything. But the truth of the matter is, my darling Henry…Mother didn't ruin my life. I ruined my life ….and ours. It was my decision to go along with her. And that gave her the opportunity to make a decision for me that changed my life forever. I wish I had been stronger to stand up to her and do what

I knew in my heart was right. Father showed me that. He taught me right from wrong. But when he died, there was just mother and me. And I was too young to resist her domineering influence and control.

"I wasn't sure there was hope for me anymore. I have done things, said things, believed things that were all manipulated for my own self-esteem. I thought not even God could bring good out of this mess. And why should He?"

Her legs began to cramp from sitting on the ground, so she rose and then sat back on the stool, massaging her calves. The pain was a welcome break.

"This week has been a most unusual week, Henry. I felt so utterly alone. Everyone had left me. You. My friends. Even God. I felt totally abandoned. Even our beautiful home held no joy for me. I wanted to give up. Henry, you would have been so ashamed of me, if you could have seen me in such despair. I was so distraught, I wanted to.....I wanted to...I wanted to die." Admitting such a thing to Bonnie was one thing. But for Nettie to admit it to her beloved husband was quite another. The agony she felt before rushed back with a vengeance. "I have been so lonely without you! You and father were the only ones in my whole life who ever truly loved me. And without you, I didn't think I would ever know love again."

"Remember, when I told you I had probably hurt Melva Jane and Myrtle's feelings over the paint color for the church bathrooms? Well, apparently I did, because they are not speaking to me. They haven't for over two weeks now. They are constantly avoiding me. At church. At the Hair Buzz. The grocery store. But, it was all my fault, really. I humiliated and alienated them by publicly voicing something very private. You know, Henry, as painful as this is to say, I think what Melva Jane said about me may be true. I *have* become my mother." Nettie gritted her teeth in agony. Nothing grieved her like admitting that she had become the very person who had brought her the most pain.

"You were the only joy I have ever known. And I wasted over 50 years of that held captive to myself and my secret. You might be wondering what brought about this bearing of the soul. Well, yesterday in my despondent state, the young girl, Bonnie, saw me at the end of my rope. She refused to leave me in such a state. I wanted her to go away and leave me alone in my misery. I'm glad now she didn't. Her concern touched me, along with the wisdom she shared from her Miz Jessie. Did I tell you about Miz Jessie? Well, if I didn't, I will at a later time. What transpired during that time was a wake up call. Bonnie told me that she understood that nothing will fill the void of you being gone, but the time and loneliness can be filled with something more healing. I'm not sure what that might look like just yet, but it did give me hope."

Smiling, she reached for his name. "God isn't finished with me yet, my dear. I am still here for a purpose. I must find out what that is. Then some day, we will be together again."

Smiling, she reached into her purse and pulled out Henry's Bible. "I read your Sunday School lesson sheets, Henry. Every one of them. They were tucked away in your Bible cover that I have kept on the nightstand. When I went to bed last night, I pulled your Bible onto my lap and opened it. There were pages and pages of notes tucked in the pockets of your Bible cover. I never knew they were there. It was like gold in my hands. So precious and painfully intimate.

I desperately needed to hear your voice through your writings. So I read them. For hours I read them, over and over. I could hear your heart in those pages. It's what you had been trying to teach me for over fifty years. That God loves me too. All those years, I could not understand that kind of love. From you or God. But now I am beginning to see. You both sacrificed so much for me. God gave His Son. You gave me your life."

"One day, my dear, I will return and tell you all about this Bonnie. And her Miz Jessie too. They have both been such a help to me when I needed it the most. Miz Jessie's wisdom helped me to see that our love for each other did not die when your body did. It is still here," she said patting her heart. "And maybe, just maybe, I will find God's love too. I think I am finally ready to search for that as well. Now, don't you go thinking I'll become "miss goody two shoes" anytime soon. I'm sure I will still be your impatient Nettie, but I do believe for the first time since you left for heaven, that I feel God tugging at my heart."

She was astonished at her vulnerability and felt a release she had never felt in her entire life. She didn't feel alone anymore. She felt Henry's love wrap around her like a warm blanket. She traced each letter in his name with her finger and said aloud, "H.E.N.R.Y. I can't explain it but I feel like something is changing inside me. I'm not really sure what that is just yet. But it feels very good."

Standing to her feet, she smoothed her skirt and kissed her hand, placing it on the top of the gravestone. "Well, my darling, thank you for always being here for me. I know deep down, you are not under the ground. You are with Jesus. But this was the only place I felt safe enough to release my burden."

Looking to heaven, she spoke to the sky. "Dear Jesus, thank You for taking care of my Henry. And thank You for showing me that love does not die. Not real love."

Looking back at Henry's grave, she whispered, "I best be going. I have many more fences to mend." With a smile, Nettie left. Instead of feeling exhausted from unleashing the burden that had weighed her down for years, she felt lighter, more alive than she had felt in a very long time.

28

The next week Nettie stood at the kitchen sink washing her hands. She caught herself humming. *I don't hum,* Nettie thought. She shook off the image and reached for the dish towel.

Feeling thirsty, she reached for a glass from the upper cabinet. There it was again! Humming. *What in the world is this?* She began humming this time on purpose. *I know that song. This is so strange.*

She took a few sips of her water and remembered. It was a song she heard all her life in church. But what brought it to mind now? And why was she humming it? Perplexed, she walked into the living room and glanced out the bay window. The afternoon shadows were signaling the coming of the end of another day. Suddenly, her eyes caught Bonnie passing by on the sidewalk. Nettie bolted for the door, opened it and shouted at Bonnie.

"Bonnie! Bonnie! Come here!" Stepping onto the porch, she waved for her to come quickly.

Bonnie's hurried steps indicated she was alarmed that something dreadful was wrong. Sprinting up the walkway, she bounded onto the porch. "What is it, Miss Nettie? Are you alright?" her eyes wide with fear.

Nettie realized she should have thought this through before scaring Bonnie. "Oh no, nothing is wrong. I saw you coming up the street this way and wanted to catch you. Do you have a few minutes to sit with me a spell?"

Bonnie nodded, clearly perplexed by Nettie's invitation. Letting out a breath of relief, she dutifully followed her to the rockers and both sat down. Nettie began rocking, fiddling with her fingers in her lap. Bonnie kept her eyes glued on Nettie, noticing the softness in her eyes and expression on her face. She was smiling. One minute she sounded distraught, and now a smile? She waited for Nettie to say something.

After a lengthy silence, Nettie spoke. "I went to Henry's grave last week. I can't explain it, but I felt like something broke inside of me."

Bonnie jumped in, "Oh no! Do I need to call an ambulance? Do you think you broke a bone? Miz Jessie used to say old folk could break bones quicker than snapping a chicken's head off."

"You sit real still and I'll go call a doctor!" Bonnie bolted to her feet, when she felt a pull on her arm.

Nettie laughed. "Sit, please. I did not break a bone."

This was the first time Bonnie had ever seen Nettie laugh. It shocked and surprised her. She gingerly leaned on the porch railing waiting to hear more.

"That is what I like best about you, Bonnie. You care about me. And I have to say it makes me feel real good that you do."

Bonnie's mouth hung open. "Are you sure you're alright?"

"Yes, I am. I can honestly say for the first time in a long time, I am fine. Please get comfortable. There are so many things I'd like to share with you."

Bonnie took her seat in the rocker once again.

Clearing her throat, Nettie picked up where she left off. "As I was saying, I went to visit Henry last week. I know you might find this strange, but I talk with Henry when I go. I know he's not really there. It is a place for me to go to feel close to him. I am reminded of the times when he would be at work in the real estate office downtown. Often, I would drop by his office to chat with him. Then, when I left, I felt happy having those few minutes together."

"Aw, Miss Nettie, that is so sweet."

Nettie stopped rocking. *Should I tell her what's on my mind? Or will she think I'm more addled than she already does?* Breathing deeply, she forged ahead. "Bonnie, I'm not quite sure how to begin. So I am going to jump in with both feet. I haven't been the most likable person in Windy Garden. I know that. I can be quite harsh and mean at times. I learned that well from my mother. She taught me to be in control and show no fear. As a result, I built walls around myself so high no one could see my pain. A pain I held for far too long." Nettie exhaled loudly.

Bonnie held her breath.

Eyes welling with tears, Nettie confessed. "It has been a miserable way to live. I am seeing that clearly for the first time in my life." She looked over at her new friend.

Bonnie's stunned expression was evident, which did not surprise Nettie. Before continuing on, Nettie felt the need for a break. She offered Bonnie a glass of lemonade.

Bonnie blew out her breath. "Um, sure, lemonade sounds good to me."

"I'll be right back," Nettie said as she stood and headed indoors.

Pondering the direction of the conversation moments before, Bonnie could not imagine what had happened to Nettie that she would feel comfortable telling her these things. Miz Jessie used to say "holdin' thangs inside eats up yer innards. It can make yer body sick as well as yer heart."

Bonnie thought back to last week when she had found Miss Nettie without hope and ready to give up. She was glad she had been there that day. Gram's voice echoed in her heart, "When us old folks need to talk, listen. Listen with all your heart and do not judge. You have never been in their shoes and do not know the depth of their hurt. Sometimes they need to voice their pain. Being old does not make us stupid. It just means we have hurt a lot longer than you have."

The front door opened and Nettie was struggling to balance a tray of drinks and cookies. Bonnie jumped up and took the tray from her. "Here, let me help." She placed the tray on the table between the two rockers. Nettie handed a glass to Bonnie along with a plate of cinnamon sugar cookies. "I got these cookies at the Apothecary a few days ago and forgot all about them." Nettie sat in her rocker and picked up her drink.

"They look delicious. Thank you." Bonnie took a took a sip of lemonade that made her pucker.

"I like mine tart. Don't you?" Nettie asked, noticing Bonne's eyes squint shut.

"Uh, it sure is tart." Her face scrunched, as she took another sip.

Nettie laughed again. "I made it myself from fresh lemons yesterday and added the tiniest bit of sugar. Sugar is not good for you, you know."

For Bonnie, the real treat was not the cookies and lemonade, but hearing Nettie laugh. Now that was a treat!

Settling back into her rocker, Nettie began again. "Bonnie, you haven't known me very long but I feel, for some reason, we have been drawn together. When you first moved to town, I was so upset over you being here. I tried every way I could to avoid you. Everywhere I went, there you were. At first, I didn't understand why your presence upset me so much. On one hand, I was curious to find out and on the other, something inside me wanted me to shut you out completely. But your care and concern touched me. Actually, it began to chip away at the wall I had built around myself. Each time you stopped to visit, I grew more and more curious about you and your Miz Jessie. To tell you the truth, after a while, I would look out my window quite often, hoping to see you walk by."

Nettie took a sip of lemonade. "After some time, I grew pretty comfortable with you and your stories of home. I hadn't allowed myself to become that close to anyone since my Henry died. Without him in my life, I felt more alone than ever. I began shutting myself off from my friends and former business associates. It wasn't until recently that I realized I had alienated everyone I knew." Every word came painstakingly from the deepest recesses of Nettie's heart. And while she felt the sting of emotional pain, with each word, she also felt release.

Bonnie could tell how much Nettie had been hurting inside.

"My Henry was such a kind man. I could tell him anything and he never condemned me. I don't know how he did it, but he had a way of rubbing the edges off my anger with such love, I'd forget what I was angry about." She smiled at the remembrance. "I never really appreciated his love like I should have. I regret that more than anything in my life."

Nettie took a sip of lemonade and paused for a few moments. Holding the glass in her lap, she continued, "I don't know if the gossip mill has spread it or not, but I hurt my two dear friends deeply. Melva Jane and Myrtle. You were there that day. You may have overheard the arguments, I don't know. But it doesn't really matter. I am ashamed I behaved so poorly. Since then, they have not spoken to me. My world has been wretchedly quiet and lonely since. You happened by the next day when I was......well, when I was at the end of my rope."

Bonnie reached for Nettie's arm and gently stroked the wrinkled skin. "You don't have to speak of that, Miss Nettie."

"But I do." Nettie placed her hand on Bonnie's. "If I don't say what I have to say now, I'm afraid I will remain the miserable person I have been to so many. And myself."

Bonnie nodded and sat back, giving Nettie time to gather her thoughts.

"I had lost every friend I had ever had. All my life, I wanted to blame everyone else for the sorry state I was in. But as usual, pouring my troubles out to Henry last week gave me a good hard look at myself. All these years, I kept blaming others for why I was the way I was. I blamed mother. I blamed the town. I blamed my friends. I even blamed God. Shocking for me to say that, isn't it?"

Not expecting an answer, she plunged ahead. "I'm not really sure if it was providential or the closeness to Henry, but I finally saw myself as I really am. I was my problem. Every attitude, every mean gesture, came from me. They were my choices. I have been ruining my life….and it was even true with Henry. Now, don't get me wrong. Henry and I had many good times together. We would laugh and tease almost everyday. He'd sing to me and make me feel like the most special person in his life. There were things I did that I can't explain to you now, but suffice it to say, I could have made our lives much better."

Taking a deep breath and looking at her glass, she asked, "Would you like more lemonade?"

"Oh, no, thank you."

"Am I keeping you from something important?"

"Not at all. I was heading to Gus' Produce for salad fixings but I'd rather stay here with you than hear about what poor judgment I have picking out tomatoes."

Nettie smiled at Bonnie's humor. "Then if you have the time, I'd like to finish what I've started."

Bonnie nodded.

"As strange as this sounds, especially to me, admitting those horrible attributes of my life was, in truth, a relief. I confessed things I had held in for so long, afraid of the consequences. The anger and fear I had held so tight kept me from receiving love. Henry's love. Even God's love. I didn't even know what love was, until you shared your Miz Jessie with me that wretched day. Her words encouraged me that love did not die when Henry died. I wanted to know more. So that night, I found Henry's Sunday School notes tucked away in his bible. Bonnie, I was so shocked! Henry had been teaching the same message Pastor Randy is sharing! I couldn't believe it! Here I've been fussing over the sermons and the truth has been living in my house for years!"

Bonnie clasped her hands in excitement. "Oh, Miss Nettie! I cannot tell you how excited I am for you. I believe Miz Jessie might say at a moment like this, "Heavens be praised!""

"Yes, that sounds like something she would say," Nettie smiled. "The reason I stopped you this morning was that something peculiar happened earlier. I came home today and caught myself humming. I have never hummed in my entire life. The song was familiar but I didn't know all the words. Then it dawned on me. You mentioned a while back that your Miz Jessie used to hum. What song was it she hummed? Do you remember?"

Bonnie was glad Nettie was asking about Miz Jessie. "Well now, let me think. It was the same tune over and over all my life. She hummed it when she was happy. She hummed it when she was sad. I thought for a long time it was the only song she knew." Bonnie giggled as her brow scrunched in search of the song. "Of course! Amazing Grace! That's it!"

"Really? That is the same song I was humming. Amazing Grace. I've heard that one most of my life, too. But I have never been one to sing or enjoy music that much. And I have the worst time remembering the words. Do you know the words?"

"Yes, I do! It goes like this......'Amazing grace, how sweet the sound, that saved a wretch like me. I once was lost, but now am found. Was blind but now I see.' I asked Miz Jessie one day why she hummed that particular tune and she said, 'it 'minds me o'er and o'er what I done been. But I ain't that no moe. I was lost, a wretch and blind. But I's now found and saved and can see!'

"What do you suppose she saw?" Nettie asked eagerly.

"She told me that too. She said she was blind to God's love.

But when she done give her life to Jesus, she see'd He'd been lovin' her all along, even when she be bad. I'm sorry," Bonnie laughed, "there I go talking like her again."

Nettie laughed right along with her. "I can see why you love her so much. She sounds like a very godly woman."

"Oh she was. I mean she is. She's still alive, probably around 70 by now. I remember asking her when I was in the fourth grade how old she was, and she said she wasn't quite sure, because she couldn't remember being born." Bonnie smiled thinking of her sweet Miz Jessie and happy to be recalling memories of their times together.

"I see. I see," Nettie whispered aloud thinking on the words. Then, like a flash of lightning, she sat straight up. "Oh, my. I think I *do* see! I, too, am a wretch and lost. And I have been blinded from loving myself all these years. I began to see that with Henry last week. I can't give what I don't have. Not a real love. Only that can come from God, who *is* love. I am beginning to see, Bonnie!" Her excitement made her feel years younger. Nettie slapped the arm of her rocker in triumph. Her smile radiated across the porch, seemingly illuminating her entire body.

Bonnie couldn't contain herself any longer. She jumped up and knelt before Nettie hugging her lap. Nettie stroked her hair and kissed the top of her head. She held on tight to Bonnie and let a peace settle over her. With her hand, Nettie raised Bonnie's face to hers. "Thank you for not giving up on this crotchety old woman."

Bonnie sat back on her heels and smiled. "Miss Nettie, it has been a hard journey trying to figure you out. From my first visit to the Apothecary, to church and around town, I kept running into you, too. I wasn't at all sure I wanted to get to know you but something kept tugging me in your direction. I do believe it is God Who has put us together."

"Bonnie, I believe you are right. There is so much more I wish I could tell you. Maybe someday I can. But right now, I feel like my heart is opening up like never before. And it feels good. I'm not sure what I have to do next, but I do know something is changing."

"Winds of change," Bonnie murmured.

"I didn't catch what you said."

"Oh, I was just mumbling to myself." Bonnie was seeing a Miss Nettie that she had never seen before. Her heart flooded with the memory in the Apothecary when Diane shared with her that, *"If you feel God leading you into her life, you know you have to step in."* I can't tell you how excited I am for you. I have been praying that God would show you how loved you are. And in case I haven't said it myself, I love you, Miss Nettie." Her eyes were brimming with tears.

Nettie stared at Bonnie in disbelief. "I....I don't know what to say. This is all so new for me."

Bonnie stood, leaned down and touched her cheek. "You don't have to say anything. I just wanted you to know." Straightening, Bonnie smiled and said, "Well, I guess I better be going."

"So soon?" Nettie rose from her rocker. "Can you wait for just a minute more?"

"Sure."

Nettie walked over to the door and slipped inside.

A few minutes later, Bonnie heard the front door open with a creak. Glancing over, she saw a familiar quilt draped over Nettie's right arm. She recognized it immediately. It was her quilt from the auction.

"I think this is the proper time to give you something I have had for a while."

"Miss Nettie! My quilt! My awful, pitiful effort at a rag quilt. Where? How? Uh, why?" Bonnie stepped closer and stroked the quilt, shaking her head in disbelief.

"I have another confession to make. At the fall festival, I believe I hurt your feelings when I commented on your quilt hanging in the auction tent. Although, to my credit, at first I didn't know it was yours, until after you left. When I stepped up to see who had made it, I read the card attached and there was your name. I looked around to see if anyone else had heard my remark and there on the other side of the stage stood Ida Mae, my best friend since childhood. She shook her head and said, "Nettie, how could you?" I didn't think much of it at first, but when she left and the tent was empty, I sat down and stared at your quilt. You had been so nice to come see me when hardly anyone else ever did, except for Ida Mae. I realized I wanted that quilt. I met with the judges and asked if I could buy the quilt anonymously. They agreed to a silent auction. But I made sure my offer would be the highest."

"Oh, but it is so ugly. Why would you pay so much for something so awful?"

The question amused Nettie. "At the time, I bought it partly out of guilt. But now, the truth of the matter seems pretty clear. Someone, a long, long time ago, paid a high price for an awful person like me."

Bonnie thrust herself into her friend's arms and hugged with all her might. "Thank you!" Stepping back, she looked at the quilt draped over Nettie's arm and said, "Miss Nettie, I would like for you to keep this. If you'd like. The story in this quilt is yours, not mine."

Nettie's hand flew to her mouth in surprise. "Are...are you sure?"

"I'm sure," Bonnie smiled.

"Oh, Bonnie, thank you! It has been hanging over my living room sofa for a over a week now, reminding me not only of the sacrifice and love Jesus has given me, but also, how lovingly it was made by a very special young lady who helped me discover love in my life again."

The two dear friends embraced as tears ran down both their cheeks in a rare and celebrated moment of joy.

With a final endearing look and a squeeze of the hand, Bonnie turned and headed toward Main Street. She fairly skipped out of sight.

Nettie settled back in her rocker and stroked the arms of the chair Henry had made her for her 40th birthday. "Henry, my dear, I have one more thing I must do, which will make you very proud."

She leaned her head back against the rocker, closed her eyes and prayed, "Lord, you really do love me, don't You? I don't know why I didn't see it before, but my Henry was trying to show me Your love for over 50 years. Thank You for not giving up on such a cantankerous old woman like me. I have been such a stubborn fool. For most of my life, I wasn't willing to let go of all the hurt from my mother. I realize now that she couldn't help being who she was either. She had her own hurts and insecurities to deal with. Like her, I gave in to anger and bitterness." Pausing, she took a deep breath. "Lord, I do not want to be that person anymore. I wish I had listened to my Henry and Pastor Randy sooner, and realized the price Jesus paid for me on the cross. I carried a weight of guilt and condemned myself for most of my life. Two things that were not mine to carry. I ask You to take over my heart and give me a clean start. Let me see Your love."

Opening her eyes and rising, she looked down the street. "Now, Lord, there are still more fences that need mending. I'm new at this, so I don't expect my friends to forgive me right away, but I do ask that You go before me and pave the way. And thank You, for Bonnie, and her Miz Jessie. They been 'mighty goods to me......'I'm jus' sayin." Nettie laughed.

The oaks were casting shadows across the flower beds from the soon to be setting sun. The day had slipped by too quickly. The sky was clear, the moon visible. A quiet settled over Nettie's heart. A sudden breeze blew across the wind chimes, sending a tinkling sound to Nettie's ears. "Winds of change. You are here, aren't You, Lord? I did hear you, Bonnie." She smiled.

Whispering to her audience of One, she said, "The moon will be a full one tonight. I see the sun setting on my past. Yet the morning promises a new day. A new day in the life of Nettie Pegram. I can hardly wait."

Nettie looked down at the tortured rag quilt. What she saw was exquisitely beautiful, because of what it represented. She carried it like a newborn baby to the living room sofa and gently draped it over the back, stroking it with care. She stepped back to admire her precious treasure, and realized she was not the least bit tired. She felt as energetic as a thirty-year-old. A thought flickered in her mind as she went to the bedroom to retrieve Henry's bible from the nightstand. Picking up the Good Book, and making her way back outside to her rocker, she thought of what Miz Jessie might say, and smiled. "Well, this be one thang I knows. To really know ya, Lawd, I best be gittin' in Yer Word." She giggled, placing the Bible on her lap, and opened it to John, chapter 1. "This is a good place to start." She read for hours under the porch light, surprised by her own happiness. Dusk had descended. The streetlights shone brightly. And the brilliance of the moon illuminated the night.

Drinking lemonade and cookies, she read until the wee hours of the morning.

Conclusion

As the winds blow among the mighty and majestic oaks that dominate the town of Windy Garden, dust from the ground is blown about and settles on the leaves and branches, inhibiting healthy growth. When stronger winds and cleansing rain come, the dust and debris are washed away, allowing light and air to penetrate the delicate foliage. The tender leaves flourish and the tree grows taller, stronger. The oak yields to the wind's prodding, and the tree waves its acceptance.

Like the mighty oaks, the winds of change that blew through Nettie's life came gently and tenderly. They came through Bonnie and Miz Jessie. Through dear friend Ida Mae, and through memories of Nettie's beloved Henry. The winds eventually intensified and blew away her pain, disappointment, and shame. Change came through brokenness. It came through truth.

For Nettie, the winds of change culminated in love and grace. She did not seek their presence, nor did she ask for it. Little did she know, they were always there.

Questions

1. What was your first impression of Nettie Pegram? Do you know anyone like her?

2. How did Bonnie's memories of Miz Jessie help the people of Windy Garden? How did they help you?

3. Why do you think some of the church-going folks harbor the same hurts and bitter feelings as those outside the church? Have you ever felt like Nettie? Have you ever been angry with a family member? A church member? Or with God? How have you handled your anger, your disappointment?

4. What kept Nettie from being set free from the hurts in her life? Those she blamed? Or herself?

5. What was the breaking point for Nettie?

6. What change, if any, did you see in Nettie?

7. How did the characters in the story affect you? Which ones did you like the most and why?

8. What change, if any, have you seen in your own beliefs after reading this book? Have you discovered any beliefs that you have held on to most of your life that have kept you in bondage?

9. If there are areas of your life that you need to let go of, in order to be free to see how very much 'you' are loved, what are they?

67107631R00200

Made in the USA
Lexington, KY
04 September 2017